MAXWELL'S CHAIN

Peter 'Mad Max' Maxwell is a very busy man. As Head of the Sixth Form at Leighford High he is trying to mark GCSE coursework on time, and at home baby Nolan claims a lot of attention, as does Metternich the cat. His 'Significant Other' DS Jacquie Carpenter has decided he has to give up his amateur sleuthing, but how can he refuse when the terminally nervous school photographer asks for his help after accidentally photographing a murder on the beach? Their discovery of a body buried in the sand dunes sets off a chain of events that only Mad Max can break.

MAXWELL'S CHAIN

MAXWELL'S CHAIN

by

M. J. Trow

Magna Large Print Books
Long Preston, North Yorkshire,
BD23 4ND, England.

British Library Cataloguing in Publication Data.

Trow, M. J.
     Maxwell's chain.

     A catalogue record of this book is
     available from the British Library

     ISBN   978-0-7505-2822-1

First published in Great Britain 2008 by Allison & Busby Ltd.

Published in Large Print 2008 by arrangement with
Allison & Busby Ltd.

Magna Large Print is an imprint of Library Magna Books Ltd.

Printed and bound in Great Britain by
T.J. (International) Ltd., Cornwall, PL28 8RW

CHAPTER ONE

It wasn't often that a night was so perfect. The water scarcely moved in the light breeze off the sea, bringing with it a promise of an early Spring. The moon was high and orange and its twin swung lazily below it, reflected in the waves. There was scarcely a sound, just a whisper from the damp, cold sand beneath the photographer's feet as he moved slightly to balance while he framed the view. If it had not been for the camera in his hands, he would have rubbed them together. He knew a winning view when he saw one and this one had 'Leighford Photographer of the Year' written all over it.

Letting his breath out slowly, he squeezed the shutter and captured the magic in the box. A few more for luck and he could get back home to a warm house, warm drink, warm wife. What could be nicer?

He slid a little down the dune side, feeling the sharp, dead, whippy grass brush his trousers. He stowed the camera away. Yes, it was a little outdated and clumsy, but he had no time for digital. He loved the slow thrill of the emerging image in the tray in his darkroom. His wife still called it the bathroom, but it hadn't seen anyone bathing for years. And so they showered downstairs.

He allowed himself a controlled slide to the foot of the dune and then made his way back to his car. The moonlight was plenty to see by when the high, wispy clouds had cleared, although he stumbled once or twice, misjudging the angle of the ground, pale beneath him. He grumbled away to himself about the things that people left lying about; this looked like a scarf, for example, and his logical, developer's mind told him that if it was cold enough for a scarf, it was too cold for the beach. As if to prove it, the wind whipped from nowhere, slicing through his anorak and taking his breath for a moment. The things he did for an award! He picked the scarf up and stowed it in his bag to dispose of later. An imaginary Little Old Lady With A Bad Leg Walking Her Dog rose up in his mind. Mustn't let her trip up. She might break a hip. Die of exposure. It would all be his fault. And a long time ago, he had learnt at Sunday school that these things mattered. If Bill Lunt had a failing, it was that he always saw the fly, never the ointment. That was something else they'd instilled into him at Sunday school. Robert Raikes had a lot to answer for.

He got into his car, alone in the car park now that it was dark, but not quite dark enough for lovers, and drove away.

Back on the dunes, where the spur called the Shingle rose to the cliffs near Dead Man's Point, nearly in the sea, the deed was done. The mouth, nose, lungs had filled with swift moving sand. The hands had ceased to clutch, the legs to kick. The dune had ceased to become a battleground, however one-sided. It was a grave. It was a crime scene waiting to be discovered, if the sea didn't get there first.

Emma Lunt was a patient woman. She endured Bill's obsession because it could well have been worse. He might have collected illegal birds' eggs or been a crypto-Nazi or a member of Opus Dei. His shop in the High Street did well. If he didn't do digital, there were plenty of people who did. And, happily for their wages bill, most of those people were school leavers. In other words, they came cheap, despite the curse of the minimum wage. So the sales of middle of the range cameras, the printing of middle of the road holiday photos, the taking of middle-aged family portraits all kept Lunt Photographic happily in the black. The winter was a lean time of course, but the days of beach photographers leaping up to curmudgeonly couples and frosty families as they trudged along the rain-lashed sea front in August, demanding money with menaces, had long gone. They ended, in fact, in 1964. And if Bill's enthusiasm for snapping Emma in unlikely poses had waned ... well, enough of that, thought Emma, was certainly enough. She'd never really liked it.

She turned her head at the sound of his key in the door.

'In here,' she called, from her curled up seat on the sofa, draped in rows of pearl and plain like a latter-day Madame Dafarge, peoples' heads bouncing squelchily around her.

'Just going up to...' his voice petered out and the one step up the stairs to the dark-room was retraced into the lounge. 'Hello, dear,' he smiled, head round the door. It was always a good idea to at least pretend that you were going to spend the evening with the wife. He was still wearing his willie hat and his ears were crimson.

'No,' she said, completing his thought. 'No, you are not just going up to develop what you have just taken. What you are going to do is spend a while with me. Let's talk about our day, why not?' She patted the seat next to her, sweeping the knitting aside and waited expectantly.

He sat down gingerly on the edge of the cushion, looking not unlike a rabbit caught in the headlights, smiling to hide the vacant space where a conversation ought to be taking shape and tugged off the hat. 'Ermm, the moon was lovely. Over the water. I've taken a good few shots. Should be up for the Photographer of the Year, no problem.'

She sighed. Photo chat was better than no chat at all. 'See anyone else down there? On the beach?'

'Not a soul. A bit parky, as a matter of fact. Not as mild as the weather forecasters make it sound.'

She chuckled. 'It *is* February,' she reminded him. 'What was that song? "John Kettley, he's a weatherman. And so is Michael Fish"? I still think Fahrenheit sounds warmer than Celsius.'

'You're showing your age,' he wagged a finger. 'Someone else thought it was chilly, though. They dropped a scarf. I've got it here, somewhere.' He rummaged in his bag.

'Why ever did you bring that old thing back with you?' she said, wrinkling her nose in disgust as a rather tatty scarf, grubby, full of holes and rather redolent of dog emerged from amongst his cameras. It wasn't a patch on her handiwork.

He looked at it in dismay. It really was rather horrible in the harsh light of his lounge. He saw something jump off it, nearly mentioned the fact and then thought better of it.

'It didn't look quite so nasty in the moon-light,' he said. 'Anyway, I thought perhaps someone might trip on it and I didn't want that on my conscience.'

Emma smiled at him, grateful that he hadn't brought the used condoms and Asda trolleys home as well. 'You soft old thing,' she smiled. 'Take it out to the bin. It's probably got a million fleas in it.'

One million, minus one, thought Bill Lunt grimly. But there was no hope of finding that one now – the Franz von Werra of the flea world. Holding the scarf at arm's length between finger and thumb, he went through the kitchen and dropped it in the bin in the utility room. He was washing his hands when she came up behind him,

'Not often I catch you at the sink,' she said, circling her arms round his waist. 'In fact, not often I catch you in the kitchen.'

He felt a bit of a sinking feeling coming on.

'So, since you're here, why don't we open a bottle, rustle up a bit of supper and sit down like grown-ups for once?'

'I've got some...'

'Not going to mention developing, I hope,' she said, tightening her grip in something resembling the Heimlich manoeuvre.

'No, no, not at all,' he said, letting his breath out in what he hoped was a silent sigh.

'Good. What have you got some of, then?'

This woman was tenacious, you had to give her that. 'Some planning. Some planning to do for the Leighford High School photos tomorrow. I've got a new idea for this

14

year. I got it off the telly.'

'What's that?'

'Buddy pictures. It's big in America, for the graduations, you know. Groups of friends together, not just tutor groups and things. Subject groups. Teams. That sort of thing. They didn't do that sort of thing when you were there, did they?'

'Have you asked Peter Maxwell?' she whispered in his ear.

'No. I'm sure he'll not be too bothered.' Bill Lunt screwed round in his wife's embrace. He needed to see her expression.

She laughed, just one, sharp bark of a laugh. 'American idea? Peter Maxwell? Not too bothered? Are you insane?'

Emma Lunt, née Watson, was a founder member of the Old Leighford Highenas. She had a pretty good idea of what Peter Maxwell would think of buddy pictures. And, as it turned out, she was right.

'Buddy?' Peter Maxwell fixed the unfortunate photographer with a gimlet stare. And he may have turned a shade paler. 'Pictures? Am I mistaken, Bill, or does this have a ring of the good ol' US of A about it?'

Bill Lunt hadn't seen Peter Maxwell for the best part of a year. They kept an annual vigil, those two. Every January, come hell or high water-rates, the Head of Sixth Form at Leighford High School would ring Lunt

15

Photographic in the High Street and ask to talk to Mr William Lunt, prop. If Emma answered, she'd go all schoolgirly again, just like she did all those years ago when Mr Maxwell explained about the South Sea Bubble and what you do when it bursts. If Bill answered, it was more to the point.

'Usual, Bill, please, your best daguerreotype of My Own, standing patiently in serried ranks as a permanent sepia reminder of the Best Years of Their Lives, whether they appreciate it or not.' Click. Burr.

That morning, a little before Valentine's Day, the man the kids had called Mad Max for half a generation looked madder than ever. He stood foursquare on what, in a real school, would have been the First Eleven Square; in fact, a little to the north-east of where Jade Minchinhampton habitually left her cheese sandwich leftovers. The brisk wind rattled through the barbed wire of his hair and his eyes narrowed as he looked at the photographer. Behind him stood the flat-roofed, red-brick monstrosity that had sent the architects' doyen Nicholas Pevsner to an early grave and that still saw furious complaints fluttering out of Clarence House on a regular basis. In the mornings, when the rain came from the east, a third of the classrooms were unusable. By the afternoon, global warming had depopulated another third. And throughout the winter, Mondays were strictly a gloves and scarf day on account of the total lack of central heating.

'Ooh,' Bill Lunt tried his level best to sound doubtful. 'Ooh, it might, you know, be a bit American, now you come to mention it.' He mouthed the words silently, as if the taste of them might give it away. 'Hmm, not sure. Anyway, what do you think?'

'I think it sounds like rubbish, Bill, if you don't mind my saying so. The Americans have given us Spiritualism, chewing-gum, Coca-Cola, George W Bush and the moronic interrogative, although those last two might just be one and the same. According to them, they also gave us some help in two world wars, although the jury's still out on that one. As for friendship groups, these kids are friends with each other for at best a microsecond. If it lasts any longer than that it is because one of them has something on the other. If they want pictures of each other they take them with their mobile phones, constantly and at every possible opportunity. Usually in Maths, where the staff seem to have only a fleeting relationship with discipline.'

'So…?'

'So?'

'So … do you want me to do the buddy pictures?'

'Bill, are you still married to the beautiful Emma?'

'Yes.'

'Did you tell her you were planning buddy pictures?'

'Yes.'

'Did you ask her what I might think?'

'Erm ... yes.'

'So, do I want you to do the buddy pictures?'

Bill sighed and hefted his camera bag higher onto his shoulder.

'No. No, you don't want me to do the buddy pictures.'

'Good lad. Excellent. Now, let's line the little buggers up and get this done before they freeze to death out here. I don't know why we do these things in February. Some EU directive, I suppose – don't get me started on that one.'

'It's because the winter uniform looks better on the pictures,' volunteered the photographer.

'Uniform?' Maxwell stepped back, aghast. 'Uniform? Do the kids here wear uniform? I had no idea.'

In his day it was all blazers and peaked caps and black polished shoes and turn-ups and fluff inspections. The assembled multitudes behind him did look a motley crew. Banned jeans were on almost every leg, piercings glinted everywhere in the thin February sun. One of them was wearing his grandad's T-shirt with 'Led Zeppelin' written on it. But

18

the chattering, like so many starlings on a wire, was cheerful and there weren't too many fights going on, just some desultory shoving from the girls in Year Eight, longing to become Year Nine when they could legitimately pinch their dads' lager supplies and become ladettes. The smartarses from Year Thirteen Physics were poised on the edges of the rows, ready to dash round and, apocryphally, appear at both ends of the photograph. Could it be done? Possibly, in the dear, dead days of Fox-Talbot, but not now, surely? The Senior Leadership Team were shivering on seats in the middle of the front row, like the race apart they so clearly were. James Legs Diamond was the Lead Learner, as Headteachers were now called by the Liberal-left, a husk of a man who was prey to nervous disorders and blown by the double winds of Ofsted and County Hall. At his right hand, all Uriah Heep and false dignity, Bernard Ryan resolutely ignored the appalling behaviour of a knot of Year Seven kids and tried to remember he was Deputy Head. To Diamond's left, his minder and hatchet-woman, Dierdre Lessing, the Cruella de Vil of Leighford High, sat like the Ice-maiden, her sub-zero body temperature the norm at last.

Maxwell patted Bill Lunt's dejected shoulder and went to take his place, front and centre, with the Sixth Form, Maxwell's

Own. Slowly, the chattering stopped and everyone faced forward, except that one strange child in Year Ten – The Syndrome Kid – who found that focusing was a trick he hadn't quite mastered.

'Say Ofsted, everyone,' cried Maxwell, cheerily.

The shutter clicked and Leighford High School, in all its glory, was captured on film for another year.

'Brrr,' Sylvia Matthews was pressed up against Maxwell's radiator in his office when he walked in after un-marshalling his year group from the photo line-up. It had been the usual thing – the kids loved it and the Senior Leadership Team recoiled in horror. Maxwell barked at them, in what was probably a passable Lord Cardigan – 'The Sixth Form will retire. Threes right. Am I hurting you, Reynolds?' he growled at a passing GNVQ student, 'I should be, because I'm standing on your 'air!'

'Why do we do these things in February?' Sylvia asked the Great Man.

Sylvia Matthews had been the School Nurse at Leighford for ever. To be fair, she didn't look all of her eighty-six years, but she sure as hell felt it on days like this. She'd long since stopped being annoyed by Peter Maxwell or the colourful displays on his walls. In the far corner, William Powell was

20

kissing a rather unlikely looking mermaid in the curvy form of Ann Blyth. Above the radiator Burt Lancaster, all hair and teeth, was dragging Audrey Hepburn over the sand in *The Unforgiven*. And behind the spider plant, a squadron of Japanese Migs was bombing the hell out of the Pearl Harbor fleet in *Tora! Tora! Tora!* There'd be tears before VJ Day.

'Warmest Feb on record, apparently,' Maxwell said, encouragingly, removing his hat and Jesus scarf and flinging them onto the top of a filing cabinet, their natural habitat when not about his person.

'Still February though, warmest or not,' she muttered, rubbing her hands together and praying he had some coffee on the go.

'Bill Lunt explained that it is because the winter uniform is more photogenic,' Maxwell explained kindly, reading her mind and switching on the kettle. Sylvia and Mad Max had been an item once, or so the kids whispered. It was a marriage of true minds in a way, but there had been impediments.

'Winter...?' Sylvia was bemused.

'Yes, yes, I know. I said that. Not very noticing for a photographer, is he? I think Bill is just remembering his training at the rather shaky hands of old Whatsisface, you know, old Thing, used to do the pictures with that pinhole camera way back when.'

Sylvia puckered her brow. 'Hmmm ... yes,

I remember him.' She chuckled. 'It didn't matter whether the kids were pulling faces or not; everything was so blurred you couldn't tell one from another, let alone what their expressions were doing.'

He laughed and turned away to make the coffee. 'Browning!' It had come to him at last, Maxwell the Historian hated not to remember the names of the dead. The living, now, were a different matter.

'Yes, that's him.'

'Every picture was the Browning version,' he said, as he handed her her mug of brown liquid. 'Bit like this gravy.'

She took a sip. 'Oh God, Max. This coffee is bad, even for you.'

'Sorry.' He took a sip too and shuddered. Crap wasn't the word. 'It's the NQT lad's turn to get the goodies in this month and I think he's on a bit of an economy drive. Short of readies.'

'Well, who isn't, after Christmas?' Sylvia nodded, knowing how appallingly newly qualified teachers were paid, 'but surely there's no need to buy this muck?'

Maxwell nodded. 'To be honest, Sylv, we're a bit worried about Gregory. A few too many car boot sales and too few essays marked, at the moment. You just can't get the staff any more. He's got till half term to sort his act out and then I think Paul is planning a word.'

'Oh, crumbs,' Sylvia attempted a William Brown takeoff, not altogether successfully in that she'd never read a Richmal Crompton book in her life. Even so, Maxwell beamed at her fondly, just for trying. He'd read them all. 'That will scare him.'

'I know Paul isn't exactly Attila the Hun,' Maxwell agreed, glancing out of his window to where Paul Moss, the Head of History, was still trying to get Year Nine back into his classroom after the photograph, 'but we have to be seen to go through all the stages. Paul is his Line Manager, so it's his call. I might take young Gregory out for a drinkie, though, and see if I can wheedle whatever the problem is out of him.'

Sylvia snorted. 'Looking at him, I think the offer of a drink with you will probably be one drink too many. Wearing my nursing hat, I think he manages drinking quite well on his own.'

'Oh? I hadn't picked up on that.' Maxwell knew that Sylvia had a gold in Gossip from the 1984 Olympics. She was worth cultivating.

'Well, that's why I wear this rather fetching uniform and you wear … whatever it is you wear.' She forgot the horrors of a moment ago and sipped again. 'Oh, yuk, Max. Tip this away, will you, before I accidentally poison myself. I must go, anyway. I expect the girlies will be queuing up with frostbite or something, threatening to sue that nice Mr Diamond for making them stand outside for a few minutes. Anything to get off games. Family all well, by the by?'

'Shipshape and Bristol fashion.' It was unusual for Peter Maxwell to go all nautical and as he said it he didn't think his Jacquie would go a bundle on the analogy.

As Sylvia reached the door it opened, and Bill Lunt came in, carrying a stiff brown envelope.

'Oh, hello, Bill. Do you know Sylvia Matthews?'

'Only by sight,' Bill chuckled. 'Through my lens, as it were.' He shook her hand.

'I'm sure she enhances any picture,' said Maxwell, in full gallant mode. She gave him an old-fashioned look and he waved as she left and ushered Bill in, all in one Head-of-Sixth-Formly sweep of the arm. 'How can I help, Bill? It can't be gestures by Year Twelve. You haven t developed the picture yet.'

'Not today's picture, no. But there's something else I'd like you to have a butchers at, if you would.'

'All right. What's this? Oh, you wouldn't like a coffee, would you? I'd poured this for Sylvia, but she has to answer her calling.'

'No, thanks,' Lunt smiled. What did he know that Maxwell didn't?

Maxwell hauled his pince-nez out of his jacket pocket, the pair he'd half-inched from

24

that nice Mr Pickwick a while back. 'I was out last night and took some pictures. Moon over the sea. Very atmospheric. I'm going for the Leighford Photographer of the Year again this year. I might even send them up to the *Daily Mail*.'

'Hmm. Gosh.' Maxwell remained noncommittal. He assumed that sending them to the *Daily Mail* was a good thing, but wasn't a hundred per cent sure.

'I developed them this morning. It would normally have been last night, but Emma ... well, you know how women are.'

'Indeed.' Maxwell was happily cohabiting with Jacquie and parenting their little boy, Nolan, in a by-and-large-argument-free environment, but he could see that that probably didn't apply globally. 'How is Emma, by the way?' Maxwell remembered Emma Watson as a bubbly little girl with buck teeth who developed into something of a cracker come AS level age. She'd developed a feistiness, too, that Maxwell rather liked. Never rude, just assertive – sort of woman who might demand the vote sometime in the future.

'Oh, she's very well. Manages the shop. But she doesn't always see why I need to develop things straight away. We photographers do get a bit obsessive, I'm afraid. So, I got up early this morning and did these. I've enlarged them, so you can see what I mean. You might still need a lens, though.'

25

'I may not be twenty-twenty any more, Bill, but...'

'No, no. I didn't mean that. I just mean the image I want you to look at is very small and a bit grainy at this enlargement. No offence meant, Mr Maxwell.'

'And none taken, Bill, I assure you. Anyway, let's have a look-see. Do you have a lens with you?'

Bill Lunt whipped out a magnifying glass from his pocket, like a poor man's Basil Rathbone. It still had a 'Lunt Photographic' price label on it. He spread out the photos on Maxwell's desk and stood back. Maxwell leant over them, magnifying glass in one hand, pince-nez in the other. He looked closely at each one, then straightened up.

'Very nice, Bill. Very atmospheric. Very *Daily Mail*.'

Bill Lunt looked crestfallen. 'Can't you see it?'

'Ummm ... I think perhaps not. Sorry.' Maxwell leant in again, anxious to please the man. Had the photographer caught the face of Mother Theresa in a sandy hillock? The second gunman on the Grassy Knoll?

'Oh, come here. Let me show you.' The photographer took the lens from Maxwell and put the pictures in a neat pile. 'Number one.' He pointed to an area in the bottom left. 'What do you see?'

'Dune.' Ever the film buff.

'Right. Number two. Same place.'

Maxwell bent closer and screwed up his eyes. 'Oh. I see... What is that?'

'I think it's an upraised arm.'

Maxwell looked at him. Then back at the photo.

'All right. I think I can see that.' It could just as well have been the Loch Ness Monster, but he sensed that Bill Lunt was a sensitive soul, especially when it came to his photos, so he trod warily.

'And the next?'

Maxwell peered. 'Nothing?'

'Right. And the next?'

Maxwell was warming to this. One more lucky guess and he'd get an A Level in Photography, sending Leighford's ALPS ratings through the roof. 'Oh, I see. The arm again. Wait, so what we are seeing is...'

Bill Lunt straightened up triumphantly. 'What we are seeing is someone stabbing a body behind the dune. In stop motion.'

Maxwell bent to the pictures again and flipped through them quickly. 'You could be right. In fact, in this one,' he pointed to one in the middle of the sequence, 'I think you can just see another arm as well, reaching up.'

The photographer looked closer. 'I think you're right.' He stepped back from the desk, slowly, rubbing his eyes. 'What are we going to do, Mr Maxwell?'

'Well, Bill.' Maxwell straightened up the

pictures and replaced them in the envelope. 'You could send them to the Daily Mail, I suppose. They're very atmospheric, as you say. Did I ever tell you about the case of the World's Oldest Photograph?'

'But ... but, Mr Maxwell. What about the arm?' Bill Lunt was aghast. 'We can't just leave it. There's been a murder.'

'Come on, Bill.' Maxwell was looking a little distant, thinking hard as he was. 'You sound like a Sassenach version of Taggart.' Bill Lunt's wasn't the best impression of Blythe Duff he'd ever heard. And after all, Peter Maxwell had sat through, not once but twice, that appalling load of tosh *Blow Up*, in which a photographer had unwittingly captured a murder. Or had he? He'd sat through it twice in order to understand the plot, *not*, he hastened to tell everyone, *just* to see as much as possible of Vanessa Redgrave.

'Can't we at least go and look?'

Maxwell pursed his lips. 'We, white man?' he said to himself in memory of the old Lone Ranger/Tonto joke. He closed his eyes and pictured the evening spent in his warm and cosy lounge with Jacquie and Nolan. Metternich the cat would be stretched out in front of the fire in all his black and white, battle-scarred glory, quietly, and against all the odds, protecting His Baby from all-comers including, quite often, the child's parents. He also pictured the chilly breeze

28

off the sea, the lining up to get the exact spot, the trudging over the damp sand carrying a spade. No contest, really.

'Pick me up at the end of Columbine at half seven,' he told the photographer. 'Bring a spade. And a torch. Oh, and a camera.'

Bill Lunt chuckled and rubbed his hands together. 'All right!' he said, grinning broadly. 'Sleuthing with Mr Maxwell! You know you've got a bit of a reputation for this, don't you? Wait till I tell Emma. Or, wait a minute. Do you think I should tell Emma?'

'It's not for me to say, Bill. But let's just say I will be telling Jacquie I am off for a quiet drink with someone from work.'

'Point taken, Mr Maxwell...' He patted the side of his nose, that grand gesture of the conspirator throughout time.

'Bill, if we are to be digging together, could you call me something else?'

'Mr M?'

'I'd rather you didn't,' Maxwell said. 'It's as though you've forgotten my name. What about Max?'

Bill Lunt was ecstatic. 'OK ... Max. See you at nineteen thirty.'

'When?' The Head of Sixth Form was aghast.

'Erm ... half past seven?'

'Excellent.'

'Oh, perhaps I'd better have your mobile number.'

'All of my numbers are mobile, Bill, if they choose to be. But if you should be talking about the number of a mobile telephone, then I'm afraid I must quote my wife here.'

Bill waited and nothing happened. 'What would your wife say, Max?'

Maxwell snorted and tossed his head, such an immaculate take-off of his pretty young wife that it made Bill Lunt's head spin, and he felt the warm glow of being with a fellow Luddite grow.

'Oh, I see. Seven-thirty it is, then.'

'Seven-thirty it is, Bill. Wrap up warm. Wear a scarf, or something. Not really bucket and spade weather, is it?'

Maxwell shook his head as Bill Lunt went down the stairs two at a time. The thing on the dunes would turn out to be a branch caught in the wind, or similar; an Asda trolley somehow washed up from Dar-es-Salaam. Except that – he cast his mind back – it was particularly calm last night. No raging storm, no writhing swell. Well, he pondered further as he picked up a pile of exercise books, it would be some seaweed or something. A sea bird. A weather balloon reflecting the moon. Part of a wrecked spacecraft from Roswell. Or, of course, just possibly, an arm, stabbing someone to death.

He opened the door to his office just as a hooded figure ran past.

'Jones. Take that stupid hood off. Stand up

straight. Don't run. And why aren't you teaching Nine Zed?' He tutted. Maths teachers might be hard to find, but really! There was surely a limit. And, whistling quietly, he was off, to teach some kids, as if they needed teaching, some more about Man's inhumanity to Man.

CHAPTER TWO

As things turned out, Peter Maxwell didn't have to be economical with the truth over his up-coming spot of sleuthing. Yes, he did have a reputation for these things and as luck would have it, Jacquie had been poached by DCI Henry Hall to collate age statistics on local ASBO holders; woman policeman meets number cruncher. He had already done the adding up, and had made the average age ninety-seven. He had done it again – three this time. Even allowing for the granny on the Barlichway who had perfected the art, to everyone's horrified amazement, of peeing through letterboxes, and also allowing for the tot who had bitten and spat his way through every playgroup in town, he knew his maths was dodgy somewhere. He was banging his calculator on his desk and was about to follow it with his head when Jacquie had wandered past and taken pity on him. All right, so Hall, all bland and unreadable behind the rimless specs, was a fast-track graduate of the new school, but electronics were nearly as alien to him as those new-fangled Belisha beacons were to Peter Maxwell.

Nolan was with the child-minder, according to Jacquie's phone message. He would be fine there until she could pick him up. The wind was a bit keen for a ride on the back of Daddy's bike, no matter how well wrapped. And the velocipede that was White Surrey was not the most comfortable ride in the world. That honour, if the graffiti behind the Sports Hall were to be believed, belonged to Jemma Davidson of Year Eleven. There was a stew in the fridge, if he fancied that. Or she would bring chips. Let her know.

Maxwell rang back and left a message with Ken Wertham, the rather curmudgeonly desk sergeant; Dixon of Dock Green, thou shouldst be living at this hour. What with 999 and 101 and practically every number in between, the last few months before retirement were hanging heavily on the desk man's hands. He toyed with not passing the message on, just to spite the stuck-up sod. What was he doing, old as Methuselah and no better than he should be, with a nice bit of tottie like Jacquie Carpenter? Then he remembered what had happened the last time he had 'forgotten' to pass on the message. His ears still rang in cold weather. He picked up the phone.

'Jacquie Carpenter.'

'Desk here, Sergeant. Your ... Mr Maxwell has just rung. Says thanks for the stew, but he thinks perhaps it's had all its useful life and even Metternich doesn't want it.'

'Cheeky.'

'I'm sure it's lovely. He says don't worry about the chips, he is going out with a colleague. Something about lesson planning.'

'Really?' Jacquie was amazed. 'Are you sure that's what he said?' Jacquie knew Maxwell hadn't planned a lesson since Mafeking was relieved. 'Lesson planning.' She repeated it because she wasn't sure she'd ever said those words before, not in that configuration anyway.

'Yes. I wrote it down.' Wertham sounded peeved and not a little apprehensive.

'Yes, yes, I'm sure you did. Well, thanks for letting me know.'

Jacquie put the phone down and tapped a pencil against her front teeth pensively.

Alerted by the cessation of the tapping of calculator keys, Hall looked up through his open doorway.

'Everything all right, Jacquie?' he called.

Jacquie Carpenter had been DCI Henry Hall's favourite detective for more years than he cared to acknowledge. She'd been a slip of a thing in uniform when they'd first met and he could still remember her, ciggie shaking in her pale hand as she stood outside her first murder scene at the ruin the kids called the Red House all those years ago. She'd long since given up the smoking and the shaking, but murder scenes? Well, some things never changed. Motherhood had rounded Jacquie Carpenter. She was an inch fuller everywhere in the literal sense, more careful perhaps with her own life, slower to judge, but quicker to leap to the defence of woman or child.

'Hmm?' She looked up and met his frown. 'Oh, yes, no worries. Umm, sir?'

Hall came over. 'What is it?' Henry Hall was a three-piece-suit man, in an age when no one wore three pieces any more. Without noticing it, the fast-track whiz kid with all the smart answers had become a middle-aged man. Promotion had passed him by because he wanted it to. Above his rank was all political correctness, quotas, community policing, ethnic understanding and glorified social work, hob-nobbing with magistrates and chief constables over rounds of golf and dry Martinis. Here it was still the cops and the robbers, ho ho. And when Jacquie called him 'guv' he listened; when she called him 'sir' he came over.

'Are there any new unexplaineds at the moment?'

'Not that I know of,' he shrugged. 'Why?'

'Nothing concrete,' she said. 'It's just that Max has rung and said he's going out with a colleague.'

Like Jacquie and Hall, Hall and Maxwell went way back. It was the Red House case, funnily enough, where they had met too. It was Hall's case, but people in Leighford with long memories still called it Maxwell's House and they didn't mean the coffee. The two men walked wide of each other most of the time, a nod, a grim smile, a small wave, even a microwave, from a car or the saddle of a bike respectively. But somehow, in Hall's inquiries and in Hall's cases, Peter Maxwell was always there, like Banquo at the feast.

Hall turned to go back into his office. 'For goodness' sake, Jacquie. Why not just marry the man and make the cliché complete?'

'No, no, guv, don't get me wrong. He can do what he likes. Does, in fact, do what he likes. It's just the rest of the message that has me worried.'

'What else did he say, then?' Hall's blank glasses turned back to her, his face somewhere behind them.

'He said they would be lesson planning.'

'I still don't quite see...' Hall knew Maxwell was a loose cannon, but teaching was a foreign country; they did things differently there.

'Guv, Max hasn't planned a lesson in his life. He has told Nolan on many an occasion

35

to shoot him if he ever found him writing a lesson plan.'

'Perhaps he's been told to. Perhaps there's another Ofsted inspection – although after last time, let's hope not.' The last time, Hall remembered, people had died. You didn't mess with Ofsted in Tony Blair's Britain. 'Perhaps...' Hall brightened, with his finger in the air. 'Perhaps it's a new directive from County Hall and he's...' Hall stopped. 'You're right. That is odd. I'm sure there's nothing pending, though.'

'Don't worry.' Jacquie picked up her calculator again. 'It's probably nothing.'

And she was talking to herself really as she started tapping in numbers and Hall returned to his desk. He sat for a moment, then made a note on a post-it and stuck it to the edge of his monitor screen. Just in case.

Maxwell stood on the corner of Columbine with his shoulders drawn up and his chin drawn down into the shelter of his colourful scarf. His habitual hat was in place, pork pie with the brim down, but it was a comfort thing; like a blanket, but infinitely less stylish. It gave very little warmth. He couldn't feel his ears at all. The sunny February day, a sure sign of global warming or a sure sign of an impending mini-ice age, depending on which ranting scientist was in the ascendancy, had begun to cool with the dark and as far as Maxwell was concerned, Bill Lunt and his nice warm car couldn't get there quickly enough. The cold was beginning to creep up his legs and heaven only knew what might happen when it got to the top.

It was the jeering he heard first and the laughter that followed. Loud, belligerent, like the SA in some Nazi town, swaggering down the street in the sound archive of his brain. Then he saw them; a knot of hoodies hunched like the camels of the night milling round a smaller figure in their centre. Instinctively, most people would walk away, cross the road, reckon it wasn't their fight. Instinctively, Peter Maxwell crossed the road too, into the thick of it. He was a Samaritan at heart.

'Thick indeed,' Maxwell's breath snaked out on the night air as he reached the nearest rough, shoving around an old man two-thirds his height and four times his age.

'You what?' the hoodie tried to vocalise.

'Let me see,' Maxwell peered at him. He didn't know the face, but he knew the type only too well. 'Yep. CAT score 74.3. SAT 69.8. Grade A GCSE in Unpleasantness. But I bet you can text on your stolen mobile faster than I can say "Leave the old man alone, you little shit, or you'll be going home tonight via A & E at Leighford General".'

The hoodie blinked and the jeering had stopped. Six pairs of eyes were on Maxwell now and the first to flicker were those of the old man. He ducked out of the vicious circle surrounding him and scuttled away into the darkness.

'Do you wanna kickin'?' the hoodie asked.

'Thank you, no,' Maxwell stood his ground, nose to nose with the moron. 'I've just had one. You know,' he beamed at them all, 'I've been rash. It was wrong of me to brand you all as low-life garbage just because you were all about to kick the crap out of a defenceless old man. That nice Mr Cameron has said we are supposed to hug people like you. So, whaddya say, guys? Group hug?' And he held out his arms.

Two of them were all for wading in, fists and boots at the ready, but the chavviest of them crossed in front of them. 'No,' he snapped. 'Not this one. It's Mad Max. Let's go.'

'Who?' one of them asked.

'What? Him?' the first hoodie jeered. 'That's Mad Max?'

Maxwell closed to him so that hat brim and hood brim touched for a second. 'Would you like to find out how mad?' he asked.

And the hoodies were gone, thudding away round the corner before the bravest of them called back, 'You're a wanker, Maxwell!'

The height of wit and repartee.

The sound of a discreetly sounded car horn made Maxwell turn.

'Mr Maxwell?' Bill Lunt had the loudest whisper Maxwell had ever heard. Even so, the cloak and dagger was a little unnecessary.

'The cloak and dagger is a little unnecessary, Bill,' Maxwell said as he climbed into the car. Lunt Photographic was obviously doing all right. Leather seats, unless he missed his guess.

'Sorry, Mr Ma ... Max,' the photographer said, as he released the handbrake. 'What was all that about?'

'Just chillin' wit me bros,' Maxwell jived. 'Talking of which, does this heater work?' He fiddled with a few dials on the car's fascia.

'I wasn't sure what you had told your wife. About tonight, I mean.'

'Not wife, Bill, Significant Other. Soulmate. Partner. Divida Anima Mea. Other Half. Detective Sergeant Carpenter. Call her what you want, really.'

Bill Lunt swerved and clipped the kerb. 'Detective Sergeant? Is this OK, then? I had no idea.'

Maxwell shrugged. 'I can't see why not, Bill.'

'Well, she's a policeman. Er ... policewoman.'

'She is, she is indeed, Bill.' Maxwell unwound his scarf to let the ends dangle. 'And as such, I'm sure she wouldn't mind two thoughtful citizens investigating a potential crime scene, trampling all over it with their clodhopping feet and obliterating all clues, making the job of the aforementioned police twenty zillion times more difficult.'

'Are you sure?'

'Of course not, Bill,' Maxwell sighed. 'She'll be livid, but that's my problem. It's not as if we haven't been here before. We've rowed about it, I've promised never to do it again, we've rowed some more. It's who we are. Don't worry. Call it a compulsion. Some men gamble. Others drink. Yet others womanise. I investigate murder. Heigh ho. Waddya going to do?' It was a perfect Homer Simpson.

'But I do worry, Max. If poking around crime scenes is what you do, worrying is what I do. Emma's always telling me about it.'

'Well, *don't* worry, Bill. I dare say you've already been told it may never happen.'

'About fifty times a day.'

'There you are, then. Everyone can't be wrong.'

'But there's so much out there, isn't there? There's accidental death, there's tripping hazards, there's *electricity!* There's bodies of water, there's ice falling from aeroplanes, there's *killer bees!*' Bill's grip on the steering wheel was getting harder; his knuckles stood out like quail's eggs under his skin in the scudding street lights. Maxwell hadn't realised that the nice, easy-going photographer of Leighford High was such a neurotic. 'There's thunder. There's lightning. There's trains, both derailed and carrying nuclear waste.'

'There's a huge Tesco lorry.'

'Yes, true, there's all sorts of lorries.'

'No, Bill, I mean, there's a huge Tesco lorry, over there, coming at us round the roundabout.'

Bill swallowed a scream and screeched to a halt. 'Oh Max, I'm sorry. That was a close one.' He sat with both hands frozen to the wheel, staring straight ahead.

'Yes, Bill.' Maxwell felt his heart descend slowly from his mouth again. 'But that's what it was. A close one. We have close ones all day long, but we negotiate the stairs, we float, we swat the bee. We even,' and he patted the man's white knuckles with a smile, 'miss the lorry. Think of all the things that happen every day to feel lucky about. Not the things that could ruin your life.'

'It's OK for you, Mr Maxwell,' he said peevishly. 'You're all right. Lovely wife … er … policewoman. Lovely baby; I've seen him on the back of your bike.'

Maxwell snorted softly down his nose and smiled. It's what he did when his natural reaction would be to let a tear roll softly down his cheek. He waited while the man found his gears again and drove on.

41

'Oh, Bill,' he said, patting the man's arm and making the car buck wildly across the carriageway for a moment. 'Bill, I *am* lucky. I *am* all right.' He let a moment pass, while he got his throat ready to speak through again. He looked out of the window, saw in the dark glass the faces of his first wife and baby daughter, torn from him when his life was so very, very all right. Before that day when the wet road had killed them, and the sharp bend and the flying police car, all sirens and flashing lights and macho bravado. He touched a forefinger tip to his ghostly baby's nose and looked away.

'Right then, Bill,' he said, rubbing his hands together. 'Are we there yet?' All in all, it was a pretty good Bart and Lisa Simpson.

The big car growled down the road that skirted the Shingle and rolled into the car park at the landward side of the dunes. The two men got out and went round to the boot. There was a brief hiatus while Bill thought he had left the torch at home. He then found it under the first-aid box, foil lined blanket and emergency fluorescent triangle without which he refused to go on even the shortest journey. He'd seen a documentary on the telly once about the Donner Party, the wagon train that had left Missouri too late and only survived by cannibalism. Yes, that was the Rockies and

1846, but try telling Bill Lunt that.

Maxwell was a patient man; Bill Lunt's luck truly was in. Anyone else would have given him a clip round the ear and demanded to be taken home. They were, after all, about to tramp across a rather chilly dunescape towards the incoming tide, looking for something that probably wasn't there. And the old, haunting refrain crept unbidden into Maxwell's mind. 'Last night I dreamt a dreary dream, beyond the isle of Skye. I saw a dead man win a fight. And I think that man was I.' Having found, or not found, that something, Maxwell was in for a right bollocking when he got home. He mulled over his options as they tramped silently, in Indian file, towards the edge of the sea, the rush in their ears becoming a roar that blotted out all else. The conversation at home was not going to be easy, he decided, If they found a body, Henry Hall was going to go ballistic. The crime scene would be hopelessly compromised and he would at least threaten to bang Maxwell up for ever and throw away the key. He had threatened it often enough, after all. As a teacher, Maxwell knew that eventually you had to do what you threatened or you lost all power, all credence. This time it would be the Oubliette, the Chateau d'If, Devil's Island. If they didn't find a body, Jacquie was going to go ballistic. She could read him like a book; something really

43

simple, like a Mr Men book. Mr Nosy. Mr Silly. Mr I-Can't-Help-Looking-For-Bodies. She would know he was out sleuthing. And he had promised he wouldn't. Had promised loads of times he wouldn't...

His reverie was broken by cannoning into the back of Bill Lunt. The photographer was rooted to the spot, stock still up to his ankles in soft sand. Maxwell sighed.

'What is it, Bill? Litter? A dead seagull?'

Bill's voice came from deep inside, a tiny, strangled thing that could hardly make it past his chattering teeth, his suddenly dry lips.

'No, not really,' he tried to whisper above the boom of the surf. 'It's a hand, actually.'

Maxwell looked around their feet, fitfully lit by the wavering torch beam. 'Where? Where's a hand?'

Lunt swallowed hard and moved to one side. 'Here,' he said, trying to sound like a grown-up, a grown-up photographer who had cleverly detected a crime. 'Here it is,' he said bravely. 'Just by my foot.' And he fainted dead away, gracefully to one side. Thoughtful, even in sudden unconsciousness.

'And so,' Maxwell said to Henry Hall, 'I looked down and, damn me, but if he wasn't right. It was a hand, sticking out of the sand, as if it was waving, rather than drowning. Poor old Bill.' It was nearly eleven now, way

44

past everybody's bedtime. Peter Maxwell had left his mobile at home, because he always left his mobile at home. He'd done the joke about mobile homes so often Jacquie wasn't listening any more. Peter Maxwell had tried to revive Bill Lunt, but on second thoughts let him sleep rather than leave him next to human remains or have the indignity of having to carry him back to the car. So he'd hot-footed it back along the sand, through the deserted car park and up onto The Shingle Road. A bit like Vinnie Jones looking for the RAC.

The old girl in Bide-A-Wee was suitably alarmed by the red-faced, out-of-breath apparition hanging on her door frame, but she'd duly called the police and the ambulance service and was eternally grateful to see the apparition vanish. And she slid the bolts shut behind him. You couldn't be too careful. He could have been a Global Terrorist.

That was then. Now, Maxwell looked back over his shoulder to where the fainting photographer was sitting on the ground, someone else's metal-lined blanket round his shoulders, sipping water from a plastic bottle. 'It's not the same actually finding a body as reading about it or seeing John Nettles finding one on the telly.'

'And you should know,' grunted Henry Hall.

'To hear you talk, Chief Inspector,' Maxwell said, 'you'd think I found them all the time. In fact, I have personally discovered surprisingly few.'

'Surprisingly few?' Henry Hall exploded. 'Listen to yourself, man. Most people go a whole lifetime and don't find any. I know dozens of coppers who've never seen a corpse.' He humphed and turned away. 'Surprisingly few, indeed!'

Maxwell fell into step with him, the path over the dunes lit brightly now by the SOCOs' arc lamps. The scene was surreal, as if a B-feature camera crew had descended on Willow Bay to film *The Creature That Was Thwarted By Peter Cushing II*. Men in white suits measured, photographed, probed, spoke into walkie talkies. Red, white and blue lights rotated across the sand.

'Well, Henry. You must know what I mean. You're always saying I get too involved in things. I'm sure my kids at school think I bump into bodies round every corner.'

Henry Hall stopped and pointed, rather theatrically for him, away to his left, landward, away from his crime scene. 'Mr Maxwell ... Max, please go home. I can vouch for the fact that you have a lovely partner. Your son's smiling face grinning up from his mother's desk is sometimes the only smile I see all day. Just for once, leave this to us. But, just before you do,' he closed to his man, 'what can you tell me about the photographer?'

Maxwell frowned and glanced back at the man. 'Not very much. Takes a darned good photo. Reliable sort.'

'How did he react when you stumbled over the remains?'

Maxwell laughed. It was nervous reaction, really. He was always amazed, even after all this time, that everybody didn't see the world as he did. And he didn't like the way the conversation was going. 'Bill? He was clearly horrified when he saw that hand. I thought he was dead.'

Hall shrugged. 'Good actor.'

'Bill?' Gobsmacked again. 'No, no, he came to me with the photographs, I told you...'

'Yes, precisely. He took photographs of a crime being committed and didn't do anything until the next day when he came to you. Is that what you would consider normal?'

It was late. It was cold. And the tide was coming in. No one was at their best.

'Chief Inspector, are you somehow implying that Bill Lunt...'

'Would you consider the time-lag normal?' Hall persisted.

'Umm...Well, it's not what everyone would do, perhaps, but understandable enough in its way.' Maxwell stood head to head with Hall, neither man inclined to give way. 'He

47

wasn't even sure what he had photographed until we had a look. It might have been a branch or anything.'

'I suppose,' Henry Hall said grudgingly, 'that at least we have an accurate time of death.'

'How, accurate?' Maxwell said. He'd read *The Romeo Error* and *Time of Death*. He knew that forensic science was going backwards and the Great Certainties were no more. The days of Simpson and Spilsbury were gone for ever.

Henry Hall smiled condescendingly. 'You probably don't know this,' he said, 'but digital cameras time and date the images to the second.'

Maxwell smiled back, the smile of a man with a surprise up his sleeve. He'd got a million. 'Thank you, Henry, for considering me a dinosaur and a very early one, just out of the primeval soup at that. I am in fact a bit of a whiz with the old digital camera. I do have, as you kindly pointed out, a particularly lovely partner and a totally enchanting son, both of whom I record for posterity at every opportunity. Unfortunately, Bill Lunt is not a digital man. He prefers steam, hand-cranked, call it what you will. His camera just about has a shutter and a lens. Apparently, it is what makes photography art.'

'Oh, fine. Just fine.' Henry Hall walked away and something in his step warned

Maxwell not to follow. He raised his voice slightly, to allow for the rapidly increasing distance between them and the annoying bellow of the surf.

'I'll be at home then, Henry, should you need me,' he called. There was no reply. 'Bye, then.' When there was still no reply he turned and made his way back towards the car park. A paramedic was just loading a white and shaking Bill Lunt into the ambulance.

'Mr Maxwell, Mr Maxwell,' Bill held out his hand towards him. 'Please come with me in the ambulance.'

Maxwell considered the options. If this was daytime telly, that nice Dick van Dyke would be waiting for Bill in Community General. If this was modern film *noir*, the ambulance driver would be psychotic old Nicolas Cage. As it was he saw the answer to a problem that had been dawning. 'Certainly, Bill,' he said, hopping aboard. 'I'll have to get off halfway, though. Sorry.' He turned to the paramedic. 'Columbine, if you would,' he smiled. 'No need to drive down the road, it'll only spook the neighbours. On the corner will be lovely.' He settled down on the vacant bed. 'You really don't look too well, Bill. Not too well at all...'

The silence inside Number 38, Columbine, the little town house that was *Chez Maxwell*, south of the Flyover, was palpable. It was the silence of two people studiously ignoring a third. Nolan's little nocturnal whitterings over the baby monitor were like sounds from another planet. Metternich, black, white, feline and neutered, who had been giving himself a thorough grooming, including all his private bits, curled up tight, nose up bum, when he heard Maxwell's key in the lock. He didn't like to take sides; this was a human thing – let them fight it out. He'd eat the survivor. Jacquie was knitting. She was concentrating furiously and her needles hissed together like tyres speeding on a wet road. No matter that she was dropping more stitches than she made, it being nearly one in the morning and all. She kept up the momentum, click, hiss, ignore, click, hiss, ignore. Motherhood may have slightly rounded Jacquie Carpenter, but it had made her more beautiful too. The grey eyes, smiling in the symmetry of her face; the lips parted in greeting. Tonight, however, was a *little* different.

Maxwell tried the jolly approach. 'Hello, Heart of Darkness,' he beamed, hurling cap and scarf in all directions. 'Got home safely, then. Nole in bed, is he? Good show.'

Click. Hiss. Ignore.

'You'll never guess what happened to me this evening.'

Jacquie put down her raddled knitting and stared at the man she lived with. 'Ooh,' she said, icily. 'Let me take a stab. You went to

50

the pub with a member of your department and spent the evening lesson planning. No, no, wait a minute. That sounds a bit far-fetched, doesn't it? Like an episode of *Hustle*. Let me think, now.' She tapped her chin with her empty knitting needle. 'Oh, no, now wait a minute. I've got it. You went wandering off over the dunes with some mad photographer and found a body.' She looked up, hands clasped now under her chin, the picture of an Angela Brazil heroine winning the hockey cup for the third time running. 'Don't keep me in suspense,' she said. 'Which of those was it?'

'You've heard, then?' he said, still smiling brightly, wondering whether he should risk a tip-toe to the drinks cabinet. After all, they called his favourite Southern Comfort SOCO these days; singularly apt bearing in mind the company he had recently been keeping.

'Henry rang,' she breezed, still in brittle, Jolly Hockeysticks mode, 'I'd just set off home, and I'd already done enough over-time for a decade, so I'm joining the team tomorrow.' Her icy resolve broke. 'Max, how could you?' She suddenly sounded like a furious mix of Margaret Meldrew and Barbara Good. 'You nearly died not ten months ago.'

'I'm allowed an accident, surely,' he muttered, taking the chance and pouring

51

himself a drink.

'Yes, an accident. Anyone is allowed one of those. But someone was trying to kill you, Max. Because you were snooping about.'

They had been indeed. And they'd got to old White Surrey's brakes just to make a point. Maxwell could be flippant about it now, although he still had the headaches from time to time.

'Yes, but Bill...'

'Bill being?'

'Bill Lunt. The mad photographer?'

'Oh, yes. Lunt. Chief suspect, according to Henry.'

Maxwell turned. 'Yes,' he said. 'I sensed a bit of a niggle there. What is Henry's problem?' he asked, exasperated. 'He'd have his doubts about Padre Pio.' A bad call perhaps – a lot of people had their doubts about Padre Pio. Except that Jacquie didn't know who he was.

'He led you straight to the body,' she reminded him. 'Apparently the footprints don't diverge from the path to it by even an inch.'

'Well, he knew where he had taken his picture from,' Maxwell played photographer's advocate. 'So he just followed his eyeline.'

'What was his landmark, then?' She leant forward, as someone laying the final trump card.

He leant back on the sofa opposite her, as

someone with an ace up his sleeve. 'The moon, in actual fact,' he said, smugly. 'He was taking photographs of the moon for the Leighford Photographer of the Year competition and the murder took place while he was doing it. Coincidentally, I mean. The murderer wasn't posing for him or anything.'

'Glad to hear it. So we've got some slavering werewolf out there, have we? Bad moon rising and all?'

Maxwell ignored her. 'So, when we got to the dunes, it was about the same time and so the moon was the same... Do you think Henry will realise that?'

'What, that the moon is the same?'

'Well, he wanted time of death. The moon in the picture will help him there, won't it? I mean, I expect there's a website or something, is there? About the moon?'

Jacquie sat up straight and looked at her man. Then she got up and went across to sit by him. She stroked his hair and gave him a kiss. 'I learn a bit more about you every day, Peter Maxwell,' she said, softly. 'You always chunter when you're feeling a bit fragile. And, by the way, the latest police think tank says that there *is* a link between the moon and psychotic behaviour.'

'Several million werewolves can't be wrong,' he nodded. 'It's like anthropy, only different. And, by the way, my money's still on Ollie Reed.'

He smiled at her and leant in to her fondling hand. 'It was a bit of a shock, you know,' he conceded. 'A hand, just by his foot. That meant, just by mine. I was right behind him.' He sighed. 'It was young.'

'Ah, sweetie,' she said, frowning and smoothing his cheek. 'It wasn't one of Yours, you know.'

He looked up at her. 'I hope not,' he said. He swirled the Southern Comfort in his glass. 'It was dirty. Young and dirty.'

'Well, it would be, Max,' she said, trying to be a bit businesslike. 'It had been buried in the sand.'

'No, not just sandy. Really dirty. Ground-in dirt, broken fingernails. Uncared for and unwashed.'

'What, you mean, someone living rough?'

'That kind of thing, yes.'

'That's not terribly common in Leighford,' she said. 'That's more of a big city thing. Big town, at least. Brighton. Portsmouth.'

'I haven't seen any kids like that around, I admit,' Maxwell said. He saw more from the saddle of his bike than most coppers saw in a month of Sundays from their patrol cars. 'I usually notice their dogs first, in fact. They've always got great big dogs, haven't they?' Metternich stirred in his sleep. His antennae had registered a warming of the atmosphere, but even so, when he had had a few more minutes' shuteye, he thought he

54

might go and sleep outside His Boy's room. You couldn't be too careful. Now the subject had turned to d★★s, he thought the time was ripe. He got up, stretched extravagantly and sauntered up the stairs. They watched him go and smiled at each other.

'Who'd have thought the old chap would go soft like that?' Jacquie said. 'You can set your watch by him these nights.'

Maxwell, who, from the quiet of the War Office, his night-time attic, often heard the last squeak of some poor rodent as Metternich did his nightly rounds, smiled at the thought of the great black and white beast going soft. Even so, he was glad he and the baby got on. It would have been a shame if they had had to get rid of one of them. He'd got quite fond of little Nolan.

CHAPTER THREE

The breeze off the sea got colder as the night wore on. The SOCO team shivered as the sweat cooled inside their plastic suits, but they had to carry on. Despite the fact that the body was buried above the tide line, the sand of the dune was notoriously unstable; a windy night could destroy even more than Maxwell and Bill Lunt had already. So, they worked on, in the harsh light of the arc lamps, the fine sand stinging their eyes, searching for the tiny piece of evidence that might nail a killer.

Slowly, the body belonging to the hand emerged. They had expected someone young – Maxwell's estimate was correct; it was young. About twenty, as far as the SOCOs could judge, though with dead eyes obscured by the sand stuck to the once damp corneas and the frantic mouth filled with a silent scream of soft dune, it was at first difficult to tell, The sex could go either way, too; the chopped hair could belong to both. Then as their brushes revealed more, it became clear – their body was female, thin and unkempt, wearing the obligatory anorak, sweatshirt with a barely discernible logo, and jeans, worn away to strings at the hem, all stained now with blood from the stab wounds in the abdomen. On her feet, a pair of trainers two sizes too big. Across her shoulder, a bag of *Big Issues;* the current copy, wet and mangled like old blotting paper only the oldest member of the team remembered from his childhood. Also in the bag, in a side pocket, was a stash of coins, clearly the takings of the day. The other stash, of some rolling tobacco and a small bag of cannabis, was irrelevant now. But it did show that this wasn't a random mugging. The clothes didn't look interfered with, so they started playing with the assumption that sex wasn't the motive either. In fact, as one shrouded figure remarked to another, there was no reason at all for her to be here, buried and dead, on the dunes outside Leighford, beyond the sweep of Willow Bay. The one thing missing was her *Big Issue* ID. Then, even that wasn't missing any more as the probing fingers of Brian Meredith found it, a tatty piece of laminated card, tucked into the back pocket of her jeans. He turned it to the light and squinted to read it.

'Lara Kent,' he read. 'No address, though.'

'I don't expect she's got one, has she?' Henry Hall loomed behind the man, bending forward from the waist to see the card. 'She was selling the *Big Issue*, for goodness' sake.'

'Yes, guv, but that's no reason to suppose she's got no address. If she's selling the *Issue*, she's trying to help herself at least.'

'Don't lecture me, Brian,' said Hall. Sometimes, he felt as old as the hills and as right wing as Genghis Khan. And he was always surrounded by Pinko-Liberals, the new policemen of the new generation. 'Is there a number or something on that card?'

Meredith turned it over. 'Yes, on the back, look.' He held it up.

'Right,' said Hall. 'As soon as you can raise someone, find out as much as possible about her. Meanwhile, get a copy of that ID photo. It's probably the best picture we'll get of her, at least for a while. If we can't scare up some relatives or friends, we may have to go door to door.'

A horrified gasp grabbed their attention. Alyson Sheridan, one of the team working off to the right of the burial site, nearer the sea, had jumped to her feet and was standing, staring at the ground, the back of her hand to her mouth. They all waded through the sliding dune to cluster behind her. There, emerging from the sand, was the body of a dog. Indeterminate of breed, it was, as Maxwell had foretold, a great big dog, thin as its mistress, with a matted coat and studded collar. It too had been stabbed repeatedly and the blood was caked around its flanks.

Hall nodded to Alyson, steadying her by the shoulders before letting her stumble off up the dune, looking for fresh air when she was, in fact, surrounded by it. 'Isn't it odd,' he remarked to no one in particular, 'how a human body just makes us pick up our brushes and cameras. A dead dog makes us feel sick.' Maxwell would have agreed and he would have reminded all and sundry that they set up the RSPCA forty years before the NSPCC. The moral? A dog is not just for Christmas; it'll get you life.

'I put it down to *Old Yeller*,' said Meredith. The film was being endlessly reshown on the Movies for Wimps channel.

'I put it down to not being professional,' Hall said, looking up the hill to where Alyson was being comforted by a WPC in uniform. He never watched *any* movie channels. 'Could someone make sure that whoever the fainting violet is is taken off live duty and sent for a bit of retraining.'

'Oh, come on, guv...' the SOCO leader began, and stopped as the blank glasses turned to him. To hide his confusion, Meredith bent to the dog's body. 'That's weird,' he said.

'What?' Hall hunkered down beside him.

'There's blood on his mouth, as well.'

'He bit someone, do you think? Or is it from the lungs?'

'Bit someone, let's hope.' He swabbed the dog's canine tooth and capped and labelled the swab. 'And ... hang on ... look, just there. It's hard to tell in this light, but is that a thread, caught in his teeth?'

Hall peered closer, but couldn't be sure. He'd been on the dunes now for nearly five hours, feeling like something out of Bloody Omaha. Life's a beach and then you die. 'Somebody bag this dog's head,' he called. 'It's priority. Take the body to the morgue with the girl.'

'Jim Astley's going to go ballistic,' Meredith said.

'So, what's new?' said Hall, letting the cold and lateness of the hour strip him of his usual professionalism. 'He goes ballistic if you wish him happy birthday. It's how he knows he's still alive. Stuck in there with bodies and Donald. It's enough to drive anybody nuts.'

One by one, the team withdrew from the murder site, leaving just some fluttering police tape to tell the world that they had been there in the first grey light of another winter dawn. The depressions that had held the bodies slowly filled up with shifting sand, as the dune healed itself. No one was there this time, to take pictures of nothing happening. Even a camera wouldn't have seen the mobile phone, two dunes away, sink with infinitesimal slowness, deeper into the sand, its battery dying, its messages hidden forever in the oblivion of its grave.

Jim Astley did indeed go ballistic. People in the corridors of power had expected him to move on, move up, move out years ago, but the old curmudgeon was still there, seeing himself as a latter-day Simpson or Spilsbury. Unlike them, however, he didn't get the headlines, but like medical men the world over he had delusions of grandeur and it was his arrogance, more than anything else, that kept him in post. True, he couldn't crouch in awkward crime scenes any more and recently his glasses had fallen into a few too many patients, but, by definition, they tended not to complain very much. Now he had been dragged out of his nice warm house, away from a nice full English. His lab at Leighford Mortuary was full of sand and the smell of wet, slightly decaying, dead dog. The girl he could deal with later, Hall had said, which was damned good of him, really. The dog was the one holding the clues.

'I think he bit someone, Jim,' Hall said from his end of the lab. He wasn't squeamish, as DCIs went, but he knew better than anyone the need to give Astley room to work – not possible elbow to elbow. 'There's thread caught in his teeth. We need to source that. And DNA the blood from round his mouth. We've swabbed that. We also need to get a breed, if we can. Add it to the door to door. People remember dogs.'

The door of the laboratory squeaked open and swung shut. Another smell vied with that of dog. It was Donald, Astley's assistant, borne in on a waft of McDonald's All-in All-day Breakfast Special. Donald had something of the Incredible Bulk about him these days, except that he wasn't green and nobody liked him anyway, whether he was angry or not.

'Donald,' Astley said waspishly, glancing at the lab clock. 'Glad you could make it.'

'No problem,' said Donald, licking his fingers and doing up his gown in a complicated movement made possible only through long practice. 'I was in the area anyway. Morning, Mr Hall.'

Hall could never work out whether Donald was extremely bright or extremely stupid. It may have been that even Donald didn't know.

Astley turned to his assistant. 'We have here two bodies, one, over there,' he tossed his head in the girl's direction, 'and the other, apparently more urgent, here.' He gestured at the dog.

Donald looked closely. 'Greyhound cross,' he said. 'Hmm, I'd say probably with something like an Airedale, something like that. About two hundred pounds worth of dog there, I'd guess.'

'Pardon?' Hall and Astley said together. Then Hall went solo.

'Do you mean people pay for mongrels like that?'

'Well,' Donald said. 'Not a mongrel specifically, you see. It's a cross-breed, but we know what breeds. A greyhound,' he traced the line of the dog's back and tail, 'and an ... mmm, I still think Airedale.' He held up the dog's matted head, showing the tell-tale square jaw and alert ears. 'People buy them for the temperament, both placid and loyal, in this case. Other crosses are bred for viciousness – Staffordshire and, well almost anything. Or for working; any of the terriers and say a cocker. They can be a bit nasty-tempered, but good for ratting, say.'

'And you're an expert in this how, exactly?' Astley spat. Not only did his lab smell like the aftermath of Crufts, but now Donald was effortlessly holding the floor. It was not a situation with which Astley was particularly familiar.

'Oh, my granddad has a farm, just outside Lewes,' he said. 'He has a few cross-breeds and I got interested.'

Hall interrupted. 'So, you could trace the breeder?' he asked.

'Not likely,' Donald said. 'You could trace the owner, though.'

Astley rolled his eyes. 'That's what we're trying to do, Donald,' he said, condescendingly.

Hall was less sceptical. He was impressed by the big man's knowledge, so carelessly shared. 'How?'

'Well,' Donald said, moving away towards the sink, to wash the dog off his fingers. Even he had limits. 'He's chipped, isn't he?'

'I don't know,' asked Hall. 'Is he?'

'Yeah,' said Donald. 'Most vets do it free these days and I think I could feel it, little tiny thing, there, on his neck.' He waved chubby fingers in the direction of the animal.

'And what does this chip tell us?' asked Hall. He had no pets. They required emotional attachment and he only had just enough to go round his family.

'Well, the chip doesn't tell us anything. But it tells us the chip company it's registered with and they can tell you the address, all that stuff, if only the owner has kept it up to date.' Donald smiled through the last, slick traces of his All-day Breakfast. 'It's a start, though, isn't it?'

Hall almost smiled, as much at Astley's discomfiture as at the progress he was suddenly making. But the DCI had a reputation and he checked himself. 'It certainly is, Donald. It certainly is. What do you do to read this chip?'

'Get a vet in. They've got a scanner that reads the information.'

Astley threw up his hands. 'Not content with a dog, Henry, you're now filling my lab with vets. What next? A stripper?'

Hall walked into the lobby and made for the lift. The sight of Donald's face brightening at the thought of a stripper would stay with him for days. As would the tongue-lashing Astley was giving Donald as Henry Hall left the building.

The nice thing about a Friday was that the next day was always Saturday. And this week proved to be no exception. Jacquie being on duty, hard at work at the crime face, unravelling the skein that Maxwell and Bill had uncovered, Maxwell was on shopping and amusing Nolan duty. With the boy strapped securely into his buggy, only his eyes visible in the Laplander cap his dad had fitted, they meandered round the town centre. Leighford in the middle of winter was a little like Byzantium just before it fell to the Turks or Magdeburg after Wallenstein (or was it Tilley?) sacked it. The rock shops were closed for the duration, as were those that sold T-shirts, which would not now be printed-while-you-wait until late May at the earliest. Mr L's Baguettes had gone to that great bakery in the sky. And three more charity shops were under new management. Yep, just like Byzantium.

None of this mattered to Nolan, who had been given the shopping list to look after, and for some reason he had eaten it, just loving that old biro taste. Because of this, Maxwell now had in his shopping bag a bottle of Southern Comfort (without which no self-respecting Head of Sixth Form could be), a bag of doughnuts (which were on special offer) and a cuddly toy version of Nolan's latest TV addiction – 'collect the set' (the financial death knell of parents everywhere). This would all have serious repercussions later, as the list had been for a small brown loaf, half a dozen free-range eggs and a chicken, although Jacquie didn't specify which came first. Never mind, thought Maxwell. Close enough.

And if Saturday was a nice thing, Saturday morning was the nicest bit. There were no kids in town to negotiate; they didn't surface until well into the afternoon, when exasperated parents kicked them out. Maxwell could browse the shops till Nolan got cranky and then they could go home, via the park for a little light swinging. There'd be no shouts of...

'Sir!'

'Take no notice,' Maxwell urged Nolan. Over the years, he'd preferred the 'straight ahead' look. 'They probably don't mean me, anyway.'

'Sir! Mr Maxwell!'

'Oh, poo, Nole. They've got me ... unless of course, it's that other Mr Maxwell, my doppelgänger,' Maxwell muttered, turning round with a smile as big as the great indoors. 'Hellooo... Oh,' his smile broadened and fixed. 'Hello, gentlemen. What a surprise. I thought you two were on a trip up the Limpopo or something similar.'

The two lads in question grinned. 'No, Mr Maxwell,' one of them said. 'We've been working in Nigeria for two months, digging wells.'

Maxwell could believe it. These were Old Highenas of recent origin and life in the great outdoors had seen them fill out, pick up some muscle and street cred since they padded the corridors of Leighford High.

'I knew it was something to do with water,' the Great Man agreed. 'Was it fun? Well digging?'

The bigger, dark-haired one answered for them both. 'It was OK,' he said. 'No women, but otherwise OK.'

His smaller, blond, more handsome companion said, 'Actually, Mr Maxwell, it was a real eye-opener. I'm really glad we went. I'll appreciate uni much more, now I know a bit about life on the larger scale.'

'Well said, Nick,' Maxwell said, patting him on the arm. Even as he did so, he could hardly believe that here was one of His Own, not a year out of school yet, and he had already forgotten that you could not fool Mad Max, not even for a moment. 'Back for long, are you?'

'Well, Mr Maxwell,' said Nick, 'I'm off to London for a bit, staying with my sister. I'm going to Goldsmith's, anyway, so it will be nice to learn my way around. You remember Kelly, don't you?' Maxwell nodded. He'd known dozens of Kellies in his time. Why did people call their daughters after rather ghastly Irish towns? There again, wasn't she from the Isle of Man? 'She works for Gordon Ramsay, well, not actually for Gordon Ramsay, more like in a restaurant he used to own. But he still pops in. She hasn't actually met him or anything, but it's quite exciting, don't you think?'

'Mmm, yes, yes, I suppose it is. He might be swearing at her any day now. I didn't realise you were interested in cooking, Nick. Had you down for a bit of a boffin.' To Maxwell's permanent disappointment, Nick, who had the GCSE grades to be anything, had for some reason fallen among scientists and was lost to History as a result.

'Oh, yeah, man, Mr Maxwell,' said the other. His name was Richard, but for some reason lost to time he was always known as Lobber. 'His prawn Creole's a legend.'

Nick blushed. 'It's not that good, Mr Maxwell,' he said. 'But I do like to cook, yes. Lob's just exaggerating, as usual.'

It was called Kid Creole in Maxwell's day; he was a different generation.

'And what're you doing, Richard, after this gap year?'

'Well, I'm not on a gap, not as such.'

'I thought you got in on clearing?' Maxwell prided himself on keeping up to date and he always remembered the frantic days in August when the results were known and the *Daily Mail* told the world how rubbish they were. Phones rang off hooks and computer keys were red-hot with emails. 'Didn't I hear something about a Foundation in Media somewhere up north?' Personally Maxwell couldn't imagine anything worse. Foundation? Media? North? He was describing the end of the world.

'Yeah, well, in the end I din't really fancy it. It looked a bit ... poncy, you know what I mean?'

'Well, not really,' Maxwell had to concede. He'd only just got used to 'gay' meaning homosexual. Already it meant something totally different. God alone knew what 'poncy' meant by now. 'But if you didn't want to go, then I'm glad you didn't bow to peer pressure. What *are* you doing, then?'

'I'm working in a shop in town. Get every fourth Saturday off. That's today,' he added, so Mad Max didn't think he was bunking off. Old habits died hard.

'Well, I won't keep you, then,' said Maxwell. 'Don't want to waste your day off nattering with me.' On cue, Nolan began to whimper. 'Oh, the little bloke's off on one. Better get him home. Bye then, lads.'

'Is he ... er ... your grandson?' Nick ventured.

'Not exactly,' Maxwell smiled. Surely, the lad *knew?* Hadn't *everybody* at Leighford last year heard and expressed amazement that the old bugger could still manage it?

'Well, bye, Mr Maxwell,' Nick said. 'See you around before I go, I hope.'

'Yes, that would be nice,' lied Maxwell.

'Seeya, Mr M,' said Lobber.

'Hmm,' Maxwell agreed through clamped lips. He didn't like lying twice in a row in front of Nolan. You heard such things about

69

early influences creating axe murderers and such. When they were safely round the corner, well away from the Early Learning Centre, Maxwell let out his breath in a huge sigh.

'Nole, my little mate,' he said, peering over the buggy so that he was disturbingly upside down to his son and heir. 'What you have just witnessed is not to go any further. You have just witnessed your daddy fibbing like anything, pretending to be glad to see those two. I can't remember two kids giving me more trouble than they did when they were two of My Own. Always up to juvenile rubbish, peeping at the girls in the shower, taking the handles off doors, letting tyres down. I bet those wells they dug never fill up with water because they've filled them with clingfilm or something. Still,' he started bouncing the buggy to make Nolan laugh, 'No one else will be up this early. I promise you, we'll have no more...'

'Coo-eee. Sir!' This time the call was much shriller and accompanied by giggling. He didn't have to turn. It was Year Nine. Probably Eff Why. And either Abi Buildingsociety or Chloe Oojar. Either way...

'Hang on, kid. We're in for a bumpy ride.' And, against all sense and reason, Maxwell broke into a run. And that was something else the kids at Leighford High didn't think Maxwell could do.

Saturday morning at Leighford nick was not so carefree. Saturdays followed Fridays with monotonous regularity it was true, but with not even a dream of a day off to comfort the murder team. They sat in rows, resignation etched on every face. The more hard-bitten among them didn't really see why they were losing good lie-in time on the random death of some homeless kid, The newer ones, who hadn't grown those essential extra skins yet, were waiting for Henry Hall to tell them more, to assign them jobs, to tell them what to do. The ones in between were waiting for him too. They were waiting for him to stick his head round the door, say it was all cleared up, no problem, that weedy photographer did it or failing that, the boyfriend, don't worry, everyone, you can all go home. Oh, and by the way, this is no longer a smoke-free zone. Bonuses and George Medals all round.

The door opened and Henry Hall entered, followed by Brian Meredith, the SOCO team leader, looking a shade more normal out of his white suit, and a trolley load of paperwork. A small but audible groan rose from the serried rows.

'We're here this morning,' Hall began, as usual without too much preamble or time wasted on greetings, 'to continue the investigation into the death of Lara Kent, an erstwhile *Big Issue* seller. Some of you may have seen her around,' he gestured to her picture, blown up big and pixelly from her ID card on the board behind him. 'She had a dog, a greyhound-Airedale cross, I am reliably informed.' Odd glances were exchanged, but nobody said anything. 'You may also re-member this. We've had some bits of luck in this case already. I'll pass you over to Brian, who can fill you in on the forensics.' He stepped aside, perching on the edge of the table.

Meredith stepped up to the plate and cleared his throat. He hadn't chosen to be a back-room boy for nothing; he hated hold-ing forth, but he tried his best. 'We were able to more or less clear the site last night, ermm, that's down on the dunes, for those of you who weren't there.' Several heads turned to look at Jacquie. They all knew who *was* there. Jacquie looked up to meet the stares before they burnt into her scalp. 'A Mr ... Lunt and a Mr ... Maxwell,' said Meredith on cue, by way of confirmation, 'found the body last night and called it in. A long story cut short, we found the ID card close to the body. Alyson found her dog buried not far off.' He raised his head from his notes to look for Alyson in the room. She was conspicuous by her absence. Not the stuff, perhaps, that SOCO specialists were made of. 'The dog seems to have blood around its mouth and a scrap of fabric in its teeth. We're having both of those analysed. Dr Astley's assistant identified the dog's breed but, more importantly, he alerted us to a microchip in his neck.'

A wag at the back of the room called out, 'I didn't know Donald had been chipped!' and was rewarded by laughter.

Meredith looked annoyed and Henry Hall tapped his biro menacingly on the palm of his hand. He understood *why* policemen laughed when sudden, gruesome death was in the air. It was the actual *laughter* he didn't quite cotton to. There was a time for it. And a place. But not here. Not now.

'To a microchip in the *dog's* neck,' Meredith continued. 'We have had it scanned and have been in touch with the company who manufactured it. This means we have an address for Lara, so no real need in the first instance for door to door.'

There was a faint but collective sigh of relief.

Hall stepped forward again. 'This may sound like a lot at this stage of the investigation, but in fact all we know is the name and hopefully, a previous address for our victim. We have a potential time of death, taking the photographs which started all this into account. We may have the DNA of the killer, which is pretty much useless until we have our killer in custody. I know lots of you think we may have a suspect, but Mr

73

Lunt, whilst not completely in the clear, would seem to be a very unlikely choice for our killer.' Jacquie smiled inwardly. Perhaps Maxwell's support of the man had hit home with the DCI. 'What we don't have,' Hall went on, 'is a motive, a murder weapon, or a murderer. So, the book is still pretty empty. Let's try and fill in the gaps. I think most of you have assignments. Jacquie, a word. Brian, can I leave you to carry on leaning on Jim Astley for a bit more detail?'

'Delighted,' said Meredith. He might not do Front of House very well, but leaning on Astley was always a pleasure.

Hall raised his voice a little. 'Is everyone clear on what they're doing?' There was a generalised murmur of assent. 'Good. Anyone unclear, check with Brian. I'm sure he's got lots for you to do. Jacquie and I will be back later and we'll call another briefing in … what shall we say? Five hours?'

Another Saturday afternoon gone west. Never mind. Leighford FC weren't very cheering to watch anyway. Not now they'd sold Beckham, Ronaldo, Owen and Rooney. Better off racking up the overtime.

Jacquie shrugged into her coat and fell into step beside Hall, making for the side door that led to the nick's car park.

'Guv…'

'Jacquie, if you are going to apologise for Maxwell again, please don't.'

'No, sir,' Jacquie lied. 'I was just going to ask what we're doing.'

He looked at her, and grunted. For all he was a copper of the new school, he hated being second guessed by an inferior. 'We're going to Arundel,' he said finally,

'Arundel?' she repeated. 'That's a bit posh for a *Big Issue* seller, isn't it?'

'I don't suppose that was a deliberate career choice, Jacquie,' Hall said. 'Anyway, we'll soon know.' He tossed her his car keys. 'You can drive. I'll close my eyes for a bit, if you don't mind.' It had been a long day's journey into night so far.

Jacquie was startled. Henry Hall never showed his human side. In fact, most people didn't know he had one. As they drove out of Leighford over the Dam, making for the Flyover, she risked a sideways glance and her face softened at the sight of her boss with his glasses slightly askew and a little bubble growing and shrinking at his lip as he breathed in and out. Suddenly he gave a snort, straightened his glasses and wiped his mouth.

'I'm not asleep,' he said, testily. 'I'm just resting my eyes.'

'Of course, guv,' Jacquie agreed quickly. A few more miles went by. Hall must have been tired. She'd crashed her gears six or seven times and he hadn't said a word.

'If anyone finds out about this,' he said in

a mumble, 'I'll know where they heard it.'

This time she allowed herself a little chuckle. 'It's not going any further, guv,' she said.

He snuggled a little down in his seat. 'Good,' he muttered, and rested his eyes some more, fully aware he'd hate himself later when he tried to stand upright again after even the briefest of dozes in that position.

Jacquie thought to herself, if I wasn't going to possibly tell a parent their daughter is dead, if I wasn't going to have to keep Max out of this at all costs, if I wasn't going to be out all weekend away from the baby, then I'd be having a good time.

CHAPTER FOUR

Maxwell sat with his feet up in his first-floor sitting room, back at Columbine, book open on his lap, watching Nolan sleep. He was much more picturesque at ad hoc naps than Henry Hall; for a start, he didn't have a pair of glasses digging into his cheek, just a dimpled fist lightly placed against his chin, where it had landed when the fingers he sucked to help him drop off had finally slipped from his mouth. He gave a little sigh from time to time, twitched his leg and carried on sleeping. Maxwell turned to Metternich, stretched at ease on the chair. At least he knew the Boy wasn't dreaming of eviscerating rodents as he slept.

'Two things, Count,' he began, giving up on the *The God Delusion* for the eighth time, 'Firstly, you know you're not supposed to be on that chair.' The monstrous black and white beast flicked a dismissive ear. Was he bothered? 'Fair enough. Just checking. Secondly, I wondered if you had any thoughts on the events of last night. Not the trouble with the Mem, I don't mean. All that frostiness is just her way of saying "I love you". I mean the body that poor old Bill and I found on the dunes. In the dunes, perhaps I ought to say. I didn't see anything, just the hand, but I'm sure it was a girl, and young, too. Jacquie says she wasn't one of mine and I hope she's right.' He sipped his coffee. The cat licked a paw, tongue searching between his toes. Fingers, since it was his front paw. 'It's odd that I haven't heard from Bill, though, don't you think?'

Metternich turned his head and stared at that plastic thing in the corner, silent now, but the blasted thing had been ringing all morning. It had almost driven him to getting up and moving somewhere quieter. But not quite.

'Hang on.' Maxwell had had a thought. 'I

haven't checked for messages. I am a fool.'
He put his mug down and got up with that
strange silent grace that parents adopt when
they are trying not to waken a child. He
crept across the room and picked up the
phone. The fractured dial tone told him the
story. He had a message. He dialled 1571;
the year of Lepanto, when Don John of
Austria had kicked seven kinds of shit out of
the Turks and set his people free. Without
that fortuitous *aide memoire*, Maxwell would
never pick up messages at all.

'This is BT One Five Seven One. You
have,' minute pause, 'fifteen new messages.
First message. Message received at today at
ten oh seven hours.'

'Max, Max, this is Bill. Are you there? Is
this one of those phones where you hear
who's on the other end? Max? Max? Mr
Maxwell? Perhaps not. Well, if you're there or
when you get this message, can you give me
a ring? Please, I mean? Only, I've had the
police round. They seem to think I did it. The
... you know, the ... thing. Murder. They
haven't arrested me or anything but, well,
Emma's in a bit of a state. Well, so am I as a
matter of fact. So ... um, yes, if you could give
me a ring. That's Leighford 879621. Umm ...
right, then.'

'End of message. To hear the message
again, press one. To save it for thirty days,
press two. To delete it, press three. Next

message. Message received today at ten fifteen hours.'

'Max, Max ... are you there...?'

And so on, thirteen more times, getting more and more frantic, more high pitched and desperate. And the electronic woman who punctuated them must have had a sore throat by now. Maxwell slowly replaced the phone. Why would he want to keep all that lot for thirty days? As a classic example of mounting hysteria, however, the messages had merit. Perhaps he'd pass them on to the psychiatric unit at Leighford General as a learning tool for their students. In any event, he was aware that he had just witnessed the unravelling of Bill Lunt. Surely, the police couldn't seriously suspect the man? He had been practically catatonic at the murder scene. And he wasn't that good at acting. In fact, Maxwell would have taken bets that he wasn't any good at acting at all.

Taking the phone with him, he went back to his seat, and his conversation with Metternich. 'So, as I was saying, Count. I have in actual fact heard from Bill, only not really because we haven't spoken. So I haven't checked what he remembers about last night. I admit I wasn't really concentrating while we were walking towards the sea. I was just watching my feet. He didn't say anything, but I think he got a message on his phone; I think I heard that beep beep thing you get. You know the one.'

Metternich did indeed know the one. It got right inside his head, like a fly buzzing round in there. He remembered the good old days, when people had left messages on bits of white stuff lying around. When he was a kitten, in those far off days before he had responsibilities – like His Nibs here, asking him stuff all the time and That Woman moving in, upsetting the male balance of nature and The Boy to be watched – he occasionally used to cut out the trip to the litter box and wee on the messages. That was fun! But wait, the mad old duffer was still whittering on.

'I must ask him if he got a message, although it probably isn't any of my business, I promised Jacquie I'd keep out of this one, Count.'

Metternich cocked a disbelieving eyebrow at him. If he had a rat cutlet for every time he'd heard that one.

'No, I did.' Maxwell sensed the cat's disbelief. 'I really am going to leave it alone.'

Metternich settled down for a bit more kip, paws over nose, nose up bum. Usual thing – the contortionist's dream, the sort of thing Louis Wain used to see without even going off on one.

Nolan burbled in his sleep and replaced his sucking fingers in his mouth.

The central heating pinged as a distant pipe cooled.

'Oh, dammit, Count. Of course I'm not. Who am I kidding?' Maxwell stabbed the numbers into the phone and paused with it to his ear.

Why did they do that? Metternich wondered for the millionth time. He'll start talking in a minute. Yep, there he goes.

'Bill. Bill, it's Max.'

The thing by his ear squawked and he wandered into the kitchen. There were some things a man didn't want his son or his cat to hear.

'Calm down, Bill.' It was a damn-near perfect Michael Winner. 'I'm sure it's not as bad as all that. Oh, is it? Why has she gone back to her mother? Surely her mother only lives in Leighford, so she hasn't gone far.' Maxwell listened, with the phone slightly away from his ear, then sighed. 'I do understand, Bill. Look,' he crossed his fingers to counteract the lie that was on its way. 'I'm sure Jacquie would love to have you for a few days. Come on round. Yes, no, really. I'll see you shortly.'

He rang off and walked back into the sitting room. Two pairs of big round eyes, brown and golden, were looking at him in what he assumed was horror.

'All right, all right. There's no need to look at me like that, either of you. I'm sure she'll be fine about it.' But it was a worried man who sat down again on the sofa. He dialled

81

once more and sat while the call connected. He looked down and found he hadn't yet uncrossed his fingers. Probably just as well.

They swept around that brave curve by the river, where the road ran on to Angmering and Littlehampton, driving over the bridge with the Howards' great castle staring down at them. Jacquie glanced to her right, to the stretch of river that followed the riverbank and remembered a night long, long ago when she'd wandered there with a boy. And he'd kissed her in the sunset's flare on the water. And she felt her heart leap again. Just a little. Just for a moment. Whatever happened to Johnny Depp? She caught sight of the gently snoring DCI beside her and it jolted her back to reality. Johnny Depp was another fantasy altogether. The lad's name was actually Tommy Gluck and he had a speech impediment. No doubt by now he had eight kids, a nagging mother-in-law and hairs were starting to grow out of his ears. Ah, the dream of young love.

She parked the Ka with a bit of a bounce, hoping it would wake Hall up. The DCI had been out of it since Leighford. She didn't want the job of having to shake him awake. He sat upright with a jerk (no reflection on Jacquie of course), straightening his glasses in a reflex movement. He cleared his throat and shrugged his jacket straight.

'Do you have such a thing as a mint?' he asked Jacquie. 'My mouth feels horrible.'

Jacquie foraged in her bag looking for one of those breath Things That Stick To The Roof Of Your Mouth and brought out a pack of Haribo Jelly Bears. She always carried some about her person; they were Maxwell's favourite, after Southern Comfort, a rarish steak, coq au vin, prawn cocktail and Black Forest gateau; well, he was a child of the sixties. She proffered the bag.

'Hmm, no thanks,' Henry Hall felt he had lost enough gravitas on this journey. This was not the time to admit he only ate the black ones. There'd be all kinds of ethnic questions over that.

'Anyway,' Jacquie said, trying to restore some dignity into the proceedings. 'Do we know who lives here? Parents? Just one parent?'

'I believe that we will be meeting a Mrs Marianne Crown, previously Mrs Kent, Lara's mother, and her husband, Lara's stepfather.'

'I see. Do we know how long ago the girl left home?'

'Well, the dog was not very old, according to the vet. Two or thereabouts. She had him microchipped, probably around about eighteen, twenty months ago at the most. So, we're looking at any time since summer before last up to last week.'

'Right.' They walked across the drive of the thirties house. Average. Everyday. Trim without opulence. Nothing out of the ordinary. Hardly the house of a murder victim. Yet Hall and Jacquie knew that was nonsense. It could be any house. Anywhere. Anytime. Jacquie knocked on the door. While she waited for it to open, she turned quickly to Hall. 'Just one last thing, guv. Do they know how she was living?'

'I don't know,' he said, then, quickly, 'Here we go.'

A shadow had appeared across the reeded glass of the door and it was eased open on a chain. One eye and a balding head partly filled the gap.

'Yes?'

'Hello, Mr Crown,' Jacquie began. 'We are from...'

'Not today, thank you,' the man said and firmly shut the door.

'No, no,' Jacquie lowered her mouth to the letterbox. 'We are from Leighford Police. We rang...'

The sound of genteelly raised voices from behind the door, followed by a scuffle, preceded the opening of the door. A pretty woman, about forty-five but not looking it, stood there. Her eyes were red, but otherwise her make-up and hair were immaculate.

'I do apologise,' she said, ushering them in. 'I try to get to the door first, but he does so love to answer it and I'm not always quick enough. Come in, come in.' She pointed to her left. 'We're through there.'

They squeezed past her into a room dominated by an enormous cream leather sofa, complete with footstools and matching cushions. Already sitting sulkily at one end was the owner of the eye and bald head. He didn't look inclined to introduce himself, so Jacquie and Henry Hall took the initiative.

'Mr Crown,' Jacquie said, 'I am Detective Sergeant Carpenter from Leighford.'

He ignored her.

'I am DCI Henry Hall,' said Hall, in the slightly wheedling tone which even he adopted when faced with the recalcitrant elderly.

Lara's mother came in behind them. 'Take no notice of him,' she said. 'He can be very rude sometimes.' She ushered them into chairs crammed into opposite corners of the room, completely overwhelmed by the sofa. She took a seat at the opposite end of the monstrous thing to the sulky old man. She looked expectantly at them.

Henry Hall began. 'Mrs Crown, I am not sure quite what you have been told, but we are afraid that we have some bad news for you. A body was found last night in Leighford and it was carrying identification which leads us to suspect it is your daughter, Lara.'

The woman nodded, appearing to be

calm, but Jacquie noticed the clenched fist in her lap. Sudden death took people in different ways. And it changed from day to day.

Henry Hall continued. 'Do you have a picture of Lara? Something recent?'

The woman got up and fetched a picture from the windowsill. It was crowded with pictures, but there was only the one with Lara in it. 'It's not particularly new,' she apologised. 'It's from when she was my bridesmaid.'

'When was this?' Jacquie asked.

'August, year before last.'

Henry Hall allowed himself a little mental tick in that box.

'Nothing more recent?'

'No. She left home a few weeks after this was taken. She didn't take to my husband much.'

Looking at the miserable old creature hunched grumpily on the end of the sofa, Jacquie could quite see why.

'She had a place at university anyway – Bath Spa – so she would have been going, but...' the woman's face crumpled and she couldn't speak for a moment. There was no move of affection from Crown, no urge to comfort her. 'But, I expected her back, you know, from time to time. Vacations. Bringing friends back. We'd have made them welcome.' The last sentence was a wail, a cry for understanding. 'But we never saw her again.

She never came back, not even for Christmas. We rang the university, but she had never even signed in there. She'd just disappeared.'

Hall was struck, and not for the first time, by the distance of families. Two of his three had gone to university and he and Margaret had driven them both there, saw their rooms, got the feel of the place.

'Did you report her missing?' Jacquie asked.

The woman looked confused. 'No. Why should we?'

The policepersons looked at each other, bemused. 'Well,' said Hall, 'she was missing, wasn't she?'

'Well, yes…'

'You'd had a row,' Hall completed her sentence. 'You knew she had left home on purpose.'

'Yes, I suppose that's it,' she said. A slightly unpleasant smirk came over her tear-stained face. 'And I was newly married. I was, well, you know, otherwise engaged.'

There was a joke in there somewhere and Jacquie could hardly prevent herself from laughing out loud. And the thought that the miserable old sod caught in the grip of that huge sofa could keep anyone engaged was unbelievable. Maybe he was a multi-millionaire with only three months to live. While everyone searched for the next, nonembarrassing, thing to say, there was the sound of a key in the front door. The door into the lounge opened and a man walked in. He was around twenty-seven or so, dressed in fitness clothes, gym bag in his hand. Jacquie had to admit it; he was frankly gorgeous. Henry Hall was not as instantly smitten as Jacquie. He stood and held out his hand.

'Hello,' he said. 'I am DCI Henry Hall. And you are?'

'Mike Crown,' the hunk replied. He turned to Lara's mother. 'Are you all right, darling?' He planted a kiss on her cheek. 'I am so sorry to be late, but we went to another set.' He looked at the old geezer. 'Dad behaving himself?'

'Not really,' his wife said, gazing adoringly at him. 'Sit down, darling. I'm afraid it *is* bad news.'

'Oh, sweetie,' he said, without a trace of emotion and turned to Hall and Jacquie. 'It's her, then. Been dead long? Since she went, I mean?'

Henry Hall could not keep the ice out of his voice. Now that the family entanglements had been sorted out, it *ought* to have been better; in fact, it was slightly worse. 'No, Mr Crown,' he all but spat. 'She has not. She has been dead just over two days. In the months between, we believe she has been living rough or in squats, with her dog. She has recently been selling the *Big Issue* in Leighford.'

Crown seemed oblivious to his tone. He may be better looking than his dad, Jacquie thought to herself, but he takes 'horrible' to new depths.

'Oh, right. We wondered where she'd gone, didn't we, darl?'

Marianne Crown had lost all semblance of distress. Her daughter may be dead, but her gorgeous young husband was still here and that was, after all, what counted. 'Well, she'd just gone off, honey, hadn't she?' she fluttered at him. 'We hardly missed her, after a bit. They grow away from you, don't they, in the end?'

Do they? Jacquie wondered, Would that little pink thing she had at home, cuddling into her neck when he was tired and twining his fingers into her hair, *ever* grow away? And what would it do to her if he did? Jesus, she realised, she'd become Marianne Crown.

'He missed her, I reckon,' came a growl from the end of the sofa. They had all forgotten Mr Crown Senior.

His son jumped up and bundled him from the room. 'Now, then, Dad,' he said. 'Why don't you go and do some gardening or something?' They could still hear him muttering as he made his way down the hall. 'Mum died a few months ago,' Crown said. 'Dad came to stay for a bit and he's proving a little difficult to dislodge. But Marianne's a wonder with him, aren't you, darl?'

She simpered. But the police pair had noted his comment and it clarified a lot of things for them. It's all very well marrying an older wife with her own home. But it's even better if she has a pretty daughter on the premises to remind you you're still young.

Neither Jacquie nor Henry Hall had much stomach for continuing the interview once Superman arrived. They took the photograph with them, carefully removed from its silver frame by Crown before he handed it over. They paid lip service to their condolences, walked silently down the path and got into the car, faces frozen in blank expressions until they were safely up the road. Only then did they turn to face each other.

'What a wanker,' Jacquie exploded.

'Now, now,' said Henry Hall, awake now, driving and in control. 'That's such a nasty, judgemental word. We never use that at home.'

Jacquie looked crestfallen.

'No, for people like Crown, we always prefer "tosser".'

CHAPTER FIVE

'But I left a message,' Maxwell was placatory. He knew he was looking his best; a bathed, changed, fed and smiley baby in one hand, a gin and tonic, ice and lemon, in the other.

'True.' Jacquie took the baby and the gin from him, not necessarily in that order. A kiss and a sip and things might look better. She tried both. No, no good, it still sounded rubbish. And it was all made worse by the fact that they were carrying on this conversation at a low hum, through the clenched teeth of secrecy. 'I don't understand why you invited a suspect in my latest murder case to stay with us.'

'I'm not sure I invited him, as such.' Maxwell, relieved of son and gin, flopped down in his chair. 'He had left about a million messages and Emma has left him and ... well, I knew you wouldn't really mind. You can't seriously think he is a suspect. I mean, go and look at him. He just doesn't look like a murderer.'

'Neither did Crippen. Nor do I, but I may well become one in a minute. I don't want to ask this, but where would I go, were I wishing to look at him?'

'Ermm … in the spare room?'

'*What?* My spare room, I mean, our spare room? Here? In this house?'

'Well, yes, woman policeman. Where else do we have spare rooms?'

'At my mother's fortunately, because I think that's where I'll have to go if he stays here,'

'Oh, come on. It isn't that serious.' To Maxwell, for anyone to consider seriously living with Jacquie's mother, there would have had to have been a nuclear holocaust.

'Yes, Max, it is that serious.' Nolan sensed the mood of the moment. His Mummy was upset. His Daddy was a prat. What's a boy to do? He put his fingers on Jacquie's lips as if to say 'Hush, now'. But she wasn't having any of it and gently turned her head away. 'William Lunt is a suspect in the murder of Lana Kent. Not a very *suspect* suspect, I grant you, but he is on file in the police station *where I work!* Max, this is extreme, even for you.'

Maxwell got up and made for the door. 'You're right. I was stupid. But he is just so … pathetic, somehow. I just *know* he didn't do it. Why should he? He didn't know her or anything.'

'How do you know he didn't? I've got the stats somewhere of the number of murderers who "find" their victims. They can't bear the wait for somebody else to happen on it and they try to control the proceedings. You only see Lunt once a year for the annual photo. Just because he is married to an Old Leighford Highena doesn't make him automatically innocent, you know.'

'No, of course not. I'm sorry. Metternich told me I was doing a stupid thing, but if I didn't ignore him sometimes, he'd be unbearable.' He moved onto the landing and started up the stairs. 'I will get him to leave. I don't think he'll mind. The shop certainly does well enough for him to afford a hotel if he can't bear it at home,'

She blew him a kiss. 'Thank you, Max. You know it makes sense.' She settled down to play aimlessly with Nolan's toes. She didn't know whether he liked it or not, but it certainly calmed her down. 'Piggy,' he gurgled, which she hoped referred to the game and not his mother's profession. She had only got as far as the porcine who had roast beef before Maxwell was back.

'Problem solved,' he said, his brow furrowed.

'Oh?'

'He appears to have gone.'

'Gone? You mean, out? Or gone, as in taken all his things?'

'Gone. Left. Vamoosed.'

Jacquie immediately felt bad. 'Oh, Max, do you think he heard us? I didn't want to hurt his feelings.' Jacquie's stomach somersaulted in the way it does for all of us at moments like these. The rational bit – that Bill Lunt had overheard their whispered conversation, taken umbrage and packed his bags, creeping noiselessly past their open door; and all in a few minutes, never entered her head.

'Does a suspect have feelings?' he asked her, one eyebrow raised. Maxwell was not one of those blokes Julius Caesar would have wanted with him on the Ides of March, that's for sure.

'Oh, please. I feel awful.'

He crossed the room and gave her an absentminded hug. 'Where's he gone, though?'

'I expect he's gone home,' she said. 'At least, I hope he has, I would imagine when they released him without charge, they asked him not to leave the immediate area.'

'Yes, I expect you're right, heart,' he said. 'He will have gone home. I mean, as you so rightly say, there was no reason for him *not* to be at home.' They sat in silence for a while. 'I wonder if he's had time to get back yet?' Maxwell added.

'It all depends when he left, I suppose,' Jacquie said, shifting Nolan onto the other arm. She suddenly got up and went to the phone. 'For goodness' sake, Max. Why don't we behave like adults? What's his number?'

'Battle of Barnet,' he said.

'Oh,' Jacquie tapped in 1471. 'Has no one

phoned since him, then?'

'No,' Maxwell said, fighting down the urge to hug her. He'd make an historian of her yet, but he sure as hell wasn't going to let her know how proud he was. On the other hand, Nolan didn't seem to have any grasp of dates at all, and he was fifteen months old next Thursday.

'It's ringing.' He could hear the tinny sound easing out round the bones in her head. 'No reply, though.'

'Leave a message.'

'Oh ... sssh.' With no hand free, she flapped Nolan at him. 'Hello? Mr Lunt, this is Jacquie Carpenter. Um ... I was just wondering if you had gone home because ... well, Max and I were wondering if you were coming back. You'd be very welcome. Ummm. Well, give us a ring when you get in. See you later. Bye.' She put the phone down and turned to face Maxwell, who was sitting with arms folded, histrionically drumming his fingers on his bicep, tapping a foot in time. 'What? Well, he *is* welcome. It's just not ... well, not very sensible. I'd still like to know he's OK, though.'

'Of course, woman policeman. I can see your dilemma. I'm sure he'll be fine. Now, would you like a shrivelled up piece of Freezer Bottom Special with vegetables glued to the plate or would you like me to phone for a Chinese?'

Jacquie leant back in her chair. 'Chinese,' she said, while the words were still leaving his mouth. 'Delivered.'

'Is there any other kind?' he asked her. He moved towards the phone.

'Heavy on the chilli beef,' she reminded him. 'And prawn crackers. And chips.'

'I'll just order the whole menu, shall I? I trust you won't be telling me you're eating for two.'

She sighed. She had promised herself she would tell Maxwell nothing about this case. He would be kept totally in the dark. He would get not one single detail from her. She sighed again. 'It's been a prawn cracker and chips kind of day, Max. It started when Henry Hall went to sleep in the car...'

Maxwell replaced the phone and, in a surprisingly limber movement for one of his advanced years, curled up at her feet.

'Say on, Scheherazade. I'm all ears.'

She cuffed him round the nearest one. 'Chinese first. Then story.'

Grumbling, he got to his feet.

'And make that extra pancakes with the duck.'

'Duck?'

'Yes. Half a one should do it. That's why I want extra pancakes.'

'You drive a hard bargain, light of a thousand camels.'

'But I'm worth it,' she replied, with a more

than passable stab at the Garnier advert. 'But if I die of starvation, you might never know.'

He dialled for all he was worth. He timetabled it in his head. Phone. Order. Get Nolan into bed; the child already had an unhealthy appetite for sweet and sour. The Yellow Peril was getting closer. Eat. Get the goods. And then twelve hours tomorrow, marking GCSE coursework. Typical! Even the Lord had a day off, but not Peter Maxwell. What a lovely way to round off a weekend. Even Monday looked good from here. Hang on, though. Lesson Three; Ten Eff Four. Cancel that.

'Hello? Mong Wing? Get an extra pencil sharpened – I think you might need it...'

Mad Max marked thirty-seven pieces of coursework that Sunday. By lunchtime, he'd lost the will to live.

The dawn that Monday was a particularly splendid effort. It was pink and pearly grey, with a mist wisping off the sea inland, making a promise of a beautiful early spring day to come. In the silence of the park that measured the length of the Esplanade, just one road's width from the sea, a listener might almost fancy that they could hear the creak of an unfurling daffodil, the whisper of a crocus opening to the morning light. That same listener, walking from the entrance of the park at the west end into the dawn light to the east would then have sensed, no fancy needed, a faint noise, coming from one of the benches along the path that meandered through the wakening lawn. It was a whimper, very faint and growing fainter. It sounded like someone saying, whispering with their last breath, 'Help me. Oh, help me. Please.' And that horrified listener, should there be one to hand, would discover that it didn't just sound like someone dying. It really was someone dying, there on a park bench, in Leighford Esplanade Park.

Peter Maxwell was in the middle of explaining to Nine Eff Gee the niceties of the War of Jenkins' Ear. He found a nice rant on the shortcomings of the Foreign Office of today vis-à-vis that of Walpole was as good a way as any of starting the week. It didn't help poor, bemused old Nine Eff Gee that the Foreign Office wasn't called the Foreign Office then, but the Department of the North, or it might have been South; no, Samantha, there wasn't a Department of the East or West, but there were, of course, wicked witches from there. No, Melanie, that was a joke – do keep up!

There was a timorous knock on the door and when it opened, there stood Thingee

One from Reception, looking strangely ill at ease without the desk she usually hid behind.

'Mr Maxwell?' she said in a tiny voice. 'You're wanted in Reception.'

'Speak up, Thingee, old chap,' said Maxwell, full of the joys of incipient spring, the scent of the chase and of Saturday's soy sauce still, metaphorically, in his nostrils. After all, Captain Jenkins had lost an ear and what with the acoustics in Aitch One... 'Who wants me in Reception?'

Thingee crept closer and mouthed a word.

'No, sorry. Can't you go back down and ring me up. I can hear you when you use the phone.'

She crawled a tiny pace nearer and whispered as nearly in his ear as she could manage, 'It's the police.'

'Is it?' he stepped back in amazement. Nine Eff Gee were agog. 'Why does Mr Plod want to see me, I wonder?'

'It's not a Mr Plod,' Thingee said, bemused (no child of the Blyton generation she). 'It's a Detective Sergeant Carpenter.'

'No, no, Thingee,' Maxwell chortled. 'That's not the police. That's just Woman Policeman Carpenter. You know, little Nolan's mum?'

Thingee smiled. They all knew Nolan. Nine Eff Gee smiled too – at least, the girls did. The lads didn't know what all the fuss was about. Nolan had been breaking hearts at Leighford High School from a few weeks old. Whenever his dad or his mum wheeled him in, there was always an adoring bevy of wannabee mums crowding round. They'd moved on from dollies years ago and their body clocks were winding up for the real thing. 'I know Mrs Maxwell ... I mean, Sergeant Carpenter, Mr Maxwell,' she said. 'But she said to particularly say this was the police. Not just Mrs ... I mean, Sergeant Carpenter.'

Maxwell looked serious, then turned to the class. 'If any of you so much as twitches a finger,' he said, 'I will continue this lesson later using a real ear. Savvy?' The last word (which Maxwell always had) was pure Johnny Depp by way of Jack Sparrow and since Nine Eff Gee couldn't tell Captain Jenkins from Captain Sparrow, that was good enough.

They savvied. No finger twitched until the bell went and they all left the lesson with a collective sigh of relief. The thing about Mad Max, you knew where you were. If he said he was going to cut someone's ear off, the only question would be; whose?

Down in Reception, Jacquie waited by the desk, making small talk with Thingee Two, Thingee One's afternoon replacement. It was odd to see them both together; perhaps it presaged death or something, the way seeing your own doppelganger was said to do. And, in a way, it did. She turned as Maxwell came into the glass booth built into a side of the Hall.

'Hello, Sergeant?' he said, managing to impose a question mark at the end of the greeting.

'Sir,' she said. She was accompanied by a rookie constable Maxwell didn't know and the niceties must be maintained. 'We are here in connection with a suspicious death.'

'Well, yes,' he said, perplexed. 'I found the body last week, if you recall.'

'Not that suspicious death,' she said. 'Another suspicious death. Is there somewhere we can go? Your office?'

He led them through the labyrinth that was Leighford High, that Sixties shell that bore the brunt of generations of school-children creeping unwillingly to school. Their faces weren't beaming anymore and nobody knew what a satchel was, still less carried one. Their black shoes left scuffs on the lower reaches of the walls and curious grey blobs decorated the carpets – thirty year old chewing gum for the archaeologists of the future to ponder.

They crossed the Quad in silence under the bare arms of the trees and took the stairs to the Mezzanine floor where Maxwell reigned as Head of Sixth Form. You couldn't hear the pandemonium from the Languages Department on this side of the building and Maxwell ushered the police people into his office, his Inner Sanctum.

The rookie stood just staring at the film posters around the wall. Jacquie plonked herself down on the ghastly, itchy, flimsy L-shaped seating as Maxwell hit the kettle switch.

'A body was discovered this morning at seven o'clock by a jogger in the Esplanade Park,' Jacquie continued, as if the trek through the school had not intervened.

Maxwell looked puzzled. 'I'm sorry,' he said. 'It's probably just me, but I don't know why a body in Esplanade Park should be anything to do with me. If I can say this without distressing your colleague here, who I am sure is of a sensitive nature, you do know *exactly* where I was from around 5.30 last night until 8 o'clock this morning. So, in short, I'm not the guy. You'll have a coffee before you go?' He turned on his heel.

Jacquie grabbed his jacket hem and pulled him back. 'Max,' she said, dropping the veneer of professionalism. 'I've come here because I recognised him.'

'So, why come here?' He was rather miffed. When he wanted to be involved in a murder, it took Kung Po Chicken to get the details out of her. Here was one he knew nothing about and he was dragged out of a lesson to be told about it. Women, eh? He threw an exasperated glance at the rookie, but realised at once the lad had no idea what a woman was, so no help there.

She drew nearer. 'I recognised him because he's one of yours.' Maxwell looked stricken. 'Not a current Yours, I don't mean. He's an Old Highena.'

'My God. Who?'

'That's the problem. I only know he came here. I can't remember when exactly or who he is. He's one of those who comes up to you in the street and tells you he always liked History and you was his favourite teacher up at the school, honest.'

'Does he belong to the group who then touch me for the price of a pint?'

'He might have done. He was found on a park bench.'

'Well,' Maxwell sat down heavily in the chair, the coffee offer forgotten and the kettle switching itself off. 'Where do we go from here?'

'Max, you know I wouldn't ask if there was any other way, but I need you to come down and identify him for us.'

'I'll get my coat.' It wasn't that he was morbidly curious. He had been connected with sudden death often enough to know that what was, to the uninvolved outsider, just a salacious or exciting news item, to the people involved always brought grief and distress, anger and regret. If this body was that of a Leighford Highena, however long ago, it meant that parents were probably still living in the area, mates might be waiting even now for him outside a pub, workmates would be looking at an empty desk, wondering whether to phone home and find out where he might be. It wasn't just a dead body. It was a dead life.

'I'm sorry, Max. But the DCI thinks you can really help us on this one.'

Maxwell suppressed a snort. Henry Hall had blown hot and cold on this very theme for years. It was as if he blew on the dandelion clock of crime. 'He helps me, he helps me not.' Now, he'd sent a woman to do a man's job; worse, the cunning old bastard had sent Jacquie Carpenter.

She touched his lapel by way of goodbye. 'We can find our own way,' she told him and she and her rookie companion went back to the car.

Maxwell weighed his options. Leighford Highenas had died before, some of them violently. Some behind the wheel of a car, some in the wrong place at the wrong time. But there was something *personal* about it always. Maxwell had gone to their funerals, on wet hillsides, wearing a pink bowtie once because pink had been the girl's favourite colour. He had made small talk with relatives and friends, offered commiserations, growled his way through the hymns. 'All Things Bright

And Beautiful' indeed. Time after time, and just too often, all things bright and beautiful were snuffed out, destroyed. He hauled on his coat, threw the Jesus scarf around his neck, dumped the shapeless tweed hat on his shapeless hair and made for the light.

'Thingee, my dear,' he said when he reached Reception, gesturing for her to come closer. 'I fear I have been picked up by the fuzz. If you could cover this afternoon for me I would be grateful. For some reason best known to the timetablers I am down for Travel and Tourism today. I have been showing them holiday-themed DVDs, I am not ashamed to admit. Let's see, we've done *Carry on Camping*. We gave up on *Lost in Translation*, since it clearly was. *Summer Holiday* was last week ... who's free to do this cover?' He smiled brightly at Thingee One.

She ran her finger down a list, printed on bright orange paper. 'Umm, let's see, Mr Maxwell.' She looked at him and winked conspiratorially. 'Would you like it to be Ms Lessing?'

'Oh, Thingee. Most fragrant of women.' Thingee blushed to the roots of her hair. 'That would be splendid. I would love it to be Ms Lessing. In that case, write this down.' He cleared his throat and dictated. 'Eleven Zed Queue. First lesson, show as much as you can of *Last Tango in Paris*. I gather that the Religious Studies department have a well-thumbed copy. Second lesson, questions to the teacher in charge of the cover.' He smiled. 'That should do it.'

Maxwell turned on his heel and made for the door, ducking his head and turning his face away as he whisked past Dierdre Lessing's office window. Out of the corner of his eye he saw her half rise out of her seat, one finger in the air, but he was in the police car and away before she could make it to the door. He'd come back for his bike later.

Jacquie rang the bell in the reception area of Jim Astley's morgue. Donald answered and was delighted to see her and said so. Maxwell, he was not so pleased to see, but, uncharacteristically, managed to keep that piece of information to himself.

'Hello, Donald,' Jacquie said, with a bright smile. 'We're here to possibly identify the body brought in this morning.'

Donald, putty in her hands, opened the door on a buzzer and waved her through. He was blissfully unaware that Jacquie had just split an infinitive. Maxwell *was* aware, but let it go. Now was not the time.

'We'll do the paperwork in a minute,' Jacquie said, reading Donald's mind. 'If Mr Maxwell doesn't know the deceased, it would be just as easy not to have his name on the forms. What do you think?'

Donald nodded. Much, *much* easier.

Donald and the Work Ethic were only casual acquaintances. And if it could be managed that Jim Astley didn't know he'd been here, that would be better still. Maxwell was impressed. He knew she was good – she had, after all, managed to get that old grouch Metternich on side in a matter of days, in his experience a unique skill. But he thought that Donald was probably almost as hard a nut to crack as the black and white behemoth.

He showed them into a corridor, dimly lit with strategically placed seats for the collapsing bereaved. He disappeared through a door and a curtain slowly drew aside. It reminded Maxwell macabrely of a cremation in reverse and he wondered how this could soothe a shattered relative.

Beyond the window, a body was laid out, decorously draped in white. The pale face was turned slightly towards the viewer, eyes closed and hair roughly combed into what may have been its usual place. The mouth was slightly open and not even Donald's nifty placement of a wad of surgical blue paper roll could disguise the lividity on one cheek and the line of the chin. Even so, and even allowing for the stubble and general unwashed appearance, it was clearly Darren Blackwell, erstwhile Leighford non-High-flyer, last taught by Maxwell when he, Darren, was a fresh-faced fourteen-year-old, chirpily deciding to opt for Geography instead of History. He opted for Science in the Sixth Form. He opted for a Modern Apprenticeship instead of university. He then decided to opt for drinking and any pills he could buy under the pier. Cop out after cop out. And now here he was, laid out. Be sure your sins will find you out. Maxwell gripped the edge of the windowsill and nodded to Jacquie.

'Darren Blackwell,' he said. 'Age ... umm, let me work it out. He'll be ... twenty-two, possibly twenty-three. His youngest brother is in Year Ten at the moment. His middle brother has just done A levels and is away at ... Hull.'

'How do you do it, Max?' Jacquie asked/ 'Do you remember everyone you teach?'

''Fraid so,' Maxwell said, with a lopsided grin. 'It's not pretty, but someone has to do it.'

'So, his family are obviously still in town.'

'Yes,' Maxwell said. 'I can't remember the address exactly, but I know it's near the seafront. They keep a chippie, or a kebab shop or something similar. They'll know at school.'

She gave him a one-armed hug. 'Come on,' she said. 'Let's get you back there.'

He returned the squeeze. 'Dear me, no,' he said, to her surprise. 'Dierdre is covering my lesson for me and I wouldn't interrupt it for the world. I imagine it is one she'll remember for quite a while.'

CHAPTER SIX

Darren Blackwell's parents did keep a chip shop – The Plaice To Be - in the High Street in Leighford. They were sitting now in the small living room of the flat above; tastefully furnished, with a flat screen television the size of a blackboard and as much electronic gadgetry as could be packed into one entertainment module, cunningly crafted from mock pine. Henry Hall sat on the chair; Mr and Mrs Blackwell huddled together on the settee. The appalling carpet swirled in reds and greens between them.

'You say Darren didn't live here with you?' he asked either of the pair.

'No,' Mr Blackwell answered. 'Not because we didn't want him here, mind. All our boys will have a home here, always. But he'd been away to live and, well ... do you have a family, Detective Chief Inspector?'

Hall nodded. He did have a family, not that he had seen enough of them as they grew up. They were good boys, never a moment's trouble, and he never ceased to give thanks for that. Other people's boys gave him more trouble than his own ever had.

'Then you'll know what I mean, I expect.

He came home for a bit, didn't he, love?' He turned to his wife for support. She nodded over her sodden hankie, balled up in a fist so tight it looked as though it might never open again.

'But, the other boys were younger then. Alex was only twelve and this flat's not that big. He and Kevin had to double back up when Darren came home; it made for arguments. He found himself somewhere, didn't he, Mother? With some mates.'

'Some mates, yes,' she whispered.

'Whereabouts?' Hall asked gently.

'We don't really know,' Blackwell continued. 'He left his address as this one. Well, it saved him having to change it, you know, with the bank and that. So, he'd come back for his post and that.'

'Did you never visit him?' Hall wanted to know.

'I wanted to,' his mother said. 'Make it a bit homey, you know. I bought him little bits, cushions and things like that. But he said it wasn't very easy to have visitors. You know, because of his flatmates. They all had to share and it wasn't easy.' She looked at Hall. 'Well, that's what he said, wasn't it?' she appealed to her husband, who nodded.

They looked so bereft, so lost, their chicks now two, not three. Ordinary people, both overweight, martyrs to sampling the chips they cooked. The fact that Darren had been a bit of a cuckoo didn't help them in their loss. He had died only a few hundred yards from where they sat now. Hall knew he would do anything to stop them finding out that the 'flat' was a series of cardboard boxes and old carpets fashioned into a hideaway in the woods out of town beyond the Dam. That in that hideaway they had found some cushions, dirty and damp; a table lamp, useless in that powerless place, its bubblewrap still in place, each small bubble crushed to flatness by Darren, in the interminable hours between his crawling into his shell and the light of dawn. Most poignant of all, a curled photograph of his parents, with their three boys, standing in a row outside the shop. No, Hall would not let them know about that.

'Did he ever say he was having trouble with anyone?' Hall asked, 'Did he owe money, that kind of thing?'

Darren's mother sat up sharply, hen defending chick, a tigress standing over her dead cub. 'No, he didn't,' she said sharply. 'And anyway,' her eyes filled up again and her lip quivered, the fight leaking out of her, 'who kills someone because they owe them money? They'll never get it then, will they? It makes no sense.' She burrowed her face into her husband's shoulder. No, it made no sense. None of it made any sense.

Mr Blackwell looked over his wife's bowed

head at Henry Hall. 'How did he die?' he asked.

Hall breathed a sigh of relief. The interview was back on the usual track. That was normally the first question asked and at last it was here.

'We are investigating at the moment, Mr Blackwell,' he said, a touch formally. 'At first sight it looks as though he may have been...' He hesitated. Stabbed with a narrow blade, Astley would be dictating any time now, leaning over the body before he went to work with his electric saw and took off the dead boy's cranium and carved the obligatory 'Y' into his chest. 'Why?' indeed. Hall had known the cause of death from just viewing the body; the shredded clothing, the congealed blood. Surely not exposure as well, although, Heaven knew, the nights were still cold. He settled for the bland, as only he could. 'He may have been murdered, I'm sorry to say. I don't know any details yet.' Cowardly, but kind. Somehow, these two parents, bereft and grieving, had touched the father that lurked deep inside Henry Hall. 'As soon as we know, we'll let *you* know,' he promised.

'I suppose you'll want us to come and identify him?' Mrs Blackwell said, sniffing.

'Er, no, there's no need for that,' Hall said. 'Mr Maxwell from Leighford High has already done that.'

They looked at each other, puzzled. 'You said a jogger found him,' Mr Blackwell said. 'Mr Maxwell doesn't jog, surely?'

Hall blinked as the picture trotted across his mind's eye. 'No, but his partner is one of my sergeants. She recognised Darren and thought that Mr Maxwell could help. As it turned out, she was right.'

Mrs Blackwell smiled bleakly, for the first time. 'Mr Maxwell's wonderful,' she shared with Hall, 'don't you think? All my boys like him. Mr Maxwell said this, Mr Maxwell said that.' She waited brightly for a reply.

'Oh, yes,' Hall grated out. 'He certainly is. Wonderful. Yes.' The things he had to do in this job, he thought, sometimes defied belief. He rose to go. 'We'll ring or come round as soon as we know anything more. I'm sorry for your loss.' The cliché perhaps helped someone, Hall thought, but not him and, looking at the pair in front of him, not the bereaved either. But somehow, it had to be said. 'Do you have anyone who could come and be with you, perhaps? Family? A friend?'

Darren's mother nodded. 'My friend is coming over. We've known each other since we were at infant school. Our boys are the same age...' She dissolved into sobs. Now, only some of their boys were the same age. One of hers was dead and her life would never be the same. He had been living rough, he hadn't always been what she

113

wanted him to be, but he had been alive. Now he was the blank look in people's eyes, he was the reason for people crossing the street, changing the subject. If she was heart-broken now, thought Hall, she would look back on this as bearable in the months and years to come.

He shook their hands and said, 'Good. I'm glad. We'll be in touch.' He clattered down the stairs and got in his car. He thumped both hands on the wheel and let out a long-held breath. Things were getting bad. Henry Hall was catching humanity. What he was not catching was a killer.

Peter Maxwell was sitting in his modelling chair at the top of 38, Columbine. This was his War Office. Nolan had been up there, always secure in somebody's arms. Jacquie occasionally went up and blew dust off things. But only Maxwell and Metternich had the run of the place.

On the desk in front of him, a white, plastic 54-millimetre soldier lay on his back beside a white, plastic, 54-millimetre horse. In the fullness of time, suitably accoutred and painted, he would take his place in Captain White's squadron of the 17th Lancers, now forming up to Maxwell's left to ride into legend. Maxwell had been collecting these figures, courtesy of Messrs Historex, modellers extraordinaire, for years. They drained his bank balance, they took up his time when he should have been marking books or dandling his baby or talking to Jacquie. But hey, they also kept him sane. And they gave him a challenge. Six hundred and seventy-eight men had ridden behind Lord Cardigan on that fateful October day back in 1854 – Maxwell was still at school then – and the figure under Maxwell's modelling lens today was number four hundred and twenty-six.

Actually, as he had had to repeat to Metternich several times now, this one was Corporal Thomas Morley, who had been promoted to sergeant shortly after the Charge and served as a cavalry officer for the Union in the American Civil War – well, somebody had to show the Americans how to ride properly. Morley was a bit of an old grouch himself, not unlike Metternich, in fact, and spent the rest of his life whingeing because no one would give him the VC.

Maxwell was feeling faintly guilty about his decision not to return to Leighford High earlier, but his brush with murder had, this time, left him feeling a bit shaken. He had found an abandoned corpse only days ago, he had mislaid a suspect, and that was only his recent History. He had had more brushes with death and destruction than any Head of Sixth Form should ever have to bear. But something about Darren Blackwell's unkempt body had made the father in him rise up and want to howl. That boy, like his, had once sat and gurgled up at his proud parents. That boy, like his, had slept on his father's chest, dribbling quietly as he did so. Then, that boy had gone wrong somewhere, had taken a turning that had led him to death on a park bench. Maxwell had needed some time out. He would be back at the chalk-face tomorrow, casting pearls before swine, but now he would watch them more carefully, looking for that moment when a wrong word might send them spinning into oblivion. Or at least, he thought ruefully, he would if only he had the time; teaching any one of the classes he had the next day needed more arms than Kali, more eyes than Argus. Then he remembered that plague was in the city; some anonymous bug was scything classes and staff down. A few less arms then, a few less eyes. But he needed a break, so here he was with the Light Brigade. And then, suddenly, he needed another break, so he put Corporal Morley down, still whingeing, and went downstairs to watch a nice episode of *Diagnosis Murder*. Ah, the bliss of daytime television. That would be followed by the rambunctious return of Nolan from his childminder and a cuddle from Jacquie. He'd be all right.

He was just dropping off to sleep – Dick Van Dyke always had that effect in the end and anyway it was the Chartered Accountant who did it – when the doorbell rang. He wandered muttering down the stairs to the door, trying to look pale and ague-ridden in case it was one of the Senior Leadership Team from Leighford High checking up on him and flung it open.

'Mr Maxwell? Thank God you're here. There's been another one. The police are after me.' Bill Lunt's machine-gun delivery had not abated while he was on the run. Not a bad imitation of Peter Lorre out of *M*.

'Bill,' Maxwell stood aside and extended a welcoming arm. 'Come in. We've been worried about you. Where have you been?'

'I needed to have a think.' Lunt was climbing the stairs like a nonagenarian, pressing on each thigh in turn to make the gradient. 'I've been sleeping in my car.'

'Just for the one night, though, Bill,' said Maxwell, not meaning to minimise his pain, but anxious for the facts to be kept straight while that was still possible.

Bill Lunt turned pained eyes to Maxwell. 'It was cold, though,' he said plaintively. 'And dark, in the woods, where I was parked. There were wild animals.'

Maxwell's eyebrows asked the obvious question. The woods were indeed lovely, dark and deep. But, *wild animals?*

'Well, foxes at least. And badgers have a nasty bite if you get too close.'

'And did you?' They were in the sitting room by now and Lunt had collapsed on the sofa, narrowly missing Metternich, who was stretched out behind a couple of cushions. The animal hissed, merely reaffirming Lunt's terror of nature, red in tooth and claw. Maxwell walked towards the kitchen. He'd been sitting on Metternich for years *and* had the scars to prove it. 'Tea?'

'Did I what?'

'Get too close to a badger.'

'Well, of course not.' Bill Lunt felt that his role as victim was not being taken very seriously. He was a man on the run. He should be looked after. He felt tears prick his eyelids. No one loved him. He sniffed. 'They've got quite a nasty bite, you know.'

Maxwell sighed and went into the kitchen. He put the kettle on and picked up the phone.

'One one eight, one one eight, how may I help you?' asked a voice.

'Ah, yes,' Maxwell whispered into the receiver. 'Lunt Photographic, Leighford, please.'

The voice registered distaste. 'Can you spell that, sir?' it said, with a smell under its nose; obviously the result of those silly moustaches they all wore.

'Ell you enn tea, Lunt, Pea aitch...'

'Oh, *Lunt* Photographic.' The voice collected itself. 'Yes, I have that here. Would

118

you like me to put you through?'

'If you would,' Maxwell said and started gathering the tea things one-handed as he waited for a reply. Like most men, he'd never managed to do that thing with the phone tucked into his neck. But then, like most men, he couldn't multi-task either and dropped the thing before retrieving it deftly.

After a few rings the phone was snatched up. 'Helpyew?' slurred the answerer. The voice seemed faintly familiar, but Maxwell couldn't place it.

'Er ... is Mrs Lunt there?'

'Yeah.'

'May I speak to her please?'

'Yeah. Emma?' The second word nearly exploded Maxwell's ear drums. Why did people never move the phone from their mouth when they shouted across a busy shop? 'Emma? 'Sferyew.' The phone landed with a crash on what he assumed was a counter.

Despite the fact that the voice appeared to be speaking Polish, Maxwell was still certain he recognised it. He waited, listening at second hand to the busy to and fro that was Lunt Photographic.

'Hello?' Emma's altogether more cultured tones came through the earpiece.

'Oh, Emma,' whispered Maxwell. 'I think I have something of yours here. It's Peter Maxwell, by the way.' He had suddenly realised he sounded rather dodgy, like those

119

old perverts who claim to be fifteen in chat rooms or have an unrivalled collection of saddles from little girls' bicycles.

'Mr Maxwell?' she said. 'What can you possibly have of mine?' She was no fool, thought Maxwell. She's on to me.

'Ha ha,' he tried a light laugh. 'Well, it's your husband, in fact. He seems to be on the run.'

'For goodness sake,' she spat. 'Of course he's not on the run. What's he got to be on the run for?'

'Well, he seems to think he's a suspect in a couple of murders, for a start.'

'A *couple* of murders?'

'Yes, well, there's been another, but, that's not the point, really.'

'Not the point. A murder, not the point?' This was déjà vu for Emma Lunt, née Watson. She could still remember all those times that Maxwell had returned A level essays to her, telling her, in the kindest possible way, that it needed beefing up or toning down or that her antithesis was not the point, really.

'No. Emma, my dear, we all know Bill didn't do anything. But he says you have gone back to your mother's and also he seems to be labouring under the misapprehension that he is public enemy number one. Dillinger, Bonnie and Clyde, that sort of thing.'

'Exactly,' the word came out on a sigh. 'That's why I went to mother's. Not because I think he murdered anyone. It wasn't because I thought he would murder me in my bed; it was his impersonation of Richard Kimble that was wearing me down.'

Maxwell beamed. That's my girl, he thought. Still a film buff, like so many of his ex-Own. They might forget the causes of the Crimean War, but they'd never forget a film. All right, so Emma's version of Richard Kimble was Harrison Ford, whereas everyone of Maxwell's generation knew it was really David Jansen, but you couldn't have everything. 'Well,' he said, 'Can you come and get him, there's a good girl? The Mem is a bit aerated at having him here and he slept in the car last night, apparently. He's a bit tearful and sorry for himself. He seems to have become unhealthily obsessed with badgers.'

'Badgers?' Her voice rose to a squeak.

'Well, precisely. We all know what that can lead to, don't we? Can you get here in, say, half an hour? Thirty-eight, Columbine. Lovely. Bye, then.' He rang off before she could argue. The kettle had gone off the boil and so he addressed himself to the Maxwell Tea Ceremony again, all white face paint and excruciatingly small shoes.

When he went back into the sitting room a strange tableau met his gaze. Stretched out on the sofa was Bill Lunt, dead to the world. Looming over him and about to poke him with the business end of a mop was Mrs B. After all, she cleaned up at the school in the afternoon. For a moment, his world turned upside down.

'Mrs B?' Maxwell said. He thought she came to do for him in the morning.

Mrs B spun round with a shriek that could curdle milk, hands grasped to her chest, fag-end flying who knew where. Bill Lunt flinched in his sleep, then subsided again. 'Oh my gawd, Mr Maxwell,' she said, the scream ending in a cough. 'Oh, my gawd, what are you doing there? I nearly died. There's a bloke on your settee. Did you know there's been another one. 'Oo is 'e? Ain't it terrible?'

Maxwell was used to the Thompson sub-machine gun that was Mrs B and he coped with it admirably. 'I live here. Did you? Yes, there is. Yes, indeed. Mr Lunt, or Darren Blackwell, depending on whether you mean the bloke on my settee or the other one. Yes, it is. Don't you usually come in the morning?' It was a gentle reminder that most people asked one question at a time.

Still patting her chest, exhaling like there had never been a Clean Air Act, Mrs B nodded. Another fag-end, unlit but half-smoked at some previous, more accommodating venue, had materialised from somewhere in her pinny and was stuck firmly to her lower lip. 'Yeah, Mr Maxwell, I do as a rule. But I got stuck at another job, din't I? That's how I know there's been another one. I clean up at one of the shops in town and that lad what they found was the son of them as keep that chippie.'

'And so that made you late because...?' Maxwell drew out his question, hoping that might start Mrs B's thought processes into something approaching coherence.

'Well, because...' Caught between a rock and a hard place, Mrs B could hardly admit that she had stood open mouthed in the doorway of the greengrocer's, mop in hand, and watched as the police had arrived, knocked at the door and been admitted to the flat above the chip shop. How she had waited until that miserable bloke, that copper with the blank glasses, had come out and driv' away, but not until he had hit the steering wheel, nasty temper that showed. How she had nabbed that woman, that one whose kid was up at the school, when she arrived and that was how she knew who it was what was dead and also why she was really late at Mr M's.

He let her off the hook. 'Don't worry, Mrs B,' he said, softly. 'I think we'll just let Mr Lunt sleep, if it's all the same to you. Just do a bit extra next week, if you like.'

Mrs B drew herself up as far as she was

able. 'I don't like to skimp, Mr Maxwell,' she said, her voice tight with offence. 'I like to do a good job.'

Struggling to keep the amazement out of his voice (he knew for a fact that there was a sixteen-year-old spiders' web in the corner of his office), Maxwell said, 'No, really, Mrs B, I'm sure we'll manage. Nolan is getting a dab hand at mopping and, as you know, Metternich always does the drying up at the end of the evening, mostly by rolling on the plates. You just run along now, or you'll be late for up at the school.'

'Well, if you're sure...' her eyes narrowed. 'Why aren't you there?' she asked. 'You bin suspended again? That Mrs Lessing, she ain't no better than she should be. It ain't fair they keep pickin' on you, Mr Maxwell, it ain't. Just 'cos you're a bit strange.'

He was shepherding her down the stairs and he toyed with a sharp push in the big of her back. They'd see it as self-defence, surely, justifiable homicide. Maybe he'd get the George Medal. 'I'm having a day off. No, I haven't. No, she isn't. No, it isn't and,' he sighed, 'I suppose I am.' By now they were in the hall and he waved her off without regret. 'Bye, now. You have a nice day now, d'you hear?' It was a pretty good Clint Eastwood, but his heart wasn't really in it.

Mrs B, on the path now with her mop at a less than jaunty angle, turned away. 'Poor old bleeder,' she muttered to herself, as she walked off to mop aimlessly up at the school. 'He's really lost it, this time. As soon as you find blokes on their settees, it's the end, that's what it is. I read about that old poof actor; what was his name – Charles Laughton? Married to that Elsa Manchester. That poor policewoman and that little baby. What a carry-on.'

Mrs Troubridge, Maxwell's neighbour, the wrong side of eighty and mad as a tree, crouched behind her hedge giving her cotoneaster a right seeing to. She nodded sagely to herself. She'd seen it coming for years and now it was here. She was disgusted and appalled, all at the same time. How exciting!

CHAPTER SEVEN

Maxwell was stirring his tea and looking pensively at the sleeping photographer when he heard the car draw up outside Thirty-eight. By the time the door had slammed and purposeful feet had negotiated the path, he was at the front door, flinging it open to prevent the doorbell from waking Bill Lunt.

'Mr Maxwell,' Emma stood on the step

and looked past him. She was a little heavier than Maxwell remembered her, a little less light of step, but running a photographic emporium and living with the man who invented neurosis couldn't have been a piece of cake. 'Where is he, then?'

'Upstairs,' Maxwell said. Seeing her surprised look, he elaborated. 'Town house,' he said, gesturing overhead. 'That's where the sitting room is. The estate agent described it as three up, three even upper, nothing down.'

'Ah.' She waited. 'May I come in?'

'Sorry,' he stepped aside. 'How rude of me. I just thought I'd warn you first. He's a bit tired and depressed. This thing has been a bit of a shock.'

'Yes, yes, I know. I'll just collect him though, if I may. I have to get back to the shop. The staff aren't all that reliable, if you leave them on their own.' She sighed. 'Just youngsters, really. But they are the ones who know all about digital.'

Maxwell suppressed a smile. Emma wasn't exactly a pensioner herself. He led the way upstairs and pushed open the door.

Hard Emma Lunt, proprietress of Lunt Photographic, disappeared before his eyes. At the sight of her husband stretched out on Maxwell's sofa, one arm thrown across his eyes, the other protectively across his midriff, fist clenched, she had dissolved into wifely mush. She rushed across to him and threw herself across his torso.

'Bill,' she wailed. 'Are you all right? I've been so worried.'

He woke with a start and had scrambled into a half sitting position in the corner of the sofa before he realised what was happening. Then, he recognised the arms around him, the head on his chest. 'Emma?' She snuggled up further on his chest and tucked her head under his chin. Everything became a little incoherent and Maxwell withdrew into the less embarrassing realms of the kitchen, where he busied himself yet again with making tea.

When he came out, the image of a Jolyons nippy, were it not for the missing apron, frilly cap and air of resignation, they had gone.

He went over to the window and tweaked aside the curtain, in his best Mrs Troubridge style. Emma was tucking Bill into the passenger seat, making sure he was comfy and belted in before driving away. Well, thought Peter Maxwell, a sort of happy ending was beginning there at least. There would still be the police questioning, the paparazzi, the short-lived notoriety, which would either make or break Lunt Photographic. ''Ere, weren't you that bloke wot found...' – that sort of thing. The *Daily Mail* would throw in a dream cottage for the exclusive rights. Al Pacino would demand to play the photographer in the film. *Kill Bill.*

Or had somebody done that already? But for now, they were driving off into the sunset on a second honeymoon.

A car was turning in to Columbine and missed the Lunt vehicle by a whisker. It was Jacquie, Nolan safely strapped in the back, home from the nick, via the childminder. Maxwell savoured the moment, watching unobserved as she pulled up to the kerb and switched off the engine. She turned to say something to Nolan – whatever it was, he liked it; Maxwell could see his arms wave and could almost hear the gurgle. She got out and went round to the back, undid his harness and lifted him out. He was getting to be a bit of an armful now; he could walk, but, like Alan Bennett's Lady Dundown, he didn't have to.

Maxwell contrived to be sitting casually, two cups of tea waiting on the table, when Jacquie walked in. Nolan slid down her and toddled across to Metternich, who welcomed him with a yawn and a stretch.

'Hello, Nole,' Maxwell called, waving extravagantly.

Nolan waved and gave his attention back to the cat, who glanced at Maxwell over the boy's shoulder with a triumphant gleam in his wicked yellow eye as if to say 'Want me to lick him or eat him?'

Jacquie dropped into her usual seat on the sofa and reached for the tea. 'For me?' she asked. 'God, my feet!'

'Of course, Light of my Life,' Maxwell said quickly.

'Not made for anyone else, like … visitors, for example?'

'No, no, just for you,' Maxwell lied.

She aimed one of those tired feet at him, missing him by miles. 'Don't give me that. I just saw the Lunts leaving. I am a trained copper, you know! They looked like love's young dream, I must say.'

'Yes, well, I admit I made it for them, but they'd buggered off by the time I came out of the kitchen. Gratitude, eh? There haven't been any lips in it or anything.' He pulled a face at her. 'Except mine, of course.'

'That's all right, then.' She held the mug to her face gratefully and swigged. 'Oooh, that's better. There's nothing like a nice cup of tea.'

'No. Except a cup of tea, of course.'

'I won't rise today. It's been a shocker. Henry Hall was really quite upset after he visited the Blackwells. He took it hard. They didn't realise the boy was sleeping rough. Thought he was with friends.'

'Sleeping rough? What, really rough, as in in a cardboard box?'

'A tent in the woods, actually.'

Maxwell put down his tea. 'Oh.'

'Oh?' Jacquie knew that look.

Nolan was crouching by Metternich, trying to engage the black and white monster in something approximating to conversation. Metternich wasn't having any, just lashing his tail. He wouldn't hurt the Boy for all the world, but the only one who knew that for certain was Metternich. So Maxwell kept an eye, just in case...

'I'll tell you now, save time,' he went on. 'Bill Lunt spent last night sleeping in his car. In the woods.'

She relaxed again. 'There are loads of woods around here.'

'Yes, but not many where you can park. For that I suppose it would have to be Silverdown Woods.'

'Well, in that case, it is "Oh".' She put the cup down on the coffee table.

'Did he die there?' Maxwell asked. 'It was in the park, wasn't it?'

'Yes. But it is a bit of a coincidence that the man who found the first body...'

'Me.'

'Not you,' she corrected him. 'You were just there. Why is it always about you?'

He chuckled.

'Where was I? Yes, the man who found the first body happens to spend the night in the same woods where the second victim has been sleeping out. Henry isn't going to just let that one go. He can't, Max. There are coincidences and there are coincidences.'

'No, I suppose he can't. But I still say Bill

Lunt is innocent. Rather like his distant relative, Bill Stickers.'

Jacquie was a little young for that one. She didn't know who Mr Chad was either. She reached for the phone. 'I'm telling Henry, Max. Then, we'll have something to eat, play with Nolan, give him a bath and watch some rubbish on the telly. And at no time during those activities are we going to speak of this case. Is that clear?'

'As crystal, dearest,' Maxwell said, and, putting his tea down first for Health and Safety reasons, he slipped down out of his chair and crawled over for a natter with his boy and his cat.

The boy took matters into his own hands by wandering off in search of his mother and food, though who could be sure they were in that order of importance.

'That's it, that's it,' Maxwell called after his receding heir. 'Leave the old man sprawling like a prat on the mat.' He bumped noses with Metternich. 'Oh, it's you.'

The cat stretched again and looked intelligent, not easy when all you have to work with are two big yellow eyes with slits for pupils and a set of white whiskers. Nonetheless, Maxwell settled in beside the animal and began the conversation. After all, he had whitish whiskers too and his pupils only differed from Metternich's by one consonant.

'Well, Count,' he said, risking a clawing by

stroking him between the ears. 'Where are we on this one? And I shall be asking questions later. Two youngsters, sleeping rough or at least homeless within the meaning of the act. One girl, one boy. Did they know each other? I wonder. One not local, one as local as they come, one of My Own. Cause of death? Were they the same? Motive, I hear you ask? Well, there you have me, Count. I have no idea what the motive could be. There was no theft, although apparently the girl had money on her. There didn't seem to be a fight or anything going on. Nothing sexual. Apart from being dead, there's nothing suspicious about either of them. No drug involvement, except for a bit of weed on the girl, which, begging the Mem's presence, isn't what even an old fart like me would call much of a crime. I should think it probably makes the long night shorter. Or at least a touch more colourful.'

He glanced at the cat, who was sitting up now, all attention.

'Don't look at me like that, please. I was young once.'

The cat stalked off in the direction of the kitchen, probably to seek a second opinion of that last comment. His eyes may be vacant, but the ears were razor sharp and they had, in fact, detected the faint clink of the business end of a tin opener making contact with the edge of a tin. Even if it should transpire that only beans were involved, he was probably all right for a titbit if he went through what he fondly believed to be his cute routine, namely placing his bum on either foot of the nearest human.

Maxwell rolled upright with that surprising energy he normally reserved for a blitzkrieg attack on the smokers behind the Sports Hall. He leant back against the chair and gazed at the ceiling. He'd just have to talk to himself, then. It was Eight See all over again.

'It's clear to me that Bill Lunt is as innocent as the day is long. There was no need for him to draw attention to the murder; it would have gone undiscovered for ever if it weren't for his photos. Yes, I agree that the...' there was a thud on the cushion of the chair behind his head. Metternich was back. 'Oh, beans, was it? Or just a can of worms? Well, I was just saying Bill Lunt didn't do it, whatever the profilers might think.'

The kitchen door swung open and shut, leaving Nolan on the other side of it. His face screwed up and he started to cry. Jacquie's head poked round the door.

'Max, can you just keep Nole in there for a moment? You know the rules, no s-e-x, no politics, no religion, no murder in front of the boy.' Her head disappeared and the three Maxwell Men heard the murmur of her voice through the door.

Stymied, Maxwell and Metternich's conversation stuttered to a halt and the three chatted about this and that.

'Did I ever tell you guys about Muffin the Mule?' Maxwell asked.

'What did I tell you about s-e-x?' Jacquie's voice came through from the kitchen.

'Ears like a bat, your Mummy,' Maxwell pretended to snatch Nolan's nose – the game of the month. Even Metternich was impressed. Although when he removed noses, the whole thing was rather bloodier.

Jacquie came back in and replaced the phone on its station. She threw herself down on the sofa and held out her arms to whoever got there first. Nolan won, by a short head. Maxwell swerved onto a chair and Metternich hadn't even heard the starting pistol.

'Henry says thank you,' she said over the boy's head to Maxwell.

'He does?' Maxwell was frankly astounded.

'Not as such, but he was grateful nonetheless. I'm afraid that means a search warrant and a fairly unpleasant night for the Lunts, Max. I'm sorry.'

Maxwell grimaced but nodded slowly. She was right; coincidence could only stretch so far. Still and all, he hoped they would understand that he had to do it.

'What did Henry think when you mentioned s-e-x on the phone just now?'

Nolan turned at that moment to his

134

mother. He'd been wondering that too.

'I put my hand over the receiver,' she said, 'Like what they taught us in the Police Academy.'

Maxwell nodded. He'd seen all those.

'He said what?' Emma Lunt exploded in the policeman's face.

'Just that your husband had been sleeping out in the woods last night, madam,' said DS Tony Deacon, unperturbed. 'I'm sure there's nothing to worry about, but I'm sure you understand that it would be better in the long run for your husband if you stood aside and let us in.'

Emma squared up to him, for all the bloke was built like a brick Shi'ite temple. 'Have you got a warrant?'

Deacon sighed. He did so wish that people wouldn't watch all those police dramas on the telly; the procedurals were usually rubbish. 'Yes, madam, we have a warrant.' He brandished it under her nose. 'We don't do searches without warrants in real life.'

'Well, don't leave the place in a mess.'

'We'll be as neat as possible, madam, commensurate with a thorough search.' He turned and called down the path, 'OK, you lot. Let's get in and search, the lady says don't make a mess.'

The six police officers marched through the door in single file, chuckling as they went, but each one careful to wish Emma Lunt a cheery good evening. Six of them, she noted. God knew what real crime was going on undetected in Leighford while these flat foots ruined her shagpile. They dispersed up stairs and through into the kitchen. Deacon went through into the lounge. He was a bit of an amateur psychologist who was creating a mental dossier on guilt or innocence based on the size of the television screen in suspects' houses. Oh dear, oh dear, oh dear, he thought. We have a right one here and bang to rights. The telly was the size of the windscreen of a moderately sized family car, black and slick as a puddle of oil. The innocent ones tended to have either a small flat screen or an old-fashioned fat telly with no gadgets to speak of. This one had extra speakers, SkyHD – the lot. Guilty as sin.

Smirking to himself Deacon went through into the kitchen, just in time to meet one of the policewomen coming out of the utility room. She was carrying a bag, heavy with some fairly bulky contents. His smirk widened.

'Well, Brady,' he said. 'Bloodstained clothing?'

'Not as such, sarge,' she said.

'Well, it either is or it isn't,' he said, slightly testily.

'Yes, sarge. It is bloodstained and I suppose it's clothing. I don't think it belongs

136

to Mr Lunt, though. I think it may belong to the first victim.' She opened the bag and he peered in. At the bottom lay a grubby scarf and in the confined space of the bag-mouth, he could tell it was none too clean. In short, it stank to high heaven.

'Oh, close that up,' he said, waving a hand under his nose. 'Where was that?'

'In the washing basket.'

'Best place for it. What makes you think it is Lara Kent's?'

The policewoman took a deep breath, tucked the bag under her arm and started to tick the points off on her fingers. 'First, it's really dirty and this house is really clean, so I can't imagine it belongs to Mrs Lunt. I say *Mrs* because it is very much a woman's scarf. Second, it seems to have sand in it and I know the body was found in the dunes. Third, it's got ... well, fleas, sarge, and I know the dead girl had a dog. So ... well, I just thought it might be hers.'

He took the bag from her. 'Well done, Brady, well done, We'll make a copper of you in twenty years or so. I'll label this and get it to forensics. Keep searching.'

And search and search and search they did, but found nothing else. Tony Deacon may have looked an idiot, but that was just a front, really, to lull the guilty into a false sense of security. Bill Lunt was a photographer, so Deacon had brought the SOCO cameraman along, just to check out the man's darkroom. The usual – chemicals, film, infra-red, a bit of dark; all very disappointing, really. Nothing sweaty whatsoever. They impounded Bill Lunt's computer just in case and asked his wife about his mobile phone. She just gave a snort. The man who didn't do digital really *didn't* do digital. When it came to mobile phones, Bill Lunt's degree of revulsion made Peter Maxwell look like he could text for England. They didn't tidy up after themselves as they had implied they would. And they didn't get even a cursory goodbye from Emma when she slammed the door behind their retreating backs. And all the time, she was wondering and worrying about what they'd taken away in the black bag.

Thirty-eight, Columbine was drenched in the sort of silence that you only get when the baby is fed, bathed and asleep. Nolan lay in his dreams, the pale stars and moons of his nite-lite twirling overhead and the room filled with his soft snoring. The cat had gone out, to paint Leighford red with the blood of rodents. The official Man of the House had done the washing up without being asked to and therefore the official Woman of the House had made the coffee and poured the drinks. Metternich being absent, it was left to Jacquie to purr softly as Maxwell rubbed her feet. When the phone rang it was as if the air was being sliced into by a circular saw at the business end of a megaphone.

They turned their heads to look at it but neither of them moved.

It rang and rang and rang and the battle of wills went on on the sofa. Maxwell continued to rub Jacquie's feet. She continued to nurse her glass and look inscrutable. The ringing finally stopped. Several minutes went by.

'Well,' said Maxwell, in his best behaviour voice. 'Who could that have been, I wonder?'

'Who indeed,' countered Jacquie. 'We will have to wait now until tomorrow, as per our agreement earlier.'

'Our agreement as to...?'

'You can't fool me like that any more, Peter Maxwell,' she said. 'This isn't the playground and I won't fall for your tricks. Seven Eff I ain't.'

'Fine,' he shrugged. 'I don't care who it was. They've rung off now, anyway. But I wonder, Woman Policeman, that you don't worry that it might be... Work.'

'They'd use my mobile,' she said smugly. 'So I know it's not.'

'In that case,' he said, triumphantly, giving her foot a final squeeze, 'our agreement isn't an issue.'

'Why not?' she said, guardedly.

'Because, if it was ... our embargoed subject ... that that call was about, then it would be on your mobile. Since it wasn't, it could be anyone. Your mother, for example, hanging by her fingernails on the edge of a precipice. A colleague of mine wanting to know a vital date or other piece of information, like the ALPS data on Thirteen Bee One. It could be someone wishing to sell us some lovely double glazing. Or that call from the Palace about my K which is so long overdue.'

'Don't touch the phone, Max,' she warned, her eyes scary slits.

'Or a conservatory, perhaps. Wouldn't that be nice? You know, that nice Mr Cameron.'

She swung her legs over and stood up. Her feet were tingling deliciously, but she really needed the loo and had to use them to get there. 'While I'm gone, don't touch the phone.'

'No, dearest. I won't move from this spot.'

'Make sure you don't.' She left the room, doing a double take round the door, to be sure. He hadn't moved, although he was secretly flattered that she seemed to think he could move that fast.

Thirty-eight, Columbine having been built, like all its neighbours, out of ticky-tacky (they all looked just the same), he could clearly hear her cross the landing and the snick of the bathroom door. Only then did he think it safe to creep over to the phone and pick it up gingerly. He pressed the green button and listened. Just the dialling tone, so no message. He scrolled down through the missed calls. Luckily for him, Jacquie was pretty sure this was beyond his technological grasp. He chuckled to himself – after all, his generation had put a man on the moon. He recognised the number, although there wasn't a date of anything important embedded within it. The Lunts. Hmm. He replaced it carefully. He wasn't sure whether or not he wasn't completely Lunted out at present. He was back in exactly the same position as before when Jacquie came back into the room, cradling the Southern Comfort and staring into where the embers of the fire would be if the Carpenter-Maxwells had such a thing. She curled up in the chair and stared at him for a long few minutes. Finally, she couldn't stand it any longer.

'Who was it, then?'

'Who was what?'

'Max, please! Not only have I known you for a frighteningly long time, but I am a trained police person. I *know* you've checked who that was.'

'Oh, ye of little faith,' he said, chuckling silently. Yes, she was a trained police person, but he had been outwitting kids for more years than she had been alive. So he was going to win this one. Slam dunk, whatever that might mean. 'That phone has not been touched.' He smiled at her and reached for the local *Advertiser*. The front page carried the story of Darren Blackwell. He brandished it ostentatiously in her face. 'Oh, dear and lawks a mussy.' It was Cleatus from the *Simpsons*, all in-bred and cornpone. 'Look what's in this paper. I can't read this. We're not allowed.' He threw the *Advertiser* aside and got up. 'I'll go and get a book, I think. Something light like Isaiah Berlin on *Historical Inevitability*. Anything you'd like while I'm on my feet? Haunch of caribou? A damn good throttling?'

'A few nibbly bits if you're passing. A few crisps, the odd olive, any little cubes of feta that come your way. Anchovies.'

'Tapas, in short.'

'You're so good to me,' she smiled. There was nothing short about tapas and it would take him ages. She could check the phone while he was gone.

'I know, but you're worth it,' he smiled back, a perfect cross between Charlize Theron and Jane Fonda. Then he would have won; if not the war, then at least this battle. The moral high ground always had the finest view.

She heard him clattering loudly in the kitchen and slid over to pick up the phone. She too recognised the number. She didn't have to use a date mnemonic. She just had that sort of mind; one that picks up the important stuff. The Lunts. She replaced the

142

phone and tapped her teeth thoughtfully. After a moment, she picked the phone back up and pressed the green button. She scrunched down into the chair as it started to ring, as if that would minimise the sound. It was answered. 'Hello,' she whispered. 'This is Jacquie Carpenter. You know, kind of Mrs Maxwell.'

The reply was soaked up by the bones of her skull and, despite the fact that, from his vantage point of a partially open kitchen door Maxwell had stopped banging sauce-pan lids together, he couldn't hear a thing.

CHAPTER EIGHT

The morning dawned grey and miserable, just to remind everyone that it was still February and Ten Ex Four had double History at nine ack emma sharp. As Maxwell shepherded his little family down the path on their way to their respective places of employment that morning – Jacquie to right wrongs, Nolan to finally sort out the baby with one eyebrow which every small child has in its life and Metternich to reduce the local volage (his day job) – he was given a rather cold shoulder by Mrs Troubridge. Her response to his cheery 'Good Morning' was a loud harrumph and a slammed door. The woman had to be Methuselah's auntie, but she could be found gardening and homing in on the local goss in all weathers. Today seemed a little different.

'Have we done something to annoy Mrs Troubridge?' Jacquie asked as Maxwell belted himself into her passenger seat. He liked Tuesdays; Jacquie had a standing arrangement that, come hell or high water, she started later on that day and so he got a lift and White Surrey got the day off, stamping and snorting in the garage that passed for the rolling meadows.

'Well,' she said, pulling away from the kerb, 'I haven't. Have you, Nole?' She turned to smile at him and he shouted 'Nononono-nonono!' his newest and most favourite and therefore most nerve-shattering response. She turned back to Maxwell and said, 'No, we haven't done anything. You?'

He thought for a moment and then shook his head. 'No. Must be Metternich. She's been off hooks with him since he took her that mouse. She trod on it with a bare foot. Apparently, if feels much like treading on a large and hairy grape. And I quote.'

Jacquie shook her head. 'She inhabits a strange world, that one. Has her sister arrived yet?'

'Sister? I didn't know she had one.' He wondered again how she got these titbits.

The woman worked all hours and then had Nolan and himself to fend for; when did she find the time? There again, she did put the multi into tasking.

'Yes.' There was a pause while Jacquie concentrated on changing lanes on the Flyover. There was a rumour that the man who planned roads in Leighford didn't drive. Jacquie thought it was far more likely that due to his severe agoraphobia he hadn't actually left the house in years so had no idea of the chaos he had caused with his imaginative road markings. He knew perfectly well that if he did leave it, someone would lynch him.

Safely on the right path for Leighford High School, she had some brain spare to continue. 'Yes. She's coming to stay.'

'I'd worked that out,' Maxwell said, rummaging behind his seat for his briefcase full of unmarked marking. There didn't seem to be anywhere else for the conversation to go on this one, so he let it die a natural death. He patted his pocket. 'Oh, bum. I've forgotten my wallet. I was planning to take young Gregory Adair out for a pot of tea and something crumby this afternoon. He's close to failing his NQT year and that would be a shame. He knows his stuff, he just seems to lack concentration. Do you have any wherewithal?'

'I have wherewithsome,' she replied. 'My

bag is by your feet. Have a scrabble.'

He did so and unearthed a rather dog-eared tenner. 'May I borrow this?'

'Borrow?'

'Well, have, I suppose I mean.' He still sometimes had to pinch himself to remember that this lovely, funny woman lived with him and was his love. Wherewithsome – for goodness' sake; that would keep him going all day, in the face of Eight Pee Oh! And the tragedy was that there wasn't one of his colleagues who would get it. Even so, he'd put on a brave face and claim it as his own.

'Of course. What's the problem with Adair?'

'Mind not on job. Always chronically short of dosh, more so than he ought to be, I mean. Looks a wreck most days.'

She tapped him on his disreputable hat, pulling a face at the paisley bow tie. 'We can't all be fashionistas, Max.'

'I think sometimes that Mussolini was right.' As far as the confines of the Ka would allow, he struck the Il Duce pose, chin out and fist across chest. 'No, all joking apart. He needs a fatherly word.'

She drew up outside Leighford High School with a flourish and leant over to kiss his cheek. Children were crawling, those who could still crawl with all that whatever going about, towards the gates, goaded by parents with whips and red-hot pincers. 'And, if I may speak for the little man in the

146

back there, you are just the man to provide it.' He leant in for a moment, storing up the scent of her hair and the petal of her cheek, against the day.

On cue, Nolan sang out, 'Dada!' His parents beamed with pride; that kid had timing that any actor would give his right arm for. Even so, Maxwell didn't care for his choice of artist.

The Head of Sixth Form bounced into school almost bursting with pride. His grin in her direction gave Dierdre Lessing quite a turn. She scowled at him from her eyrie and her scrawny old neck bent low over her slaughtered chicks. She'd be circling the skies again come lunchtime.

Once ensconced in his office, Maxwell leant back and closed his eyes. It would be all of fifteen minutes before the first skirmishers of Ten Ex Four, the Forlorn Hope, would dribble into his classroom next door. He spent the time picturing Jacquie's drive to work, via the childminder. He pictured her walking out, down the path, checking her watch as she went. He pictured her driving, very carefully, to Leighford nick, parking, tripping up the stairs into the office she shared with a gazillion other detectives, just outside the bigger, emptier office of Henry Hall. In his mind's eye she took off her coat, brushed her hands quickly over her hair and sat down at her desk. Although the slower start on a Tuesday was nice on the home front, he knew she hated anyone stealing a march on her. He pictured her leaning her head towards the computer screen, doing things on keyboards he could only wonder at. He dialled her number.

'Carpenter.'

'Hello, Carpenter. Maxwell here. So, what did the Lunts want?'

'Whatever do you mean, sir?' she said archly.

'Come on, don't shilly your shally at me, Woman Policeman. I know you rang them last night. I meant to ask you in the car.'

She blew out in exasperation. 'I can hardly tell you that from here, can I, Max?' she said, tightly.

'Email me.'

She held the phone away from her ear and looked at it in amazement. 'I'm terribly sorry,' she said, restoring it to her ear. 'I thought you were Peter Maxwell, dinosaur of Thirty-eight Columbine and Leighford High School, not necessarily in that order.'

'The same.' He bowed low in his chair.

'Well, you just used the "e" word at me. What were you thinking?'

'I'm thinking I want to know what you said to whichever Lunt you spoke to last night and that this may be the only way I get to know before the end of today. And I'm morbidly curious. And I have a lovely Teaching Assistant here who is dying to teach me how to use the email system, when she's not tearing off my clothes, of course.'

Jacquie ignored the last part. 'It will be rather private for that, Max.'

'I can read, you know. I just can't pick up emails. At the moment. How hard can it be? Bernard Ryan sends them all the time. And he's a vegetable.'

She was still in shock but heard herself say, 'I don't even know your email address. Do you?'

'Naturally not. But I know a woman who does.' The phone went quieter and he heard a shouted, but muffled conversation. 'Apparently, it is maxwep at lfdhgh dot sch dot gov dot uk. Have we all gone completely mad?'

She scribbled furiously. 'Yep. Got that. Not that I will necessarily send you this email, mind you. And if I do, it may not contain what you want it to, so be prepared.'

'Maxwep?' she heard him say. 'What kind of email address is that? I want to be crimeaman at Sebastopol dot co dot uk dot and carry one or something. Maxwep?' She pictured him looking round the room helplessly. She heard another conversation, less muffled. Then he was back on the line. 'Apparently, it is the first five letters of my surname followed by my initial and then the rest of the gobbledegook is which school etc. God, the world is absolutely barking. Anyway, bye. Look forward to receiving yours electronically of today inst.' As the phone went down, she heard a final and distant cry of 'Maxwep?'

Sighing, she turned to her computer and logged on. Finally the ancient thing groaned into life and she began composing her email.

Max, I don't see why this can't wait until tonight, but here goes. Yes, all right, you win, I did speak to Emma Lunt last night. As I thought they searched the place and took away his computer. I asked about his mobile phone and, as I'm sure you already know, he doesn't have one. They also took something from the laundry basket – she wasn't very clear really but I think she thinks it was a scarf. But they didn't take any other clothes. Anyway, good news is – we didn't arrest him or anything, but we have made an appointment for him to come in and see us today to make a revised statement. OK, now? You do realise that I will be emailing you all the time from now on and you'd better answer. J. She pressed 'send' and sat back. There was no chance that he would get that, she thought. He's still looking for the crank handle to start his laptop. But no; apparently not. She Had Mail.

J (how formal) you dark horse. You never said a word and I was sure you would have. Well done! But what's this about no mobile

150

phone? I was sure I heard his go beep on the dunes. Well, it was probably a rare seabird like the Lesser Spotted Wheebling Gannet or something. Got to go. I quite like this means of communication, by the way. Why have you been keeping it from me, all of you? It's a conspiracy. That's my theory, anyway. M.

Bless his little heart, thought Jacquie. Although getting him to carry a mobile phone was like pulling hen's teeth, he always assumed everyone else had one. It probably was the Lesser Spotted Whatsit, but even so, it was something to mention next time she saw Henry Hall.

A shadow fell across her desk. She looked up and saw Henry Hall. She cocked a Maxwellian eyebrow at him.

'Is there anything I can help you with, guv?' she asked. It wasn't like Henry Hall to loom.

'Yes. I need you to do a bit of sleuthing for me.' The man, unusually for him, had taken off his blank glasses and was cleaning them. He had eyes, after all.

'Errrm. Isn't that my job? As a detective, am I not supposed to sleuth pretty much nine to five?' And often much more, a tiny voice added in her head.

'No, I mean *sleuthing*. The kind of thing Maxwell does. A bit of covert activity. You know the sort of thing.'

'I haven't caught it off him. Perhaps he could do it for you.'

Henry Hall heaved a huge sigh, crossed his fingers behind his back so the next bit didn't matter and said, 'You can take him with you if you like.'

Jacquie knew what was happening now. She should have known before. First, Maxwell asks her to send an email, then Henry Hall asks her to work with Maxwell. Clearly, this being Tuesday and her only late start, she was still in bed and dreaming. She gave herself a sneaky little pinch under the desk. Ow! No, she was awake.

'Are you totally sure, sir?' she stammered. 'I mean...' how could she put this without being disloyal to the man she loved? '...you know how Max can be.'

Henry Hall did indeed know. But occasionally, even a sensible policeman, steeped for years in hatred of the amateur detective, can see who the best man for the job must be. Maxwell wasn't a fictional detective like Sherlock Holmes or Mike Hammer. He was real, for Christ's sake and he got results, even if some of his students didn't. 'I basically need to get a bit of info on some kids. There have been several reliable sightings of some hooded types in the area of both murders. I thought that Maxwell would be the one to ask. About a kid-related problem, that is.'

'He'd be great if we had the kids banged up. He could tell you everything you would need to know, down to their ingrowing toenails and what their dad said to the school nurse in 1982. But even he doesn't know random kids in hoods. There are other schools in Leighford, you know. As well as buses into Leighford, visitors to Leighford...'

'If you don't want to do it, Jacquie,' he said, the light sparking off the glasses, shining again to mask his face, 'you just have to say so.'

'No, no,' she said. 'I'll *do* it. It's been a strange enough day already so far. I might just as well let it have its head.'

'Anything strange that I ought to know about?'

'Yes and no. The no bit is that Max asked me to send him an email. You may not realise how odd that is...' she paused.

Henry Hall did not know Maxwell that intimately, but he had never had him down for a technical type. 'Assume I do. So what else is strange?'

'It may be nothing. Tony Deacon took a computer from the home of Bill Lunt last night. The lads checked for his mobile, of course, standard, but he doesn't have one. But Max says he heard a phone beeping as they walked over the dunes on the night they found the body.'

Beeping.

'You know, that beep they make when the battery is low or when a text comes in.'

153

'He's sure?'

'No. That's the problem. He's not exactly a phone expert. He has one, but it doesn't get many outings. It's for emergencies, he says, though the emergencies that are likely to happen to him while standing in the hall next to the table would be fairly few, I should think, He's better at carrying it now we have Nolan; he always has it then.'

'So, it might not have been a phone?'

'He said it might be the Lesser Spotted Wheebling Gannet, but it's more likely to have been a phone.'

'Carried by Bill Lunt?' Hall didn't have time for Maxwell's inanities and if he had, he sure as hell wouldn't smile about them.

'I don't think he actually gave it that much thought.'

'He naturally assumed... Oh, I see. You think it might have belonged to Lara Kent?'

'Yes, I do.' He picked up the phone and stabbed at the numbers. 'I think we'd... Oh, hello? Tony? I need to get some men down to the dunes. SOCO for preference. Yes. Nearby, basically. A phone. Mobile. No idea. How many mobile phones can there be buried on the dunes? Point taken, but... OK. Well, as soon as possible, by which I mean immediately. Who knows what will happen to it after a few dunkings in the sea? Oh, really. Well, I don't have much time for walking, personally.' He slammed down the phone. 'Know-all,' he hissed uncharacter-istically, and went back into his office and slammed the door. Seconds later, he opened it again. 'Jacquie,' he said. 'Sleuthing. Get the details from Alan Kavanagh,' and he waved in the man's general direction. The door shut again and she got up and put her coat back on. The place was humming already, like Bedlam in slowmo. Phones rang, keyboards clacked. From everywhere the clatter of heels and the grinding scream and slam of filing cabinet doors.

'Out and about?' asked Alan Kavanagh smugly as he gave her a very slim file. 'Nice weather for it.' Judging by the paperwork on his desk, Alan Kavanagh wasn't going out and about – or indeed anywhere – for some time yet. He was one of those unfortunate people whose hair had left him before he was twenty-five. It gave him the air of a thallium victim.

Jacquie just nodded and went out. She had her explicit instructions from Henry Hall. Take Maxwell sleuthing and take Max-well sleuthing was just exactly what she intended to do. However, Maxwell didn't finish school until 3.30. Plus he was plan-ning to take Gregory Adair out for a crumby thing and a fatherly chat. That would mean the Toasted Bean on the top floor of what passed for a department store in Leighford, since everything else closed at about three o'clock. Which in actual fact meant that the hoovering started anytime around two, the cashing up at half past one. The joy of living in a tourist trap, she thought to herself. All of the amenities which a normal town would take for granted twelve months of the year only opened in Leighford from April to August. Less, if it was cold. Or wet. Or the owner was on holiday. Still, and she gave herself a secret hug, she could nip off home and have an illicit late morning in, by herself. She loved her menfolk dearly, but a few hours on her tod were like hens' teeth.

She almost skipped down the back steps of the nick.

Down on the dunes, the mood was less jolly. The weather was closing in, a dank sea mist which felt to the digging men as if they were wearing a damp blanket. It seemed to creep down inside their clothes and chill their important little places. What with that and the fine sand which clung to every inch of exposed clammy skin, they were cursing whoever set them on this search. It didn't help the SOCO team that their boss, Brian Meredith, had succumbed to the lurgy and phoned in sick.

'Why are we digging for this phone, exactly?' Dave Wallace wanted to know.

'That bloke of Jacquie's,' Tony Deacon sniffed, the beads of moisture getting to him. 'You know the one. Well, he reckoned he heard a phone on the night him and that photographer found the first body.'

'So? I expect it was Lunt's.'

'Doesn't carry one, apparently.'

'Says he doesn't,' Tim Fryer snorted.

'There wasn't one in the house,' Deacon reminded them.

'Not that we found.' Tim Fryer could be Mr Negativity on days like this.

'Well, Hall is taking...' Deacon was interrupted by a sudden shout from over the next dune.

'Sarge! Over here.'

Spades were thrown down and Deacon and the rest ran round to where the shout came from. And there was a sand-covered Peta Brady, unrecognisable in her white suit, holding aloft a mobile phone.

'Well, bugger me,' said Deacon. 'I suppose we're all allowed to be right once in a while.'

Tony Deacon had had the misfortune to have tangled with the Maxwell logic more than once, and he thought grimly that the mad bugger seemed to get it right more than once in a while. And he lived with that cracker Jacquie Carpenter. And he got long holidays. Jammy git!

Peter Maxwell prided himself on being an avuncular sort of chap. He didn't have a pastoral role as such among the young staff

– they'd given that job, incomprehensibly to the Deputy Head – but they seemed to like him. It was probably because he didn't try to bond with them, like Bernard Ryan did, with random cries of 'Hi guys, how're you doing?' Maxwell was interested, but not embarrassing. He was the uncle who gave you a fiver, not the one who did the Mash with all the actions at family weddings. And that sweet little Human Resources girl meant well, but you couldn't go to her with much more than Women's Trouble.

So it came as rather a shock when Gregory Adair refused his offer of a crumby thing after school as if Maxwell had made an indecent suggestion. Adair bore a vague resemblance to Reinhard Heydrich, but without the charisma, the fencing, boxing and riding skills and hopefully, the full-blown anti-Semitism. It would be a cold day in hell before anyone referred to Greg Adair as the Blond Beast.

'I don't eat cake,' he had said, shortly.

'Everyone eats cake,' Sylvia Matthews had butted in, passing the pair in the corridor just outside the staff room after lunch. 'I've just had roast with all the trimmings but I could still eat a cake.'

'There you are,' smiled Maxwell, hands spread wide. 'Nurse Matthews could eat a cake. And she's had medical training. So, what do you say?'

'I said,' said Adair, rather bluntly, 'that I do not want to come out for cake. Or a drink. Or a chat. Or any of the things that the senior staff in this school have been offering me over the past few weeks. I don't have a problem. I haven't broken up with my girlfriend. I do have a girlfriend. I like girls and if I didn't I still wouldn't mind. My car goes. My flat is small but adequate. My degree is real. I know my History. I just don't quite see why everyone else wants to know it.' With that, he turned on his heel and walked off, slamming through the double doors to the car park and nearly taking Dierdre Lessing's nose off in the process.

'Well, nothing wrong there then,' Maxwell murmured. 'Do you think that means he's not coming over?'

A rare thing then took place. Dierdre walked up to Maxwell and touched his sleeve. Things weren't as frosty between them as they had once been, but she still wouldn't have featured on a list of Maxwell's one hundred favourite people, nor he on hers. And as for mouth-to-mouth, both of them prayed it would never come to that.

'Can we have a word, Max?' she breathed in his ear.

'Certainly, Dierdre,' he cried, full of bonhomie, though following Adair with his eyes as he made his way through the parked cars, the newer, nicer ones belonging to the Sixth

Form. 'What word would you like?'

'In my office,' she said, 'and please don't say that that is three words because I may scream. I have been trying to attract your attention for several days now, and you have been ignoring me.'

'Dear lady!' he said, ushering her into her own office at the end of the notice-strewn corridor. 'Never! Now, what would you like to talk to me about? If it's that business about *Last Tango in Paris*...' He was about to launch into his perfect Brando when she closed her eyes and held up her hand. Nuff said. A nod was as good as a wink to a blind Head of Sixth Form.

Dierdre Lessing had been on the Senior Leadership Team for ever. It had once been called the Senior Management Team until someone realised they couldn't actually Manage anything. Neither, it transpired, could they Lead very much. And so, SMUTS had become SLUTS. Heigh ho!

'I think that Gregory may be having an unfortunate relationship with ... someone,' she said, as she sat down behind her desk.

Maxwell stood by the window. Gregory Adair had not got into his car but was walking out of the gate. Age had compensations and incredibly long sight was probably the most useful. 'He just said he preferred girls.'

She gaped at him. 'Whatever would have made him say that?' she asked. 'What had

160

you said to him?'

'Good Lord, Dierdre! How long have you known me?'

She pursed her lips. He was a funny age and Mrs B did her office too. Rumours spread around the corridors of Leighford High like wild fire.

'No,' he continued, 'I just asked him out for something crumby at the Toasted Bean and he was ... well, let's say, rather adamant that he didn't want to come. He listed all the things that are all right in his little NQT world.'

With a rare moment of insight, Dierdre offered, 'But not what was wrong?'

Maxwell was secretly impressed. 'Got it in one, Dierdre. On the nose. But what is all this about an unfortunate relationship?'

She coloured and clammed up. 'I spoke out of turn, Max. No, really, just me being a little over-zealous. As long as someone has noticed he isn't quite what we were expecting from his references, that's all I want.'

'We are on his case, Dierdre,' Maxwell said. 'Paul Moss and I are trying to help him, but if he doesn't want to be helped ... what can we do?'

There was not a lot Paul Moss could do about anything really. He was the Head of History in the unenviable position of having, in his Department, a man who had lived through most of the periods he was trying to teach.

'Nothing. Of course, nothing. It's just that ... he seemed to begin so well. And I've seen him a few times, in the evenings, you know...'

'When you're on your way back from "Pottery Class".'

The nearest thing to a pottery class that Dierdre Lessing had been to was that time she applied for a job in Stoke. Maxwell couldn't resist a spot of fly-fishing for the hell of it, especially where Dierdre was concerned. Rumour had it, on its way through the corridors of Leighford High, that she was seen on her broomstick, floating over many a beach hut on her way to the Sabbat.

'That sort of thing, yes.'

Dierdre Lessing had never heard of Matthew Hopkins, the Witchfinder General, but she might have been looking at him now, reincarnated in the shape of Peter Maxwell, Factfinder General. For a brief moment, the Head of Sixth Form toyed with running Dierdre around the room until she collapsed with exhaustion and then forcing her to recite the Lord's Prayer backwards. Ah, the good old days.

'Well, what is he doing, when you have occasionally seen him?'

'Gregory tends to mix with the students, Max. And I don't think that's always a good idea.'

'Well, no. But let's not forget, Dierdre, they aren't that different in age.'

'That's not at all the point, Max, as well you know.'

He sighed. She was right. He and Dierdre were more or less of an age. When they were both bright young teachers at the furthest ends of the universe, a surprising number of young staff knocked off their sixth formers. It sometimes made lessons a little awkward, but the results were generally better. As it was, those days had gone and a righteous right-wing press echoed high court judges with stern phrases like 'positions of trust'. For all Maxwell knew, that was page 32 in the Kama Sutra. To admit such things today was tantamount to confessing to having been a guard at Auschwitz.

He'd have to consider what to do with this information. Without, of course, giving away Dierdre's potting secrets, or the shed she may have been doing them in.

At the end of the day, baulked of his Crumby Thing, Maxwell cadged a lift home from Sylvia Matthews. These two had been an item way back, at least from Sylvia's point of view. They had gone their separate ways since then, in the maelstrom of human relationships, but they were allies forever and stood foursquare together against the monster that was modern education. By the time they reached Columbine, they had put the world to rights. Kids should leave school at ten, be pushed up chimneys, sent down coal mines, chained to the oars of galleys and *then*, realising how ghastly the world can be, come back to school for the comfort and safety of the classroom and the incalculable bounty of learning.

Sylvia dropped him at the end of the road. She'd run the gauntlet of Mrs Troubridge's disapproving gaze in the past. She knew when she was beaten. Those gimlet eyes could freeze a basilisk right off its perch.

Maxwell let himself in and threw his hat randomly down the hall. Humming to himself, he trotted up the stairs, all ready for half an hour or so of illicit modelling. Bridles were a bitch at the best of times and he needed to be moderately awake to get them right. The whingeing Corporal Morley's, he just knew would be worse than usual. As he passed the sitting room door, something unusual caught his eye. It was, he would almost be prepared to bet, the sight of his Good Lady, curled up on the sofa reading a book, with Metternich curled up similarly leaning on her legs. The cat wasn't reading, but otherwise their looks of contentment were identical.

He stuck his head round the door.

'Hello?'

They both looked up. One of them said,

'Oh, hello. It's you.'

'Have a care,' he said, going into the room and sprawling in a chair. It was the line delivered by murder victims without number on daytime television. 'I'll have to shoot you if you're not careful. What are you doing here?'

'Likewise,' she said, She was particularly honed on the clichés, having just pigged out on a double dose of *Murder She Wrote*. 'As a matter of fact,' she straightened up, dislodging Metternich, who growled at her and half-heartedly flexed his claws. 'As a matter of fact, I am waiting for you. We are to go sleuthing.'

He sat up and looked at her askance. 'I beg your pardon?'

'Sleuthing. Henry Hall's specific instructions. I am to sleuth and I am to take you with me.'

'Hang on a second.' He went to the window and looked out. 'No, no flying pigs. The moon is up already and it doesn't look blue.' He turned to her. 'What's going on?'

'Apparently,' she put the book down, 'there have been reliable sightings of some hoodies near the sites of both murders and Henry wants us to check out the gangs in Leighford.'

Maxwell swept his hands down his body with a flourish. 'No problem, I'll fit right in,' he said. 'Just let me listen to some gangsta

165

rap and get back to the silly walk. Perhaps I could give Ross Kemp a call?'

'I think he means you might know these kids. I told him you don't know every kid in Leighford, but...'

'I can save us a cold night out,' he said, suddenly remembering. 'I broke up a little light mugging activity the other night. The night we found the body, as a matter of fact. And I didn't know those kids. Although I seem to remember that one of them knew me. There's no reason to suppose they were the ones, but it proves your point.'

'We'll have to go out for a while, Max,' she said. 'I can't make up *all* of a report. And Henry did ask for your help. Sort of.'

'Yes, he did,' Maxwell conceded. 'Something of a red-letter day. But only as grass. Stoolie. Nark.'

She walked over to him and pulled him to his feet. She put her arms around him and hugged him tight. 'My grannie told me about *The Sweeney*,' she laughed. 'John Thaw and Dennis Waterman running around randomly hitting people. I feel as if I'm living in an episode sometimes. Without the hitting, of course.'

'Shut it,' Maxwell snarled, Regan to the life.

'Let's go,' she said, 'before I forget what I said about the hitting.'

CHAPTER NINE

Brushed clean of sand, the mobile phone sat in the middle of a boffin's bench in the SOCO lab, perched under the eaves of Police Headquarters in Chichester, one of those square, vast buildings they'd put up when Lord Trenchard ran the Met and despite there being millions of unemployed, at least Police Headquarters served to remind everybody that Mr Baldwin was at No 10 and God was in His heaven,

It was a Nokia so bog standard that it was currently available in supermarkets as a pay-as-you-go for free if you bought your recommended five portions of fruit or vegetables in one go. Since the kids thought that meant tomato sauce and baked beans, it was even cheaper. Its one concession to individuality was a small purple star hanging from a loop at the bottom corner. A be-gloved technician called Angus was poking it with the end of a pen.

'Well?' Henry Hall was tapping the edge of the bench testily. 'What does it tell us?' Hall knew better than anyone that if murders weren't solved in the first three days, chances were they wouldn't be solved at all.

'Battery's dead.'

'Well, yes, so I assumed, after all this time. What else?'

The technician looked up, his expression full of contempt. 'I said,' he said, moving his gum to the other side of his mouth, 'battery's dead.' Angus McCall was one of those irritating people one step out of reach of the law. He worked (when it suited him) *with* the police, not *for* them.

'Well surely,' Hall could hardly keep his temper in check, 'you can get another one?'

Again, the contempt. 'Well, of course. Jess on the switchboard has a phone like this and we've had hers in there.'

Had? Hall was incredulous, but tempered his voice to patient. He had, after all, had years of experience. 'Why isn't it in there now, if I may ask?'

'Gone home, in't she?'

'I don't know,' Hall said, through gritted teeth. 'Has she?'

'Yeah. And she needs her phone, like, for emergencies.'

Hall looked around, desperately. 'Is there anyone else here?' Surely, a human being was somewhere handy.

'All gone home, in't they?' the technician said. 'I'm here for a bit because of the flexi-time. I start late on a Tuesday, then I can finish stuff up when the others go home.'

'And what are you finishing up, exactly?'

Hall hardly wanted to hear the answer, but the question had to be put. It was likely to be Level Twenty-eight on the *Lara Croft Does It Again And This Time It's Digital* game.

McCall poked the phone again with the end of his pencil. 'This,' he said and stared at the thing again.

'Do you know anyone at the path lab, you know, the morgue at Leighford?' Hall asked.

'Yeah. Everyone knows Donald. He's a good laugh.'

'Are you related, by any chance?'

'To Donald? Nah! You must be joking. Why'd you ask?'

'No reason. Just making conversation. So, you don't know anything about the phone yet, then?'

'Yeah. Loads. Report's over there, in that basket.'

In his imagination, usually so grey and colourless, Henry Hall launched himself at the lacklustre idiot, throttling and squeezing until he lay dead on the floor, his pencil embedded, via his nostril, in his brain. Angus, RIP. In reality, he just said, tightly, 'Thank you. May I take this copy?'

'You DCI Hall?'

'Yes, I am.'

''S yours, then. Got your name on it, anyway.'

Hall flashed his blank lenses at the sky and muttered an almost silent imprecation. The technician heard it however, and bridled.

'There's no need to be like that. We're here to help you lot, in case you didn't know. Back room boys, that's us. Never get no...'

But the door was swinging from Hall's departure and he never did get to know what forensic technicians never got any of. If Hall had his way, it would be any work, ever again.

Jacquie and Maxwell were out on the town, such as it was. They didn't do it often and, when they did do it, were not sorry it was a rarity. They had lots of excuses; pressure of work, difficulty in finding babysitters, a 'y' in the day, but, in truth, they just preferred a nice quiet evening in. Maxwell was kind of slow on the turns these days and found himself dozing even in the loud bits of *Pulp Fiction*. They were both on top of their work, the queues to babysit Nolan stretched round the block and the 'y' in the day excuse only worked on Ten Emm Five, whose grasp of spelling was of the most tenuous kind.

They were sitting at that moment at a table that had had a cursory wipe from a surly child in a red uniform topped by a cap at a rakish angle. If its purpose was to prevent exchange of dandruff between its wearer and the clientele, it was failing spectacularly. If its purpose was to make its wearer look a complete idiot, it was doing very well indeed. Maxwell's idea had been to go to a rather nice pub on the edge of the town centre, perhaps the Blue d'or or the Castor and Pollux that had speciality beers on tap and those rather nice crisps, which, whilst not any more expensive per pack than the ordinary kind, made up for this by only containing six actual crisps, giving their consumer an air of elitism associated with the very best universities. Jacquie had pointed out that hoodies in gangs did not usually meet up in pubs called the Blue d'or, the Castor and Pollux or even the Laptop and Ferret and so the burger bar it was. And not a nice generic burger joint like McDonalds' or Burger King either; no, they were greasily ensconced at the worn formica of Terry's Burgers, subtitled, to the disquiet of the rare American tourist, You'll Love Our Buns. It was the sort of place where you had to choose carefully for flavour between the food and its cardboard packaging.

'Do you have a description of these lovely lads we are watching for?' Maxwell asked the light of his life.

'Boys in hoods.'

'Tall boys in hoods? Short, fat, thin, black, white? Red hoods, brown, grey, purple, sky blue pink? Lincoln green?'

'Any and all of the above,' sighed Jacquie. 'Although I'm not sure they are a merry bunch who hang around Sherwood Forest.

171

I'm sorry, Max, but when people see a sea of hoods, they avoid eye contact and move swiftly away in the opposite direction. The behaviour of these lads is often a self-fulfilling prophecy; you think they are going to shout and jeer, so you take avoiding action. They see you do that and, guess what, they shout, and jeer.'

'That's very social-worker of you,' Maxwell observed.

'Just trying to see all sides,' Jacquie said. 'A bit like that kid you tell me about, you know, the one with the divergent squint.'

Maxwell snorted and sent his Extra-Thick-Chocochocochoco Milkshake spraying all over the place. Jacquie wiped her front with a napkin and wished she had come with Nolan; he wasn't so messy.

While they frittered away a minute or two more, tearing their Terry's Special Everything On It Burger into small pieces so it couldn't be served to the next punter, who, after all, might not be in for several days, Jacquie kept her wits about her and her eyes everywhere. Suddenly, she kicked Maxwell under the table.

'I think that may be them,' she hissed out of the corner of her mouth. 'Don't turn round.'

Maxwell swivelled in his seat. 'Where?'

'For God's sake, Max,' she hissed. 'I said *don't* turn round.'

'That's all very well, heart,' he said, reasonably. 'But there isn't much point in your saying that it may be them if I can't get a bit of a butchers. And I only have eyes in the back of my head at school.'

'I thought you were good at this sleuthing lark,' she said.

'I've had a bit of luck, yes,' he said, modestly. Then, 'And a good few beatings up as well. Plus the attempt or two on my life, I suppose. So, I wouldn't be surprised if some people would say I'm pretty rubbish at it.'

'Well, anyway,' Jacquie said, 'despite your strange behaviour and the totally appalling food in here, they seem to be coming in.'

The door flung back on its hinges and the cold night air carried with it what seemed to be a horde of teenagers, all shapes, all sizes, all hooded. They sprawled around at as many tables as they could occupy to cause the maximum disruption and ordered the smallest amount of food that would allow them to stay. The dandruffed youth disappeared quickly behind the counter and had a whispered dialogue with someone out of sight. Whoever it was wisely stayed backstage.

'Do you know any of them, Max?' she asked, in a hoarse stage whisper.

'Can I look now, then?' he asked, a little petulantly. She thought again of how much less trouble Nolan would have been on this junket.

'Of course,' she said. 'That's why we're here.'

He raised his head and looked sideways at the lost boys. They were aged between about twelve and sixteen, well within the remit of Leighford High, but he didn't specifically recognise any of them. There wasn't even a family resemblance to any of his kids that might give him a clue. No reptilian tongue, no third eyelid. Not even a webbed foot. He turned back to Jacquie and shook his head. 'I don't know any of them,' he told her. 'Not even a maybe.'

She gathered her coat and bag and made to leave. 'Well, on to the next dive,' she said and made for the door, while he struggled with the twists of his scarf.

'Hello,' said one of the lads, sticking out a leg. 'Out for a nice burger wiv your dad?'

'Let me by, please,' Jacquie said in a neutral tone.

'Are you dissing my homie?' asked another spotty lout, whose nearest contact with a New York street gang had to be a million light years.

'No. I just want to go,' said Jacquie, avoiding eye contact and doing everything a normal member of the public might do. Her natural instinct was to deck the little shit and have done.

'Well, what if I says you can't?' said the first boy, stepping into her path. He was thin as a reed, but tall and anyway, they out-numbered Jacquie and Maxwell by six to one. To the Head of Sixth Form, of course, this was par. He was usually outnumbered thirty to one in a classroom and yet he was, somehow, always the last man standing.

'I don't want to make this something it's not,' said Jacquie, sidestepping.

Then, everything happened really fast. The boy lunged at her and tried to pin her arms. Maxwell grabbed him by the hood and lifted him off his feet, yanking him backwards and throwing him across a table, scattering cartons and other hoodies in all directions. In a scream of sirens and a flash of rotating blue lights, uniform arrived like the Seventh cavalry. And a quiet voice in Maxwell's ear said, 'Hello, Mr Maxwell. I never expected to see you in this kind of place.'

Everything was really quiet. Jacquie had gone off with the ringleaders of the gang and the arresting officer, having silenced their jeering with a single sweep of her warrant card. The pair's covert sleuthing was over until either they found that the police had their man or they had to begin again. Maxwell sat back at their table, wiped properly by the boy sitting opposite. The blinds were down and a closed sign hung at the door. Maxwell and the boy each had a cup of real coffee, staff reserve, in front of them. The dandruffy youth swept ineptly in a corner. He'd never seen a bloke as old as Maxwell move so fast in his life.

'So, Nicholas,' Maxwell said, leaning back in his seat as far as the rigid, fixed steel legs would allow. 'You love to cook, hmm?'

The lad had emerged from the innermost recesses of the kitchen when the balloon had gone up. He looked nearly as much of a plonker as Mr Dandruff in his red uniform, but Maxwell knew better.

The lad looked down and blushed. 'I do like cooking, yes. But I also want to have a bit of money behind me when I go up to uni, Mr Maxwell. All those fancy restaurants in London, they'll take you on, but you have to pay for the privilege. And it's not as if it's what I want to do. Well,' he pulled a rueful face, 'it's what I *want* to do, but it's not what I'm *going* to do.'

'Parents?' Maxwell asked, with the lift of a sympathetic eyebrow. He'd had some of his own once and he knew they were the real problems in schools, not the kids.

''Fraid so,' Nick replied. 'I know they mean well, but they say you can be a research chemist who cooks for pleasure, but you can't be a chef who does a bit of biochemical research on the side.'

'There's no arguing with their logic,' Maxwell conceded. 'But I wonder whether Delia Smith ever wishes she could split an atom from time to time.'

'Exactly, Mr Maxwell,' the lad beamed. 'I wish you were my dad. When you taught me at school, it was brilliant. You made it all seem so interesting. I loved History, you know. Working out how one thing leads to another, just like the butterfly flapping its wings causing...'

'...the invention of the world-infamous Terry's Special Everything On It Burger,' laughed Maxwell. The boy may have loved his History, but he was going to be a research chemist nonetheless. Nick smiled too, genuinely now, and Maxwell could see how he would go through the girls at uni like a hot knife through butter. 'Seriously though, Nick,' he said. 'Don't be railroaded. You'll work for forty-three years of your life – make it something you at least don't dislike.'

'I've got to give it a go, Mr Maxwell,' the boy said quietly. 'I can't disappoint them.'

'I'll give you credit for that,' Maxwell said. 'But please think it over before you end up tied to a lab bench. Once the bills and things start multiplying, it gets harder and harder to change direction.'

'You sound as if that happened to you.' The boy sounded incredulous and Maxwell was once again aware that, no matter how popular a teacher might be, he was never fully human to a student.

'Not really,' Maxwell smiled again. 'Circumstances are funny things, Nicholas. Yes, I wanted to be Stephen Spielberg before they invented Stephen Spielberg; to make historical epics that would make *Lord of the Rings* look like *Noddy Goes to the Toilet*, but, like you, I had parents who had other ideas. Anyway, I didn't sit down to depress you – I wanted to say thanks for calling the police. Lightning reflexes on your part. I wasn't sure I could throw six of them around the room.'

'Well, they were out of hand, Mr Maxwell. I didn't want your ... your...'

'Yes,' Maxwell helped him out, smiling. 'I have that trouble too. I hate the whole 'partner' thing myself. A partner is somebody you're in business with. Girlfriend seems a little silly at my age. The mother of my child seems a touch formal. And she's not my wife.'

'Oh.' Nick was taken aback. The old devil! It was the old generation-gap thing. Nobody over thirty could possibly have a live-in-lover.

'Thanks, anyway. You didn't want my Significant Other to be hurt. I appreciate that.' A tinny tune rang out from among the boy's clothing. To Maxwell's amazement, he recognised it. 'I didn't have you down for a Diana Ross fan,' he said, as the lad foraged in amongst his chef's whites and scarlets, bought for twenty-stone Terry and looking a little voluminous on eleven-stone Nicholas.

'What?' he said to Maxwell, then to the

178

phone, 'Yeah? No. I've closed up. Bit of trouble. Yeah, the usual. I'm with Mr Maxwell at the moment. Yeah, OK. Later.' He stowed the phone away and smiled at Maxwell. 'Lobber sends his,' he said. 'He'll be round in a bit, to pick me up now we've shut for the night.'

'You've closed? Just because of a few spotty hoodies? What will your boss say?'

'He's on holiday, that's why I'm in charge.'

'So the old guy in the kitchen with you wasn't Terry?' Maxwell had noticed the man hovering as the police effectively emptied the place of customers.

'Him!' Nicholas laughed. 'No, that's Alf. He's my sous-chef! No, Terry won't mind – he only needs to sell about twenty burgers to cover the staff.'

'How many have you sold?'

'What did you have?'

'A couple of Everything-on-its.'

'Two of those, then.' He spread his arms. 'We are not an eaterie where gourmets gather. It's the chucking out trade we rely on and there's a late shift for that, comes on in about an hour and a half. They'll open up.'

'Do you have much trouble like we've just had?'

'Not as a rule. Certainly not when Terry's here. He's built like a brick shithouse and just wades in. That lot though – I didn't recognise them. They must be from out of town.'

'That's what I thought. Not Leighford High. I've seen a few groups around lately. I even broke up a bit of a mugging the other day. As I'm sure you are already aware, I do tend to look at faces, sort out trouble-makers, give them a bit of a hard time the next day.'

Nick had just seen how hard and Maxwell hadn't even waited for the next day. He pressed his hands on the table and pushed himself back, the chair squeaking on the greasy floor. 'Oh, yes, Mr Maxwell,' he laughed. 'We *all* knew that. It's in the un-official *Guide To Surviving Leighford High*.'

'As it should be,' Maxwell grinned, won-dering where he could buy a copy. He got up. 'I'll leave you to finish up. It's way past my bedtime.' He went to stand by the door. The Dandruff Kid shot the bolts for him, careful to keep at arm's length, and he sauntered off up the road. The night was still now, apart from the odd car whose tyres hissed across the standing water of half a day of rain. The truth was, he didn't really want to meet the unlovely Lobber, Nick's oppo. He had always been a menace at school and just because he was now in the world at large, he wasn't much better. Maxwell just hoped he didn't sell anything expensive, like houses or cars, in his High Street employment. He personally wouldn't buy a stamp from him; it was bound to have been booby trapped in some hilarious way that only Lobber found amusing. He had no idea why the two of them were friends, except that presumably opposites attract. He was just glad they were soon going their separate ways.

As he rounded the corner, he saw a furtive figure slip into a doorway. Most men would have gone home to their cosy firesides, thanked the babysitter profusely, slipped her an extra fiver and hunkered down with a large SoCo to await the arrival of the Mem, all hot and handcuffed from a hard evening at the nick. But this was Mad Max and something about the profile made him follow the shadow and as he made the same turn, he realised he was following Gregory Adair up a narrow alley. Maxwell and the NQT were not alone; there was another figure sidling along between them, past the skips and piles of rubbish and, suddenly, Maxwell didn't really want to know. He had spent the evening in the most sordid setting; nothing new for him, as it happened, but he had had enough. Perhaps he wasn't as Mad as all that and suddenly wanted to be back in his nice warm house, paying off a nice babysitter and doing a little modelling in his attic until his nice warm ... he didn't even know what to call her in the privacy of his head. He would really have to work on this one. Anyway, he was going home. That's it, as Billy Crystal was wont to say, when not throwing Momma from the train, and that's all.

The babysitter was long gone, the modelling drying nicely now that blue-jacketed Corporal Morley could sit his horse, the glass of warming SoCo drained and the cocoa mixed and ready to zap when Jacquie finally got home. Processing a load of unhelpful yobs was not her idea of a good evening out, but she was sure that Henry Hall would be satisfied. Quotas. Lists. Results. A little heavy community policing. Now they could all be lined up for David Cameron to hug. They couldn't *all* have alibis for the Night in Question and it was now only a matter of time before the two cases were wrapped up and Leighford could slumber again for a while. It would be something like that, the stupid, sad bastards egging each other on, looking for trouble and finding it. Yes, Leighford could slumber at least until the season began and holiday-makers arrived, with their fights on the promenade, fatal divings from the pier, light-hearted stabbings under it, drug deals in the Little Tots' Playground. She threw her keys on the table and collapsed on the sofa.

'Well, that was a short bit of sleuthing,' she said, as she eased off her shoes without untying them, to Maxwell's irritation. She caught his expression. 'What?'

'Do you never untie your laces?'

She looked down. 'No, not really. I untie them when I put them back on, you Old Peculiar. Just as I don't undo my pyjama buttons or my blouse. Waddya going to do about it? Anyway, as I said, that was quick. We finally got them all processed and I reckon we've got our man. Men. Boys. Whatever they count as, their ages are pretty varied. That was a pretty slick back flip by the way, down at Terry's. Bearing in mind the Leighford rumour machine, by morning you'll have sliced him in half with the roller blades attached to your knee caps.'

'It's nothing,' Maxwell shrugged. 'They should see me when I really get Mad. So,' Maxwell steepled his fingers. Now *that* really irritated *her*, along with people who say 'In the final analysis' and 'At this moment in time'. 'You think you've got the perp, do you?'

'Haven't we?' Jacquie raised her eyebrows. When Peter Maxwell used a phrase like perp he was probably sniffing something.

'Hmm, can't be sure. Haven't asked the cat yet – he's usually pretty sound. But I don't think so, no.'

'Go on then, Sherlock,' she said. 'I'm all ears.'

'You'll have to bear with me,' he said, stirring his cocoa with a biro, 'because I don't have a single scrap of evidence here, but it's just a train of thought. Sort of thing old AJP Taylor used to come out with. You say their ages are pretty varied. Between what?'

'Between fourteen and ... um, seventeen, I think. You'd have to ask the desk sergeant.'

'Right. Are they local?'

'As Henry Hall suspected and you confirmed, they are from out of town. One from Tottingleigh, the rest from Littlehampton. And I don't reckon they're the ones you had an earlier run in with the other night, the night you and Bill did your Resurrection Men bit. You said one of them knew you.'

'Called me a wanker,' Maxwell remembered.

'Must have known you pretty well, then.' Jacquie smiled.

'So this lot tonight got here, how? In cars?'

'Oddly enough, we don't have a joy riding pack here, though I thought we might. They came on the bus, bizarrely enough. A couple even had Rover Tickets.'

'How frugal,' he smiled. 'So, why did they make their way to lovely Leighford?'

'They've all got ASBOs or restraining orders of some kind, stopping them from creating any kind of havoc where they live. A couple of them are tagged. They're a lovely bunch.'

'Tagged *and* bus-passed,' Maxwell tutted,

shaking his head. 'Says it all about our schizoid society. Still, I expect their mothers love them.' But even as he said it, he doubted it.

'I expect they do, except the one put in hospital by her little boy last August. That was the one who squared up to me. The one you threw across Terry's. I understand his mother's sending you a medal.'

'Issues with women in authority,' Maxwell said gravely. 'I expect he was once spoken to harshly by a cinema usherette. So, they came on the bus. From where?'

'The Littlehampton Cruiser Service, apparently.'

'Do we know their bus timetable?'

'Um … not as such.'

'Which means not at all, I assume.'

'Well, I expect they know it down at the nick. I don't know it off by heart, sitting here wrapped round some cocoa – which is excellent, by the way – no, sorry. I last knowingly caught a bus in 1992.'

'Ah, you motorists, you're all the same. Encyclopaedic as my knowledge is, I don't know bus timetables either, but I can soon find out.' He got up and went along the landing to the study, little used as they both preferred to work within smiling distance of each other. She could hear distant clicking as she switched on the telly, rummaging through the channels. *Cold Case. New Tricks. Taggart* (again) Plus One. Why was it always

shop? He was soon back. 'I Googled Leighford buses and, amazingly, got their timetables.'

'Why amazingly?'

'Well, I usually get an offer to buy Leighford on eBay, or sell me three new and used
Leighfords from Amazon. And then, of
course, Luscious Lesley from Leighford has
a camcorder and is dying to chat to me. But
I'm getting the hang of the thing, I think.
Anyway, it's on the screen.'

'Couldn't you have printed it out?'

Maxwell looked horrified. 'Print it out? Of
course not. My skills begin and end with
Googling. Apart from Google Earth. That
makes no sense at all. I have people to print
things for me, up at the school.'

Jacquie sighed and put down her cocoa.
She pointed at it. 'That had better not have
a skin on it when I get back,' she said, 'And
before you ask, there's nothing on. *A Matter
of Life and Death*. *The Magnificent Seven*.
Citizen Kane. And *Metropolis*. Same old tut
every night.' She came back in moments,
without a printout and picked up the mug.
She poked the surface of the drink tent-
atively. 'Hmm, you're very lucky,' she said,
sitting back down, 'It's touch and go.'

'Well?' He hadn't fallen for her lure. Be-
sides, he knew every word of the *Metropolis*
screenplay.

'You're right. They could have done the

186

first one, but not the second. Assuming they travelled by bus, of course. We have sightings that the bench was empty till well after midnight. Their last bus goes at 10.12.' Despite the seriousness of the moment, she couldn't help a little giggle. 'For goodness' sake, a gang that travels by bus. They're a bit pathetic, aren't they?'

'They wear thin hooded sweatshirts in the middle of winter. They talk like New York street gangs although most of them have never been further west than Bournemouth. They have ASBOs because they have wee'd in the street. Of course they travel by bus. But they haven't murdered anyone. I'm afraid I am going to add – yet.' Maxwell sipped his drink. 'Back to the sleuthing, is it?'

Jacquie shook her head, 'No, I don't think so, actually. I think the whole sighting thing is a bit of a red herring. They stand out, don't they? If someone asked you who you had seen at a particular time of night, in a particular place, then you wouldn't mention the quiet bloke with a carrier bag, the two women walking fast because the night is cold, the little granny-type with her shitszu. You mention the gang of hoodies.'

'True. Very true.' They both stared into their mugs and let their minds wander. Dr Crippen could have been the man with the carrier bag, just before he cut off his wife's head; what *did* he do that with, by the way?

The two women walking fast were the Lapin sisters, on their way to gouging out the eyeballs of the women they worked for. And as for the little granny with her shitszu... Then Maxwell added, 'What does Henry think?'

'We didn't get him in. He's really been working all hours and the gossip is he was ready to strangle the late-night guy in the lab this evening when he messed him about over this phone thing.'

'Ah, Angus,' Maxwell nodded. 'So there was a phone, then? I wondered. Is it any help?'

'How do you know Angus?' Jacquie asked. 'He works in Chichester.'

'Indeed,' Maxwell nodded. 'But he lives in Tottingleigh and once attended a series of WEA lectures I ran on the Role of the Nutter in History. He fitted right in. The phone?'

'Hmmm, not much use,' Jacquie shook her head. 'We're assuming it belongs to Lara Kent. If so, we will be able to trace calls made, calls received, texts, that sort of thing. But these pay-as-you-go phones, you know, they're ten a penny. You don't have to tell the truth when you register them. In fact, most of them you don't have to fill anything in at all. You just top them up with the card that comes with them. If you do it with cash, that's it. Untraceable.'

'Why would she want an untraceable phone?'

'No, no, not *her*. Her murderer.'

Maxwell sat up sharply. 'Are you suggesting that she knew her murderer? That Darren knew his murderer?' He looked at her in the lamplight. 'This is probably stupid, but I thought these killings were random.'

'Why did you assume that?'

'Well, she was from out of town, living ... what, in a squat or something? He was local, living much rougher than squatting. She was trying to make a go of things, *Big Issue*, that kind of thing. He just seemed to have given up. Even street people have a hier-archy, a pecking order, don't they? I just don't imagine they would move in the same circles.'

She laughed. 'Max, for someone who is around kids all day, sometimes you have no clue. There are no circles. They go out when they have a bit of money. They go out and cadge when they haven't. They go where their favourite bands are. They go inside for the warmth. If they are at the bottom of the heap, they'll go inside for the off chance of a half-eaten pie. I'm not saying they were friends, but I bet they would have recognised each other.'

'Polly Nicholls, Annie Chapman, Liz Stride, Kate Eddowes, Mary Kelly,' Maxwell murmured. 'All victims of Jack the Ripper. Did they know each other? I wonder...'

They were silent for a moment, imagining

189

the cold, lonely world of both of the murder victims, random or planned, it made no difference. Once, they were beloved children, hugged, fed, kept warm. Someone had hopes for them, looked forward to seeing them grow up. Then, in what was just a heartbeat in the scheme of things, they were mysteries sent for solving on a pathologist's slab.

As one, they got up and went into Nolan's room, where their little son lay sleeping. Together, silently, they wished on the stars circling his bedroom ceiling and leant their heads together. It didn't matter that they couldn't tell their wishes; they both knew they were just the same.

CHAPTER TEN

Wednesday was the usual thing; middle of the week sort of time, so all the flakeys from both staff and pupil cohorts had gone down with a touch of the usual. But that was over and above the Plague of the Spanish Lady, Bird Flu, e-coli or whatever else was decimating the south coast that winter. Maxwell's cover requests were, as usual, completely insane. Wednesday was supposed to contain two lessons of what teachers laughingly call protected time, so obviously, he had been asked to cover a dance lesson and a child-birth module for Health and Social Sciences. One of those he was a dab hand at; but who wants to learn the foxtrot these days? And he could be struck off for trying the Lambada (although in his day, the word had meant 'scooter'). He palmed off the dance class onto the Teaching Assistant – totally illegal, but since she had a degree in drama and dance, it seemed the natural choice. As Maxwell would have said, had he been known for his puns, she had De Knees for it. The mystery was why Denise was a teaching assistant in the History Depart-ment; another cracking appointment by Legs Diamond and his Flying Monkeys of the SLT. The childbirth class he gave to Juliette Simmonds of the English Depart-ment, a woman so extremely pregnant that she could become a hands on example at any moment – Minnie Ha Ha, Breaking Waters.

Metaphorically dusting his hands together to celebrate a job well done, he ensconced himself in his office with cries of 'I owe you one' and picked up his phone. He jabbed the speed dial and waited, humming a tune he couldn't quite get out of his head. If only he had been concentrating in the Sixties, he might be able to put a name to it. The Cambridge History Tripos was all well and good, but the real world had passed him by.

He was forty-six before he realised the Doors were anything more than part of the furniture. With this particular tune he could get as far as 'De dum de di di di di de de de dum,' but after that it was a dead loss.

'Yes?' Someone had picked up at the other end. 'History office.'

'Oh, Paul, Max. Are you free at all today?'

'No, I've been given lots of cover. Would you believe two in one day?'

'Tsk, tsk. Well, everyone's off with a touch of that thing that's going around. Skivers' disease, that's the one.'

'Was it anything important, Max? Only, I've got reports to check. Oh, not yours, of course. Immaculate as ever.'

'Oh, still? Never mind, Paul. I just wanted a word about...' Maxwell's door opened and Gregory Adair walked in and sat down opposite the Head of Sixth Form, '...setting Year Nine.'

'In February? Are you bonkers, Max?' Time was when Paul Moss would never have dared ask the Great Man such a question. Even now, he felt his heart stop the second he'd said it.

'Well, yes, of course,' Maxwell smiled. 'Hence the name. Bye now.' He looked up at the NQT, sitting stiffly in the chair. 'Can I help you, Gregory? Only, this is my protected time, you see, and...'

'Look, Maxwell,' the man snarled. 'Stop

following me, right. I'm fed up with it. I saw you last night.'

Maxwell looked at him levelly. 'Before you make an idiot of yourself and also force me to report you to your mentor, I feel I must point out that that is exactly what I did do. Stop, I mean. I was just going to say hello, like you do when you meet a colleague out and about, but you disappeared up that passageway quicker than a rat up a drain-pipe and I let you go.'

'Lost me, you mean,' snapped the NQT.

Maxwell leant forward and in a voice that generations of children had learnt to dread, said, 'Listen to me, sonny, and listen well, because I will say this only once.' The chilling thing was that there was no sign of *Allo! Allo!*, no funny voice at all. 'I don't care what you are doing in your spare time, but I suspect that it is both sordid and underhand. For all I know it may actually be illegal. You are this far,' he held up his thumb and forefinger pressed together, 'from failing your NQT year. What say we speed everything up and make that happen now?' The fingers clicked and Adair flinched backwards. 'However,' and Maxwell leant back, clasping his hands behind his head, 'you do seem to know a hawk from a handsaw, as our English colleagues would once have had it when they knew enough to quote from anybody, and so I think we'll give you another chance. But I suggest that you stop skulking in passageways after dark and especially that, if you see Ms Lessing of an evening, you smile politely at her and make sure you are not doing anything untoward.'

'Ms Lessing?' Gregory Adair was confused. Sweat stood out on his brow and upper lip.

'Oh, yes. Her spies are everywhere, and so is she. Don't annoy her, Gregory. Don't annoy me. Walk wide of us both. Don't annoy *anyone* and you might just make it. Right,' he shuffled some papers on his desk. 'Off you bugger now, I have work to do.'

The NQT could hardly get out quickly enough and actually collided in the doorway with Paul Moss.

'Oops!' A born raconteur was Paul Moss. 'What are you on about, Max?' the Head of History asked as he closed the door.

Maxwell nodded his head towards the departing colleague. 'I wanted a word about the great pedagogue there and he came in,' he said.

'Oh, right.' The light dawned. 'I'm sorry, I thought you'd gone a bit nuts.'

'And as I concurred, I probably have. But I really think we need to keep an eye on him, Paul. I saw him in town last night, behaving very oddly. He was meeting with someone and I couldn't see who.'

'That's not a crime, Max,' Paul reminded

194

him gently. Perhaps in Maxwell's day, NQT's weren't allowed company. In Maxwell's day of course, such people were called probationers and those eccentric Wright brothers were mucking about on Kitty Hawk beach.

'No, I grant you that. But he is over-reacting to everything anyone says and if a kid did that, you'd suspect them immediately. And rightly so.'

'I'll put it in his record. We'll talk again in a week or so.'

'You're the boss,' said Maxwell, although neither of them really believed that. He waved his hand as Moss left his office. Now then, priorities. First, coffee; not the awful stuff that Adair had provided, the sweepings of some supermarket floor, but some of the good stuff from home. Then, a bit of brain-storming with Nursie. When it came to life's failures, Sylvia Matthews was an expert. They all came to her, at some stage. Either they thought they were pregnant and wanted out. Or they thought they might be gay. Or, in one case that had kept the staff room agog for weeks, they *had* thought they were gay, but were now pretty sure they weren't. Everybody was waiting for the first gay pregnancy, such was the speed of genetic engineering these days. Sylv would know the ones who were having trouble at home, had left home or hung out with those who had. Maxwell needed to know whether they should be looking out for anyone. It had come pretty close to home with Darren Blackwell and he didn't want it any nearer to his doorstep than that.

Jacquie had paperwork again. Surprise, surprise. As Henry Hall had said, when you bring in a job lot of hooded ASBOs, you must expect the odd bit of paper to come your way. She was perfectly sure that they had not murdered Lara Kent or Darren Blackwell. But they had clearly done something, and if she could pin it on them, then perhaps their ASBO radius could be increased to include Leighford. And Brighton. Then it would be London, Colchester, Belgium and all points east.

'Jacquie?' a voice said, rather too close to her ear. She looked up into the unlovely nostrils of Alan Kavanagh, leaning into her personal space, brandishing a file.

'Sorry, Alan,' she said, backing away out of range of his coffee breath. 'Miles away. What can I do for you?'

'I've got this file on a missing person. I thought you ought to see it.' With a conspiratorial wink, he placed it across the pile of paper already on her desk. She could hardly complain. Across the entire acreage of Leighford nick, similar piles of paper stood like so many towers of Babel, all clamouring in urgent tongues and all of them failing to reach heaven.

Gingerly, she opened the file. She read the first line and, mesmerised by its contents, groped for her mobile phone, hidden in the depths of the bag hanging on the back of the chair. She hit the first speed dial button and got through to an interminable answerphone message, giving her so many options her head swam. 'To speak to the Premises Manager, press one. To leave details about your child's absence, press two. To express amazement that anyone can doubt machines have taken over the world, Press a flower.' She must be catching this technophobe thing from Maxwell, she thought. She always used to be able to cope with stuff like this. But then, she hadn't always just had news like this.

'Hello? Leighford High School, Reception.' Finally, a human being.

'Hello, Tansy?' Trust Jacquie not only to know both Thingees' names but be able to tell them apart. 'It's Jacquie Carpenter here. Can I speak to Mr Maxwell, please?'

'He's in a meeting at the moment,' Tansy came through loud and clear. 'With Nurse Matthews. Can I give him a message?'

Jacquie knew perfectly well that this was not a meeting *per se*, more a bitch session, but there again, Maxwell wore his heart on his sleeve and for all his world-weary

197

exterior, if he and Nursie were interviewing some kid, there was a reason for it. 'Um. It's very difficult, really,' said Jacquie, chewing the corner of her thumbnail in her anxiety.

'Oh,' breathed Tansy sympathetically. 'Is it something to do with,' she dropped her voice to the edge of inaudibility. Any lower and only whales could have heard her, 'your work?'

'In a way,' Jacquie said. 'It involves us as neighbours. Our next door one has disappeared.'

'Oooh,' Tansy was thrilled to be surfing the breaking wave of police news. 'Do you think she might have been ... you know, murdered, or something?'

'Almost certainly something,' Jacquie said. 'But could you get Mr Maxwell to ring me as soon as he is out of his meeting?'

'Straight away,' Tansy said. Even her voice was wide-eyed.

'Thanks,' said Jacquie, but the phone was already halfway down and she was re-reading the front page of the file. It was dated the day before, quite late, and the details were scant. But the name leapt out at her; 'Troubridge'. The description could not have been more accurate and also more general; there had to be hundreds of small, mousey-haired, slightly infirm but still pretty good for her age ladies in Leighford and its surrounding area. If they put an APB

198

out for her, the nick would be swamped with grannies within hours. She sighed and felt quite melancholy. If only there were other boxes to tick. Accent you could use to engrave titanium. Tick. Attitude that you could strike matches on. Tick. Ability to hold a grudge until hell froze over. A really, really big tick. Those extra things were what made Mrs Troubridge what she was. A cantankerous, miserable, nosy, basically kind at heart but, most of all, missing old lady. Peter Maxwell would already be re-running scenes from *The Lady Vanishes*. But the absent heroine there was a spy. You don't think Mrs Troubridge...?

Jacquie glanced across the room to where Alan Kavanagh was trying to look at her out of the corners of his eyes whilst appearing to study his computer screen. He obviously didn't know that Jacquie was quite fond of Mrs Troubridge. That the mad old dear was their cat-feeder and plant-waterer in chief. And whenever she could would cuddle little Nolan and slobber over him, regressing his language development by many months with her baby babble. All Kavanagh knew was that the address was just one number different. That it would look to the powers that be that Maxwell had, yet again, managed to get shit on his own doorstep. He would immediately have added, of course, had anyone been privy to his thoughts, that he didn't wish the old besom any ill. Even so ... a sly smile was beginning to twitch the corners of his mouth.

Jacquie turned the page. Another thinly filled out pro forma was all that remained of the file. There was a photograph pinned to the corner of Mrs Troubridge in a rather unexpected hat, looking a little like Mrs Pankhurst and squinting into the sun. It had clearly been taken some years before and Jacquie thought, irritated, that they almost certainly had a better picture of her at home than this one. It would have also included Nolan at various sizes and Metternich in various attitudes of disgust, but they could always crop it for the paper. She made a mental note to get that sorted.

Last seen; bus station. Bus station? It was a well known fact that Mrs Troubridge rarely left the confines of Columbine. Some kind soul shopped on line for her, and although Meals on Wheels had made any number of overtures, the old lady had made it plain she wasn't ready for *them* yet. You had to be *really* desperate. She found that all the gossip she could possibly need beat a path to her door. And she did own a telephone. The first tick in the box marked 'unusual behaviour'. Time of last sighting; 21.30. That let the hoodies off the hook – they were tucked up waiting for processing at the nick by then. But... Jacquie tapped her teeth with her pen, a habit Maxwell hated, except when doing it himself... Why were they so set on the idea that there was only one set of dodgy teenagers in hoods in town? Red herrings swam in more than one shoal, after all. And Maxwell had clearly encountered at least two. Contact name and ... her phone rang and she snatched it up.

'Carpenter.'

'Hello, Carpenter. What on earth is going on? I've just had Thingee One in here even more incoherent than usual. Something about next door. Is it on fire? Have they saved my summer hat? It's not Metternich smoking in bed again, is it? If I've told him once... Oh, Jesus, not the Light Brigade?'

'Max. Stop a minute and let me tell you. It's Mrs Troubridge.'

'Mrs Troubridge is on fire?'

'No, Max.' Jacquie hardened her voice. It was the only way to bring him back on track. 'She's missing, actually.'

The silence on the other end of the phone was thick with embarrassment. 'Oh. How do you know?'

'I work in a police station, Max, in case you had forgotten.'

'Yes, I know that, but how do you know this small fact? You don't work on the front desk. You're working on the murders so surely they wouldn't give you a misper to deal with.'

'Misper? Max, I'm going to stop you watching television. No, they wouldn't give me a missing person to deal with, except that for some creepy reason I don't want to dwell on, Alan Kavanagh knows where I live and put the file on my desk.'

'Do you think it has any connection with the others? The deaths, I mean.'

'I don't see one. I can't see one between the first two, let alone between them and a little old lady. I think she may have just gone a bit more doolally than usual and wandered off.'

'She has been a little bit strange lately, you said so the other morning.'

'Max, I said she was off hooks with you and probably Metternich. That is perfectly normal on planet Troubridge. I expect you looked at her funny or Metternich used her cotoneasters as a urinal, that's all. Even so, I'll spend a bit of time on it, go the rounds and see if I can find out a bit more. I'll have to speak to Henry, but I don't see that it would be a problem. Apart from anything else, we've got much better pictures of her at home than this one on the report.'

'Do you need me to help in anything?'

'Not right now. I ... I just wanted to tell you straight away. I know you're quite fond of the old trout in fact.'

Maxwell chuckled, a quick back projection of his years with Mrs Troubridge playing on the screen in his mind. 'We go back a way, I must admit. I hope she's all right. I really wouldn't want any harm to come to the cantankerous old biddy.'

'Same here,' said Jacquie. 'I'll find her, Max. Don't worry. Love you,' and she put the phone down quickly. She knew his lighthearted response masked a real concern over the old dear's possible plight. She had been there when he first moved to Columbine, his grief over the loss of his first family healed over, but still raw in the long watches of the night and the hours of weekends and school holidays. Sparring with Mrs Troubridge was a hobby that kept the worst of the pain away in those days. Jacquie considered the options. Best case scenario, the old lady had got on a bus to somewhere and was wandering dazed and confused in Devizes or some such place. Worst case, she was about to be washed up on a beach somewhere, with unexplained dents in her head. With fingers crossed, Jacquie tapped on Henry Hall's door.

'Come.' God, how she hated that. How much breath did it take to also say 'in'?

'Guv, I wondered if I...'

'No, sorry Jacquie, you can't.'

'I'm sorry, perhaps if I could tell you what...'

Henry Hall looked up at her, two perfect little fluorescent tubes reflected in his lenses. 'No, you can't have time off from two murder investigations to look into the disappearance of your neighbour.'

Jacquie looked crestfallen. 'Sorry, guv, I didn't know...'

'No, well,' his head was down to his paperwork again. 'I try to keep abreast and I know it can't be easy for you. But, no, sorry. Perhaps when we have this cracked.' He almost smiled. That in itself was such a rare occurrence she didn't know what to make of it. Was it sardonic? Cynical? Wind? Who could say?

She stepped back out into the communal office and felt at a bit of a loss. Her first thought was to ring Peter Maxwell. He always knew what to do, in or out of a crisis. Then, she thought again and on those second thoughts, what could he do? He couldn't leave school yet; it was Wednesday – Ten Gee Four. Nobody could manage Ten Gee Four last thing in the afternoon, except Liberty Valance – and Peter Maxwell. And then, they were horribly short-staffed, weren't they? Perhaps he'd have to do bus queue duty or something. And he knew nothing of the circumstances; better to leave it till they went home. Then perhaps they could do a search of the town themselves, looking for the places only Mrs Troubridge would go. She looked back at Hall's closed door. What a shit! *Someone* had to do something.

Alan Kavanagh's phone rang and he spoke into the receiver for a moment. Then, he covered the mouthpiece with his hand. 'Jacquie,' he called across the office. 'That murdering toerag Lunt is in reception. D'you want to just tell the guv'nor for me? Save my legs.'

She looked at him as if he had crawled out from somewhere and turned on her heel. 'Run your own errands, Alan, there's a good boy,' she said over her shoulder. 'I'm off to the canteen. I've heard a rumour we get coffee breaks.' And she went down the back stairs to avoid meeting the Lunts. Sometimes, even nice people take the coward's way out.

At Leighford High School, tucked away in the sanctuary of Matron's office, Maxwell was sitting thoughtfully. Sylvia Matthews knew how fond Maxwell was of his old neighbour, although she herself would not have wee'd on her if she was on fire. You read about these things all the time in the papers, families looking fruitlessly for missing grannies, granddads, more sadly, uncles, aunties, friends of their old dad's from way back who now had no one. And now, here it was, happening to someone she knew. She avoided platitudes and just waited for him to speak. That was why she was so popular with anyone in trouble. Her advice, when sought, was sensible, well thought out and optional.

'Well,' Maxwell finally said. 'Whatever was the mad old besom thinking? Going off like that?'

'Who reported her missing?' Sylvia asked him. 'She doesn't speak to the Other Side, does she?'

Maxwell was confused for a minute. He had no idea that ouija boards and similar were in the armoury of the State Registered Nurse. Then he realised what she meant. 'No, no, she doesn't. Ever since their youngest kicked a ball over.'

'I assume it did lots of damage?'

'No, not a bit. But it might have done and so they stopped speaking. Mrs Troubridge is very old school. Children should be seen but not heard. Come to think of it, in her book, they shouldn't even be seen. Apart from Nolan, of course. He basically can do what he likes!'

'How long ago was that?' she prompted.

'Ooh, let me see. Their Lucas is ten, now, so it must be... God, twenty years ago. Twenty-five? It was when the houses were pretty new, anyway.'

Sylvia was puzzled. 'If their Lucas is ten ... how can it be twenty-five years ago?'

'No, no, it wasn't *Lucas* who kicked the ball. No, it was his dad when *he* was about ten. She can bear a grudge for England, that woman.' He lapsed into silence again.

'But, still,' Sylvia comforted. 'I'm sure she'll be OK.'

Maxwell shook himself and sat up straighter. 'You're right, Sylv,' he said. 'Anyway, Jacquie's on it, so it will all be sorted soon.'

'Of course it will,' Sylvia said. 'Now, was that all? Only, I've got my girls to check on soon.'

'Any girls in particular?'

'The pregnant ones, Max. My usual contingent of about seven.'

He looked amazed. 'Seven pregnant girls? In the school? Right now?'

She laughed and poked him with her pen. 'How can you have missed them, Max? Jasmin Yelland is due in seven weeks. She can hardly walk about.'

'Jasmin Yelland? But she's in my History set in Year Eleven.'

'Precisely, Max. That's why I find it hard to credit you haven't noticed. Do you take any notice of these kids at all when you're teaching them?'

'Of course I do. But they tend to hunch down in their desks, you know. They all look the same shape from the front of the room. I was telling them only the other day about pregnant women avoiding the Drop in the eighteenth century by pleading the belly. Jasmine didn't turn a hair.'

She ushered him out. 'Perhaps that's because she's not sitting in a condemned cell as we speak. Take a closer look next time you see her. I think you'll be surprised.'

'I think *she* will be if I take *too* close a look. Do they know who the dads are?'

'Sometimes. Jasmin does, but she's not telling. A few of them are in therapy about it, if you know what I mean. Keeping it in the family. One of them seems to be implying the Angel Gabriel came to her.'

Maxwell nodded. 'I blame the *Da Vinci Code*. So, that's why the list was so long when you asked me if any of these kids are in trouble. It would have been easier to list the ones who aren't.'

Maxwell found himself on the other side of her door. He was gobsmacked. He found himself looking at midriffs as he walked through the crowds of students thronging the corridor and had to give himself a mental shake. All that glittering metal was making his eyes go funny. He'd be getting an odd reputation, if he went on like that.

White Surrey, patched and worn but not beaten, delivered Maxwell home at the end of another eventful day. People had teachers all wrong. They thought they just swanned around with a cup of coffee in one hand and a good book in another, then spent forty-five minutes with their feet up on a desk, drinking one and reading another while thirty dear sweet children quietly absorbed knowledge from impeccably covered text books packed full with up to the minute information perfectly crafted to help them in their courses. The truth was very different, but who would believe it; crap coffee, no books, good or bad, and as for thirty well-behaved children – it was a myth as elusive as the Holy Grail, but apparently there was a school somewhere, up north, the legend went, that did actually have thirty well-behaved children in it. But not all at once, of course. That would be silly.

But, although the day had been tiring as always and his sleuthing with Sylvia had been less than useful, throwing up as much red herring as a Grimsby trawler in spawning season, he still spared a minute for short reflection outside Mrs Troubridge's dark home. He hoped that he and Jacquie wouldn't be the only people to miss her. That would be sad. Then the cold of the late afternoon seeped in a bit too far and he went inside, to be greeted by a lovely disembowelled offering, which Metternich had artistically spread on the rug. That cat is just *too* generous, if he has a failing, thought Maxwell and shut the door, looking for the dustpan and brush to wipe up after Hannibal Lecter's nastier brother.

The grey weather had not let up all day and now it was almost dark. The sun was setting low in the west just to remind everyone it still existed and the sky was pale pink, barred with dark clouds scudding across it in the strengthening wind. February Fill Dyke, February brings the snow; call it what you like, it was bloody cold.

So Mike Crown had his head tucked well down in his sweatshirt hood as he jogged along the old railway line, derelict since the days of Beeching, his torch ready to light to help him over the last half mile or so until the lights of home shone out to him. You didn't keep a body like his without a bit of work and jogging relaxed his mind. It also kept him out of the house, away from his mad old dad and his clinging wife. He preferred older women as a rule, always had. A bit of cash, a bit of experience, a bit of gratitude. But perhaps marrying one had been a bit of a mistake. Still, moving on should be easy; there was always another one ready to make him comfy.

The next older woman he met, though, made him far from comfy. From her less than convenient resting place across his path, she made him fall over, wrench a knee and badly graze his hands. At least she wasn't clingy or needy. She was just dead.

CHAPTER ELEVEN

Maxwell had the house nice and warm, lamps low, pie in the oven, table laid, all ready for when Jacquie came in. As a former bachelor of some standing, he was a dab hand at the culinary arts and so opening a box was a piece of cake to him.

Jacquie looked weary as she climbed the stairs and flopped against him as they both had a little think about Mrs Troubridge. If she was wandering about, she'd be dead by now, thought Jacquie, rather illogically. The night was really cold and was limbering up for the snow that often fell at half term, now tantalisingly near.

Nolan, delivered by his best friend's mother from nursery, was bathed and delightful, full of organic lamb and rice, which looked and smelt indescribable, but which he always hoovered up with squeals for more. He and Maxwell had watched a Mr Men DVD, rewinding again and again to hear the late, great Arthur Lowe intone that there was a goose loose in the lane until they nearly split their sides. There had been a brief and manly chat about the day, with obviously a little more detail in Maxwell's version, and so

Jacquie sat at peace, cuddling her little boy and leaning against her big one. Maxwell had covered Hegel's Dialectic with the boy last week, so today's mano-a-mano had been very much a post-revisionist thing.

When Nolan's eyelids could no longer even pretend to be open, they mentioned Mrs Troubridge out loud for the first time. Nolan was the apple of her eye and she of his, so they didn't even want to mention her name in case he wanted to see her straight away, as he often did. And spelling the old girl's name out, *à la* 'w-a-l-k-i-e-s' as people did for the more discerning dog, was an intellectual rigour neither of them was quite up for by that time of a Wednesday.

'I can't believe it, Max,' Jacquie said. 'According to the file, she just disappeared at the bus station.'

'I can't quite work out why she was... Wait a minute. Do I not remember you saying her sister was coming to stay?'

'Oh, God, you're right. Or was she going to stay with her? I can't remember and you know how she goes...' there was a pause as they both reconsidered the present tense but she let it go, 'on about things. I tune out.'

'Well, that would explain the bus station. I suppose she had gone to meet her, or check times or something. Perhaps that's it, perhaps she has just gone to stay with her sister. We're worrying for nothing.' Maxwell sighed and sat back, problem solved. It was the Marie Celeste and the Creation of the Universe all rolled into one.

'Then who reported her missing?' Jacquie's timing was impeccable. 'It must be her sister and so she can't have got there.'

'True,' Maxwell nodded. 'Damn you, Holmes, I was beginning to feel quite hopeful, there. What else did the file say?'

'Well, that's it. Nothing. It's very early days and if it wasn't for the address, I don't know whether it would have got to us at all yet. After all, it's not as if she's a frantic DIYer and we've stopped hearing the Black and Decker through the wall. We have to wait a while before we start working on any missing person.'

'Even someone as old as Mrs T.'

'Yes. I agree, there should be different rules, but there aren't.'

'So, basically, she went to the bus station and disappeared into thin air.' As Jacquie had surmised earlier, the cinematic that was Maxwell was indeed conjuring up images of the tweedy Miss Froy, caught up in a world of espionage as dated as it was daft. But then, a grimmer thought struck him. 'Our hoodies came by bus.'

'Wrong timing.' Jacquie had got there as well. 'We already had them in the nick by then.'

'God, yes. Anyway, I shouldn't think that

even that number of them could make someone disappear into thin air.'

Deep in her bag down the side of the sofa, Jacquie's phone rang. They looked at each other with resignation. It had to be work, that was what the phone was for, except calls from Maxwell and it clearly wasn't him.

'I have to answer it,' Jacquie said. 'It might be about ... you know...'

'Go on, then,' Maxwell said. 'I'd rather know.'

Jacquie rummaged for her phone and got there just as it stopped ringing. Classic. She hit redial and waited. No reply – she looked up at Maxwell in exasperation. 'They must be leaving me a message, I hate that.'

'Oh, yes,' Maxwell said, encouragingly. 'I always hate that.'

She raised an eyebrow at him. They both knew he thought that messages ought to be brought by a Galloper on a lathered horse from Some Other Part Of The Field. She waited impatiently for the text to tell her she had a message. It seemed like ages. Then it was another æon until the voicemail answered and then another millennium until she got to the newest message.

Which was from the night sergeant at the nick. 'DS Carpenter. DCI Hall asks can you give him a ring. It's ... um, it's not good news, I'm afraid.'

She rang off and sat down. Her legs had

gone all wobbly. She thought she could bear these things, she who had seen bodies, sometimes strewn over a fair distance. She had had to break news far worse than this to more parents, husbands, wives than little Nolan, for instance, had had hot dinners. She always thought of Maxwell when she did so, hearing that worst news of all, all those years ago, when the tyres screamed on the wet tarmac and his world turned upside down. She had to give herself a moment before she rang Henry Hall.

Maxwell stood up and came and wrapped his arms around her. Thank goodness for those arms. Without them she would have sunk long ago. After soaking up all the love she could, she carefully unwrapped him and picked up the phone. She dialled Henry Hall's direct number.

'Jacquie. Thanks for getting back.' Jacquie knew perfectly well that Henry Hall had a house, a wife, kids. Yet somehow he always seemed to be there, in his office, behind his desk, glasses blank, his mind an enigma.

'Guv.' Jacquie's throat was dry and her lips felt stuck to her teeth. 'What's going on?'

She heard him sigh at the other end. 'We've just had a call from the Arundel nick. Mike Crown has just tripped over a body.'

She nearly passed out with relief and put a thumb up to Maxwell. He grinned and silently clapped his encouragement. 'Mike

215

Crown as in...?'

'Lara Kent, yes. That's why they rang. If you remember, we asked them if he had any previous before we paid them the visit.'

'Yes, that's right. But ... a body. That's a bit of a coincidence, isn't it, guv?'

'You know I don't believe in those, Jacquie. When someone says it's a coincidence, I always get suspicious. And you're about the twelfth person to say it. So now I'm *very* suspicious indeed.'

'My message said it was not good news, guv. I think this sounds pretty good – he's obviously lying about the tripping over. We wondered about him from the start; he's a much better bet than Lunt.' They had and he was. There was a pattern about murder. The old cliché about killers returning to the scene of the crime was just that. But some of them never left it, 'finding' the body, offering help, volunteering for searches, being that *teensy* bit too helpful, too ready to please. 'So why not good news?'

'Because... I'm sorry, Jacquie, I don't mean to condescend. Is Maxwell there?'

'Yes.' She was puzzled now. Henry Hall never wanted to speak to Maxwell at the best of times. And this was in the middle of a break in the middle of a murder inquiry. Hall was usually ready to consign Maxwell to the deepest dungeon about now, the oubliette of the Chateau d'If.

'Can you put him on?'

Mutely, Jacquie passed the phone to Maxwell.

'Hello, Henry. How can I help you?' Maxwell was pulling all sorts of interrogative faces at Jacquie who answered with some of her own. Thank God they still hadn't quite perfected the technology of Phone-o-Vision.

'Sorry ... Max.' The name was dragged out of him with red hot pincers, by the tone of Hall's voice. 'I just felt it would be better to tell *you*. The body that was discovered earlier this evening – Jacquie will doubtless be telling you the circumstances – is described as being of an elderly woman. We are obviously thinking it may be your Mrs Troubridge.'

'God.' Maxwell was struck as dumb as he ever would be, not because Hall had called her *his* Mrs Troubridge, but because, after the briefest of hopes, it could be the old lady after all. 'Where was this, did you say?'

'Arundel. A disused railway line.'

Maxwell felt hopeful again. 'That's not her usual kind of stamping ground, Henry, I have to say. I haven't known her leave Columbine for years.'

'No. But since when did murder victims behave normally? The only person to behave more oddly than a murderer is usually their victim.' Maxwell concurred. What was Evelyn Hamilton, the first victim of the wartime blackout killer Gordon Cummins doing sit-

217

ting in an air-raid shelter when there wasn't an air-raid on? And why did she have £80 in her handbag, a colossal sum for those days. Always questions; never answers.

'Yes, I accept that. But, Henry, she's a very old lady.'

'But perfectly hale and hearty, I understand.'

'Well, yes.' Maxwell paused. This wasn't going anywhere and he needed to tell Jacquie what was going on. 'All right, Henry. If you need us for anything. Identification, that kind of thing.'

'Thanks. We probably will. According to our records, she just has a sister. A bit younger, but not by much. If you're sure you won't find it...' but Henry Hall knew that was a platitude that didn't apply to Maxwell. He also knew that he would walk over hot coals rather than let Jacquie do it. 'Yes, well, thanks again. It's a different nick, so we may be a day or two. Paperwork, collaboration, you know. We'll be in touch.' And he cut the connection.

'That was odd.' Maxwell turned to Jacquie. 'He says the body was an elderly woman.'

Jacquie didn't answer, just sat there staring at him with eyes like saucers.

'He thinks it may be Mrs Troubridge. But I don't.'

She got up and rested on his chest again. 'That's sweet, Max, but we must face facts.'

'She was found on a disused railway line, Jacquie. What on earth would Mrs Troubridge be doing on a disused railway line?'

'What was she doing at the bus station?'

'Point taken.' He moved her away and looked into her eyes. 'If it's possible, let's try not to dwell on this. Henry says it could be a day or two, so we may be worrying unnecessarily. I don't even know why the police force there got in touch with your blokes. There must be loads of missing people.'

Jacquie had to think for a moment just how much Maxwell might know. Usually, the answer to that question would be 'everything', but probably not on this occasion. She decided to put it in a nutshell. 'The bloke who found her is the stepfather of the body you and Bill Lunt found on the dunes,' she said, all in one breath. 'Henry doesn't believe in coincidence, so when a name crops up again in any investigation, he gets to sniffing around. It was the finder, not the body that made them ring. Henry just put two and two together.'

'Let's hope he's making five,' Maxwell said. 'Since the subject has cropped up, how did Bill's interview go?'

'Something and nothing,' she said, recognising a change of subject when one bit her on the nose. 'The phone has rather changed things. They have got the numbers off it and none relate to him. They are mostly pay-as-you-go, non-registered things. They really should stop that; it's just too easy for anyone a bit crooked. One in particular was there more than others, along with a few saucy texts; nothing David Beckham wouldn't be proud to send. Bill is almost sorry his fifteen minutes of fame are over. Emma came in with him. She's like a Rottweiler when she's riled, isn't she? I wouldn't like to cross her. She'll be in the frame next if she's not careful.'

'Emma? She wouldn't hurt a fly,' Maxwell chuckled; but then, in the context of History lessons at Leighford High, he'd never seen her with her dander up.

'No, but she'd certainly give it a good telling off,' Jacquie asserted. She had seen Alan Kavanagh actually change colour when he had met them on the stairs as they left the building. And that was when Emma was feeling calmer.

The baby alarm in the corner burbled and then exploded with a wail. A diversion – that child really *did* have excellent timing. They tossed a coin, Maxwell's famous two-headed zloty. All right, he won, but he went with Jacquie anyway.

At eight a.m. precisely that Thursday a strange thing happened to Peter Maxwell. Well, perhaps not that strange, as his recent professional life had been peppered with suspensions, warnings, sudden and mysterious deaths and other alarums and excursions, but this was definitely a first. Just as he was getting himself together to brave the February weather, choosing the old Jesus tie to complement the old Jesus scarf, the radio whittering in the background, a few words in the whitter attracted his attention.

'Whitter, burble, flatter, Leighford High School, natter rhubarb.' It was almost like S4C's News programmes, but he had caught the gist now and gave it his fuller attention. '...a previously unprecedented move, Leighford High School has been temporarily closed due to the large numbers of staff absent. The Head Teacher, James Diamond, spoke this morning to our reporter, Anne Fallows.' The grey tones of Legs Diamond filled the kitchen for what Maxwell hoped would be the only time. 'Yes, Anne.' Maxwell chuckled. 'Yes, Anne' – what a media tart that man was. 'The staff and students at Leighford High School have been hit by the recent virus that is going round. Due to the large numbers of absences, which my remaining staff have been working tirelessly to cover, I have no option but to close the school for the rest of this week. I would therefore ask parents to not send their children in this morning, or tomorrow. Over the weekend, we will be contacting all families affected by this with detailed plans for the immediate future. We'll be in touch by phone and email. Supply cover is at breaking point all over the county and it takes time to mobilise the various Agencies.'

Peter Maxwell knew perfectly well that Legs Diamond couldn't organise a piss-up in a brewery, much less mobilise anything. It was rather like the Russian army at the start of World War One, but not so well organised.

'But what if a child has already set off?' Weren't the media annoying, raising ticklish issues like that?

'Thank you, Anne, that is a very pertinent point.' Maxwell could almost hear Diamond rising on his toes and closing his eyes in that pompous way he had. 'There will be staff at the school this morning, both to advise pupils who arrive and to plan the next few days. I do stress that this situation is unlikely to last beyond tomorrow.'

'Thank you, Mr Diamond. Back to the studio.' Maxwell could hear the disappointment in her voice, but then few who spoke to Legs could avoid it. She had wanted juicy gossip. He had provided dry bones. Virus going round, indeed. It was just terminal disenchantment. It was a wonder there was a school in the country open. And if that school happened to be run by Legs Diamond, it was a wonder more people weren't hurt in the struggle for the main gates.

Slurping a coffee which no longer had to

be on the run, Maxwell ambled into the sitting room and picked up the phone. Before he could start to dial, it rang. He always hated it when that happened; he called it his touch of the David Blaines. He had, after all, been walking on water for years. He answered it anyway.

'Hello? War Office.'

'Max, glad I caught you before you set off. Sorry, it's Bernard Ryan.'

'Hello, Bernard.' Maxwell was equally sorry it was Bernard Ryan. As Deputy Heads go, Bernard Ryan didn't and that was the problem. 'You're not one of the viralled, then?'

'Er … no, but it seems to me like everyone else is. Are you well?'

That sounded like a very loaded question to Maxwell. He toyed with doing his urban squalor tuberculosis impression, the one he always did when teaching Year Nine about the 1840s slums, but he couldn't really be arsed for Bernard. 'Yes, same as usual. Rude health.'

'Er, good. Glad to hear it. Umm...'

'Come to the point, Bernard, there's a good Deputy Head. I'm on my way. Saddlebags packed. Chalk and cane on board. There was no need even to ask.'

'That's the thing, Max. We … that is, the SLT, have decided that we're OK with the staff here already. So … have the day off, why don't you? You've been doing so much cover, you deserve it.'

You lying bugger, Maxwell thought. There were three things wrong with that sentence. Ryan had used an initialism, which was rapidly destroying the English language. He had employed the ghastly Americanism of OK, thus confirming that the end of civilisation was nigh. And above all, he was being *nice*. 'Bernard, you spoil me,' his mouth said. 'Now, are you sure?' He'd never been told to stay home before – except when he'd been suspended, of course.

'Quite sure, Max, thank you,' Ryan said, relief spilling in gouts through Maxwell's phone. The Deputy knew of old what a pain in the bum the Head of Sixth Form could be in crisis moments, taking charge, doing everything, making it all work. That was the last thing he wanted.

'Well, thank you,' Maxwell said, equally gushing, equally insincere. 'I hope you get it all sorted soon. Don't be a stranger, now. Bye, then.' He put the phone down. What were they planning? There were rumours that the Powers That Be wanted to create a faculty system at Leighford High, to build Humanities where it had not existed before. Perhaps they'd bring in some Business Studies lightweight to overlord it all; in which case, as Maxwell had said loudly at a recent staff meeting, such a person would be a crime against humanities. On the other hand, did he care? He decided not and went off to top up his coffee. A whole day free. Like Jacquie, he loved his family. Like her, he relished the odd day without them. Space and time, that old continuum that Bert Einstein was always banging on about. He *could* go and get Nolan from the child-minder, but it was still a touch cold for the bike. He *could* go upstairs and do some modelling, anchoring Corporal Morley to his lance-cap, for instance, but he found the muse was just not on him at 8.10 on what should have been a school morning. Anyway, he'd got to the highlights on the horse bit and that took *total* concentration. He *could* go into town and do that boring shop for all the non-edible items out of which they had run – he knew Jacquie hated to do that. Forty quid and not a bar of chocolate to be seen. He *could* do all those things ... but what he *would* do was take a bit of a train ride to Arundel, just to see what was going on. If asked, and he would be asked, he would just point out what a lovely town he found it; antique shops, deli, nice Chinese restaurant for lunch, castle for the afternoon. He knew no one would buy that, especially since the castle would be closed out of season, but he had to have something ready.

His musing was interrupted by the door-bell. He went down the stairs, hoping it wasn't some colleague come to fetch him after all. Bernard Ryan had the staying power of a gnat. He flung open the door and that was when the second strange thing in fifteen minutes happened to Peter Maxwell.

CHAPTER TWELVE

'Is everyone here?' Henry Hall scanned the room, sweeping his blank gaze from side to side.

Everyone looked to their left, then right. Although chairs weren't allocated as such, over time people started sitting in 'their' spot. They knew when someone was missing. Gradually, heads nodded as all were accounted for.

'All right, then,' said Hall. In Maxwell's mouth, that would have become a Jim Carrey take-off. In Hall's, it was just three words. 'I want this meeting to briefly touch on the phone found on the dunes. Then, we'll go on to the Arundel connection.'

Eyebrows rose questioningly all over the room.

'Only some of you know this so far, which is why I have the screen up. Colin has prepared a Power-Point presentation gathering all the threads and we will go through this in due time. First, though, we have the phone.'

He held it up, sealed in its evidence bag. 'At last, we have everything this phone has to tell us. Numbers, names to go with those numbers, although that doesn't apply to many. We know where it was bought and when. We have the ringtone. Now, I don't know how many of you bother with all the little bits your phones will do. I admit that I use mine for calls and the odd alarm if I'm away from home for the night. But, apparently, it is possible to assign a ring tone for different callers. So, for example, you might have a telephone ring sound for your mother, a piece of music for your wife or girlfriend.'

'Different music for each one, though, guv, otherwise you might get caught out!' called DS Bob Davies, always quick with the backchat, from the back of the room. Muffled chuckles.

'Yes,' said Henry Hall flatly. In his world, a wife and a girlfriend were mutually exclusive. 'So, we've tried out the ring tones to see if she has anyone she wants to keep from anyone else. And, sure enough, we found she had one number that was different.' He pressed a key on his laptop on the desk in front of him and absolutely nothing happened. Colin leant forward and whispered something. 'Oh, yes.' Henry Hall pressed another button first, then the first one. A jangling tone with an irritating computerised voice shouting 'Hello' made them all

227

jump. To everyone's relief, he pressed the button again. 'That's the main tone,' he said. 'But for just one number, she had programmed in this.' He looked down helplessly and then gestured to Colin, who went round behind the desk and did his stuff. This time the noise was less jarring, but still annoying, as the tune was one of those on the edge of everyone's memory, but not quite memorable enough. All over the room, people were clicking their fingers, closing their eyes and mouthing words they couldn't quite recall.

'Do we know whose number that is, guv?' asked Alan Kavanagh.

'No, unfortunately. That is one of the pay-as-you-go ones. Now, any other questions before we go on to the next item?'

Heads shook. Those who did and those who didn't know what was going on next were equally agog. Arundel was where Lara Kent came from. Seat of the Earls of Norfolk, sleepy little town. Nothing much happened there, ever. The phone was Lara Kent's. Some of the newer hands were hoping that Darren Blackwell wasn't being back-burnered, but anyone who had known Henry Hall for any length of time knew that the dead boy was as much in Hall's head as the dead girl. He might not be too good at pressing buttons, but his brain had the best computer system they knew; nothing forgotten, nothing beneath his notice. He would have been shocked had he known how like Maxwell he was, deep down there where the little grey cells jostled each other for position.

'Arundel, then. Last evening, just as it got dark, a jogger tripped over a body on the disused railway line just outside the town. This wouldn't normally be anything to do with us, of course, but there are two things that make it rather our business. First, we have a missing woman, reported just the day before this body was found. Second, the jogger who tripped headlong was none other than the stepfather of our first victim.'

'A hell of a coincidence,' said the usual voice at the back.

'No such thing,' barked Hall. 'A name crops up twice, it crops up for a reason.'

'Bill Lunt,' muttered Alan Kavanagh.

'Yes,' admitted Hall. 'But he seemed almost to ask for it. This guy ... well, Jacquie and I met him and immediately had alarm bells ringing. The mother seemed dodgy too – she's not the sort to grass on her old man. She's too pleased with herself for catching him in the first place. For "old man" read "toy boy." He's being questioned under caution now in Chichester and as soon as they've had their crack at him, I shall be going up to have a go myself.'

'Do we have a positive ID on the victim yet?' This from Jacquie, trying to keep her partiality under wraps, but having to ask the question nonetheless.

'Not as yet,' Hall said. 'We aren't certain it is our missing person, but, as I said, I don't believe in coincidences.'

'Anyone going with you, guv?' Kavanagh had his hand in the air, like a crawling schoolboy, but without the shining face.

'Yes,' Hall said shortly. 'Well, everyone, I think we can say that's all for now. Collect your updates from the desk at the...'

A cough from Colin brought him up short.

'Sorry, of course, yes. Colin here has produced a Power-Point presentation of the facts as we have them at the moment. He will run you through it, I'm sure.' He personally didn't think that the presentation would give them any more facts than they had already. He knew, as Peter Maxwell knew, that all Power-Points did was show off somebody's ICT skills – they advanced the condition of mankind not one jot. A suspect, a really dodgy suspect, had 'found' another body. Sealed and delivered, as far as he was concerned. And no, he wasn't going to take Alan Kavanagh, who he personally couldn't stand. The man invaded your space and Henry Hall of all people hated that. He would, of course, take Jacquie. And, if he knew his man, they could give Maxwell a lift home at the end of the day.

Bill Lunt walked into his own shop as if into the lions' den. He never felt entirely happy out there with the staff he called his, in the shiny world of digital cameras and their paraphernalia, in that smell of plastic and brushed metal, new and heartless. And an endless succession of punters who claimed to know more than he did and who all seemed to have exclusive, never-before-seen photos of Diana that they would reveal to a disbelieving world one day, when the price was right. Photography to Bill Lunt was a dark, arcane art, chemicals, red dark, old leather and sweaty fingers trying not to blur the image with their excited trembling as the perfect shot swam into focus in the tray. He'd read a while ago the theory that da Vinci, the cryptic old bastard, had taken photographs four hundred years before Niepce. He couldn't get the idea out of his head.

The staff, all two of them, gave him what he assumed was a warm welcome. They were fairly charmless, both of them, but they knew a pixel from a pixie and in the modern camera shop, that was basically all they needed to be able to do.

'Hello, Mr Lunt,' the lad said, dark hair flopping over his earnest face. Lunt always thought of him as looking rather like a pork pie, rather shiny, rather greasy, rather flaky.

'Hello, Richard,' he said and, rather to his surprise, found himself shaking hands with the boy. 'Umm...' How did you continue a conversation that by all usual standards ought to go 'I'm sorry I've been out of the shop a bit the last week, but I am a murder suspect and you know how it is. Busy, busy.'

'No worries, Mr L,' the lad said. 'We knew you didn't do it.'

'Yeah, right.' The girl slouched over and stood in front of her boss, one hip stuck out, her arms folded in front of her, propping up a tiny bust and allowing her pierced navel to just show beneath her sleeve. Swirls of blue and white make-up made her eyelids heavy. This was her day-wear. By night, she was a Goth. 'We all knew you never done it.'

'Thank you, Jade.' Emma had materialised at his elbow. 'Mr Lunt is very grateful for your loyalty, but I think a little printing is probably called for. There seems to be getting quite a backlog.'

The girl swapped hips, but otherwise didn't move. 'What was it like, Mr Lunt?' she breathed at him on a wave of nicotine, inadequately hidden by gum. 'Was it gruesome?'

'Well, I hardly...' but he didn't have the chance to complete his sentence. Emma had shooed the girl back to her post at the computer over which she had, against all the odds, complete mastery. Gum and Goth. It was the beginning of the end of civilisation. Emma shook her head; God alone knew

232

what Mr Maxwell would make of it all.

'Don't encourage them, Bill,' she hissed. 'They do little enough as it is.' Sighing, she picked up a pile of delivery notes and went to check the stock. Somebody had to keep the wheels turning.

Feeling a little like a lost soul, Bill Lunt went behind a counter and stared lifelessly out into the grey February morning. He wished now he'd never mentioned anything to Peter Maxwell; wished he'd kept his mouth shut.

Jacquie and Henry Hall were, yet again, in a car heading towards Arundel. This time, though, Hall had all his faculties, which was just as well since he had volunteered for the driving on this occasion. And they were in his Lexus, which gave him space and elbow room. Jacquie's Ka gave him an elbow up his nose. They drove in silence for quite a way, Jacquie's nerves making the interior of the car crackle with tension. Finally, she had to ask the question.

'Guv, have Chichester really not identified the body yet?'

'Jacquie, why would I lie to you? No, they haven't. They are trying to contact Mrs Troubridge's sister, but so far with no luck. Until they've given that their very best shot, they can't announce anything. And, because it is quite likely to be her, they've not issued a description or anything to the media. I would imagine Mrs Troubridge is quite frail?' He looked enquiringly at Jacquie.

She was puzzled, and then sorted it out. 'Oh, I see. *Our* Mrs Troubridge weighs about six stone wringing wet and has the attitude of a brick shithouse. There is nothing and nobody she won't take on and there are usually no prisoners. The sister, I don't know at all. Until the other day, I didn't even know she had one. But if genetics means anything, I shouldn't imagine she's too easily shocked. On the other hand, having your sister's face plastered everywhere would be quite stressful for anyone, frail or not.'

'There was an element of bruising as well, though stabbing was the means.' He risked taking a hand off the wheel and passed it over his face, a sure sign of his frustration. Henry Hall was strictly a two hands at ten to two man, even when stationary in traffic as they now were, negotiating Chichester. He saw the spire of the cathedral to his left and the chill-looking water in the low-lying fields. 'A photo, even made up, would be a bit distressing. But I'm sure she'll turn up soon and we can progress this, Jacquie.'

They didn't break their silence again until they got to the nick. Hall knew this one well. Jock Hazelton used to run it when Henry was a rookie. Ex-Met, ex-Para, tough as nails. He'd retired one Friday and they found him dead in his car on the Sunday morning. Nothing suspicious. Nothing untoward. Nothing to live for. They'd cleaned the place up since Hall was here last, but it had the usual posters, the usual missing and the damned, the usual spider-plant to trap the unwary who might sit too close and become enmeshed in its cobwebs.

There were introductions all round and the visitors were taken to the not-very-secret secret room behind the mirror in the interview room. It was life imitating art. No police stations had these until dear old shouty Trevor Eve used one in *Waking the Dead*. Now, they were de rigeur.

Mike Crown wasn't looking his usual toned and tanned Lothario self. He sat at the pockmarked Formica table in police station issue white suit, looking at his hands, locked together with tension in front of him. Even from the distance and allowing for the darkening effect of the mirror, he was deathly pale and there were distinct beads of sweat on his forehead. A policeman sat silently in a corner. There was no brief present, because Mike Crown was pretty sure he didn't need one.

The door to the interview room opened and DCI Helen Marshall walked in and sat opposite Crown, her back to the two Leighford coppers. Helen was about as different from Jane Tennison of *Prime Suspect* fame, as it was possible to be. She was thirty something, with two kids, a loving husband, a Lhasa Apso, no drink problem and no hang-ups. If she wasn't real, you couldn't invent her. She'd impressed Hall as soon as they met at the annual West Sussex conference three years ago. And you didn't get to impress Henry Hall by being flaky.

'Now, then, Mr Crown,' she said on a sigh, pressing her palms flat on the table and leaning back, flexing. 'We haven't got terribly far, have we?' Helen Marshall had the tone of a rather disappointed infant school teacher off to a fine art. Everyone she questioned had been to infant school once; it was astonishing how often it got results. 'All we have so far is that you jog every day, unless you are working out at the gym and sometimes even then. So yesterday evening, you were just doing your usual circuit when you fell over a body in your path. Have you any idea what the odds are of doing that?'

Crown bit his lip and shook his head. He looked close to tears.

Jacquie nudged Hall and leant closer to mutter, 'He looks almost human, guv.'

'Don't let looks deceive you, Jacquie,' said Hall with his usual dose of cynicism. 'Especially his. He's been using them since he was in the cradle, I don't doubt. He's our man, no problem.'

Meanwhile the DCI was pressing her

point. 'I must insist, Mr Crown, that we find it a little beyond normal coincidence,' Jacquie heard the hiss of indrawn breath from Hall, 'that you should be involved in two murders in one week.'

'Involved?' Crown was outraged, sitting upright now, staring the woman in the face. 'Involved? My stepdaughter was murdered when neither her mother or I had seen her in over a year. And then I trip over, *trip over*, a body while I am out jogging. And you call that involved?' He showed a bit of spirit by folding his arms and burying his chin in his chest. 'That's it,' his muffled voice came, 'I'm not saying anything else until my solicitor gets here.'

'That is your right, Mr Crown, of course,' said Helen Marshall, brushing her hair back from her face. She smiled at him, nasty policewoman becoming nice policewoman before his very eyes. 'But if, as you contend, you have nothing to hide, then why not answer just a few more questions and then perhaps you could go home.'

'Naughty,' muttered Hall. 'I'll have to pretend I didn't hear that.' He knew as well as anyone how magic that word 'home' sounded to a man who might not see that particular place again for twenty years.

'Inspired to send a woman,' Jacquie said, as impressed as Hall by the DCI's technique. 'She'll get more out of him than any man would.'

'Not so much inspired as essential,' Hall muttered to her. 'She's the guv'nor here. And she's good. And attractive. And therefore, disliked by almost everyone in the station.'

It's a shame Alan Kavanagh didn't come after all, thought Jacquie. They would have that in common, at least.

Crown had lifted his head again. This was a woman, for Christ's sake. Women were only good for one thing. He wasn't going to let her browbeat him. He squared up to her. 'Listen,' he said, sharply. 'I am not perfect and I suppose that we might just as well say here and now that you will uncover lots about me that isn't very nice. I am married to a much older woman and I did it for the money. And her pretty daughter, who actually turned out not to come with the package, but no matter, because the money was nice. I also have various mistresses scattered around the county; I won't call them girlfriends because that would be silly, bearing in mind their ages. I put the one into one night stand and I'm not ashamed of any of it. And they aren't local, because I don't shit on my own doorstep. So, as I sit here, I am looking at the end of my marriage, because my wife is besotted but not that besotted. But what I am not looking at is going to prison for murder, because I *haven't killed anybody!* I've got alibis from here to Land's End, if you'll let me have my diary.'

Helen Marshall sat back smiling and flicked a cheeky glance at the mirror on the wall.

Hall shook his head. 'I hope you're making notes, Jacquie,' he said. The DS was rapidly going off the woman as he spoke.

'Well,' the DCI went on. 'That's a nice piece of character self-assassination, Mr Crown, but you see we've heard it all before. Paint a black picture of yourself, admit to being a slime-ball of the worst water and hope we'll think "Wow, he's an honest guy. He can't possibly be guilty". Because all your "confessions" don't amount to a hill of beans, do they?' She was leaning forward now, arms still folded, face hard in the neon light. 'Humping housewives isn't a crime unless the housewives object. If being married to a shit like you keeps your wife happy, then, hey, who cares? Fancying her daughter isn't a crime either ... unless of course you tried it on, she wasn't having any and you killed her.'

'No,' Crown shouted, thumping the table with his fist. The constable in the corner shifted, but a single hand gesture from Helen Marshall kept him in his place.

'Alibis,' she said, leaning back, calm as the ripples on Willow Bay in summer, her voice soft, her gentle alter ego in the driving seat.

'Can't you just give me your alibis?'

'No,' he admitted, backing off himself, sensing the heat evaporate from the moment, though the blood still pounded in his ears. 'I need my diary to say where I was on each day.'

'It wasn't very long ago, Mr Crown,' the woman prompted gently.

'I know, but sometimes I ... well, let's say that it can get a bit hectic, sometimes. I mean, just as an example, I got home the other day and there were a couple of coppers from Leighford in the house. It was about Lara. I had completely forgotten they were coming and I'd got ... tied up. That happens. Sorry.' He looked at her and saw no response. 'Look, I've got expensive tastes, OK. I have to make a bit extra where I can.'

'He's even worse than we thought, guv,' Jacquie whispered. That was what Maxwell loved about her. Underneath the CID exterior, there was still a little girl who, if she could no longer be shocked by anything, could at least disapprove.

'Guiltier,' agreed Hall. 'I'm not sure that "worse" would cover it. He is a piece of work, though. His tracks won't be easy to follow. He's probably got a Mrs Robinson in every town in the county.'

'They'll all give him an alibi, guv, you're right,' Jacquie sighed. 'If he can get to them first, that is...'

'Mike,' Helen Marshall was saying; if it weren't for political correctness, she'd be offering him a ciggie about now. 'I am not trying to frame you on anything, pin something on you you didn't do. But you can surely see our position. What we have here is a person – yourself – who has been involved in two murder enquiries in a very short space of time. You claim that you are only involved involuntarily, as it were. You were related by marriage to one and tripped over the other.'

He nodded sulkily. This cheeky tart was playing with him, having a smug joke at his expense. And he'd seen *Waking the Dead* too; who was watching all this from the other side of the mirror?

'But, you see, it goes deeper than that.' Helen Marshall was tracing little patterns on the Formica with her index finger, as though she was trying to work her way through the latest Sudoku. 'We know that you have been in Leighford recently; your car was caught on CCTV in the town centre.'

Jacquie and Hall sat up straighter. This was progress.

'It's not far,' he blustered. 'I was shopping.'

'Hmm, if you say so, of course. It's a girly thing, I suppose, but I'd have thought Chichester, Arundel, even Littlehampton, had better shops. However, that leads us on to a few other things. A young man, Darren

Blackwell, was murdered in Leighford earlier this week. At first we thought that had no links with your stepdaughter, but I have just received word from the Leighford forensic team and apparently, in tracking the numbers on Lara's phone, they found that of Darren's younger brother.' She turned her head towards the mirror, as if asking apology from the two Leighford cops concealed behind it. She didn't mean to steal their thunder, but it was too good a chance to miss. Helen Marshall was as much in awe of Henry Hall as he was of her. Stealing a march was the name of the game.

'So what?' Crown said. 'Lara was a pretty girl. She attracted the boys, always did. Got that from her mother.'

'Yes,' Helen agreed. 'She certainly was a pretty girl, but she didn't mix in the same crowd as Darren Blackwell and he and his brother didn't socialise. A slight family problem, I understand.'

Oh yes, thought Jacquie. A slight problem when your brother is sleeping rough in a wood. Socialising is not perhaps quite the right word for it then.

'Still don't know the name Darren Blackwell,' Crown told her. 'I don't usually take much notice of men, if you see what I mean.'

'Then,' she ignored him and carried on listing her suspicions, almost as though he wasn't there, 'the body over which you tripped,' Maxwell would have applauded the grammar, thought Jacquie, 'is, we think, a missing person from Leighford. So, as you see, Leighford keeps on cropping up. All roads seem to lead there, don't they?'

'So I see,' said Crown, leaning forward. 'But I don't live there, do I? So I don't see where I come in to this chain of events.'

'It may be because of the woman you have been seeing in Leighford,' the DCI said suddenly.

Crown leant back again. He mimed zipping his lip. 'I'll have my lawyer now, blondie, if you don't mind,' he said and stared resolutely at the ceiling.

'Oh my word,' breathed Hall. 'He's in trouble now!'

The DCI got up slowly and walked to the door. She turned before she went through it and looked straight through the mirror. The grin she gave to Henry Hall was a facsimile of the last thing the unluckiest wildebeest sees as it goes under for the last time, just short of the banks of the Zambezi.

Peter Maxwell didn't need a lift back from Arundel, because he hadn't gone. Henry Hall caught radio newsflashes too and anyway, Leighford nick was routinely apprised of school closures in the area, so he knew the current Head of Sixth Form would not be at the chalk-face. And he knew they'd found a potentially neighbourly body in Arundel, so Hall naturally assumed ... but was not on the money there. What he did need was a sit down, a glass of water or a large Southern Comfort, whichever was the sooner and a whole heap of explanation. Opening his front door had been so easy. Just grab the knob, twist and fling. It was what was on his doorstep that was giving him trouble. There stood not one, but two Mrs Troubridges.

They were dressed differently, he admitted, but the general style was the same. Pudding basin hat, pulled low on the brow. Scarf, one pale pink, one beige, tucked into a tweed collared coat, worn just long enough to top the ankles. Gloves, to match scarf. Fur topped boots, brushing the hem of the coat. This was February. The weather could be treacherous. But Maxwell knew, from very many years' experience, that at least one of them would be wearing this selfsame ensemble until at least June, on the principle of cast ne'er a clout till May be out.

'Mrs Troubridge?' he almost whispered. Years of teaching had taught him to hide shock, horror, disgust in order to keep ahead of the little bastards who had caused it, like when he'd fallen down the stairs in the Tower Block or that nice Mr Vincent had been run over by the ambulance that time. He'd just dusted himself or Mr Vincent down and carried on as if nothing had happened. But this was beyond even his finely honed powers.

'Yes,' they chorused, shades of Tweedle-dum and Tweedledee. Surely, Lewis Carroll at his maddest had foreseen this very moment and laid it down for posterity.

'Which one of you is ... my Mrs Trou-bridge?' How else could he put it? The answer was immediate. The one who was giggling and poking him in the arm with one begloved hand.

'Oh, Mr Maxwell,' she tittered. 'I am. And this is my sister, Araminta. Technically, she is Miss Troubridge. As you know, I married our cousin – wags said it was so I didn't have to have my handkerchiefs resewn. We're twins,' she added, somewhat super-fluously, 'although I am, technically speak-ing, the elder by seven minutes.'

'Are you?' he replied, recovering himself a little. 'Yes, now I come to look more closely, indeed you are.' He stepped to one side. 'Do come in, ladies. I'll make you some tea, or something. I...' again he was lost for words. 'I'm really glad to see you, Mrs Troubridge. And of course you, Miss Troubridge, And I'm so glad you came round to see me. Jacquie and I were afraid I had upset you in some way.'

'Not at all. Don't mention it,' they spoke as one. It was as if they had bestowed an honour on him and he shook his head to dispel the feeling of being down the rabbit hole. Mrs Troubridge threw him a puzzled glance, but her brow soon lightened. Though she was an expert at grudge-holding, she had already forgotten the news of the sleeping man on his sofa, vouchsafed by that ghastly little woman with the cigarette who seemed to visit her neighbour rather often, for reasons on which she tried not to dwell.

He led them up the stairs and he heard behind him the twittering whisper of the Miss Troubridge to the Mrs, 'You've done so much more with yours, dear.' And the answering murmur of, 'Long years as a bachelor, dear. Bound to take its toll.'

Clenching his teeth, he turned to them with a smile as they trotted into the sitting room and sat disconcertingly at either end of the sofa. 'Tea, is it then, ladies?'

They nodded.

'And how do you take yours, Araminta?'

'Just the same as I do,' Mrs Troubridge replied.

That put Maxwell in a bit of a quandary. He couldn't remember how she took hers either. Arsenic, was it? Old lace? Oh well, tray, pot and all the fixings it would have to be.

While the kettle boiled, he hovered in the kitchen doorway. The Troubridges had occupied the sofa like a couple of bookends. Maxwell was just grateful it was Metternich's day off. He wasn't sure a cat of his years could quite handle all this. Inevitably, the question had to be asked. 'Where have you been, Mrs Troubridge?' he said. 'We all thought you had gone missing.' Unasked, the question ricocheted round his head, 'Who did Mike Crown fall over last night?'

'Well,' Araminta began. 'It was all a bit of silliness, really.'

'I went to meet Araminta off the bus...'

'But I arrived early, so...'

'...she went off to get a little drinkie, and I arrived on time and found her not there.'

'So she, silly girl,' Araminta smiled fondly, 'set off to look for me.'

'So Araminta couldn't find me and booked into a hotel...'

'...and she went off to see if I was still at home, hurt or something. Fallen down the stairs or some similar accident. As if!'

'But before I did, I reported her missing...'

'Wait.' Maxwell held up his hand and broke the chain. 'So it was *Araminta* who was reported missing?'

'Yes, of course,' Mrs Troubridge said. 'Dear me, Mr Maxwell. Don't tell me you thought it was me.' The pair of them laughed like two demented budgies.

'Well, yes,' he said, hardly able to keep the amazement out of his voice. 'Of course we did, Mrs Troubridge. We didn't know until recently that you had a sister, let alone a twin.'

'Had I not mentioned it?' Mrs Troubridge was puzzled and sat there, one finger to her chin, casting her mind back, where it was happiest. 'Not when I mentioned the late Mr Troubridge even?'

'Because,' Araminta couldn't help herself, 'that's when we stopped speaking, of course. When she ran off with Mr Troubridge. You do know we were cousins?' she asked, dropping her voice.

Since Mrs Troubridge had reminded him not four minutes ago as well as at regular intervals over the years, he clearly did, but he couldn't help thinking that there had probably been a lot of that sort of thing in the Troubridge family. You got a lot of that sort of thing in Tottingleigh in the old days. He nodded, smiling weakly. Finally, he said, 'So, let me get this right. When you, Mrs Troubridge,' and he pointed to his neighbour, 'married Mr Troubridge, more years ago than you care to remember, you stopped speaking to *you*, Miss Troubridge.' And he pointed to her sister.

'Mr Maxwell,' Araminta said with a sigh. 'You've got it all wrong. Of course that wasn't how it was. *I* stopped speaking to *her!* I was affianced to Mr Troubridge first, you see. Then, my sister came home from spending some time abroad and he took one look and fell in love. Well, she was the elder by seven minutes and that will always tell, don't you think? So like Victoria and Albert, only in reverse. She couldn't resist and the rest you know.'

Mercifully for Maxwell's future sleep patterns, he didn't know and didn't want to – there were limits, after all, even to encyclopaedic knowledge such as his. 'How ... sad. But you have forgiven her, Araminta?'

'At last. After all, life is short.' The twins smiled at each other and, reaching across, took each other's hand and clasped it warmly.

A distant whistling brought Maxwell down to earth. 'I'll make the tea,' he muttered and went gratefully into the normality of his kitchen. Cups, plates, the toaster – all the outward trappings of sanity. But round and round in his head went the question – who is the body and is there still a link? Suddenly, the phone rang, almost in his ear.

'War Office.'

'Max,' came Jacquie's voice. 'You're at home.'

'I don't want to carp,' he said, 'but today is very strange. If you didn't expect me to be here, why have you rung? Metternich isn't taking calls. And anyway, it's his day off.'

'I rang to leave you a message,' she said. 'For when you got back from Arundel.'

'Arundel? I'm not in Arundel.'

'No, but...' she had the grace to sound

embarrassed and he had the sense to keep quiet about his thwarted travel plans. 'Never mind. It was just to say that we don't know yet if the body is ... you know, Mrs Troubridge.'

'I do.'

'You do what?'

'Know if it's Mrs Troubridge.'

'We're not talking hunches, Max, or making me feel better. We're talking about a murder.'

'I'm talking about Mrs Troubridge and also Miss Troubridge who are both sitting large as life on our sofa.'

Jacquie went silent for a second then, 'What? Are you all right, Max?'

'I think so. Admittedly, I had a bump on the head playing silly mid-off for Jesus all those years ago, but it is all making sense in a very Troubridgean sort of way.' He filled her in on the bus-station meanderings, trying to keep the element of farce to a minimum. 'I think you need to be here to get the real impact. For now, perhaps you could pass the news on to Henry. It might help.'

'Umm, yes. I will. And it might. I'll see you later, Max.' A pause. 'Are you sure you're all right?'

'Positive. But you might like to see if you can find out who the body is. Because, now, we're looking for someone who *isn't* missing, if you catch my drift. And as I am sure you know, yin of my yang, that is always so much more difficult, rather like meeting a man who wasn't there. See you later.' And Maxwell put down the phone, suddenly full of foreboding. Pulling himself together, he assembled the tea, broke open the Tesco's Finest Hob Nobs and made the best entrance he could muster into the sitting room. 'Hob, Miss Troubridge? Nob, Mrs Troubridge?'

The sisters twittered and giggled like girls and Maxwell, recovered now from the virtually heart-stopping shock they had given him, smiled benevolently. Having a missing Mrs Troubridge was one thing – quieter for a start and less confrontational. Having a dead one would have been much nastier and he was glad that moment was staved off until the next time he felt tempted to push the old trout down the stairs.

CHAPTER THIRTEEN

Jacquie flicked her phone shut with a thoughtful expression on her face and went back into the office where Henry Hall was waiting.

'Everything all right?' he asked. He knew her looks of old, the slight, imperceptible swings of mood that made for good days or better days. Henry Hall – and Peter Maxwell, come to think of it – had never had it so good.

'Yes,' she said. 'In fact, I think this is where I say there is bad news and good news. Which would you like first? In fact, if I give you the good news, you will be able to guess the bad, I think.'

'Go on, then,' Hall said, clasping his hands in front of him like a Victorian schoolmarm. 'Please don't keep us in suspense.'

While Jacquie had been in the corridor on the phone, Hall had been bringing his opposite number up to speed, especially on the Troubridge connection. Helen Marshall and Hall went back a bit. In fact, despite her husband and family, she had always carried a bit of a torch, being a sucker for the strong, silent type. Well, the silent type. He, safe behind his blank lenses, had always been unaware, much to the amusement of everyone else, who could tell at a thousand paces. She lived with it these days and even had a laugh sometimes. Looking at him now, she still wanted to smooth that little wrinkle between his brows, brush the piece of lint off his jacket. That didn't stop her from wanting to beat him at every turn, of course, just to prove that she could. She settled for getting him a cup of coffee and a piece of shrink-wrapped carrot cake. Where was Jamie

Oliver when police canteens needed him?

'The thing is, Helen, our missing person may well be Jacquie's next door neighbour.'

'That's a bit of a co...'

'Don't say coincidence, please,' he warned her. 'There's no such thing.'

'OK, then. I won't. But it is, don't you think? And, don't I remember hearing some-where that her other half's a bit too involved sometimes? He's not like one of those nutters who phones it in when he's done it, is he?' Helen Marshall had known men like that – and it *was* always men, funnily enough, for whom the lure of fifteen minutes of fame was too great. They weren't all serial killers with more previous than Harold Shipman, they were just sad old misfits who wanted the world to notice them, just once. She demol-ished half her cake in one bite.

'No,' he said, shaking his head. 'There was a time when I thought so. There are staff in my nick who wish it were so. But ... no. He's just a bit too nosy, a bit too easily able to get Jacquie to tell him everything. And a bit too right, for some people's taste. But,' he could almost feel his throat closing over as the next words took shape, 'his heart's in the right place. He's very, *very* bright and he knows almost everyone in Leighford and their cat. So, he's got a bit of a march even on us. And, before you ask, it's not him.'

'Right. That's one we can tick off. Just a

couple of hundred thousand to go, then.'

'Why stop there,' he asked, dryly. 'The population of the country is ... let's say sixty million, to keep the maths simple. Half women, so thirty million. Half too old, fifteen million. Half of that too young, seven and a half million. Most of those not related to the first victim. Make that one. Mike Crown.'

Helen Marshall screwed up her face. Henry Hall could whittle down the wind in terms of suspects, but she wasn't happy. 'I don't like it, though, Henry. He's a nasty piece of work, I'd be the first to agree. But ... he's too selfish to be a killer, if you know what I mean. He would only do it for gain, and there doesn't seem to be any. We don't even know who she is yet.'

'Mrs Troubridge, Jacquie's neighbour.'

'Perhaps. I'm not sure she fits the description that well, but ... well, we'll soon see. The PM will give us chapter and verse.'

'Has Crown seen her?'

'No. He was too squeamish to look closely after he tripped over her. All he did was call it in and then wait for us. When we went to the location, he was at the end of the path, green as grass and shaking.'

'Perhaps he should.'

'Have you gone all medieval on me, Henry? Do you want to see if the wounds bleed?'

'Surely they've stopped bleeding by now.'

'I was just speaking metaphorically,

Henry. They used to see if the presence of the killer... You know, in Chaucer's time – "Murder will out"... Oh, never mind.' Sometimes she thought she might have had a lucky escape.

The door opened and Jacquie came in.

'Go on, then,' Hall said. 'Please don't keep us in suspense.'

'Well, the good news is that Max is at home, entertaining.'

Hall looked blanker than ever. A blow by blow account of her partner's social life he could do without. And of course there were those in Leighford nick who didn't find Peter Maxwell entertaining at all. 'So, he's not snooping around at the scene of the crime, then,' said Hall. 'That *is* good news, but not earth shattering, Jacquie.'

'That's not the news. The news is, he's entertaining Mrs Troubridge.'

'What?' Hall and Helen Marshall said together.

'Yes, quite,' Jacquie said. 'And also her sister. Apparently, she was expected the other night and wandered off for a coffee or something and confusion ensued. Max was a little incoherent, with mixed annoyance and ... well, being thoroughly Troubridged, I should think, I'm sure I'll get the details tonight.'

'Have I missed something?' Helen Marshall asked. Like all attractive women, she was always on the alert when there was another one, a younger one at that, in the room. 'What's the bad news. She's not suddenly died has she? Poisoned coffee, something like that?'

Jacquie could also be arch. 'Mrs Troubridge only drinks tea,' she said. 'No, the bad news is that now we have absolutely no idea who our body is. We're back to minus square one on that one, guv.' She addressed herself exclusively to Henry Hall.

He was not the most sensitive of men, but even so, he wished it would stop. Not for nothing did the police service delay the introduction of women officers for as long as it could. 'I think it's time we interrupted the forensics team,' he said to the DCI. 'We need to get a photo of the victim to Mike Crown and watch very carefully as he views it. And we need to have a look ourselves.'

'That won't help, though, Henry, will it?' Helen said. 'There's now no earthly reason why she should be known to you. The Leighford connection was always fragile. Now it doesn't really exist, except between Crown and his stepdaughter.' She stood up and extended a hand. 'I'm afraid I must go and get ready for the press conference,' she said, looking briefly at her watch but not really focusing. 'We'll be in touch if we think you can help us further. Henry.' She shook his hand briefly and then sat back down. 'Detective Sergeant.' She nodded at Jacquie. 'Can you find your own way out?' and she bent to the paperwork littering her desk.

Hall stood in the corridor wondering what had gone on in the last few minutes. He asked Jacquie.

She patted him on the shoulder. It was more than she would usually do, but she had watched this man sleeping and that gave a woman leeway. 'Guv,' she said. 'If you don't know, I can't possibly tell you,' and chuckling quietly, she made her way to the stairs. Turning her head, she threw back one last remark. 'Our good news is her bad news. And that sounds good to me.'

Henry Hall, still puzzled, followed her down to the car park and they soon were driving through the February day back to Leighford. Back to the safe ground. All in all, it was probably a woman thing.

The forensic team in Chichester toiled on, unaware of the politics in the air. They had found a well nourished female of indeterminate age, certainly well cared for, lifted, tweaked and enhanced in various subtle ways. They had scanned her for DNA, of which they had found an ample quantity, in fact, an unusually large amount. They assumed she worked in an environment where she came up against a lot of people. But one set of DNA was there in particularly copious amounts. The lab boys differed in their opinions. One said it was only to be expected, as there had clearly been reasonably close proximity, if only for a brief moment. Hairs fell, spit flew, it was fair enough. The other said that that was all very fine, but it was the places that the DNA was found that clinched it for him. Under the skirt waistband. Under the bra strap. Under her nails. It would have had to be a pretty comprehensive trip for Mike Crown to have left his DNA all over the victim's body. In the mental list the lab tech carried in his head, he put a big tick against him – they had the killer. All they needed now was the name of the victim. He picked up the phone and dialled. It was time Mike Crown was confronted with what he had done. They might have this sewn up by teatime at this rate. Job done.

The Troubridge sisters had gone home by the time Jacquie arrived later that Thursday afternoon. Maxwell still had the habit of closing one eye and looking askance, as if recovering from a blow to the head. Johnny Depp had picked that one up from him to play Jack Sparrow. After he gave Jacquie all the details of his surreal encounter, sounding like something scripted by Mervyn Peake for *Gormenghast*, he waited with breath well and truly bated for her recital of *her* morning.

'Nothing doing, Max,' she said. 'It's got no link to Leighford any more. It's the job of the Chichester police to sort it out.'

'*Mi casa, su casa,*' Maxwell shrugged. 'Not only are all you boys wearing the same blue, but it's the same police authority, damn it. And anyway, it was the stepfather of our victim...' Maxwell's sentence had become plaintive. He and Nolan often exchanged notes on how to get their own way, updating at regular intervals. Currently, Nolan had it all to do when it came to wheedling. But he had a cuter nose than his dad, so it was even stevens really.

'Firstly,' Jacquie said, as severely as she could, 'what's with the "our" victim?' Conversations like this always had an air of déjà vu about them. She and Maxwell had been there and got all the T-shirts. 'Secondly, despite what Henry says, I don't think the guy did it. He's truly horrible, preying on ladies who need a bit of reassurance, shall we say, to be kinder than he was about them. But I don't think he's a killer. I think he genuinely did trip over a body. It must happen all the time, taken all in all.'

Maxwell's eyebrows rose into his hair. 'All the time? In that case, I really must jog more. Well, all right, jog. But, in *that* case, if it's nothing to do with our victim,' he persisted in his description; he had taken ownership, as he was constantly being told to do by the SLT, 'you can tell me every-thing, can't you? It can't possibly matter. Eh,' he nudged her, 'Eh, go on, you know you want to. Eh? Eh?' Maxwell's Eric Idle was not totally lost on Jacquie, although she barely remembered the original.

She sighed and sat down heavily. 'Max, today has been a bit of a rollercoaster. When I went to work, I thought Mrs Troubridge was dead.'

'And now we've got two for the price of one,' Maxwell remarked.

'Yes, that's right. I also thought we had found our murderer.'

'And now you discover you've just got a really clumsy jogger,' he added.

'If you say so.' She suddenly grinned. 'It was quite funny, though,' she said, snuggling up. 'The DCI at Chichester really fancies Henry.'

'Does he now?' Maxwell said, wondering what part of the bland policeman could attract anybody. 'I suppose that's all right among today's PC PCs, is it? Gaily speaking?'

She swiped him round the head in a playful sort of way. 'The DCI at Chichester is a woman, you sexist pig. DCI Marshall, God rot her, has smashed her way through the glass ceiling.'

'Ah,' Maxwell caught just a tiny flash of green in his love's grey eyes. 'Does Henry know this woman has the hots for him?'

'No, that's the best bit. She wears it like a badge. Doesn't like me at all.'

'Of course she doesn't.' Maxwell chuckled, 'Successful women never do like other women. Look at Dierdre Lessing, for instance. I believe she sticks pins in wax images of all the other women on the staff if they are younger, more attractive or more intelligent than her.' He was silent for a while, then, 'She gets through a lot of pins.'

Jacquie chortled at the thought. 'Even so, it was a bit annoying, you know. She kept calling me Detective Sergeant, like it was an insult.'

'So, if she was so horrible, why not tell me all about the case?'

'Nothing to tell, Max. Stop it, now. Mike Crown fell over a body. They are working on ID as we speak.'

'And this Amazon will let Henry know who it is?'

'Unlikely. She really froze him out, at the end. Gave us the bum's rush, in fact.'

'So,' he leant back, hands behind his head. 'That's it then, is it? Our little bit of excitement all over?'

'Why do you say that?'

'Well, is he the guy? Do you think he killed his stepdaughter, Darren Blackwell and this unidentified woman? He must be a random nutter, if so.' Maxwell was fully up to speed with current psychological jargon.

'Why?' Jacquie asked. 'He seems almost too down to earth. He just wants money, that's all.'

'Well, there's no link, is there?' Maxwell reasoned, wrestling with it all out loud. 'Two young victims, one older. Two women, one man. Two in Leighford, one in Arundel. Has to be random.'

'I don't know about this last one, but apparently Lara Kent had Darren Blackwell's brother's number on her mobile.'

Kerching! Maxwell looked slyly at her. She was sipping a coffee and had her nose in the cup. She couldn't see him coming, prowling up through the Serengeti grass. In a minute, his teeth would be in her throat and Metternich would be proud of him. 'That's odd,' he said, his voice low. 'Still, I expect they just met at a club, or something.'

'Isn't Darren Blackwell's brother still at Leighford?' Jacquie asked. 'A bit young for a club?'

'Bless your little heart,' he smiled. 'Without under-age drinkers, there wouldn't be a single viable licensed premises in the whole town. And your oppos in uniform would be out of a job come chucking out time. Yes, Kevin is still at Leighford High and no, what we need is to find out who this third body is and link it with the other two.' As he spoke, he knew his mistake. He had said the dreaded 'w' word. We; drat it, now he would have to start stalking all over again. It could take hours.

Sure enough, her head came up and she sniffed the wind, like the startled little wildebeest she was. 'Max,' she said, sitting up straight and looking him in the eye. '*We* don't have to do anything. *I* possibly will be involved with such an investigation and *when* and *if* it is in the newspapers or on the TV, you might then also find out. Until then, my lips are sealed.'

Damn! Bugger and poo! Back to hiding in the long grass, until she dropped her guard, dipped her nose to the water once too often. But he'd get her. Oh yes, Peter Maxwell always got his woman. A small piece of bribery might be in order.

'Now Mrs Troubridge is restored to us,' he said, rubbing his hands together like George Peppard in *The A-Team*, loving it when a plan came together, 'we have a babysitter. What do you say to a nice night out?'

Suspicious, she looked into his eyes. There was guile there, certainly, but a thousand years of teaching will do that to a man. Why not? They had only been out sleuthing this week and a nice evening out, with no strings, might be a nice change. 'Why not?' she smiled. 'I'll go and ask her ... them. It will be an excuse to meet Miss Troubridge, even if they say no.'

'Araminta.'

'I beg your pardon?'

'Araminta. That's Miss Troubridge's name.'

'What were they thinking?'

'I have the full story, but, really, Queen of Puddings, it would be too much for a youngster like you at this time of night. Go, marshal the Troubridges, Mrs and Miss. Oops, did I say Marshall? Sorry. Then come and put your gladrags on. Something Nexty. We'll party like it's 2007. Or at least go for a drink.' He patted her on her way. 'Go on. Chop, chop. I'll go and warn Nole. The poor kid will think his eyes have gone funny, otherwise.'

Smiling, Jacquie went down the stairs, across the dampness of the lawn that briefly separated the drives and rang the bell next door. Twittering noises broke out overhead as the Troubridge twins wondered aloud who it could possibly be, at this hour. Poor Nolan, thought Jacquie. But it will make a man of him. Or else he'll be in rehab for ever.

Helen Marshall was still at her desk long after her team had gone home. She didn't do it for effect, she did it because she had to. It was still a man's world in the police and if she didn't drink and swear and smoke like them, she just worked harder than they did. She was trying out various ways of getting back into Henry Hall's good books, without too much unseemly grovelling. She had sent him and that little Detective Sergeant more or less packing when she found they were of little use to her. That was both impolite and, as it turned out, unwise. She did need them, after all. She reached out for her phone several times and then found something to distract her from making the call. A mug-ring to wipe away. A pencil to sharpen. A calendar to cross a few days off. Anything. Finally, she wiped her hands down the sides of her skirt. She hated that Henry Hall could make her feel like a silly teenager; in itself, that was bad enough. But she was going to have to ask him a favour. And she hated that much, *much*, more. She picked up the phone and dialled. It seemed to ring for ever. She breathed a sigh of relief. He'd gone home. Excellent. She could leave it until…

'Hall.'

'Oh, Henry. You *are* still there. Good. I am glad,' she lied. 'Look, I wonder if I could ask you a favour? It's Helen Marshall, by the way.'

Henry Hall was terser on the phone than in real life. His lenses kept the world at bay when face to face. When separated by miles of whatever gubbins British Telecom saw fit to lace the country with, he was ice. 'Possibly.' He didn't get hurt by people's rudeness, but he did sometimes get even.

'We've had prelims from the forensics team and … well, because of your…'

'Jacquie.'

'Yes, her neighbour being, as we thought, missing, they were looking specifically for the Leighford link.'

'Yes.'

'Well, they found one.' She waited while it sunk in.

Eventually he said, trying to keep the smugness from his voice, 'That was a bit unexpected from your end, I assume.'

'Well, yes. Look, Henry, I can't help thinking we're on the wrong foot here. I didn't mean to be so ... dismissive, this afternoon.'

'Good. Jacquie and I would hate to think you had done it on purpose.'

Ouch. On so many levels, Henry Hall did not mess around when getting even was an option. Helen Marshall marshalled her thoughts. 'Well, there we are, Henry. Water under the bridge, shall we say?' There was no reply, so she just said, 'Good. Right, the Leighford link. The forensics team found a cinema ticket, all rolled up as if someone had, you know, rolled it and unrolled it repeatedly, you know how you do, when you're waiting or something.'

'Not really.'

'It's a common nervous reaction.' She found herself getting annoyed and knew it would get her nowhere with Henry Hall. She took a deep breath, in through nose, out through mouth, yoga style. 'It took them a while, but they have managed to decipher it as a ticket for the deluxe screen at the Leighford Multiplex.'

Henry Hall brightened. There really *was* a Leighford connection. And one that could be traced, quite quickly. 'Do you have a date?'

'Yes, it was the twelfth.'

'Monday? I'll get right on it.'

'Right on it? How can you tell who went to the cinema on Monday?'

'The deluxe screen here in Leighford is by booking only. It only holds about fifty people all told and because there's a bar in the lobby area, they don't allow under eighteens, no matter what the film is. We use it quite often, as a matter of fact.' He had often sat a few rows back from Peter Maxwell, and had been very tempted to do something juvenile with a few well aimed bits of popcorn, but so far had managed to resist.

'Heavens, Henry,' Helen said, and suddenly their relationship was back on track. 'I never had you down for a film buff.'

'Oh, I'm hardly that,' he said. 'But when I go out I would rather not be looking for people breaking the law, and somehow the extra two pounds fifty and having to book keeps the law-breaking in the deluxe screen to a minimum.' Peter Maxwell, of course, was always the exception.

'So, can you get a list, do you think?'

'What showing was it?'

'They didn't say. Just that it was the twelfth.'

'They are showing *Music and Lyrics* this week. I've avoided it, because Mrs Hall is not a great Hugh Grant fan.'

'Otherwise, you might have been sitting next to a potential murder victim,' Helen Marshall said.

'I think we all do that, at some time in our lives,' said Hall. 'The trick is not to be one.'

'That's very deep, Henry,' said the DCI. 'I think I'll just get off home and leave you to do the digging at your end. Or I could send someone, if you like?'

'No, it's quite all right, Helen,' Hall said. 'I'll pop round myself. It's on my way.'

CHAPTER FOURTEEN

Henry Hall waited in the foyer of the Leighford Multiplex with gritted teeth while a school party milled around him. He was useless these days at guessing children's ages, but from the height of the line of snot and ice-cream dribble gradually building up on his jacket, he thought they were probably around about seven. He looked with admiration at the teachers shepherding their charges and wondered that they looked so well on it, though one did seem to have quite a serious tic under one eye. He couldn't move through the tide of little sweaty, screaming people, so decided to just ride it out. Actually, it could have been worse. What he was witnessing was Year Five of Tottingleigh School getting their reward for a recent Ofsted success. Had the virus not been stalking the land, their numbers would have been greater.

He closed his eyes, to make the time pass more quickly. That way, he couldn't see the tired decor, the only slightly bent life size figures of stars of forthcoming attractions. Tobey Maguire swung above his head, sadly just within the reach of the passing wag who had adorned his black spider suit with an extra willy made of half-chewed gum. He made a note to get the speech bubble which was written on the Drew Barrymore figure wiped off – the community police officer would be on to that first thing tomorrow. Spelling was pretty good, though. If you vandalised something today, thank a teacher. On the other hand, he could definitely get the manager under the Obscene Publications Act. The tide of children swept round him and down the stairs, the sound of their chatter dying away like a radio with its battery fading. Then, suddenly, it was cut off by the final closure of the swinging exit doors. Henry Hall heaved a sigh and turned towards the deluxe screen doors. There was a God.

'Henry Hall! Well, swipe me pink,' said a familiar voice just near his left shoulder. It might have been the late, great Tony Hancock, but it wasn't. Hall hadn't expected the day to get worse and yet, somehow, it just had. He turned, pasting on a smile.

'Hello, Mr Maxwell. Jacquie. Fancy seeing you here.

'No, no, we're always here,' said Maxwell. 'Film Buffs Are Us and we thought we'd celebrate the return of Mrs Troubridge by a visit to the cinematographic emporium.'

'Humm ... how appropriate,' said Hall.

'It is,' said Jacquie, feeling the need to fill in the detail. 'She's our babysitter.'

'Oh, I see.' That made some sort of sense. What made no sense was the fact that a deranged old lady, newly returned from the Missing Persons List, was deemed by these otherwise intelligent people to be suitable for looking after their child. 'Here for a bit of Hugh Grant, then?' Henry Hall tried to make light conversation when he could. He'd get the hang of it one day. Also, he was trying hard to avoid the question he knew was lurking on Maxwell's lips – 'what are you doing here?' He wasn't to know that was a question rarely asked *Chez Maxwell/Carpenter* without laughter and collapsing. It was always followed in the TV cop shows by a grisly murder, thereby implying, with all the subtlety of Charlotte Church, that the victim knew his killer.

'Good Lord, no,' Maxwell said, chuckling. 'We don't do the Hugh Grant thing, do we, Jacquie?'

'No,' she said, looking a little crestfallen. 'No, we don't. Not really.'

Maxwell gave her a sideways glance. 'Well, perhaps later. On DVD, dear. Where I have the option to take the cat for a nice, long walk or start reading *War and Peace* to Nole.' He smiled at Hall, man to man. 'No, no, we're here to watch *Hot Fuzz*. Came out last week and we fancied a laugh, after the last few days.'

'So ... watching a police film is relaxation, Jacquie?' Hall suddenly felt lonely, here in the giant foyer with the unlikeliest and yet the happiest couple in Leighford and surrounding area.

'Hardly police, guv!' Jacquie laughed.

'I watched *Shaun of the Dead* with much enjoyment,' said Maxwell, 'and so did *all* my zombie friends. Anyway,' Here it comes, thought Hall, 'that's enough about us. What are *you* doing here?' For a reason Hall did not understand, Maxwell raised a hooked finger and pointed it at him, with a recoil effect. Hall remembered doing something similar in the long, long ago, when playing cowboys and Indians with his sisters; never a very fulfilling game, as he spent a lot of the time tied to a tree. Jacquie grinned and nudged Maxwell.

'Oh, you know, just booking a seat at the deluxe.'

'Deluxe? Ah, I see – Hugh Grant. Are *you* a fan, then, Henry?'

'No. It's Mrs Hall,' he lied, without compunction.

'Lovely,' Maxwell beamed. 'We've got a few minutes before we have to go in. We'll tag along. Then, perhaps you'd like to join us for one of the scrummy three squillion varieties of ice cream served by a surly Leighford Highena in this very foyer? With average luck it'll be Wonky Wendy tonight, class of '97.'

Henry Hall briefly felt like a rabbit caught in the headlights, then mentally shook himself. 'That sounds a very attractive proposition,' he lied. 'But after booking my seat, I really must get along home.'

'Of course,' said Jacquie. 'And we must go and get to our seats. See you tomorrow, guv. Come along, Max, we'll be late.'

'No,' he said. 'Plenty of room in the one and nines. We've still got...'

'Really, Max. We'll be late,' and she dragged him off through the turnstile that led to the Seats for Common People. Henry Hall slipped through the door for the Posh.

'What's he *really* doing here?' Maxwell hissed in her ear.

'He's really booking seats in the deluxe,' Jacquie said. 'Really, Max, you must get out of the idea that Henry lives at the police station. He actually does have a life outside, you know.'

'Nah,' said Maxwell, perfectly echoing any one of Ten Eff Zed when asked if they knew any History, any History at all. 'He's on to something and I'm going to find out what.' He pulled against his captor but she was trained in safe restraint and her grip was fierce on his sleeve. She pulled herself up so her nose was as near to his as she could get it without stepping on his toes.

'Listen to me, Peter Maxwell,' she hissed, menacingly. 'We are going into that cinema now, we are taking our seats. We are watching a film. If you do not laugh in the funny bits, I will know you are thinking about Henry. If you laugh when no one else does … all right, I'll give you two of those, but if you do it repeatedly, I will know you are thinking about Henry. If you think about Henry, you will get a pint of ice cold Coke in your lap and half a ton of popcorn up your nostrils – and that's for starters. Understand?'

'I love it when you're strict with me,' he put on his best pervert smile. 'And yes, I do understand.' He knew when the end of her tether was in sight. They gave in their tickets to yet another surly Highena; Zoë Bigtits, class of '94. 'She's a policeman,' he said by way of explanation to the spotty girl as they went into the dark. The usherette wasn't surprised. The only surprising thing was that, having arrested the mad old sod for nameless crimes, she was taking him to the pictures.

Maxwell sat through the adverts. He sorely missed Pearl and Dean and their slightly out of focus, slightly too loud ads for things no one could ever want. He wriggled only slightly when being admonished to turn off his mobile phone or have his nuts put in a vice by a rather scary woman dressed in bondage wear. He watched patiently through the forthcoming attractions, none of which he wanted to see particularly, because they were not attractive and probably not very forthcoming. Especially not a special-edition-digitally-remastered-extra-CGI-with-knobs-on edition of *The Da Vinci Code*. He'd guessed it was dear old Ian McKellen the first time. You don't get a Knight of the Theatre and give him a bit part these days. He did a bit of generic glaring when there was some crackling of paper to his left, unnecessary throat clearing to his right. Whenever Jacquie caught his eye, his expression was truly beatific. Finally, the film began and he gave less of his brain to the question of what Henry was doing; sometimes as little as ninety-nine percent.

After a while, he leant over to Jacquie and whispered, 'Sorry, sweetness, but that pint of ice cold Coke is taking its toll. The one I drank, not the one you threatened me with, obviously,' he clarified.

'Max. Your bladder's like a carrier bag. Don't tell me you're going to the loo, because I won't believe you,' she hissed back.

'No, really, I do need to go. Even carrier bags have a limit and I didn't go before we came out.' He sounded like something out of the old Zafira ad and pulled a rueful face. 'Sorry. Plus, don't forget I'm at a funny age.'

She turned to look at him. He looked quite genuine, but this was Mad Max and who could tell? He wasn't in catheter country yet, but still, she weighed up the options and came to a decision. 'All right. But come straight back.'

'Yes ma'am.' He sketched a salute and was gone, loping up the stairs all of one at a time and out through the curtain at the back. He stopped to check for Hall. There was no sign, so Maxwell slid through the doors of the Deluxe. Sure enough, a current Highena sat behind the desk, but, Saints be praised, one of the more intelligent this time. Well, in this job, you had to write, so if it wasn't an Oxbridge hopeful the whole system would crash and burn.

'Hello, Sophie,' Maxwell beamed. 'I didn't know you worked here.'

'I don't do many hours, Mr Maxwell,' she hurriedly told the Head of Sixth Form. 'Just two nights and I don't go out otherwise. I...'

'Sophie, Sophie, Sophie,' Maxwell shook his head in sorrow. 'I'm not here to check on you, dear me no.'

'Oh ... right. Sorry, Mr Maxwell. Only...'

'Only what?' He smiled encouragingly.

'We've all heard that story of you and that girl behind the till in Waitrose.'

'Well, she had been warned,' he said. 'And she would do it. And anyway, she gave me the wrong change. So she wasn't concentrating on her maths, either. That's a really old story, though, Sophie. Just how old you might guess from the fact that the wrong change she gave me was eight and sevenpence three farthings. Ah, the dear, dead days. I'm much more mellow now, as you probably have noticed.'

Another smile and she still wasn't convinced. However, she had a job to do ... for now.

'So, how can I help you, sir?' she said, singing from the Multiplex hymnbook. It was not the 'sir' of the classroom and corridor, but the 'sir' of customer relations.

'Well, as you probably know, Sophie, my other half is a policeperson.' He waited for her nod. 'And her boss, Mr Hall, was in here just now. Well, I'm afraid that DS Carpenter was supposed to get her own copy of the ...

thing you gave him. But she forgot. She's out there now, terribly upset, because she will get into trouble. So, Sophie, can you help me out?'

The poor girl looked from side to side but there was no help to be found. 'Ummm, Mr Maxwell, I'm pretty sure I shouldn't do this.'

'Oh, but, Sophie. DS Carpenter will get into such trouble. You've met our little baby, have you, little Nolan? Quite big, nowadays, toddling. Saying words.' He looked up from under his lashes. 'We sometimes need a babysitter, of course. Nice job. Good pay. Wall to wall DVDs.'

'Oh, Mr Maxwell. There's no need for bribery,' she said. He was proud of her for spotting it. He'd brought her up well. She reached under the desk. 'Here you are. I printed two by mistake.' She winked at him. 'Your ... policeperson ... might as well have the spare.'

'Sophie, you are a marvel,' he breathed. 'Thanks.' Time was marching and he had to be back in his seat pdq or there would be trouble. He shoved the paper into his pocket and dived back through the door and spun round the corner, through the curtain, down the stairs and into his seat with hardly a pause for breath.

Jacquie looked up. 'That was quick,' she said, feeling bad that she had doubted him. 'Better now?'

'Much,' he said, nestling down into his seat, aware as if it was on fire of the paper in his pocket. 'What've I missed?'

'You'll soon pick it up,' she said and turned her concentration back to the screen and her popcorn.

And pick it up he did. Almost as soon as Simon Pegg blasted the entire auditorium with his Uzi. It kept his mind off the two nagging itches in his head. One; what was on the paper? Two; he really needed a pee.

The paper in Henry Hall's pocket was also almost on fire. Outside the Mulitplex he paused irresolute. Home or office? Office or home? He was still dithering there, indecisive, when his phone beeped at him. It was his wife, who had mastered texting with the alacrity of a teenager. Bring milk and bread. Well, that was one decision made for him; he turned his blank glasses in the direction of his parked car and headed back to the office.

At that time of night, Alan Kavanagh was in the canteen as Hall popped in for a coffee and something sustaining. He hated cross checking lists; Jacquie was the woman for that task, but she was tucked up in the cinema with Maxwell. He couldn't disturb her, could he? It hardly seemed fair.

'Hello, guv,' Kavanagh's space invader approach meant that the simple phrase was threateningly near his ear. 'I didn't expect to see you here.'

'No. I was planning on an earlyish finish tonight, Alan. I might say the same of you – surely it's not usual for you to be here this late?'

'Oh, I often stay late. I nip down to records, or to the library.'

'We've got a library here?' Hall was puzzled; he thought he knew this building inside out.

'No, no. I mean the *library*. The one down the road. Leighford Library. I get out a few legal books and then come back here to read them in peace. It's a bit loud at home.' He saw Hall's blank look. 'I share,' he said. 'With two junior doctors and a professional musician.'

Hall looked suitably sympathetic and almost managed to mask his surprise.

'Anyway, guv, perhaps I could help you with whatever it is that has brought you back.'

Hall mulled it over. He would have to drag Jacquie away from her film and he had run her a bit ragged lately. Plus, if he used Kavanagh, he would keep Peter Maxwell out of the loop for just that bit longer – perhaps a vital bit longer. He looked up at Kavanagh, still looming over him and made a decision. 'All right, Alan. We'll go up to my office and do a bit of name crunching, shall we?'

Alan Kavanagh almost burst with excitement. 'That would be great, guv,' he said. 'I'll just go and finish my sardine and onion sandwich and I'll be right with you.'

Hall got up and went over to the machine in the corner. Two packets of extra strong mints should do it. No, wait, better make it three.

Up in his office, Henry Hall arranged the chairs to give himself the maximum space between his nose and Kavanagh's sardine breath. It was a fine balance between being as far as possible and not having to shout. Finally, the chairs were arranged to his satisfaction and he spread out his files on the two cases and gave Kavanagh the list from the deluxe.

'Right, Alan,' he said. 'We are looking for two things and I want you to decide on some kind of code system to tell them apart on the list.'

'Sorry, guv. I don't get you.'

Hall sighed. Jacquie always knew what to do. She used ticks, crosses, asterisks and initials to tell one category from another. He didn't have to tell her or explain and at the end, by glancing down the list she could, sometimes seemingly miraculously, tell him what he needed to know. Patiently, he explained the principle to Kavanagh and eventually he got it. Suddenly, Hall knew why they'd invented computers.

'Oh, I see, guv. What you want is for me to

put, say, a tick against anyone who appears on the list and in the file on Lara Kent. Then a cross on anyone who appears on the list and in the file on Darren Blackwell. Then ... something else against...'

'I think you have the basics there,' said Hall. 'Shall we get on?' he glanced at his watch. 'It's getting late. Even for me. Mrs Hall will have died of thirst or hunger, depending on the state of the fridge.'

Kavanagh nodded and bent his head to the list, pen enthusiastically at the ready. 'Right, guv,' he said.

'This may be a slow process,' said Hall. He waited but Kavanagh didn't speak. 'Ummm ... Alan, can I have the first name?'

'Sorry, guv. I thought you would give me a name and then I'd do my ticks and that.'

'No, Alan. *You* give me a name and then I tell you if I have it in my files. That's the quickest way.'

'Oh, right. Let's see ... Mrs Smith.' Kavanagh looked up brightly, waiting.

Hall slammed shut the file in front of him and, taking off his glasses, rubbed his eyes. 'I don't think this is going to work, Alan. Do you?'

'Why not, guv? We've only just started.' Kavanagh was wounded.

Hall replaced his glasses and gave himself a shake. 'Sorry, Alan. It's been a long day. Let's try a few more. After Mrs Smith, who do we have?'

'Mr N Leopold plus one.'

'There now, that's better, isn't it? A nice unusual name. It's not in my files, but perhaps we can look it up to see if he has a phone. There's only a mobile number here in the contacts column. So, Alan,' Hall was watching Kavanagh's pen and it didn't seem to have done anything. 'Are you going to put a mark of some kind?'

'What shall I put, guv? We didn't have a category for checking numbers.'

'Let's just write "check", shall we? It doesn't have to be a symbol.' His voice sounded strained, coming as it did from behind clenched teeth.

Kavanagh wrote the word and inwardly seethed. Why did things always have to be so difficult? It might be years before he made DCI at this rate. And he had planned to be there before Christmas.

'Let's just do a few more,' Hall said, 'Then call it a day. I think I've got a headache coming on.'

Kavanagh snorted quietly down his nose. It was time these old fogies got out of his way. He could go all night, ticking, crossing, finding murderers. What could be easier? 'Adair plus one.'

'Not on my list,' said Hall. 'Just write "check".'

Eventually, the system started to work and

Hall and Kavanagh ticked, crossed and silently cursed the evening away, while Mrs Hall's hedgehogs did without their bread and milk and Kavanagh's house mates had a small celebration, as they always did when he was working late.

Maxwell and Jacquie stood blinking in the foyer. They enjoyed going to the cinema most in the winter. Coming out of the cosy darkness to a bright sunlit evening, the magic passed quickly; coming out to a cold, dark evening, better still, a snowy one, the special occasion feeling lingered all the way home. And Peter Maxwell could still remember, even if Jacquie could not, hacking his way along the pavements of his childhood – all the three musketeers rolled into one; and one for all.

Jacquie gave Maxwell a squeeze. 'That was a lovely idea, Max,' she said, leaning up to kiss him. 'Just what I needed.'

Smiling, he kissed her back. 'Everyone needs a good laugh now and again,' he said. 'But I can't think of two people who need it more than a teacher and a woman policeman.'

She leant against him and heard a crackling from his pocket. 'What's this?' she said, delving.

'That? Oh, nothing. Jesson models or some such nonsense,' he said, clamping his hand over it, trapping hers. 'Tracking the untrackable. Just school stuff.'

'You haven't been at school today,' she said. 'That wasn't there when we set out, because I had my hand in that pocket after a hankie, remember?' Not for nothing was Jacquie Carpenter a signed-up member of the CID. She'd already been kicked out of the KGB for being too nosy.

'Yes, my little snotty one. How is that cold?' Solicitousness could often win the day. It was tantamount to changing the subject.

'I don't have a cold,' she said. 'The hankie was to wipe the seagull poo off my car door handle. What is it, Max?'

'Please,' he said. 'No scenes in front of what appears to be the whole of Year Ten.' A million eyes were watching from the queue to see what the mad old sod was going to do next. With the school closed – they hoped forever – they had to get their fix of embarrassing adult behaviour from somewhere else, and this was as good as anywhere. Any minute now, the mobile phones would be out, taking illicit pictures to be beamed around the chat rooms of the world. And the men in black from the General Teaching Council would come calling, as unexpected as the Spanish Inquisition. 'If you must know...' he looked round furtively, 'a copy of what Henry was here for.'

'What?' she hissed. 'What are your limits,

Max? That's police business. You've no right.'

'Well, you'd have found out tomorrow.'

'Precisely,' she said coldly. '*I* would have found out tomorrow. Now, I'm going to find out tonight. Give it to me.' She held out her hand, like a junior school teacher waiting for half chewed gum. 'I shan't move until I have it, Max, so let's not make a scene.'

Brain whirling with half formed plans, he handed it over. As she stalked away he watched her go. His eyes narrowed and he made a small bet with himself. Before the night was out, he would know who was on that list. Before the week was out, he would know who the victim was. Before the weekend was over, Jacquie, courtesy of the little grey cells of Peter Maxwell, would have the murderer behind bars. He rubbed his hands together and did a small, internal jig, not unlike the famous footage of the Führer, elated on the patio of the Berghof, because the Wehrmacht had kicked French arse yet again. Jacquie Carpenter, you just don't know how lucky you are, he thought. A feather in your cap is about to be handed to you on a plate. Only at moments like these did Peter Maxwell allow his metaphors to become entangled. He broke into a reasonably dignified trot to catch her up, scarf streaming in the wind like a latter day Isadora Duncan. The queue slumped back into torpor. The first section of the night's entertainment was over. Peter Maxwell had left the building.

CHAPTER FIFTEEN

Jacquie parked the car with a flourish and went up the drive ahead of her Dearly Beloved, demoted temporarily to Him. She put a brave face on it for Tweedledum and Tweedledee, as she couldn't help but think of the Troubridge sisters, shepherding them downstairs with twitterings and hyperbole, while Maxwell checked the boy and the Light Brigade, just for good measure. She agreed that Nolan was a dear little boy, handsome, bright and loving, but Araminta's assertion that he was destined to be king seemed a little unlikely to be accurate. Prime Minister, certainly. That she could imagine. She paused outside the sitting room door to rearrange her expression. Give Maxwell an inch and he would take an ell.

'Seen the ladies back home?' he asked. 'To the door? Don't want them going missing again, do we?'

'Stop it, Max,' she said. 'Stop trying to soft soap me. You're not seeing that piece of paper and that's the end of it. Do the cocoa, if you want some and either watch TV, model or have an early night. There is positively no point in hanging round me, I shall be in the study.' And out she went.

Maxwell sat still for a moment, then caught the jaundiced eye of Metternich, sprawled out on the sofa. A faint odour of pilchard tainted the air and the huge beast looked, if possible, even more smug than usual. Metternich had often given Mrs Troubridge little unexpected gifts, which, to his distress, had not always met with her approval, if the screams were any guide. But *Miss* Troubridge, the one who had made Metternich want to close one eye to help with the focusing, had been very appreciative of his purr, his handsomeness and his thick and lustrous coat. The pilchards had just been the icing on the cake. And to him a metaphor was surely there to be mixed. He was full and happy and ready for any meanderings Maxwell wanted to throw at him.

'So, Count,' Maxwell began, sprawling on the chair opposite in as near to a postural echo as someone of a different species could manage. The cat smiled, as only cats can, pouching his cheeks and narrowing his eyes. 'What names are on that list? And is the murderer's name there, or the murderee? Both? Or, for goodness' sake, neither? It's the *List of Adrian Messenger* all over again. Only totally different. She might have been wearing someone else's coat. Or have been put in it. Remember what happened to dear old Edgar Allen Poe.' Metternich didn't, but he wasn't giving the old duffer the satisfaction of admitting it. He started to get up, then subsided. 'Oh, Metternich, go and get it, will you? She'd probably give it to you, no messing. As far as I can see it, we are looking for Lara Kent's stepfather's name, or anyone they could find from Lara Kent's phone. Also, it could be anyone connected with the Lunts. The Blackwells. Someone who had once bought chips or a camera. The whole population of southern England, in fact.' He looked at the cat, stretched full length and dozing off. He poked him in the soft bit just under his arm. 'Don't go to sleep when I'm talking to you. I need ideas. I need...'

The door flew back on its hinges and Jacquie stood there, the list screwed up in her fist. 'Max,' she said. 'You must see this.'

He turned his head away. 'Must I?' he said, in his hurt voice. 'Shouldn't you discuss it with Henry first?' He was bridling better than Kenneth Williams.

'I'm phoning Henry in a minute. For now, *you* must see this.' She thrust the piece of paper under his nose.

He pushed it away. 'Not so near! You know my arms are too short for my eyes.' He groped for his newspaper reading glasses, shoved down the side of the chair and smoothed out the paper. 'Hmmm ... Mrs Smith. I don't *think* so! N Leopold. Unusual name for Leighford. More suited to the Belgian Congo. Hmmm...' He sat up straight. 'Adair plus one! Blackwell plus one! M Crown. No plus one – that's odd. Oh God, Jacquie!' He looked up into her eyes. 'Dierdre Lessing. Also not plus one.' He remembered the police description. 'A lady of a certain age. You don't think...'

'I hope not, Max. We've been lucky once. Let's hope it's our week to be lucky again.'

Maxwell sat thunderstruck. It didn't have to be Dierdre. In fact, it would be easy to check if it was Dierdre. He picked up his little black book of school numbers, also stashed down the side of the chair. He dialled. No reply. But that meant nothing. Dierdre filled her leisure time with the mad absorption of a woman who didn't want to think too much. She was probably out, crown green bowling, potting, watercolouring ... something improving at Leighford Tech. He put the phone down slowly and got up.

'Ring Henry, Jacquie. We need to check this. And also the fact that Gregory Adair was there. Dierdre has had problems with him for a while. Apparently she has seen him around with someone she feels is inappropriate and ... well, seeing their names together like this on the same list, it makes me wonder.'

'Mike Crown is there too,' Jacquie reminded him.

'And probably, further down the list, a Mr R Herring. Before we get too far into this, let's get an ID on the victim. Then we might well have another suspect who fits the frame much better.'

Jacquie looked into his eyes, often so flippant but now deadly serious. She flipped out her phone and touched one number. She looked up. 'It's ringing,' she mouthed. Then, 'Guv? Hello, it's Jacquie. Umm...' she looked up at Maxwell and shrugged, apologising in advance. 'Well, the fact is, guv, Max has been a bit naughty.'

The phone twittered angrily.

'No, no. He's here, not snooping about. He did that earlier this evening.'

More twittering and Maxwell was sure he heard the word 'list.'

'Yes, guv, as a matter of fact, he did get the list. Oh? Of course, if you'd like to, you're more than welcome. When we see you, then. Bye.'

Maxwell didn't need to have the giant intellect he in fact possessed to know what was happening next. 'He's coming here?'

'Yes. Apparently, he was about to ring. He thinks you might be able to help the police with their inquiries. In the nicest possible way, of course.'

'Don't worry about setting my mind at

rest. I haven't always helped them in the nicest possible way. It's sometimes got quite nasty. And sometimes, *you've* been the nasty policeman!'

She had no answer. In the past, sometimes she had had to be. But somehow, she felt that the DCI would not be a nasty policeman either this time. Henry Hall had been touched by this case as she had never seen him touched before. He had shown a human side she had always suspected was there, but had never been allowed to witness. His boys had just got to the age when they were only dropping in these days, busy with their own lives, their own problems. She had a baby, totally trusting and dependent on her. Was there something about being at these extreme ends of the parenting curve that made them see each other in another light? And made them want to weep for the two dead youngsters, on the edge of the society most people inhabited?

She went to sit on Maxwell's lap and slid into her favourite place, tucked between him and the edge of the big armchair. His arm was round her and his cheek on her head. Everything was all right when she was curled into the curve of this man. And he felt safe too, with the warm, scented reality of her pressing against his side. They both could cope, like this. Something which had been bothering Maxwell rose in his mind and he turned his head to speak.

'Jacquie?'

He sounded so serious that she pressed herself against the arm of the chair to twist round and look into his face. 'What?' Her heart felt cold and heavy. He was about to say something to rock her world and she wasn't sure what it could be.

'Will...?' The bell sounded. She hopped off his lap.

'That will be Henry,' she said and rushed off down the stairs. 'He didn't waste any time.'

'That will always be Henry,' Maxwell muttered, getting up and putting on his 'welcome Henry' face. 'Come on, Count,' he said to the cat. 'Move yourself. Visitors. Either smarm around the ankles or go for the jugular. Your call.'

The animal looked round lazily, focused on Hall as he came into the room and subsided again. As long as it wasn't those two mad old biddies who made his eyes go funny, he didn't care who it was. As a gesture, he tucked one leg up a bit. He didn't fancy Hall's ankles after all and the man's jugular seemed a hell of a way above cat level of a February night.

Maxwell stepped forward. 'Come in, Henry,' he said, smiling. 'Take a seat. Just move the cat.'

The room held its breath. Just move the

cat? Hall sat gingerly alongside the huge black and white thing and then, to everyone's amazement, not least Metternich's, the animal began to purr and instead of clawing Hall's leg off, just leant against it and went back to sleep.

'Well, there you go,' Hall said. 'Cats don't usually like me much.'

'That will explain it, then,' said Jacquie, folding herself onto a stool at the side of Maxwell's chair. 'Metternich isn't really a cat, in the normal way. He's ... well, he's sort of Max's familiar, I suppose.'

'That's odd,' Maxwell said, sitting. 'I always thought I was his. Greddigut, Pyewackett, Pecke-in-the Crown all rolled into one.'

That's enough small talk, thought Henry Hall. He had wasted his usual weekly ration on this man already tonight. Business now. 'I understand you have the list,' he said.

'That's right, guv,' Jacquie said. 'I'm really sorry.'

'Don't be. It may save time. I've been working on it with Alan Kavanagh, but to be honest, it hasn't got me far. I suppose all this evening has done has given me a serious aversion to sardines. Sorry.' He looked down at the cat and was rewarded with a lordly nod. 'Do you have your copy? I have a spare.'

'That would be useful,' Maxwell said. 'Then we can all have one.'

Hall handed the piece of paper over and

Jacquie smoothed hers out.

'Right, then. There are some names we can immediately discount. Do you agree?' He looked up at them from his notes,

'Yes,' Maxwell said. 'Mrs Smith, for one.'

'A real Mrs Smith, in fact. I rang her. She enjoys Hugh Grant films and never misses, apparently.'

'Bless,' Jacquie breathed. 'N Leopold?'

'I've tried the number but there's no reply. It is a mobile and I suspect pay-as-you-go, as they don't usually have voicemail and this just rang until it cut off.'

'Is there any way to trace the number?' Maxwell asked. The niceties of mobile phone tariffs were a closed book to him.

'There may be. I've put Alan Kavanagh on it for first thing tomorrow.'

'Leopold is a bit of an unusual name. Is he in the phonebook?' Maxwell was still a great believer in the telephone directory. And cheque books, blue bags of salt in crisp packets and the thud of planes as they crashed through the sound barrier.

'No. Nor on the voting register. He could be just a visitor to town, I suppose.' Hall sounded doubtful and it was true that Leighford had little to offer the off-season visitor except ice cold winds off the sea and a firmly closed outdoor swimming pool. Perhaps some writer looking for local colour. After all, it had worked for John Fowles.

'Then we come to the names we know,' Jacquie said, moving it on.

'Yes, quite. Crown and Blackwell. Quite a coincidence,' Hall said.

Maxwell and Jacquie exchanged glances. 'And more than that,' Maxwell said. 'We have Gregory Adair, an NQT at Leighford High School, plus one, who could be the girlfriend of whom he speaks but whom no one has ever met. And Dierdre Lessing, a lady of a certain age who also works at Leighford High School and who has complained to me of Adair's personal lifestyle choices, that is, he is knocking about with people who she thinks are inappropriate.'

Hall continued to look at them, his expression unchanged.

'So,' Jacquie said, leaning forward, 'we don't want to think this, but we do; we think that the victim might be Dierdre Lessing.'

'Murdered by this Adair?' Hall checked. 'Why? Because she doesn't like his girlfriend? Isn't that a bit thin? And anyway, how do you know she's missing? Was she absent from school today? Was he?'

'That's the point,' Maxwell burst out. 'Leighford High was closed today because of huge numbers of staff absent. This bloody winter bug that's going round. So I don't know. And he's really short tempered. He even lost his temper with me, and everyone knows that that isn't a good idea. A man, I'd say, with a problem. Something to hide? Something that keeps him awake at night?'

'So let me get this right.' Henry Hall was nothing if not pedantic. He risked crossing one knee over the other, aware always of the sleeping Behemoth beside him. 'Despite the fact that there are two names on this list which have cropped up already, you have chosen two more to be the victim and murderer of the Arundel case.'

Maxwell beamed. 'Got it in not many more than one, Henry.'

'You are both entitled to your opinions, of course,' said Hall, preparing to get up and leave. 'But I think you are making the whole thing unnecessarily complicated.'

'Don't go, Henry,' Maxwell soothed. 'That's just one idea. Let's go down the rest of the list. See what else we find.' He felt Jacquie tense against his leg.

Hall settled back onto the sofa, with care as Metternich had encroached rather into the nice warm, space he sensed Hall was about to leave for him. 'Well, if you think...'

'Henry, thinking is what I do best,' Maxwell said and bent his head, to all appearances willingly, to the list. 'What else do we have, then? Hmm, quite a quiet night, Monday. Ooh, look. Hall.' He looked up, enquiringly.

'My eldest son, I believe,' Henry said tightly. 'Girlfriend's birthday.'

'How lovely. I suppose it is too much to

hope that he noticed anything.' Maxwell was all smiles. He didn't know the boy in that he had not gone to Leighford High; one of the very few under-twenty-fives whom Maxwell did not recognise.

Hall in his turn was suspicious of Maxwell when he was smiling, but he decided to take the question at face value. 'I'm afraid it is,' he said. 'He's a student and not terribly observant when out with his girlfriend.'

'Oh, a student? Lovely. What of?' Jacquie asked.

'History, as a matter of fact,' said Hall, a little crossly. 'With Archaeology, though,' as though that made it all all right.

'Historians usually make excellent witnesses,' said Maxwell. 'But if he has only just started at university, perhaps he hasn't had the Observation Lectures yet. Where is he?'

'Bath Spa.'

'Sorry,' Maxwell smiled. 'I thought you said university.'

Hall grunted and they continued down the list. Finally at the bottom, they all folded their respective pieces of paper and sat back, expectant. It was Hall who broke the silence. 'Well, any other thoughts?'

'Not really, Henry,' Maxwell said. 'Either it is Crown or Blackwell, though my money is not on Blackwell. I doubt the parents were at the cinema the night after their eldest son was murdered. In fact, I think if it were possible to check this list, it would turn out that Blackwell Junior wasn't there either. He certainly hasn't been in school this week. Although with the plague running wild, who knows? So, if my theory won't hold water, then it has to be Crown, and the victim has to be one of the female names on this list. Or, of course, one of the females not on the list but represented by "plus one". I do think, though, that anyone who takes someone to the cinema and then carelessly lets them get murdered by another member of the audience is actually a little remiss. Not much of an evening out, is it?'

'So, if it *is* Crown we're talking about, and if it is a named woman, then it has to be...' Henry ran his finger down the list, 'either N Leopold, who doesn't have a sex allocated...'

'...but was with someone,' Jacquie pointed out.

'...but who was with someone, or...' he looked up, beaten. 'Or, Dierdre Lessing.'

Maxwell tried not to look triumphant.

Jacquie leant forward and looked Hall straight in the glasses. 'Please, can't you get in touch with Chichester, guv? We've got school photos here, you could email a scan of one. Just to put our minds at rest.'

Hall hesitated. He didn't want to spin the case out. But if he did this he was helping Helen Marshall solve her case and probably not getting on much with his. Unless it was

Crown, of course, in which case he was dealing with a random nutter, in which case ... if the case wasn't spinning, his head certainly was. 'All right, Jacquie. Just to put your mind at rest.'

Maxwell looked at Jacquie and said, with little conviction, 'Can I help at all? With the ... scanning and things.'

She patted him on the shoulder. 'No, Max. Don't try and fool Henry that you know a scanner from a fountain pen. Just pour some drinks and hang on for a bit.' To Hall, she said, 'I'll just ring the nick, guv, and get the email for Chichester. Won't be long. Amuse yourselves for a bit, won't you?'

The two men sat looking into the space over each other's left shoulder. The room was so quiet that Metternich's breathing was the loudest thing. Occasionally, one of them would stir, as if to speak and then subside again. Their minds were nests of similar scorpions, writhing and twisting with all the possibilities of the situation. Almost on the edge of hearing, they could hear the soft whine of the scanner, the tap of keys.

They heard Jacquie go up to Nolan's room, on the floor above, heard her softly cross the bedroom floor. Only Maxwell knew when her footsteps stopped that she was hanging over the cot, softly stroking one soft cheek with one soft finger. Then, they heard her come back down the stairs in response to the soft beep that said 'you've got mail'. The wait seemed endless until she came back into the room, but neither man felt inclined to discuss the weather.

'I've heard back from Chichester,' she said, her voice strained and quiet. Neither man really needed to ask her what the answer was, but it had to be said out loud.

'And?' Maxwell asked; his voice sounded as if it was coming from the bottom of a well filled with jelly.

'I'm sorry, Max,' she said and a tear slid down her cheek. 'It's Dierdre. I'm just so sorry,' and she knelt at his feet and buried her face in his lap.

Hall cleared his throat. 'Were you close friends?' he asked Maxwell.

'Not in the least. In fact, over the years, she has been a thorn in my side so huge and embedded she has nearly been the end of me. But ... in recent years, we had developed a *modus vivendi*, shall we say. We rubbed along. But I'll miss her, I'll admit that. And no one deserves this. Murdered, dumped, unidentified. No one knew she was missing. No one tried to find her. Even the Troubridges looked out for each other and they hadn't spoken in decades. What's the world coming to, Henry?'

Henry Hall, who had seen first hand what the world could do, could only shrug. Maxwell was right after all, but Hall knew it would give him no pleasure. He had been involved in the case from the beginning and had obviously been bending his mind around it. But now it was personal. Now he was going to get results.

CHAPTER SIXTEEN

Peter Maxwell was helping the police with their inquiries. Not, this time, in the comfort of his sitting room, in the company of his cat and his policewoman, his baby son asleep upstairs. This time, he was in Interview Room Two, a stony faced Henry Hall across the table from him, a noticeably snide DS Bob Davies at his side. Peter Maxwell was not under caution. There was a tape running, but only because it had to be, courtesy of the politically correct brigade and a galaxy of smart lawyers back in the eighties who knew lucrative human rights lawsuits when they saw them. The sad fact was that, in all the world, Peter Maxwell knew more about Dierdre Lessing than anyone else the police could find.

'I still can't believe that her neighbours wouldn't help you,' Maxwell said to Hall.

'Apparently,' Hall said, 'she liked to keep herself to herself.' That wasn't quite what the neighbours had actually said, but as he saw it, there was no need to burden Maxwell with the actual wording. She lived on the new executive development off the Little-hampton Road, known to the hoi-polloi as Fort Rich Bastard. Dierdre, of course, must have had family money; there were plenty of bastards in the teaching profession, but none of them was rich. The women of Fort Bastard had been a little more blunt than the men, but it boiled down to the fact that, although Dierdre hardly had the time of day for the people who lived nearby, her bed-room door had been a revolving one. Henry Hall was old-fashioned enough to think that a senior teacher, and one who was looking retirement squarely in the face, should have a little more gravitas. But that said more about the teachers he had had in the long ago classroom than about any moral stance he chose to take. They lived in cupboards then and the raciest of them went to the yet-to-be-exploited Tenerife for their holidays.

'The Dierdre I knew was a bit more complicated than that,' Maxwell said. 'She was a martinet at school, but by all accounts she could give most men a run for their money in her day. Even now, she could usually catch them, however fast they were running. We had a conversation at school the other day and she ... implied, shall we say, that she saw Gregory Adair when she –

and he – were both out on the town.'

'Did she have anyone regular? A man in her life?'

'These days, I think not. Dierdre was, in the hackneyed phrase, a bit needy on the emotional front. She pushed people away, but was always looking for affection. When she got it, she didn't know what to do with it. She has caused a lot of unpleasantness over the years; she was the queen of innuendo and ill founded gossip.'

Peter Maxwell was being as honest, but as kind as he could. He didn't mind speaking ill of the dead; as an historian he'd been doing that for years. But Dierdre and he went back a long way, sparring partners in the ring of nastiness that was a school staffroom. He had always said that her office was littered with the bones of the lesser men she had chewed up and spat out. Now, she would soon be bones herself. And he thought of all the little moments when he should have been more generous, more chivalrous, behaved more like the public schoolboy he was. Now, as he saw it, he had a job to do – to help Henry catch her killer. But even as he sat facing the man, Peter Maxwell was a little ashamed. Perhaps he always would be.

Davies piped up. 'But you, Mr Maxwell, can't be a stranger to that sort of thing.' He tapped a thick file in front of him on the desk. 'This is all about you, you know.

Suspicion. Rumour. Innuendo, as you say. You can't blame people for beginning to think there may be something in it.'

'All those pages,' Maxwell beamed mischievously. 'Well, it's nice to know I've made an impact.'

Hall turned to his DS, then spoke to Maxwell over his shoulder. 'Excuse us a moment, Mr Maxwell, would you?'

The chairs scraped back and they were gone. Maxwell sat for the required moment. He would have loved to have flicked through the file on the desk, but he knew that eyes would be watching behind the two-way mirror. And he wouldn't put it past Hall to leave the thing there as a trap for the unwary. Next, Maxwell toyed with performing a series of antics in front of said two-way mirror, culminating in a sign originated by the archers of Agincourt and made famous (the wrong way round) by Mr Winston Churchill. But that would have been childish. In the end, he just sat.

In the corridor outside, the DCI lowered his voice, but just a touch. 'Look, whatever your personal beliefs may be, Mr Maxwell is here of his own free will to help us get some kind of handle on the victim. He was a colleague. He is upset. We will not be doing any bullying.'

'At this time,' added Davies.

Hall closed to his man, the blank glasses

inches from Davies' nose. 'Or at any time. Please bear that in mind. Peter Maxwell could have you for breakfast, Davies. And if he doesn't, I'll have you for lunch.' He led the way back to the interview room. 'I'm sorry about that, Mr Maxwell. You were saying?'

'Well, Detective Chief Inspector Hall. I really was just saying that hardly any of us knew Dierdre on a social footing. She said she saw Gregory Adair out in Leighford with someone she considered unsuitable. He took offence when it was raised but we don't know who this unsuitable person was or where they met. It may have been a random sighting in the street. This is a small town, as they go.'

'What do you think of Mr Adair?'

'Well, I hardly know him, either. As I told you earlier, he lost his rag when I asked him about what Dierdre had seen. I saw him myself as well, on another occasion, but couldn't see who he was with. Teachers have to be careful, but he's young, not much older than the Year Thirteens he teaches. I don't think the sky would fall in if he mixed with them socially. Anything more, of course, would be different.'

'You'd say he has a hot temper?'

'Well, he's rather moody,' Maxwell mused. 'But I don't think he would hurt Dierdre. Let alone kill her and transport the body to leave it on some disused railway line. And if you're trying to link the three killings together; well, what would be his motive for Lara or Darren?'

Davies snorted. 'Well, it's that bleeding photographer, innit, for those two? It's just pinning it on him.'

Hall, without turning, spoke. 'Davies. Get out.' All the finesse had vanished now. He'd given the man some rope and now he'd hanged himself; there was nothing to do but wait the statutory hour of old to make sure that death had occurred and cut the moron down. 'We do not "pin" things on people. Mr Lunt has spoken to me at length and I am confident that he is not the murderer. Or an accessory.' He had seen, out of the corner of his eye, Davies open his mouth to interrupt. 'Please send Alan Kavanagh in.' The detective sergeant made no move to go. 'Now, if you don't mind.' There was a gravel in Hall's voice that Maxwell hadn't heard before. He was impressed; maybe he'd be able to handle Eight Eff after all.

Davies stamped out and Hall and Maxwell yet again were left facing each other, an awkward silence blossoming out from their closed mouths, palpable as a fog, mixed as a metaphor.

Finally, they both spoke together.

'I hope you didn't mind...'

'I hope you didn't mind...'

'No,' said Hall. 'Please. You first.'

Maxwell inclined his head. 'Thank you. I hope you didn't mind me half-inching that list. I did it by stealth, you know. It wasn't Sophie's fault,'

'I had no doubt that she was Maxwelled into it,' Hall said. 'And how can I mind, when without your meddling we would still be no further forward in identifying the ... sorry ... Dierdre? Chichester are very grateful, even if it has made further investigations much more complex. I was going to say I hope you didn't mind my calling you down here, on a school day and everything. It's just that you seem to know her best.'

'No problem,' Maxwell said. 'And it isn't a school day, as it happens. The school is still closed, due to so much staff absence. Viruses. Death, I suppose. Possible absconding, we have to allow for. They never tell graduating students school could be this interesting. I'm sure they'd have more recruits if they did. Stuff the golden hello – just tell them it's like an episode of *The Bill* and they'll be queuing round the block to sign up. At last there would be a reason to be a teacher other than long holidays, the undying gratitude of generations of talented children and their parents, the phenomenal pay and no heavy lifting.'

'You're taking this very well. I know it's just your way, but it's also why DS Davies and the others think you're ... well, they often think you did it.'

Maxwell laughed. 'And one day, I will have done. Just as I long for the day when Angela Lansbury becomes the mad axe-woman of Cabot Cove and Peter Falk says "Just one more thing" before arresting himself. Your problem, Henry, will be to know when that day comes.' They were silent again for a moment, then Maxwell added, 'And thank you for noticing. I'm never happy when someone dies. And I'm very sad for Dierdre. It's the thought of her all on her own, over in Chichester. What was she doing there? Not even a local end.'

'We're all on our own in the end, Max,' Hall said. It was hard to say which was the more surprising; that Hall had used Maxwell's name or that he had feelings on life's transience. Fortunately, before any further cliché could be added, Kavanagh walked in on a wave of last night's garlic and chilli.

'Did you want me for something, guv?'

'DC Kavanagh. Thank you for coming in. We are interviewing Mr Maxwell, not under caution, but simply because he was a colleague of the victim of the Arundel killing.'

Maxwell looked down at the pitted table top and traced a long gone coffee cup's memoir with his finger. Already it was 'was'. Poor Dierdre. He had spent years trying to work out what made her tick and now he probably never would. Unless the identity of her killer gave that final clue which made it all plain. Hall was filling Kavanagh in.

'We may be looking for one Gregory Adair, who was known to have some animosity towards Ms Lessing.'

Kavanagh looked blanker than Hall's glasses. 'Pardon, guv?' He reached for the safety of a chair.

'Adair. Didn't like Miss Lessing.'

'Oh. Right. Sorry, I just didn't ... hear.'

'That's all right,' Hall sighed, wondering anew what the hell they were doing in training these days. Maxwell knew perfectly well; he'd seen *all* the Police Academy films. 'Do try to keep up. Could you go and see if you can get Mr Adair's address from the school, or from County Hall if the school is completely closed?'

'Yes, guv.' Kavanagh was still looking at Maxwell with the stare that said 'you've done something and I'll get you for it'.

'Now, if you don't mind. Also, while you're checking with the school, can you see if you can find out what days Adair and Miss Lessing worked this week. Whether they were off sick or anything.' Kavanagh still stood there. 'Now.'

'Yes, guv.' The policeman seemed to come to and stepped smartly out into the corridor. He glared back at Maxwell through the viewing panel in the door.

Maxwell stared right back at him and the

man turned sharply and was gone.

'He doesn't like me, Henry.' It was a pure statement of fact.

'No. He does like Jacquie, though.' Fact again.

'Oh. The young lion wanting to rip the old one's throat out.'

Hall looked at him. Yes, he could see what Jacquie saw; an interesting, funny, intelligent and caring man. He also could see what his entire detective force saw; an irritating old git who had snared the best bit of tottie in the station. His casting vote was still officially an 'undecided'. 'A bit like that, yes. But more of a young lion wanting to bang the old one up for anything he can lay his hands on. However, we have gone off the point. You don't think Adair could have done it?'

'No. He would have stoved her head in and left her in her office. He is quick-tempered, but he's your spur-of-the-moment rocket man, not intrinsically nasty. What did he do? Kill her in a lay-by somewhere, take the body to Arundel, just to muddy the waters? Or was she killed there? Of course...' Maxwell was uncharacteristically coy.

'Come on now, Max,' Hall said. Having said the name and not had the heavens fall, he was getting more comfortable with it. Maxwell noticed and hoped the next stage would not be 'snookums' (they were both at a funny age). Not for a while, at any rate. 'Of course what?'

'It was a badly kept secret that Dierdre rather liked male company. She was very discreet, never brought anyone to staff do's or anything like that, but she certainly had been round the block a few times. And she preferred them young; by which I don't intend to imply anything that would be incompatible with her teaching position, but ... well, I'm not much of a one to talk, am I?'

Hall inclined his head in agreement.

'She didn't tend to keep her golden lads long though. They turned to dust quite quickly. I think she liked the novelty of the chase and just found the whole thing a bit boring when she had them in her clutches.'

'So. Lara Kent's stepfather was a bit that way, wasn't he? Enjoyed the attentions of the more mature lady, as he probably puts on his message board.'

Hall was stunned. Maxwell had just made an Internet connection.

'Don't look at me like that, Henry,' Maxwell chuckled. 'Just because I can't do it doesn't mean I can't speaka da lingo. I can't climb the Eiger either, but I've read accounts of men who have. If I couldn't, most of my classes and I would have lost any common language years ago. But, do you see my point? Dierdre went out looking for toy boys. Mike Crown went out looking for older women. In a smallish world, they may well have met. And I suspect that on at least one occasion, that meeting took place in the deluxe screen in the Leighford multiplex. Hence, no plus ones for either of them. Didn't you ever go to the pictures for nookie, Henry? I didn't, of course; I went to see the film.' He sat back, arms folded.

Maxwell still didn't think Mike Crown did it. He still believed all three murders were connected, logically, not by virtue of them all having met the schizophrenic madman that Mike Crown would have to be under his urbane exterior. But it would give Hall something to chew on while he, Peter Maxwell, got on with the business of finding the real killer. He needed time, time with Metternich, time with Jacquie, time with his plastic Light Brigade, chewing over time, when he could link all the loops of mail and knit himself something a bit more cast-iron than a tune going through his head and a nagging suspicion that he had missed a glance, a nuance, a touch of a hand. It was like having an itch in the middle of his brain. He needed to get home to scratch it.

Henry Hall got up slowly. He extended his hand. 'Thanks for coming in,' he said blandly. 'We'll keep in touch.' He switched off the tape recorder.

So, thought Maxwell. That's what it boils down to. Get the answer and get rid of Maxwell. Never mind. 'Don't mention it, Henry.

Glad to have been of help.'

As soon as Maxwell let the door swing closed behind him, hurrying towards the light, Henry Hall reached for the phone. 'Get me Helen Marshall at Chichester,' he said. 'Put her through to my office. I'm on my way back there now.' He stood up and looked thoughtfully at the chair just vacated by Peter Maxwell. They were old sparring partners now and for a moment he wondered whether this was just a Maxwellism to throw him off the scent. He shook his head; no, this time he must want the wheels to move smoothly. This time, it really *was* personal. He went off to get his phone call.

Maxwell went down the steps of Leighford nick, settling his scarf more tightly round his throat. It was now hours until half term, the most dreaded one, when snow and weather mayhem most often hit. He remembered one, many years ago. The school was just reaching that peak of hysteria that prefaced any break-up day, no matter how short the coming holiday was. The air was electric with suppressed excitement. The half term slog from Christmas up through the wet and miserable months of January and February had been long and tiring. Mock examinations, unit tests, parents' evenings, coursework collection. Suddenly, the cry went up. 'It's snowing!' Thirty Year Eights had

313

overturned desks and chairs and run to the windows, where they pressed their little winter-snotty noses to the glass. And there, like feathers floating down, were the biggest snowflakes Maxwell had ever seen. They didn't drive stabbing on the window like the little frozen bullets that usually came this late in the year, halfway between rain and slush. No; they came down lazily enough, but with the clear intention of muffling the whole town in a white blanket of beauty, covering everything and making it new. In that year, he had no Jacquie to go home to. Metternich wasn't even a twinkle in some evil tom cat's eye. Nolan was a dream not to be dreamt, for fear of it never coming true. So, he had let the kids go early and had walked out after their dancing feet, to ride home slowly on White Surrey through the thickening flakes. The whole town was clothed in white and great gouts of snow hung on every branch. Roads were almost impassable within half an hour and Leighford ground to a beautiful halt.

Fairyland turned to nightmare when he got home; it was the Night Before Shopping, and, all through the house, there was nothing to eat, not even a mouse, this being pre-Metternich. That weekend, Maxwell tried to kid himself he was empathising with the starving defenders of some beleaguered Crusader castle. Did it ever snow in Jerusa-

314

lem, he wondered? Or Malta? In fact, he was eventually reduced to eating a very elderly tub of glace cherries at the back of the cupboard before the thaw set in on the Monday and he was able to get out. He had felt a bit of a wuss actually. His own schooldays were in the Midlands, which were sodden and unkind. In the Granta days, he had stood at the gates of Jesus with Cambridge winds whistling in from Siberia. But the usually warm south had knocked all that grit out of him.

This morning he could feel the chill of impending meterological disaster in the wind off the sea. So much for global warming. So, with his near starvation in mind, he was turning towards Asda when he heard his name being called in a hoarse stage whisper. He turned in the direction of the voice.

'Max. Over here.'

'Jacquie?'

'I'm over here, in the smokers' shelter.'

He made his way round the corner of the building and there stood the light of his life, wrapped against the weather and ankle deep in dog ends.

'Max. What did you tell them?' She kissed him briefly.

'Just that Dierdre rather liked younger men. And that Mike Crown liked older women. The rest, Henry made up for himself.'

'Max, that wasn't very nice. About

Dierdre, I mean.'

'Jacquie, my love. Dierdre *did* like younger men. They were her hobby. Instead of, oh, I don't know. Knitting. Embroidery. Persian cats.'

'No, honestly? I always thought that was just you being rude.'

'No, that was me being honest. She would probably have told you as well, if you'd have got her as drunk as I did at the Christmas Party 1989.'

'Max!'

'Well, she got herself drunk. I was just there when she decided to tell someone. I may have told her the punch was alcohol free, but what I meant to say was that it was alcohol and it was free. The rest is History.'

'So Henry is off to interview Mike Crown?'

'He didn't say. But I expect so.'

'So ... you really have solved the case!' She leant up and kissed his cheek. 'Well done!'

'Your congratulations are a little premature,' he said, 'but thank you for them all the same.'

'Well, it will soon be all tied up.'

'No, I mean, it isn't Mike Crown.'

'What?' She stepped back and crushed an abandoned Zippo underfoot.

'No, it's a lot more sinister than that. I think there is a link between the three killings. There have been too many links in this chain and I keep catching them out of the corner of my eye, so to speak. I just feel that someone is dropping clues for me, like Hansel leaving crumbs in the forest. And so far, either I haven't seen them all and I've taken a wrong turning, or the murderer is being a bit mean with his bread. But I'll get him.'

'Or her?'

'No, not her. I don't think these are women's crimes.'

'Sexist pig.'

'Very possibly.' He rearranged his scarf and squared his shoulders. 'But meanwhile, I am going into town for provisions, against the day. Don't like the look of that sky.'

'Max, I did a huge shop only two days ago.'

'Do we have milk?'

'Plenty.'

'Bread?'

'Freezer's full of the stuff.'

'Cheese?'

'Smoked, mousetrap, e-number squeezy and goat.'

'Goat? Oh, Jesus! Cocoa?'

'Are we planning a war movies weekend again? 'Cos Tesco were fresh out of Spam and Snoek.' Maxwell was quietly impressed that his light o' love should be familiar with the ghastly rations of the People's War, but he'd die rather than show it.

'No,' he said. 'We're planning a snowed-in

317

weekend. Believe these old bones and this long memory and remember where you heard it first. There'll be ice on the Front – "the foreskin of the sea" to quote R D Blackmore, who I always thought had a rather odd take on beach management. I'll see you *Chez Lui* later. Are you fetching Nole?'

'He's being delivered. Apparently, there's a party.'

'A party? What a little roué you have given birth to, Detective Sergeant Carpenter.' He turned to face her. 'As a matter of fact, on that subject, will you...?'

The door swung open behind them. The sour-faced DS Davies stood there, Benson and Hedges already between his lips. 'Oh, hello. Interrupting something, am I?' he sneered.

'By no means,' said Maxwell, smile pasted on. 'I'm not sure you have the intellect to be a gooseberry. I was just going.' He kissed Jacquie goodbye and strolled off in the direction of town, raising an arm in farewell to the nick in general. A bit of light provisioning and a lot of thought; it was what a walk on a cold February morning was made for.

He walked past several supermarkets as being too crowded. Asda was crawling; Tesco crammed to the doors. Lidl never sold anything he recognised and Somerfield was so cheap they regularly organised trolley saunters. Waitrose he passed because since

318

the change incident he was unofficially banned. Finally, he came to the shop he wanted; a nice little deli with doughnuts to die for and a rather nice line in hot chocolate, made with rather nice actual chocolate, not freeze-dried floor sweepings. Doughnuts and chocolate wouldn't keep the wolf from the door for long, but it would make the evening go with a rather cholesterol heavy swing and, who knows, oil the wheels of logical thought.

He pushed open the door and went in, to the spicy, slightly oily warmth of the delicatessen. The counter of chilled foods drew him as usual and his short list grew by several items. Marinated anchovies, obviously. Some nice chorizo, for one of Jacquie's eye-popping cassoulets, just the thing to keep the cold out. A nice piece of Stilton, to be eaten in secret by him, before she got home, the only British thing he could see. Jacquie had never quite embraced the idea of a cheese allowed, no, encouraged, to go mouldy. What was the point on a sell-by date when the stuff had mould all the way through? He looked up and stepped back in amazement.

'Nicholas! My word, what a hard-working chap you are. Is this your day job?'

'No, Mr Maxwell. It is my *job* job,' the boy smiled. 'I left the burger bar. Too violent and too greasy, in the end. And this is *proper* food, isn't it? What can I get you?'

Maxwell gave him his order. 'Oh, and six

doughnuts, jam, that is, none of that glazed nonsense. And a jar of that rather nice organic cocoa you do here. Thanks.'

The boy handed the carrier bag over the counter and took Maxwell's card in exchange. 'If you'd just like to enter your PIN, Mr Maxwell. Thanks.' A distant burst of music came from his jeans back pocket. A look of annoyance came over his face and he pulled out his phone and switched it off. He looked up to see Maxwell looking at him rather oddly. 'Not allowed at work,' he said, by way of explanation. It was the deli equivalent of those little blue bits of tacky kids had to wear over their piercings in the more populist establishments.

'No, I should think not,' said Maxwell. 'Or at all, in my opinion.' The boy remembered Mad Max's opinions from Leighford High. There was a rumour the old curmudgeon had a bucket of water in his office to act as a repository for phones such as Nick's. He took his card and raised the carrier bag in salute. 'Thanks, Nicholas. Um, tell me, do you youngsters still go to the cinema much?'

Nick laughed. 'If it's a good film, yes. Something that would be better on the big screen. *Spiderman. Lord of the Rings. 300.* Those sort of things. Otherwise, we usually wait for the DVD. Or the game.'

'Game?'

'You know, XBox, that kind of thing.'

'Oh, I see. But not all films are made into games, I shouldn't think. Like, ooh, a Hugh Grant film, that kind of thing.' He watched with interest as the boy blushed, a rising tide that washed up from the neck of his faux-Italian waiter shirt right to the roots of his hair.

'I shouldn't think so,' he muttered. 'Well, Mr Maxwell, I must get on,' and he bent over the chilled cabinet and started re-arranging random meats.

'Of course, Nicholas,' Maxwell said, making for the door. 'Ciao.' He thought it was a suitably delicatessen sort of signing off. Well, he thought to himself, I wonder who he was on that list on Monday night. Which of the plus ones represented Nicholas Campbell? He walked off up the street to the bus station, humming a very old Sixties song and feeling very much closer to something. He just hoped it was a solution.

CHAPTER SEVENTEEN

Friday night. Traditional Catholic fish and chips at Columbine, courtesy of Jacquie on her way home from the nick. Maxwell smelt the smell of grease and carbohydrate with a little less than his usual enthusiasm; five doughnuts in six hours will do that to a man.

'Max,' Jacquie called from the kitchen. 'Chips!' She stuck her head round the door. 'I got you a pickled onion.'

'Wonderful.' Maxwell tried to summon up his taste buds. 'I got you a doughnut.'

The crinkling of greaseproof paper came from the kitchen. 'It's an awfully big bag, Max, for one doughnut.'

He joined her, gathering salt, vinegar, sauces, both brown and red and some glasses for the obligatory Coke. He kissed her ear. Not deliberately; he was aiming for her cheek but she turned to get the plates from the cupboard. 'It had a friend. Some friends. I've been doing some thinking and somehow they just got eaten. Sorry.'

She turned and smiled at him. She patted his stomach, still amazingly flat bearing in mind his lifestyle. All right, he always taught standing up, but modelling was another matter. You can't do a Light Dragoon shako justice standing up, he always said. Nobody listened. 'A three doughnut problem; it must be serious.'

He pulled a rueful face. 'Worse than you think,' he said. 'It was, and remains, a five doughnut problem. Marvellous, isn't it? How we've come on since Conan Doyle's day? Changing the subject, is it snowing yet?'

'Max,' she said, moving him aside. 'It isn't going to snow. It's February.'

'Which often has snow. And what will poor Robin do then, poor thing?'

'As you say. But it isn't going to snow. Global warming.'

'Ha! A fallacy promulgated by the sellers of air conditioning. And Geography teachers who have so little to fill their lives.'

'If you insist. However, you'll excuse me if I get on with my chips and leave the snowshoe search until later.'

'That seems reasonable. What else have I got, other than a pickled onion?'

'Cod and mushy peas. I've got a pie. Swap?'

'No. Cod is fine. Food for the brain. Table?'

'Lap?'

'Lap it is.'

They took their meals into the sitting room and sat, trays on laps, for the usual Friday ritual. Except that this evening it was not as usual. It was the last day of a half term, so Maxwell would be at home for nine days, with a mind whizzing back and forth looking for mischief. Nolan was at his party, getting high as a kite on excitement and e-numbers. Any minute now he'd start jostling his hosts for the goodie bag. Metternich was next door, the still confused recipient of Miss Troubridge's adoration, shamefully wondering from time to time if he could, after all, get all her head in his mouth in one go.

Jacquie's pie was too hot to allow for simultaneous speech. The joys of the microwave. Maxwell's brain was otherwise engaged and so it was a silent meal. There was an air of expectation, of something waiting to be said and, finally, steak and kidney vanquished, Jacquie said it.

'So, who dunnit then, Max?'

Maxwell fiddled with a recalcitrant fishbone for a moment, not the best take-off of the Queen Mother he had ever done, then looked up. 'Dun what?'

'You know,' she said. 'Nolan is whooping it up somewhere else; he's not here to overhear you talking felony. So, tell me. Who's your money on?'

He finished up his last bit of batter and mushy peas and put down his tray with a contented sigh. He turned to her. 'Nothing quite like fish and chips, is there?'

'Max!'

'All right. Well, now. It isn't Bill Lunt.'

'We all know that, I'd like to think. Who else isn't it?'

'Me.'

'As before, I think...'

'Quite a few of your colleagues would like it to be me. Alan Kavanagh for one. Bob Davies for another.'

'Max? You've always enjoyed being in the frame before.'

He laughed. 'Yes. It's always about me,

324

isn't it? But, seriously, Jacquie. They really resent me, because they all fancy you.'

She stopped eating and looked at him. 'Oh, come on. Where did that come from?'

'Eyes, mainly. As you know, I invented body language. The languid smile that turns to a leer, that turns to a tongue on the floor – you know the sort of thing. But not just that – Henry Hall as well. Look, Jacquie, don't you think we might...?'

But Jacquie was off on one. 'I've never heard anything so ridiculous. They're colleagues, that's all. I've never given them even the slightest reason to...'

He clapped his hands, his way of getting the attention of anything from a cat to a king, by way of Nine Pee Queue. 'Jacquie. I wasn't suggesting you encouraged them. I was merely pointing out that they are seriously annoyed at having their most gorgeous woman policeman shacked up with an old git like me. Moreover, an old git who is closer than they would like to rather a lot of dead bodies. The way they see it, sooner or later, I will, in fact, be the guy.' He had to stop watching *Monk*. One day, he just knew there'd be an episode called Mr Monk and the Very Irritating Teacher.

Jacquie came over to him and sat on the arm of his chair. She rested her cheek on the top of his barbed wire head. She put her arms round his neck and murmured, 'Is that true?'

'What?'

She laughed and kissed him. 'That I'm gorgeous.'

He reached round and pulled her onto his lap. 'Damned straight. Now, woman, just take these plates out and come back and help me ferret a murderer out of my head. I know he's in there somewhere and I just need to think it through.'

'It's a shame there isn't some kind of Internet database like the one for TV and film, where you can just put in a few vague details and the answer pops out.'

Maxwell looked questioningly at her.

'You know, Max. You want to know an actor, for instance, and you know a film he's been in, so you put that in and you scroll down and find him. Then, you can click on him and ... what?'

'Well, for goodness' sake, you don't need to be Barry Norman to know that any film buff worth his salt could do that without clicking and nonsense. I can give you key grip, best boy and even wardrobe mistress for most of them, by the way. And so it should be with this damned case. I have so many facts it's embarrassing. I actually *found* the first body, for heaven's sake. There are so many people, so many clues, phones, scarves, lists ... but no links.'

'There are some.'

'I know there are similarities. Such as Lara

Kent and Darren Blackwell were homeless, she less so than him, but still of no fixed address. But what about Dierdre? She was hardly a down and out.'

'There's more than that. Darren's brother's phone number was on Lara Kent's mobile.'

'Did I already know that?'

'There's no reason why you should, but nothing would surprise me.'

'Why was that, do you think? Kevin Blackwell is still at school. He's unlikely to have met Lara Kent.'

'Again, Max, I must ask you if you actually work with children or just know about them on principle. They may behave tolerably well in school, especially if they know you are on the case. But they are all after one thing...'

'I know all about that. Apparently, it has actually been known to happen in some lessons. Maths, mainly. And mostly towards the back. In my day, it was all about bike sheds.'

'...and that is to be taken for someone years older than they are.' She ignored him. 'They probably met in some pub, or club or something.'

'That would hold water if Kevin Blackwell looked older than his years,' Maxwell sipped his Coke as if it were a rare Benedictine. 'But in fact he is particularly fresh-faced, except for the spots, which presumably are the result of being impregnated with chip fat. He works in one of his parents' shops some nights, I believe. The Cod Delusion – down on the Front. Against my wishes, needless to say.'

'Well, it's down to him that you got that free pickled onion,' Jacquie pointed out.

'Generous to a fault; I teach him critical thinking, document handling, a thorough understanding of the intellectual pursuits and he gives me a pickled onion. Has he been questioned?'

'Everyone whose numbers we could identify has been questioned. Most of them – and there weren't that many – were just acquaintances. Kevin couldn't even remember her. He said he tends to just put numbers in his phone when he meets someone and then forget them, likely as not, the next day.'

'And had he?'

'Had he what?'

'Put her number in his phone.'

'That's not really the question though, is it? She had his number.'

'Now, *there's* a double entendre. But that doesn't mean he gave it to her. What if *Darren* gave her the number? What if *Darren* met her and wanted to stay in touch? He didn't have a phone. But his brother did. Before Darren could get to Kevin to explain what he'd done, he was killed himself.'

Jacquie looked him in the eyes, comprehension dawning in her face. 'I really don't know if we even checked that,' she admitted. 'I must...'

'Don't say you must ring Henry,' he said, almost sharply. 'Let's just get on with this brain storming...' He looked upwards. '...sorry, Gods of Political Correctness, I mean thought showering ... and see where we come out, shall we? So ... we have a possible connection between Lara and Darren. All we need is one between Lara, Darren and Dierdre and we've solved the case.' He sat back, content.

'Just one tiny thing, though, Max,' Jacquie pointed out.

'Yes? And that is?'

'Who murdered these linked people? And, more importantly, perhaps, have they stopped?'

Maxwell looked serious. 'I hadn't even thought about that,' he admitted. 'Why do we do that? Always assume a serial killer has stopped, with each killing. Of course he hasn't stopped. These killings might be just steps on a road, links in a chain that... Oh, there it goes again!' He stopped, and clutched his forehead.

'Max! Oh, Max, what is it?' Jacquie, heart in her mouth, flew to his side.

He looked up at her, with stricken face. 'Oh, sweetheart,' he said, 'I didn't mean to frighten you. There's nothing the matter. I just had another of those half-fired synapse moments. I *know* I know something. I just can't quite call it to mind. I'm fine. Really. There's life in the old dog yet.'

Relief made her snappy. 'Well, just don't be so melodramatic, Max. It scared me.' Sometimes, in the winter firelight, he looked every second of his ninety nine years. Other times, he was younger than Nolan – he could still outrun him. She went back to her seat. 'Where were we?'

But Maxwell had moved on, to something even more important than murder. 'I've been thinking, Jacquie. Perhaps we should...'

The doorbell broke into his sentence. Jacquie jumped up. 'That'll be Nole back from his party,' she said and they both went down the stairs to gather their little carousing boy into their arms.

Sure enough, the little bloke was at the door, fast asleep, covered almost from head to foot in sticky, chocolaty goo, on the shoulder of one of the nursery staff.

'He had a lovely time, Mr Maxwell,' said the girl, recognisable under her knitted Inca hat as a recent Highena. 'Mrs Maxwell. He might need a bit of a wash.'

Maxwell leant closer. 'Are you sure it's the right one, Rebecca?' he asked the girl.

She looked shocked, then recovered. This was, after all, Mad Max. She chuckled. 'Definitely,' she said. 'He's the only one left so he must be yours, by a process of elimination.'

Jacquie took the boy from her and his head lolled against her shoulder, into his, and her, favourite spot. 'Come on, little'un,' she murmured to him. 'Bed, I think. The wash can wait until tomorrow.' Maxwell secretly wished *he'd* had a mummy like Jacquie. She kissed his chocolate cheek. 'Mmm, chocolate.' Her Homer Simpson was coming on in leaps and bounds. Maxwell watched them go up the stairs and turned to Rebecca, stamping her feet and rubbing her hands together.

'Cold enough for snow, Rebecca?' he asked her.

'It's February, Mr Maxwell,' she said. 'A bit late for snow, isn't it?'

'Aah, a child of the global warming generation,' he said, fondly. 'I'll be proved right, just you wait and see.'

'Well, goodnight, Mr Maxwell,' the girl said. She held out her hand and for a moment he almost shook it. Then he realised she was holding out a brightly coloured plastic bag, adorned with a tag. 'Nolan's goodie bag. From the party.'

'More chocolate?'

She grinned. 'No, no. Some parents have a no chocolate clause with us. So it has non-edibles in it. A door plaque, a toy ... suitable for his age, of course.'

'How thoughtful,' muttered Maxwell, actually thinking darker thoughts to himself. A no-chocolate clause? The world had gone mad and he hadn't even noticed.

'Not all parents are as...' she was stuck for a word.

'Casual? Hippy? Dangerous?'

'...normal,' she continued, 'as you and Mrs Maxwell. They read a lot of magazines,' she confided. 'We have to be careful. Anyway, night night.' And off she went down the path, the tassels on her hat bouncing cheerfully.

Maxwell closed the door and went up the stairs. 'Me and Mrs Maxwell. Normal. Hmmm.'

He went into the sitting room and poured himself a Southern Comfort. It was early, but it was cold and his brain needed a bit of soothing. He swirled the liquid in the glass and stared into its amber depths. He could hear the burblings from the baby alarm in the corner, soft snatches of singing, a single sharp cry from Nolan, shushed by his mother and then just quiet breathing and the distant sound of a door softly closing and footsteps on the landing getting quieter. Then they got louder, but in the real world, not through the fluffy filter of the loudspeaker. And Jacquie was in the room, a smear of second-hand chocolate on her cheek. Maxwell decided not to tell her about it. It might come in handy if he got hungry later on.

'Asleep?' he asked her.

'Like a log. I'll give him his bath in the morning. I've never seen chocolate in so many places before. It's even up his nose. He must have bathed in it.'

'He's your son, all right.'

'I expect he'll come on to Southern Comfort soon enough,' she smiled, tapping the glass as she sat down opposite him. The soft thunk of the cat flap downstairs announced Metternich's arrival. They glanced at the clock. 'He's early,' observed Jacquie.

'Because of the snow, I expect,' Maxwell said.

'Max.' Jacquie threw her head back in exasperation. 'It isn't snowing. It isn't going to snow. It's February.'

'As you say. But we'll see. Anyway, to get back to these murders.'

'Yes. Where were we?'

'Links.' He crossed to the drinks cabinet and poured her something or other left over from Christmas. Southern Comfort he only kept for special people. 'How are they linked? We suspect a link between Lara and Darren and it will be easy to check on whether Kevin has her number on his phone. We need a link between Lara, Darren and Dierdre.'

'Or just Darren and Dierdre.'

'Sorry?' Maxwell looked puzzled, cut off

in mid stream.

'Well, you said they are like links. Links only attach to the next one along, not to all of them. If that was how it worked, you wouldn't get a chain, just random tangles.'

He sat up straight, slopping his drink on Metternich who had curled up on the pouffe at the side of his chair. 'Sorry, Count,' Maxwell said absently. All in all, the cat was used to it. 'That's it! We should be looking at a link from Dierdre for the next murder. It might be just as tenuous as that she taught Darren at school.'

'That means it could have been any one of sixty or so people, then. I don't suppose she was his only teacher. It might have been you, anyone.'

'No, not me,' he told her. 'Darren chose sciences, before he gave up on everything that is.' He subsided back into his chair. 'Rats! Sorry, Count,' he said again, on a reflex. They usually spelt out rodent-related words to avoid over-exciting the great black and white animal. But Metternich was intent on licking Southern Comfort out of his fur and might not be coherent for the rest of the evening. 'That's not it, then.' He sat, pulling thoughtfully at his lower lip.

'If it was simply that Lara and Darren met somewhere, could that not be the link between Darren and Dierdre. You did say she preferred...'

Maxwell sprang to the dead woman's defence. 'No, no. Don't misunderstand me. She preferred men younger than her, not boys. I mean, *I* came into the younger than her category. Though, I admit, only just. Thirties, even forties, were her choice. Just a bit less...' he patted his midriff regretfully, thinking of the doughnuts and grease he had packed into it that day, '...spongy, than the men in her generation.' He looked up and smiled, the boy peeping through the age-old eyes.

'I didn't mean to insult her,' Jacquie said, recognising the tactic, deflecting the serious with the comic. 'I just wondered. Perhaps they might have just ... I don't know, chatted in a bar, or something.'

'That's certainly possible,' Maxwell said, 'Where, though? And when? And who saw them? It would have to be someone who knew who Dierdre was, wouldn't it?'

'Not necessarily. She was quite memorable, I suppose.'

'Yes. She certainly had a rather unique lizard-like quality not often seen in the urban setting. Third eyelid and so on – the basilisk stare.' He thought for a moment. 'And she did like a little drinkie, so I'm told.'

'Like at the 1989 Christmas party?'

'Very like that,' he agreed, raising his drink in honour of Jacquie's CID memory. 'So, we need to find out where Darren liked to drink and see if it was Dierdre's kind of stamping ground. I don't think she was much of a slummer.'

'But, if she was meeting people ... younger men, Mike Crown perhaps, then she wouldn't go to her normal haunts, would she? What if she met someone she knew? You're always warning people about shitting on their own doorsteps, but then, you know some funny people.'

'True. Oh, round in circles again. You know, Supreme Being, I almost begin to hope for another murder. It's hard to see a pattern with only three.'

'Max! That's terrible!'

'Agreed. And, to save having to wait for someone else to die, why don't you check for anything *before* Lara Kent. See if that fits the pattern.'

'And how do you suggest I do that?'

'Nip in to work and look on your Differencing Machine. Print it off and bring it back here, to the nerve centre, the giant brain. The Count and I will watch the boy and await your return with bated breath.'

'No. I won't do it. Henry would go mad. Everyone will have gone home. It's Friday, after all, and the investigation into Dierdre still belongs to Chichester.'

'Yes, and when I've had a coupla drinks on a Saturday, as the old song goes, "Glasgae belongs tae me." So they will all have gone home. Smashing. You won't be disturbed, then.'

'Max, I just won't do it. And that's final.' She reached over and took a swig of her drink. 'There! I can't go, now. I've had a drink. I can't drive.'

'You had one mouthful of Tia Maria on top of pie and chips and a doughnut. I think you're still all right to drive.' He closed his eyes and began to whistle soundlessly. After a minute he opened his eyes. 'Are you still here? Oh, wait! What's that sound. I don't … no, I've worked it out. It's the sound of someone being strangled, bludgeoned or otherwise being done away with. Oh, good. That's something else to help us catch the killer of three … oh, no … four people.' He closed his eyes again and this time, hummed a tune, in a very Maxwellian – in other words, tuneless – way. It sounded vaguely Stravinsky.

She stared at his impassive face for a moment and then suddenly stood up. 'If I get found out, Peter Maxwell, you are going to be *so* sorry.'

'Yes, indeedy. But you won't be found out, will you?' He opened his eyes and smiled. 'Hurry back. Or you might get snowed in.'

'Snow, be buggered,' she muttered and then threw a cushion at him before storming off down the stairs.

He heard the door slam. 'Right, Count,' he

said. 'Let's get that brain of yours working. We need to have more or less solved this one before she gets back. Or no more pilchards for you.'

The cat twisted his head round to fix Maxwell with his golden eyes.

'I said no more pilchards. The Bobsey twins spoilt you, but I won't.' He met the amber gaze implacably. 'I won't.' Metternich extended a lazy paw, velvet wrapped around iron-tipped claws. They flexed into the sensitive bit just inside Maxwell's knee, 'The hell I won't.' John Wayne had never moved so fast as Maxwell as he leapt to his feet. It was also unlikely, or at least had never appeared in any biography, official or unofficial, that John Wayne had ever opened a tin of pilchards. But if he had, it would not have been with as much panache as did Peter Maxwell.

CHAPTER EIGHTEEN

Jacquie drove to the nick, her brain almost steaming with mixed feelings of annoyance and excitement. Looking back was something that almost always happened automatically when a murder was detected. But the speed with which the three in this group had happened had somehow interrupted the flow and, as far as she knew, no check had been made into similar crimes in the recent past. And of course, as bloody always, Mad Max was right. Like everything else in life, killing took practice. You learnt as you went. The time, the place, the target. Nothing was certain, nothing could be left to chance. But the first time was always going to be trial and error. There was no blueprint, no murder simulation room with mock-up victim and a *Murder For Dummies* lying on the table. If this was a serial killer, the chances were that Lara Kent was his *second* victim, not his first.

The good news was that there was only one car in the CID area of the car park. The bad news was, it was Alan Kavanagh's. Still, she thought as she made her way up the back stairs, he was not likely to be in the office. He was probably just in the canteen, prior to going home. She pushed open the fire door at the end of the corridor and saw, with sinking heart, that a light was on in the incident room. Never mind, just brazen it out.

'Hello, Alan.' Breezy, workmanlike, that would suit the situation best.

He looked up and his face lit from within. 'Jacquie! What brings you here?' He checked his watch,

She had the urge to say, 'Not you,' but decided against it. In fact, suddenly, she felt it necessary to give him the accurate, un-adorned truth. 'Max and I were talking and he had an idea. So, I'm here to check it out.'

'A bit of freelancing, eh?' Kavanagh said in what he imagined was a roguish way, trying to remember if he'd combed his hair that day. 'Can I help?'

Again, she considered her options and decided on the simplest. 'Why not?' She needn't tell him much. And, as not exactly the brightest copper in the small change he wouldn't add much of his own, but as another pair of eyes, another scrolling finger, he might serve. 'I need to look back to see if there are any recent murders that might have a link to Lara Kent.'

'What sort of link?'

'That's the problem. I don't know. I think if we start with really recent, such as in the last ... what do you think, three months? Murders, of course, but assaults too. Anything with a youngish victim for starters.'

Asked for an opinion, he was rather stuck, so settled for a simple, 'That should do it.'

'And South Coast based. Let's not go into London, that would be too wide.'

'OK.'

'So, Alan, let's get this clear. November, December, January. South Coast, certainly no further north than Reading. No further west than ... let's say Bournemouth. Don't bother with Kent – excuse the pun – I think that's too far. Don't worry about category for now. So, any age, either sex. And, Alan?'

'Yes?'

'Unsolveds only, obviously.'

'Obviously. Er, why only unsolved?'

She sighed. This might take longer with two, when the two included Alan Kavanagh. 'Because, Alan, if the crime has been solved, then that person cannot have committed our crimes, hmm?'

'He can if the person they got didn't do it. No crimes committed in the last three months have come to trial yet. So, they might have the wrong man. Or woman.'

Jacquie was stunned. She did a quick reappraisal of Alan Kavanagh. 'True. Well spotted, Alan. All right, solved and unsolved.' She bent to her screen as her computer ground into life. Blimey! What a dark horse. Then, her preconceptions were replaced, intact.

'How are we going to do this, Jacquie?'

'Pardon?'

'How are we going to look these things up?'

'Using HOLMES, Alan. How else?'

'But, don't we need DCI Hall's say so before we log on to HOLMES?'

'Yes. As a rule. But we're doing a bit of personal work here, Alan. That's what it's all about – thinking outside the box.'

He put his hands in his lap, like a sulky

child. 'I'm not comfortable with this, then, Jacquie,' he almost whined.

She used her best Nolan-controlling voice. 'Alan. For goodness' sake. We are helping in this case. We will save valuable hours. We may even,' she lowered her voice so he had to lean closer, 'save a life.'

His eyes were like saucers. Jacquie was encouraged. She was obviously getting better at this. She had never managed to make it work on Nolan before. 'Whose?'

'Whose what?'

'Whose life?'

'Well, if we knew that, Alan, we wouldn't be doing this, would we? We could just put a police guard on them and then they would be all right. It's because we don't know who the next victim is that we are looking for clues in past cases.' She looked across him as he sat in front of his computer and saw total confusion. She sighed. 'Just log on, Alan, would you, and look for murders in the parameters I just set.' She thought through her last sentence. 'Look for murders where I told you, for those months.' Her screen was active and she finally logged on. 'Let's go.' She smiled up at him. 'Come on, Alan. Don't be shy. DCI Hall will be chuffed and it will be one in the eye for the others when you come out with the info.'

'You'd let me tell him?' Kavanagh was ecstatic. She must fancy him after all!

Jacquie saw a window from which she could leap to escape the undoubted fire of Henry Hall's anger. 'Why not,' she said, with faux magnanimity. 'I can see that sergeant's job for you, after all. After this you could name your price.'

'Cool!' Kavanagh bent to his task and soon his fingers were blurs. But, sadly, his printer remained silent, as did Jacquie's. Nothing seemed to fit and their initial enthusiasm began to dim. The room was filled with the tap of keys and the odd exclamation of delight, followed by the groan of disappointment. Whose idea was this, anyway?

Jacquie broke the silence. Without pausing in her tapping, she said, 'By the way, Alan, how did it go?'

He *did* pause. Multi-tasking was not his forté. 'How did what go?'

'Finding Gregory Adair. You know, the chap from Leighford High? The one we think may have been involved with Dierdre Lessing?'

Blank incomprehension.

'Alan? Do you work here? Are you *from* here? As in Earth?' She realised the extent of his confusion and made her question plainer. 'Alan. Did you do as I believe DCI Hall asked and try to find Gregory Adair?'

His reply was virtually inaudible, but she could read lips well enough.

'You forgot? Alan, I don't believe it. He only asked you to do one thing. How could you forget?'

He was distraught. 'I came out of the interview room and ... and DS Davies asked me to go and get a file. It took ages and, well, when I came back to the room, he'd gone and then ... well, I forgot.' He looked close to tears. He'd never be a DCI now. From where he was, even human being seemed to be in the dizzying heights above.

'OK, Alan, let's think this through. It might be all right. DCI Hall and my ... Peter Maxwell had a bit more of a chat after he sent you to find Gregory Adair. They may be on another tack, so try not to worry. But I think, in the morning, it might be an idea if you try and find him.'

'But tomorrow's Saturday,' he whined.

'Indeed it is, Alan. It is the day when DCs who can't find their arse with both hands catch up on the messes they created Monday to Friday. Meanwhile, get looking. There must be *something* that matches what we want.' And to show him how, she bent her head to her screen again and let her fingers do the walking.

Maxwell Junior had woken up. The chocolate on his cheeks was traced with the lines of angry tears. He was confused. One minute he was at some kind of mad running

344

about place, with chocolate falling from the sky and the kid with one eyebrow who darkened everybody's life, like the scythesman at his elbow. The next, he was hot and grumpy in a dark room. No people. No light. No chocolate and, worst of all, no mother! What was happening to his world? Why was he sticky? Where was everybody? Even the kid with one eyebrow seemed to have vanished. There was one quick way to answer all his questions and that was to yell. So he yelled.

Downstairs, deep in thought, Maxwell Senior nearly died of shock. The room had been so quiet, with just the slight static hum of the baby monitor and the pilchardy snoring of Metternich to break the silence. The sudden scream was so disorienting it took Maxwell a microsecond to remember that it came from his ex-sleeping son. He was up the stairs in double quick time, Metternich on his heels, although what the cat thought he could do being minus opposable thumbs, Maxwell was at a loss to guess. Perhaps the old black and white bugger intended to sink his fangs into Nolan's scruff and see how it went.

'Sshhh, Nole. It's all all right, old son. Daddy's here. Look at you, all chocolaty.' Maxwell looked down into the cot. 'Just like your bedsheets.' He held him further away. 'Oh, and your jamas. And daddy's shirt. How lovely. Mummy made a bit of a duff decision there, I think. Let's get you changed and washed and see how you feel then, shall we? Count, pass me a clean pair of jamas, would you? You can't? Oh, well, come and tickle Nole with your whiskers. You're good at that. Look, Noley, Metternich.'

The cat obligingly jumped up onto the edge of the changing mat and played 'Catch Metternich's Whiskers Without Getting Maimed' – Nolan's favourite game and one which he always won, thanks to the un-expected good humour of the most feared quadruped in Leighford. When you got to Metternich's age, you didn't get mad, you got mellow.

Maxwell, grateful for the help, changed, wiped, re-pyjamaed and soothed the little boy, but, after all the attention, he was awake and wanting more. More Daddy. More chocolate. More of something, which he sensed wasn't forthcoming. His lip trembled as Maxwell laid him back in his cot.

'Hmmm. What do you want, my little one?' Memory came to help him. 'A new toy? Would you like something new, Nolan? Bad lad, but still, we all have our off days, eh?' He picked him up and put him over his shoulder, as he had since the boy was one minute old. 'Let's go and see what we can find, shall we?'

'T'nick. Dada.'

'You've arrived,' Maxwell said to the cat, over his free shoulder. 'You are higher in the pecking order than me. Clever boy,' he said to his son. 'I'll assume that in fact you were after starting a conversation about the late, great Chancellor of Austria, rather than calling the cat. Come on, let's see where Daddy put the toy.'

Nolan had woken up totally now and was leaning over Maxwell's shoulder, grabbing air in the direction of the cat who, in his own quiet way, was chuffed to death that his Boy knew his name. A vole would go free tonight, in honour of this momentous day. It would be called Nolan's Day and it would be remembered for ever.

Going into the sitting room, Maxwell cast around in search of the lurid bag that Rebecca had handed him earlier. A small corner was sticking up from under a sofa cushion. One day, Maxwell promised himself, I will go through this furniture and become a multi-millionaire in small change. Meanwhile, he rummaged one-handed in the bag and finally brought out a small soft toy in the shape of a giraffe.

'Look, Nole. A giraffe. What shall we call it?'

''Raffe.'

'That seems fair enough. Though George would have been funnier. George Raffe. Get it? Surly film actor of yesteryear. Did that thing with a coin between his fingers. Oh, never mind. Shall we take the giraffe to bed? He looks tired.'

Nolan looked at the giraffe and then at his father. Was the old duffer daft or what? It was a stuffed giraffe and not very convincing at that. How could the thing look tired with its eyes stitched open? Hadn't his dad seen *A Clockwork Orange?* He stole a glance at Metternich, who winked one eye, imperceptibly. Nolan got the message and yawned extravagantly, as did the cat.

'Yes. That's it. You *and* the giraffe are tired. Up to bed we go.' Maxwell hoisted the boy aloft again and took him upstairs. To Nolan's astonishment, he was, in fact, shattered. It had been a hard day, what with socialising and such. He was asleep almost before his head hit his still chocolaty pillow.

Maxwell crept from the room and back downstairs. He was sorry now that he had sent Jacquie out into the night. Not only was it cold out there, but he needed to crystallise his thoughts. Still, he had Metternich. He wasn't great on ideas, but he was logical enough and a great listener. As sounding boards go, he made a good mouser. Maxwell threw himself down on the sofa and leapt up again almost as quickly. He had sat on the bag that had once contained Nolan's giraffe and now just contained his door plaque.

He sat down again, more carefully, and examined the piece of wood. It was rather well made, rectangular and, inevitably, painted blue. The child's name was in the middle in a rather fanciful script, which the teacher in Maxwell thought rather unhelpful to the boy, should he be searching for his own room and relying on the label. However, in the scheme of things, it was probably a little more landing-enhancing than a straight lower case n-o-l-a-n. Around the edge, there was a repeating pattern that seemed random at first. Then, as his eyes focused on it better, it resolved itself into Nolan's name, in the same letters, but joined together so that it ran together, on and on, until it joined up with itself to make an unbroken frieze. It then further developed as he looked harder, so that he could see that it still read, with a little imagination, the name upside down as well. How clever. Although his Light Brigade were to a man works of art, Maxwell wasn't artistic in the accepted sense. But, rather like Pope Thing XVI, he knew what he liked. And he liked this. He knew what it was called, as well. He had dipped into the *da Vinci Code* DVD at school; it was useful on so many levels in cover lessons. SRS, pondering the meaning of Christianity; History, learning fascinating facts about da Vinci, Isaac Newton, Alexander Pope; Maths, er ... you had to be able to learn *something* from Maths. You could even use it, he had discovered, to put whole classes to sleep. This thing was called a ... what was it, now, a chain ambigram? You couldn't do it with all names, just ones with a repeating letter or close to a repeat. Nolan wasn't perfect, but the 'o' could look like an 'a' if you added a little tail. Some names were impossible. Peter, for instance, unless your p's were very unusual; Jacquie; Henry. He started going through all the names he could think of as an idea began to form in his mind. Alan, as in Kavanagh. Possible, in fact really good, as the a's could intertwine. This also worked for Lara. Darren would need work. Maxwell pulled a piece of paper towards him. Yes, that would work, with the 'n' given an extra curl and the 'e' upside down looking like a Times New Roman 'a'. He scribbled faster. Dierdre was a gift. He hardly had to fuss with that at all. He rubbed his hand through his hair. What else? Oh God, what else? Emma. That worked. Greg. He reached for the phone and jabbed the speed dial for Jacquie's mobile.

'Hello?' Jacquie sounded far away.

'It's me. I know who's next.'

'What?' Jacquie stopped scrolling and flapped a hand at Kavanagh to stop tapping his keys. She wanted to be sure she heard this. 'Who?'

'Emma Lunt. Or Greg Adair. Or Alan Kavanagh.'

'Oh.' Jacquie couldn't help but look up at the unknowing colleague trying to look helpful across the room. 'So, anyone involved with the case, in other words.'

'No. Just them at the moment. I'm working out the ambigrams.'

'Pardon, Max. The ambiwhats?'

'Ambigrams. They can be used as a sort of code, but I think here they have been used almost as a ... well, a sort of divining rod, to choose who goes next. Look, Jacquie, just come home. Perhaps you could warn Alan Kavanagh if you have his number.'

'Oh, I do have his number. But wait.' She raised her head and looked at Kavanagh. 'Alan. You may be the next victim.'

'What?'

'Alan says "what?",' she said into the phone.

'He's there?'

'Yes. He's helping me look for previous. He's actually being quite useful.' It was hard to tell who was the most amazed to hear that, but only Kavanagh blushed.

'Well, bring him home with you, then. At least we'll know where one of the potential victims is if he is in our spare room.'

'Max, first Bill Lunt, now Alan Kavanagh. Thirty-eight is turning into a protection unit Safe House as we speak. Are you serious?'

'Deadly. Both of you, come home now. I know who might be next and I also know

351

who did it. Well, I know who it might be. I've got to tie it down a bit more first. I certainly know the general area where we ought to look.'

'Max, I...'

'Just get home, Jacquie. The Count and I will have it all sorted by the time you get here.' And he rang off.

Jacquie sat opposite Alan Kavanagh silently digesting what she had just been told. Which was, she had to admit, rather little and rather garbled. Even so, she came to a decision and stood up, reaching behind her for her coat, thrown over the back of her chair. She'd heard Maxwell's rendition of Charlton Heston's Major Dundee often enough to know when the man meant business – 'I have but three orders of march – when I say come, you come; when I say go, you go. And when I say run, you follow me and run like hell.'

'Come on, Alan. Log off, there's a good constable, and let's get out of here.'

'Where are we going?'

'Back to mine. When Max says I am sitting opposite a possible future murder victim, I don't leave that person sitting like a duck.'

'Me?' In a strange way, Kavanagh was quite elated. Someone cared enough to want to kill him. If only he had known how many minds that thought had been through, he would perhaps have been less pleased. It had begun with his childminder all those years ago. He tapped a few keys and stood up. 'Let's go.'

They clattered down the back stairs and out into the cold night. Frost ringed the windscreens of their cars and the waning moon shone through a halo.

'Shall I follow you?' Kavanagh asked, through chattering teeth.

'Keep close,' Jacquie said. She was keen to help Kavanagh avoid being murdered, but his choice of sandwich, on the most recent occasion clearly cheese and onion, made sharing an impossible option. 'It gets complicated after the Flyover.' The Ka purred out of the car park, watched by Ken Wertham, the desk sergeant in his glass boothed eyrie inside the front door. Kavanagh's Peugeot was in hot pursuit.

'Lucky bastard,' he muttered under his breath. Ken Wertham could jump to conclusions for England. Then he chuckled. Nice to see that bloody smartarse Maxwell getting one in the eye. Wait till the lads heard this!

CHAPTER NINETEEN

While he waited for Jacquie to get back, Maxwell did what any amateur detective would do, with a few minutes spare at their disposal. He got sheets of paper and headed each one with the name of victims, both actual and potential. He then threw them away as being far too anal, much too similar to writing frames for the less able and Bernard Ryan.

He picked up the phone and then sat there with it in his hand, uncertain of who to ring. He knew that Henry Hall would have been in touch with Leighford High. And anyway, despite all his years there, he had never been copied in to any of the really important phone numbers. Legs Diamond was so dogged by prank callers that he was so ex-directory he didn't even know his own number any more. The others, Year Heads and their Assistants, were ex-men. In fact, in a supreme irony, the only SLT member's number Maxwell knew had been Dierdre Lessing's, and he knew she wouldn't be there. He decided to ring Sylvia Matthews and dialled her number, which he had known off by heart since Adam was in the militia.

'Hello. You've reached the number of...'

Bugger and poo. But wait! He could progress along the 'find-the-victim' path by a rather circuitous route. He dialled Paul Moss's number and waited through what seemed a hundred rings. Finally, he answered.

'Moss.'

No matter how often Maxwell heard him say that, he always wanted to snap another member of the vegetable kingdom back at him. 'Lichen. Dandelion'. He restrained himself and simply said, 'Paul? It's Max.'

'Oh, hello, Max. Are you one of the stricken?'

'No, no, I'm fine. How are you?'

'I'm coming down with it, I think. Sod's law that I would, now it's half term.'

'Oh, that's too bad. Look, Paul, do you have Greg Adair's number?'

'Is this a wind-up, Max?'

'No. Should it be?'

'No, I suppose it wouldn't really be your style. But ... don't you know?'

'Come on, Paul. This isn't a game, you know. Have you heard about Dierdre?'

'No. What about her?'

'She's dead.' There seemed no other way to put it.

There was a long pause. 'Dead? An accident?'

'Murder. And I think Greg may be next.

355

Or at least, nextish.'

'Max, you're not making any sense. How can Greg be next?'

'Why shouldn't he be?'

'Well, he could be, I suppose. But he's in the high dependency unit at the hospital. He's got pneumonia. You can't murder somebody that way, can you? It started with the same virus that's going round, but it went a bit haywire. He called the doctor several times and just got given the whole "take paracetamol" routine from some paramedic Level Two type. By the time he was found, he was in a really bad way. It's touch and go, apparently.'

'My God.' Maxwell was genuinely gobsmacked. 'When was this?'

'Hmm. Must have been ... what's today? It puts me out when we're not at school.'

'Friday.'

'Right. Well, it must have been Wednesday evening he was found, then. But he'd been a bit off colour all week.'

'He was certainly very snappy when I spoke to him. He stormed off. He bumped into you, I seem to remember.'

'Well, I would imagine he already felt grotty, then. I know he went to the cinema on Monday and had to leave because he felt so unwell.'

That answered one question and asked another. It confirmed he was at the cinema, but raised the point that, unless Dierdre Lessing was totally mesmerised by the screen, she would have seen him, yet again, with his unsuitable other, giving him more reason to kill her. But, if he was already ill on Wednesday, he couldn't have killed her. He sighed. 'Thanks, Paul. Well, at least we know he's in safe hands.'

'Max, he's in an NHS hospital. How can you say that?'

'True. Well, safe as opposed to the hands of a murderer, anyway. Have a good break, now, and don't answer the phone to any strange men,' and he rang off, feeling more certain than ever that his sneaking suspicion might be the right one.

He had one more call to make. He was halfway through dialling when he heard Jacquie come in, talking in the hall in her usual way when she was not alone.

He stuck his head out of the door and called, 'Up here,' and carried on dialling. Again, the phone rang on and on. But this time, no one replied and the answerphone clicked in. He listened to the message, right through, but, after a breathy pause, rang off. As he did so, he realised he had just left an anonymous heavy breathing phone call. But, at this stage of the game, what could it matter?

He turned as Jacquie and Alan Kavanagh came in, rubbing their hands together and heading for the gas fire,

'It's really cold out there,' Jacquie said. 'But, before you say it, we are not going to have snow.'

'We'll see,' Maxwell said, smugly. He held out his hand and Kavanagh shook it. 'Glad to see you, DC Kavanagh. May I call you Alan?'

'Yes.' Kavanagh was pleased to see that Maxwell seemed quite normal. The house was not a Black Museum of all the cases he had worked on illicitly, with death masks of those Mad Max had sent down. There were no displays of weapons or poisons; not a chainsaw or six pack of strychnine in sight. In fact, the house was quite ordinary. He was suddenly aware that he had sounded perhaps a tad abrupt. 'Please do.'

'Any further forward?' Jacquie asked Maxwell. She lifted a bottle towards Kavanagh. 'Drink?'

'No, thank you.' Kavanagh was in best Sunday school tea mode, only speaking when spoken to and politely declining all offers of food and drink, for fear he should seem greedy. He was not nine stone wringing wet for nothing.

'I have discovered that Greg Adair is in hospital,' he remarked.

'What?' the policepersons chorused.

Maxwell raised his hands. 'It's all right; he's in Community General in the safe hands of Dick van Dyke. It's pneumonia. Since Wednesday. So, not only is he not in the frame any more, he is also, I should have thought, safe from any murder attempts. Although, come to think of it, it doesn't stop people in *Diagnosis Murder*.'

'So that leaves ... who?' Jacquie asked, daytime television not being part of her regular experience.

'Just Emma Lunt, by my reckoning. Although I suppose there may be some we don't know of yet.'

'Explain how you came by the list,' Jacquie said. 'That will be a start.'

So Maxwell gathered them round and, using two colours for simplicity, carefully drew out the chain ambigrams using the names of the previous victims and those he saw as potential ones. Alan Kavanagh had all the hallmarks of a Grade E GCSE; colour coding would help him enormously.

When he had finished, Jacquie pushed herself away from the table and blew outwards. Kavanagh was just silent. This was Jacquie's call. The old geezer was obviously barking mad.

'Well, Max,' she began. Here it comes, Kavanagh thought. She's thinking of a way to divert his attention while they waited for the men in white coats. 'It would take someone like you to spot that.'

Nice one, thought Kavanagh. Lull him

into a false sense of security before tying him up with a spare clothesline.

'We didn't look at the names. We looked at the lifestyles for a link.'

'Uh?' Kavanagh was puzzled. This wasn't how it was supposed to go. She seemed to think the mad old bugger was right. Perhaps she was still humouring him.

'Do try to keep up, Alan.'

Why did everyone keep saying that to him? He wasn't slow. He had an A level in Philosophy and Ethics to prove he could think. And critically at that.

'Did you not understand the ambigrams?' she said kindly. 'Would you like another explanation?'

'No! No, of course I don't. How can a fancy way of writing someone's name make them a murder victim?'

'Well, it doesn't,' Maxwell said kindly. 'It's just that, in a random population, where everyone bumps into everyone else all the time – crowded buses, supermarkets, pubs, clubs – if you, the murderer that is, if you just decide to kill people who have briefly met each other, you'd never be able to track who you were going to bump off next. But if you had some other criterion to go by...'

'...such as their name fitting a chain ambigram...' put in Jacquie, getting excited.

'...then that makes your choice easier.' Maxwell smiled at him and held out his hand, inviting comments on his theory.

Kavanagh was struck dumb. Finally, he found his voice. 'But ... why should you...'

'...the murderer...' Jacquie helpfully interposed.

'Yes, the murderer, why should you *want* to kill people who had met randomly in shops and places? Why would you choose them at all?'

Maxwell and Jacquie looked at each other and then at Kavanagh. It was Maxwell who answered him.

'Well, because you're mad, of course. We didn't want to think like that, because that makes the potential list of killers so wide. The whole population, allowing for age, sex etcetera. I think we're talking about someone who is playing a game. Murder is a sort of intellectual exercise, like timing yourself on *The Times* crossword or working out a cryptic code. You know better than I do, Alan,' Maxwell condescended, 'most people are killed by people they know. That's *why* they're killed. And that's what leads you guys to a solution, Now, a *random* series of killings, based on something general like an ambigram, well, that's a bit of a bitch, isn't it? But, because of the victims, it is possible to narrow it down.'

'How?' Kavanagh could feel himself being sucked in to this morass of insanity.

'There are various clues that link them

together,' Jacquie said, 'but only when you have everything laid out. Lara Kent had Darren Blackwell's brother's phone number on her mobile, along with others, from anonymous pay-as-you-go handsets. But when Henry checked with him, he hadn't taken her number and had no recollection of having met her. So, we worked out, she had actually met Darren, who had no mobile and so had given her his brother's number.'

'She must have met loads of people, though. She was a pretty girl, she'd have been swapping numbers all the time,' Kavanagh reasoned.

'Agreed. This is where the names come in. You can make a chain ambigram out of Darren, but not of, say, Shaun. So, he was chosen.'

'I think I see. But the murderer would have had to know his name, then, to choose him.'

'Precisely. So, then, the murderer would have seen Darren speak to Dierdre Lessing. Which he would do, if they bumped into her. Highenas always talk to staff, it's a kind of invisible club we all belong to.'

'Hyenas?' Kavanagh's head was beginning to hurt.

'Ex Leighford High pupils,' Jacquie filled in the details.

'Yes, Highenas. Where was I?' Maxwell appealed to Jacquie.

'Darren. Dierdre. Highena.'

'Yes. So, again, we have a hint as to who the murderer could be, or at least, which group in the population they belong to.'

'And it is...?'

Maxwell looked sympathetically at Kavanagh, but even more sympathetically at Jacquie; she had to work with the idiot.

'I'm sorry to have to say it, but I think that the murderer is either an ex Leighford High pupil, or a member of its staff.'

Kavanagh couldn't help it. 'Like you, for example.'

Maxwell admired his cheek, if not his intellect. He smiled and turned to Jacquie. 'Is this the time?' he asked her. 'Am I, after all, the guy?'

She stroked his cheek and Kavanagh had that feeling of having a door closed gently in his face. 'No, Max. You're not the guy.' She turned away and then paused. 'Not this time.'

'So,' Maxwell continued. 'I've looked at the names in the frame so far, although of course it might be someone completely different. But I think our murderer is coming to the end of the game and knows it. Even so, the compulsion to complete the pattern may still drive him to murder someone who fulfils the criteria. There weren't many names that did – yours, Alan, and Greg Adair. And Emma Lunt. But I can't get an answer from her. I've tried.'

Alan Kavanagh surprised himself by saying, 'I'll go and see if she's all right.'

Jacquie laid a restraining hand on his arm. 'But, Alan. What if it isn't her. What if it's you?'

'It isn't,' he said, with finality.

'Why so certain?' Maxwell asked.

'My name isn't anambithingy. It doesn't work.'

'Well,' Maxwell began. 'It's not perfect, I grant you. You have to tweak the 'l' and the 'n' a bit, but in general...'

'My name's not Alan.'

'It's not?' Jacquie said. 'You mean you use an alias?'

'No, of course not.' He grinned. 'I use my middle name.'

'So, your name is....?'

'Horace.'

Maxwell and Jacquie guffawed and instantly silenced themselves. Kavanagh laughed too. 'What were your parents thinking?' Jacquie asked.

'They named me after my grandfather,' he said. 'It was only after I was registered it turned out that he hated the name as well. So anyone looking me up, on a staff list or something, would think my name was Horace.'

'The murderer might have overheard someone call you Alan,' suggested Maxwell.

'I don't get out much,' Kavanagh replied

sadly. 'I don't really seem to fit in Leighford. Or anywhere, much.'

Maxwell and Jacquie both mulled this statement over. There seemed little to add.

'Well, now,' Maxwell said, a little too heartily. 'In that case, Alan, old chap, perhaps we will take you up on your offer. Meanwhile, Jacquie and I will see if we can break down the list of possibles. It is still pretty huge. Now, do you know where the Lunts live?'

'I think so. I've got the address in my phone, from when I thought I might have to go and arrest him.'

'Ah,' beamed Maxwell. 'Technology, eh? Let us know when you get there. Let us know if she's all right.'

'It's nice of you to be so concerned,' said Kavanagh, shrugging on his coat,

'She's a Highena,' Jacquie said. All three of them stopped in their tracks. Did that make her a potential victim or more likely a potential murderer?

Too late now, thought Kavanagh. He had cast himself in the role of chivalrous defender and so off he had to go. 'Bye, then,' he said as he went down the stairs. 'Speak later.' Jacquie and Maxwell stood at the top of the stairs and watched him go.

As the door closed behind him, Jacquie turned guiltily to Maxwell. 'Will he be all right, Max? He'll use his nous and take back-up, won't he?'

'Yes,' he said, slightly doubtfully. 'He's done the basics, presumably – side head chancery, testicle stranglehold – use of one of those lovely metal jobbies you bash doors in with. Or should that be with which you bash in doors? But, I tell you what. Why don't you ring Henry and tell him where Horace has gone? That way, he can keep an eye. Just in case.'

'Don't call him Horace,' Jacquie exploded with laughter. 'I've got to face him on Monday.'

'Sorry. But tell Henry all the same. Then you'll be sure of facing him on Monday. Chop, chop.'

Jacquie picked up the phone while Maxwell wandered away, humming.

He was in the kitchen, nibbling unenthusiastically on a piece of crispbread when she found him.

'He's not answering. I left a message. What are you doing?' she asked, unwrapping a KitKat.

'I'm trying to think. There's this tune that keeps going through my head. It's a ring-tone on a phone.'

'Go on, then. Hum me it.'

'Hum me it? Is that even English?'

'All right. Please, by putting your lips together and expelling air, attempt to convey to me the tonality of the piece of

366

music with which you seem obsessed.'

'Better,' he said, 'I'll da daa it. It gives a more rounded impression.' He cleared his throat. 'Dada dada dada da da da da da. Da da da da di di ... oh, it's no good. I just know it's by Diana Ross.'

'"Chain Reaction."'

'Sorry?'

'"Chain reaction".' She burst briefly into song. 'I'm in the middle of a chain reaction...' Maxwell was impressed. God, this girl was good. She'd named that tune in less than one. Still, it had to be said, modestly of course, that his da-daaing was among the finest in the world.

'You weren't born when that came out. Let alone the kid who has it on his phone.'

'Indeed not,' Jacquie agreed. 'Not when it came out first. But it's been covered, most recently by Steps. It's a free download.'

'Ooh, I expect so,' Maxwell said, sweeping phonespeak under the rug.

'I'll tell you something, though. Lara Kent had that as a ringtone. For just one number.'

They stared at each other, thoughts zinging madly through their brains. There suddenly seemed to be not quite enough oxygen in the room.

Jacquie recovered first. 'Max. Whose phone was it?'

'Nicholas Campbell. Chef, student, film buff. All round good hard worker. You've met him. He worked at the burger bar. Remember? And, since then, at the deli.'

'Yes, I do remember him.' She frowned. 'Not what I was expecting.'

'No, nor I. But perhaps he isn't the murderer. What if he is a link in the chain, but who didn't fit because his name doesn't make an ambigram?'

'If so, he's a lucky boy. Even so, we must check which number makes his phone ring like that. It may be the same one as on Lara's phone.'

'Let's go.'

Jacquie pointed overhead. 'A small matter of a boy upstairs.'

Maxwell looked startled for a moment and then shocked that he could forget his son. 'Oh, sorry. Could the Tweedle sisters help out?'

'They're probably in bed by now, but I'll go and ask.' Jacquie raced down the stairs.

Maxwell paced the room. Finding Nick Campbell wasn't going to be easy, but he thought he had a system that would work, starting with the burger bar. The deli would be closed by now. That should be enough, although it was unlikely that he would be at home on a Friday night. Nice looking boy like him, bound to be out on the town. The sound of twittering in stereo from below almost made him shout with pleasure. He went to the head of the stairs, already thanking the Troubridge sisters.

'Ooh, Mr Maxwell,' one of them cried. 'It's no trouble. Nolan is such a dear little boy.'

'A dear *sleeping* little boy,' Jacquie said, by way of instruction. 'I know it's very late for you both, you are such dears to help out.'

The twittering reached a crescendo as the two sleuths hurried down the stairs.

As they buckled up in the Ka, Jacquie said, 'Where to?'

'The burger bar, my man, and don't spare the horses.'

'The burger bar?'

'Nick Campbell's address?'

'Right,' and Jacquie threw the car into gear and they sped off in a squeal of rubber, both of them fully aware that Baby Jane and her sister would, even now, be dropping loud things on the floor and poking Maxwell Junior to make him wake up.

CHAPTER TWENTY

Alan Kavanagh should have called for back-up. Bill Lunt he'd met before; a mild, inoffensive type with a predilection for photographing murders. More, the man was a martyr to hysteria and nervous disorders.

Hardly the killing type. But then, Alan Kavanagh had been immersing himself in the classic cases of late. Who would have said that nice Mr Christie of 10, Rillington Place, was burying victims in his back garden, in his kitchen cupboards, under his floor boards? And he was a copper, for God's sake!

Mrs Lunt, Kavanagh didn't know at all. She was one of Maxwell's Old Highenas; that much he did know. But they bred a funny lot at that school. What would she be? Bonnie Parker, Ma Barker and Old Mrs Bender all rolled into one, as handy with an iron bar as she was with a Thompson sub-machine gun? Again, it seemed unlikely. And yet ... and yet ... Alan Kavanagh should have called for back-up.

He left the car in a side street, his head whirling with ambigrams. Could it be Bill Lunt after all, trying to divert attention by putting himself in the frame at first, then distancing himself and killing Darren Black-well and Dierdre Lessing with impunity? But Alan Kavanagh wasn't focusing so much on Bill Lunt as the long words he'd used to himself in the time since he'd parked the car. Predilection. Impunity. Good, good. Just use those in the nick now and then, and in front of that old bastard Maxwell, and in the press conference when he took the credit for catching...

There were no lights on *Chez* Lunt.

Nobody home. His breath snaked out on the night air and he pulled his coat round him as a car snarled past and the first of the evening's revellers were on their way to a piss-up. He'd try the back. There was a gate, flimsy, wrought-iron, leading to a passageway, totally black. Shit! He'd left his torch in the car, but he wasn't going back for it now. He eased the gate open, heard it screech slightly on its hinges and vanished in blackness.

Jacquie's Ka bounced to a halt outside Terry's Burger Bar and Maxwell dashed in. All should be simple; ask Terry Nick's address, get address, go to address. No problem. He had it all mapped out in his mind as he crossed to the counter, wading through the wall of grease and squelching on those hideous little packets of tomato ketchup.

The spotty child in the unfortunate cap approached from the greasy depths beyond the fryers. 'HowmayIhelpyou?' Clearly, Terry spared no expense when it came to customer service. This was not a Highena, old or current. There was no glimmer of recognition in the dull, dead eyes.

'Is Terry in?' Maxwell felt like a runner for the Krays, delivering the line from the corner of his mouth.

'Who?'

It was destined to be a long night. 'Your boss? Terry?'

'He's not here.'

'Is he ever here?'

The lad thought for a while, then said, 'No, not really.'

Maxwell counted under his breath until he felt calmer. 'May I speak to the person who is in charge tonight, then?'

'Yes.'

Feeling as though he may be trapped in some kind of hidden camera reality TV show, Maxwell gave the lad a wintry smile. 'I'm guessing that's you.'

'That's right.'

'Who's cooking, then?' He daren't ask 'what'.

'My mum. She helps out sometimes. But I'm in charge.'

Very tribal, thought Maxwell. Here he is, the man, the mammoth slayer, the hunter. Mum's out back, picking berries and sewing skins together. That's progress for you. 'So, again I'm guessing, Terry is your dad.'

'Yes.'

'In that case, let's cut to the chase, Terry Junior. May I call you that? Do you have a record of the address of Nicholas Campbell, who was working here until very recently?'

'He works in the deli now.'

'Yes, that's right.' Maxwell's patience was now paper thin and cracks were beginning to appear. 'But it's shut, being nearly nine o'clock and all. And I really need Nick's address now. It's really, *really* urgent.'

'We don't keep records here. We keep them at home.'

'Above the shop?'

The boy bridled. 'Certainly not. We live out beyond the Dam. Four bedrooms. And a hot tub. Waiting on fries,' he called to a woman jostling at Maxwell's elbow.

If only he got to use it once in a while, Maxwell thought. But he said, 'How lovely. So,' he turned to go, 'you can't help me on Nick's address, then?'

'Oh, yes. I know where Nick lives.'

Maxwell turned back, grinning like a death's head. 'Could you tell me, please?'

'Why?'

It was that tone. That single wheedling word guaranteed to get right up the nose of any teacher the length and breadth of the land. Maxwell's answer was usually 'because I say so, you snivelling little toad' but it would have been syntactically unsound here, as well as unhelpful. 'Because ... I used to be his teacher and I want to ask him something. Something about ... cooking.' It was desperate, but it was all he had left in his armoury other than pulling young Terry across the counter and battering him to death with a fish slice.

'Yeah, he's a good cook, Nick. Anyway, I 'spect you'd like to know his address.'

'Please. If you would.'

'Some of us are waiting for food, y'know,' the woman at his elbow said.

'Why are you here, then?' Maxwell felt constrained to ask. He wasn't usually so blunt, but he had a killer to catch and even being in a fast-food outlet made him deficient in attention.

'It comes free with a Terry's Mega-hot Burger.' What a salesman this guy was.

'If it must.' Maxwell reached for his wallet. 'How much do I owe you?'

'D'ywanna drink with that?'

'Umm, yes, I suppose so.'

'What?'

'Diet Coke with Lemon.' Mad Max was a man of the world.

'We only do Pepsi.'

'A Diet Pepsi with Lemon then.'

'They don't do with lemon.'

Maxwell's teeth were nearly welded together with the pressure. 'Diet Pepsi.'

'Regular or large.'

'Regular.'

'The address only comes with large.'

'Large, then.'

'That will be six pounds ninety-five, please.'

Maxwell handed over a ten pound note. 'Please keep the change.'

'Yeah, I was gunna. Anyway, Nick lives in Albemarle Road. Number forty-seven.'

'That's pronounced Aumerle, Terry

Junior. And don't you forget it.'

Maxwell ran out of the shop like a rat up a pipe, to where Jacquie was waiting, engine revving like she was a getaway driver. The lad called after him plaintively.

'Don't you want your burger?' The only reply was a swinging door. 'It's mega-hot.'

'I'll have it,' said the woman.

Terry looked her up and down. 'We're waiting on fries,' he reminded her.

Back in the car, Jacquie had been wondering where he was and said so, in no uncertain terms. 'Carrying out a health and safety inspection, heart?' she asked.

'Aumerle Road. Forty-seven.'

'I don't think I know where that is,' she told him.

'What? Call yourself a woman policeman?'

'No, not as a rule. That's what you call me.'

'Oh, God. You probably pronounce it Albemarle. Does *no* one have any culture any more? You know, Cholmondley is Chumley, Featherstonehaugh is Fanshaw.' She looked at him gone out. 'No time to argue. I know where it is. Just go that way.' He pointed in the general direction of Brighton.

'Is it in the one-way system?'

'How should I know? When you are on foot or on a bike it doesn't matter whether it is left, right or straight up in the air. Let's

375

hope not. Haven't you got one of those flashing light thingies you stick on the car roof?'

'No,' she told him. 'Nor a can of Mace, an American nightstick or a Glock. Just little ol' me.'

He tutted. 'It'll have to do.'

In the darkness, Alan Kavanagh's eyes took a while to cope. There was a wall to his left and right and another wrought-iron gate ahead. He glanced backwards, checking for the normality of the night. The street lamp lent its usual orange glow to Windermere Avenue. An old boy wandered past, walking his dog. Kavanagh eased open the gate. Now he was in a yard, half covered by a corrugated plastic roof and there seemed to be a bike leaning against a far wall. Beyond that the garden was huge and tree-ringed and black.

This had to be the back door. He tapped on the glass gingerly. There was no bell. It swung inward, beckoning him in and he felt the warmth of central heating in the hall. He could make out the orange street light at the end of a long passageway – Windermere Avenue again and he'd got his bearings. What was it now? Nine? Half past? It couldn't be more. Nobody the right side of eighty would be in bed yet. But if the Lunts had gone out, why leave the back door open? An oversight.

We've all done it. He'd noticed, trained snooper that he was, a burglar alarm on the front wall. Either it was a faux or defective; whatever, it wasn't working. Thoughts whirled in Kavanagh's brain. He ducked right, into the kitchen. In the pale light of the electronic gadgetry, he read the time. Nine twenty three. The fridge sighed as inanimate objects will when left to their own devices and Kavanagh moved on. Ahead of him, to his right, a dining room, its six chairs like sentinels around an expensive circular table. He couldn't make out the décor, but there were clearly photographs on the walls. And a very nasty wallpaper, swirls and circles. All the garish opulence of the nouveau trend.

There were two more rooms on the ground floor and he eased himself into the lounge. He could have put his shared flat down in one corner of it. At the far end, brightly coloured fish darted with neon stripes through the electric blue of their environment. There's a pretty castle. There's a pretty castle. Then he was back in the hall, with just the stairs to go...

It was Maxwell's turn to wait in the car. They'd tossed a coin earlier (not the famous double-headed zloty), as the Ka purred through the one-way system beyond the Flyover and Maxwell had lost. Jacquie was right though. If Maxwell had gone to number Forty-seven, it would have been a chorus of surprise to see Mr Maxwell there, a trip down Memory Lane from the Campbells and confirmation that Nick had always liked Mr Maxwell; in fact, he'd made him what he was today. Then it would have been some vague, uneasy lie why Mr Maxwell wanted to speak to their Nick and why it had to be now. As it was, Jacquie flashed her warrant card and asked the bewildered parents a straight question. And she got a straight answer, in a quarter of the time it would have taken Maxwell. All right, so Nick Campbell's parents were worried. But perhaps they had every right to be.

'He's in Leighford General,' Jacquie said as she slammed the car door and buckled up. 'Visiting a sick friend.' And they roared into the night.

He counted the treads, trying to place his weight evenly so that the boards didn't creak. There'd probably be a bathroom, straight ahead, he reasoned – yes, there it was. Now, to the left, along the landing, two bedrooms. And, around the corner, the third and fourth. The first one would be small, box or guest, call it what you will. And the second... A sudden scream literally threw Kavanagh back against the wall. He bounced off it, kicking in the second door with a well-aimed boot and fumbling for the light switch.

A woman with dark hair sat on the bed with her back to him. Her head was thrown back and her legs were parted. Bill Lunt was lying under her, thrusting away for England.

'Oh God,' the woman wailed, coming down from the high of her orgasm. 'Yes, yes, Bill,' she flopped forward so that her dark hair cascaded over his face, 'Darling, that was amazing.'

Alan Kavanagh shuffled out backwards. As awkward entrances go, that had been one of his best.

The woman screamed again, realising suddenly that the bedroom light was on and that Bill's ardour had equally suddenly disappeared. He looked like a rabbit caught in the headlights. She rolled over, snatching the duvet up to cover her embarrassment. 'There's a man,' she shrieked, pointing through the door.

'Not really, Emma,' said Bill Lunt between clenched teeth, snapping out of his frozen mood and suddenly furious. 'That's DC Kavanagh from Leighford Police Station. And he'd better have a bloody good reason for being here.'

It was nearly chucking out time at Leighford General. Jacquie squeezed the Ka into a handy little place she knew between the ambulances outside A&E. It was one of the perks of the job – a stone's throw from the front door and it avoided parking charges.

There was no need for coin tossing now. The Campbells hadn't known exactly who their boy was visiting, so Maxwell took the male wards and Jacquie the female. They were unaware that, behind the scenes for months, a battle royal had been fought among the hapless members of the National Health Trust to keep the wards that way. It was all about dignity and decency and standards. Had Maxwell known he would have approved – perhaps there was a God after all. The problem was that each of the consultant surgeons who flitted in and out of Leighford General thought that was him.

Knots of visitors were drifting down stairways and staggering out of lifts, most of them as decrepit as the poor souls they were visiting. Maxwell manoeuvred swiftly round a wheelchair and padded along a corridor festooned with signs without number. Princess Anne had opened a new wing apparently in 1991 but not this one. This was opened by Edith Cavell before the Germans shot her and there was much tutting in *The Advertiser* about demolishing the place and starting again. Even so, every ward in the hospital carried the Princess Anne photo and there she was on the wall with the Hospital Manager (since then, Maxwell remembered, struck off for embezzlement), the Lord Lieutenant (now in rehab) and other Great and Good of the County.

Jacquie opted for the stairs, only too aware that Campbell might have slid past her in the lift and flashed her warrant card at the cluster of nurses at their station.

Without a warrant card, Maxwell's progress was inevitably slower. 'I'm afraid we're about to close to visitors,' a large Jamaican nurse told him.

'I'm not staying,' he called. 'Visiting a visitor.'

'You still have to wash your hands.' She effectively blocked the doorway with her bulk. 'Infection,' she pointed to the various MRSA warnings that littered the wall.

'Madam,' he said. 'If Florence Nightingale had worried about little things like viruses, do you think *any* of our brave boys in the Crimea would have come home?'

'Infection,' she repeated, the mantra of the NHS.

'Of course,' he beamed and squeezed the smelly jelly over his hands. Old boys without number lay propped in excruciating-looking beds on both sides of the ward, the Catheter Brigade. Dotted among them, younger blokes with splints and plasters and there, at the far end, his quarry, young Nick Campbell emerging from behind a glass partition, about to go.

'You don't have to leave on my account,' Maxwell said, barely faltering at all when, looking round the screen, he saw who was lying on the bed. 'Gregory,' his smile was like the silver plate on a coffin, 'I heard you were laid low.'

Gregory Adair looked like shit, to use correct medical terminology. Maxwell had had pneumonia as a child and he still remembered the delirium it brought. Always, when he relived it in his dreams, he was walking up an endless Escher staircase, around the four walls of his room, on and on, towards a dim light in the distance. And it stayed in the distance, no matter how many stairs he climbed. Rationally, the light had to be his parents' room and the stairs represented the intolerable loneliness and isolation of his illness, 'splashed,' as GK Chesterton had once written, 'with a splendid sickness, the sickness of the pearl'.

Looking at the grey pallor of Gregory Adair, it all came flooding back. The man's face was drawn, his eyes sunken, a plastic mask over his nose and mouth. But he recognised Peter Maxwell and half-extended a hand. Maxwell caught it, patting it with his other hand. 'You hang on in there, Greg,' he said, softly.'You can send your cover work in later.' And he winked.

'Er ... I've got to go, Greg,' Nick Campbell said, checking his watch and sensing the hospital staff massing at the ward entrance. 'I'll see you tomorrow.' His hand lingered a little longer than Maxwell expected as the boy took his farewells. Maxwell tactfully turned his back and didn't see the soft kiss Nick planted on Greg's forehead. Kismet, Hardy. By the time the pair were rinsing their hands in goo again, under the watchful gaze of Mrs Seacole, tears were filling Nick Campbell's eyes.

'He's not going to make it, Mr Maxwell,' he trembled. 'He's not. I know it.'

Maxwell looked at the boy. He was a wreck. He put his arm around him, like the father he was and led him down the stairs. He was still leading him through the hospital when Jacquie turned a corner into view. Maxwell saw her and shook his head. She nodded, realising the moment and gesticulated that she'd be in the car.

Maxwell took the boy out by the side door, past smokers' corner where the more addicted hospital staff gathered to indulge their disgusting, sordid habit, dragging on the ciggies that New Labour now only allowed them to smoke on alternate Fridays if there was an 'r' in the month and then only strictly to the south-west of the Town Hall. The night air hit crisp as the pair shambled up the grassy rise to the lily pond. Ducks bedding down for the night looked at them through beady eyes under beak-enfolding wings. No, there'd be no bread from these two. Over the years the hospital duck population had learnt to recognise mean buggers when they saw them. One of them quacked in disapproval.

Maxwell sat the boy down on the park bench that had been erected in memory of Arthur and Elsie Hudson who, against all the odds, had loved this spot, Maxwell having the presence of mind to remove the pigeon-poo first. 'We need to talk, Nick,' he said softly.

Nick Campbell had heard those words before. The first time he was eleven and it was his very first encounter with Mad Max. He'd been sliding down the banisters at Leighford High, a little prank he'd learnt at junior school and happened to collide with the brick wall that was the Head of Sixth Form. Nick didn't slide down banisters after that.

'I've caught you at a bad time,' Maxwell said.

Nick just nodded. 'It's just a bug,' he said, 'that's going round. Everybody's got it.'

Maxwell nodded.

'Why has it hit Greg so hard? Why him?'

'That depends on your take on the meaning of life, Nicholas,' he said. 'Whether you think it's all part of God's Great Design or just some pointless, endless round of natural selection. But Greg's young and tough.' He patted the boy's hunched shoulder. 'He'll be all right. These things take time.'

He watched as Nick's head came up and he looked out over the lake, his eyes glistening with tears, his breath on the night air a reminder that spring was not here yet.

'I didn't realise that you and he knew each other.'

Nick sniffed. 'We met last September,' he said. 'I'd just left Leighford High and he'd just started. We had that in common and had a laugh about it. Taking the piss, I'm afraid.'

Maxwell smiled. 'Present company excepted, I hope,' he said.

Nick did his best to smile too, but it wasn't altogether successful.

'I love him, Mr Maxwell,' he said. 'Greg. That's all right, isn't it?'

Maxwell looked at the boy, his face solemn and almost grey in the half light from the hospital wing. Forty years ago, son; thirty; even twenty in some circles, they'd have beaten you both to a pulp and your parents would have had to move. Poof, queer, nance. All the uncaring words of hatred of Maxwell's boyhood echoed through the darkness. But now ... well, different days.

'Of course,' he said. 'Of course it's all right.'

'Mum and dad don't know, although I think they suspected it with Lobber.'

'Richard?'

Nick suddenly got up from the bench and paced around. 'Greg isn't the first,' he said.

'Lobber and I ... well, you know...'

'You were ... an item ... at school? I didn't know.'

Nick laughed, a brittle, short sound that echoed in the night. 'Hardly an item,' he said. 'We had sex, that was all. And never at school.'

Maxwell was grateful for that at least. 'I saw you as a couple,' he said, 'but, I must admit, never in that way. You were always surrounded by girls.'

'Poofs usually are,' Nick said and the word jarred. 'We're not a threat, you see. We can talk make-up and emotions and lend a shoulder to cry on without any real sense of rivalry. Unless we're after the same bloke, of course.' He winked at Maxwell. This was better. The boy was coming out of it now, coming to terms with what hovered over that hospital bed. 'Why did you want to see me?' he asked,

Maxwell had almost forgotten in the flurry of activity of the last few minutes, but the itch was still there, the need to know. '"Chain Reaction",' he said. 'Tell me about "Chain Reaction".'

Nick looked confused. 'I don't understand,' he said.

'It's a very old pop song,' Maxwell explained. 'Diana Ross, although I am reliably informed it's been done since.'

Nick shrugged. 'Still don't get it,' he said.

'I heard it only the other day,' Maxwell said. 'It's like one of those fleeting memories you get sometimes. You know, a smell, a taste, a sound. You can't quite put your finger on it, but it takes you back. I've been around a lot longer than you, Nick; I have more moments like those than you do. But I do know when I heard it last. It was in the deli the other day, the day you served me. And it was coming from your back pocket. It's a ringtone, isn't it?'

'Is it?'

Maxwell looked at him. 'You know it is. Who was ringing you?'

Nick looked vague. 'It could have been anybody,' he said. 'I've got lots of people who ring me up.'

'I believe that person also rang Lara Kent,' Maxwell said.

'Who?'

'Nicholas, Nicholas,' Maxwell shook his head. 'You don't watch the news, do you, dear boy? Lara Kent was the body found on the beach last week.'

'The *Big Issue* seller,' Nick said,

'Precisely. The police have checked her mobile phone. There was one in particular they couldn't trace in this pay-as-you-go topsy-turvy world of ours. It had been given the ringtone "Chain Reaction".'

'Coincidence,' shrugged Nick.

'Do you know Detective Chief Inspector

Hall?' Maxwell asked him.

Nick shook his head.

'My Better Half's boss,' Maxwell explained. 'Doesn't believe in coincidences. If he had his way, he'd have the word expunged from the dictionary. An unidentified caller calls a girl who was subsequently murdered. That same caller – or at least someone designated the same ringtone – calls you.' Maxwell got up from the bench and stood in front of the boy. 'Who was it, Nick?' he asked.

For a moment, Nick Campbell stood there, the willows dark over the pond behind him and the chill breeze from the east ruffling the waters. Maxwell saw the boy's eyes bright in the reflected light and saw the muscles in his jaw flex. Then he said, 'Lobber.'

The word was almost inaudible. Maxwell took the lad's arm and led him back to the bench. 'Do you want to tell me about it?' he asked.

Like a kid with his hand in the cookie jar, it all came tumbling out. 'It started with you, Mr Maxwell,' he said.

'Me?'

'Your GCSE History lessons, the last time Lobber and I were in the same class together. You remember, Crime and Punishment?'

OCR 1935; Maxwell remembered it perfectly.

'There was one case you talked about...

Well, it became a bit of an obsession with us. Leopold and Loeb.'

'Leopold,' Maxwell repeated as the deluxe list leapt into his mind. 'N Leopold, of course. You.'

Nick shook his head. 'No,' he said. 'No, that was just the point. It was all talk, theory, that's all it was. Didn't you ever have something like that, with a mate of yours, something you talked about doing, but never did?'

Maxwell smiled. 'As a matter of fact, yes,' he said. 'When I was in the Sixth Form, a group of us read about Borley Rectory, "the most haunted house in England" and even though the place was a ruin, we were determined to spend the night there, camping. We planned it like a military operation, even down to the sandwich fillings we'd take.'

'What happened?'

'Nothing,' Maxwell chuckled. 'We didn't go. It all fell apart because we couldn't borrow a car. On such chance happenings, Nicholas, empires fall.'

'But that was Leopold and Loeb's problem too, wasn't it? The car. Leopold hired it to pick up their target, using a false name. He hadn't reckoned on the amount of blood there'd be in the vehicle, though. Didn't let the chauffeur clean it, giving some guff about the stains being spilt wine.'

'Chauffeurs? Hire cars? Spilt wine?

389

Doesn't sound *quite* like Nicholas Campbell and Richard Underdown.'

'Well, it was only an idea,' Nick agreed. 'We researched the case carefully. Leopold and Loeb were spoilt rich kids from Chicago, law students. They looked down their noses on everybody else and decided to choose an inferior to kill, just because they could. Lobber – that's why he got the nickname, of course; we invented it – Lobber decided we should choose some low-life, a down and out probably.'

'You know you're confessing to murder, Nick, don't you?' It was the nearest thing Maxwell could give by way of a caution.

Campbell shook his head. 'No, I'm not,' he said. 'It's no more than crime writers do every day of their lives. I haven't noticed Val McDermid or Robert Goddard being arrested lately.'

'But you carried it out, Nick,' Maxwell said.

'No, Mr Maxwell, that's the whole point. *Folie à deux*, isn't it? That's what you told us when you talked about the case first. I can remember it, clear as day. It was in Aitch Eight, a Tuesday morning and you said – I can remember your exact words – *"Folie à deux* means the madness of two. Take either individual on their own and they wouldn't hurt a fly. Put them together and it's fatal."'

'I'm impressed by your instant recall,'

Maxwell smiled, although he knew perfectly well he would actually have said 'His or her own.'

Nick's face suddenly darkened. 'I had a phone call from Lobber last Thursday. He told me he'd done it. He'd killed a girl on the beach, just out beyond Willow Bay and left her body in the sand.'

'Like Leopold and Loeb left Bobby Franks in the culvert,' Maxwell nodded.

'I thought he was joking,' Nick went on. 'We'd talked about carrying out a murder for the best part of two years, on and off. We'd refined it in all sorts of ways, hammered out scenarios. Then, and this was after we came back from Nigeria, it all got a bit nasty.'

'In what way nasty? I got the impression you were still best of friends when I saw you both in town.'

'We had only just bumped into each other when we saw you. Since I met Greg... I knew it was the real thing. I had to put some space between me and Lobber. He wasn't taking it well. He'd always been a bit possessive and we were going our different ways soon. I was off to university and he was working at the Lunts...'

'The Lunts?' Maxwell repeated.

'The photography shop in the High Street.'

'Of course,' Maxwell clicked his fingers. It

391

was his version of Homer Simpson's 'D'oh'. 'I *knew* I recognised the voice. I rang the other day to talk to Mrs Lunt and he answered.'

Nick nodded. 'I bet that put the frighteners on him. Knowing you were on his case.'

'You flatter me, Nicholas,' Maxwell said.

'Anyway, I realised that Lobber meant business. About the murder, I mean. You know, Leopold and Loeb planned to kill their target between them, looping a rope around his neck and each pulling one end.'

'Except it didn't happen that way.'

'No,' Nick said. 'Leopold was behind the wheel of the hire car, Loeb in the back with Bobby Franks. It was Loeb who shoved a gag in the kid's mouth and hit him with a chisel. The rope was never used.'

'So you're telling me...?'

'Lobber,' Nick said solemnly. 'Lobber chose the girl at random, followed her, picked her up on the street, took her to the beach – "Just for a walk," he told her, "No funny business", and stabbed her to death. Then he walked home, cleaned himself up and rang me.'

'And what did you do?'

Nick put his head in his hands. 'That's the point,' he said. 'Nothing. At first, of course, I thought he was joking. You know what he was like at school, nicking door signs, gluing computer keys down. Then I caught the radio. There *was* a girl dead on the beach. And I still did nothing.'

'You are an accessory after the fact, Nick,' Maxwell said.

'I know. I went to see Lobber. We had this screaming row. It all got very personal. He didn't know about Greg, of course, and it all came out. He said it was my turn to carry out the next one.' Nick looked at his old Head of Sixth Form. 'This wasn't part of the deal, Mr Maxwell. Leopold and Loeb killed once. Lobber went on doing it. When I asked him why, he said "Because I can" and accused me of being all kinds of shit for letting him down. Life's funny, isn't it; Leopold and Loeb were eighteen and nineteen, exactly our ages today.'

'And still you didn't go to the police?'

'I was on my way,' the boy said. 'I was psyching myself up to do it, when I found Greg... I went to see him, tell him about it, ask what I should do. I found him semiconscious at his flat and rang for an ambulance. Mr Maxwell,' he held the man's sleeve, 'Lobber's mad. I don't understand what he's doing now. After he'd killed Darren Blackwell, he went after Ms Lessing. Of all people. He picked her up in his car, with some ludicrous story about her boyfriend, what's his name, that Crown bloke? He needed to see her, Lobber said, urgently. How the woman fell for that I don't know, but it's my guess she got into the car and bang, he walloped her. Then he took her body out to those woods at Arundel and dumped her on the old railway line. He knew Crown jogged there – and when – so it was likely he'd find the corpse first.'

Maxwell shook his head. 'I had no idea Richard Underdown was such a devious bastard,' he said. 'Is this what schoolboy pranks lead to?'

'What happens now?' Nick asked.

Maxwell looked at him. All in all it had been quite a week for the boy. He looked drained and old beyond his years.

'Now,' he said, 'you go home, Nick. You can leave this to the grown-ups now.'

The grown-ups were having a slightly bizarre conversation of their own as Maxwell reached Jacquie's car. She waved to him to be quiet as she talked into her mobile. It reminded Maxwell of an old Bob Newhart record.

'I see, Alan,' she was saying. 'And what happened then? You went into the house. Without a warrant card. Without back-up. Hmm. And then what?' She waited. 'Mr and Mrs Lunt were in the bedroom. Decorating, were they, Alan? With the lights off? Huh-huh.' She pulled a pained expression at Maxwell, belting up beside her. 'Well, of course they might,' she said. 'No, I'm afraid

Mr Hall will have to know, Alan. Me? Well, I'd have rung the front doorbell; but that's me for you.' And she rang off before collapsing with laughter.

'It's not Emma Lunt,' she said when she could, between sniggers. 'She's at home, enjoying a quiet moment with her husband, just before they sue the arse off Alan Kavanagh for conduct likely to cause a breach of the peace.'

Maxwell hit the dashboard, growling to himself.

Jacquie looked at him. 'I didn't know Alan meant so much to you,' she said.

'If Emma Lunt isn't our next victim,' he said, 'then, frankly, my dear, I'm stumped.'

'How do we know there's going to be another one?' she asked.

'Because I feel it in my water. There's a smell of unfinished business in the air. And Lobber Underdown doesn't know when enough is enough.'

'Lobber Underdown?' she looked at him. 'Who the hell is Lobber Underdown?'

'It's a long story,' Maxwell said. 'But after what Nick just told me, he's our man. We need to ring Henry.'

Jacquie checked her watch, always more reliable than the car's clock. 'It's late,' she said. 'And it's Friday. I'll try the nick, but it's more likely he's at home or spooning and sparring with Helen Marshall.'

'Who?' Maxwell sat bolt upright.

'Don't start,' she warned him, stabbing buttons on her mobile. 'We've had this conversation.'

'No, we haven't,' he said. 'Ring off.'

'What?'

'Why didn't you tell me DCI Marshall's name was Helen?'

'Er...' Jacquie ran through all the options in her head. 'I thought I did? I didn't know it myself? I know how you hate the H word? Max, what are you talking about?'

'Ambigrams, Jacquie. Ambigrams. The thing that links our victims in Lobber's deranged mind. Nick told me he thought Lobber is choosing victims at random, but we know he isn't. The links in the chain are all about ambigrams. That which is first shall be last. And we haven't come across a better example yet than Helen.'

'Who is Lobber?' she screamed at him, exasperated.

'Richard Underdown,' he told her, solemnly, 'was one of My Own, not the pleasantest of people I've met, though I wouldn't have had him down as a serial killer. He and Nick Campbell were fantasising about an action replay of Leopold and Loeb.'

'Leopold,' she said, 'the name at the deluxe.'

'Yes, yes,' he said testily, having been there himself only ten minutes before, 'and Loeb-

Lobber, get it? But *folie à deux* became *folie à un* and whereas for Nick it was a harmless, if macabre, topic of conversation, Lobber meant it. It's his ringtone on Lara Kent's phone – Chain Reaction. And that's what this is all about. A chain reaction of individuals linked by a chain ambigram. Not only did I miss the signs of psycho in Lobber, I missed his apparent intellectual thrust as well. What the hell's he doing working in a photographers? That's where we're going now.'

'Where?' Jacquie kicked the Ka into action.

'The Lunts. Good God, is that the time?' In a heart-stopping moment he realised that they had left Nolan with the Tweedle Twins. 'Nole!' he cried.

'Don't worry,' she said, as she pulled slowly away from her parking place. 'My time waiting for you wasn't wasted. I rang them and asked if they would sleep over if we were late.'

'And?'

'I put the phone down on their delighted twittering.'

'Going into a tunnel?' he asked, suggesting the favourite excuse of mobile users.

'Battery,' she answered. 'Off to the Lunts, then. I'll phone for back-up.' She fumbled in her pocket for her phone.

'Back-up?' Maxwell repeated. 'What are you talking about? We haven't got time.'

397

'You may be right,' she said. 'Are you sitting comfortably? Then I'll begin.'

The Ka raced through the sleeping town, Jacquie noting the Paddy Wagon bundling in the drunks along the High Street. She took the short cut through the town square and along Cadogan Street before cutting down the one-way system the wrong way, wishing she had, after all, one of those flashing light jobbies she could stick onto the car roof and they screeched to a halt outside the house in Windermere Avenue.

'Front or back?' he asked her.

She laughed. 'You stay with me,' she said. 'We're doing this by the book; or at least partially by the book in that you shouldn't be with me at all.'

They crossed the lawn and she rang the doorbell. As Kavanagh had found it, the house was in total darkness and it took a while for a rather dishevelled-looking Bill Lunt to shamble to the door in his dressing-gown.

'Bill,' Maxwell beamed. 'Sorry it's so late. We're not interrupting anything, are we?'

Jacquie glared at him. 'Mr Lunt, I am DS Jacquie Carpenter, Leighford CID.'

'Yes,' said Lunt, confused. 'I know who you are. I was staying in your house, briefly.'

'Sorry,' she said. 'We have to do this formally. I need some information, Mr Lunt.'

'Not a few days ago, you people had me in the frame for a murder,' he said. 'Now you want some information? You know, we've had one of your blokes round here already, breaking into our property, watching ... us. We will certainly lodge a complaint.'

'Bill, what's the matter?' Emma appeared at the man's elbow. 'Mr Maxwell? What's going on?'

'Mrs Lunt,' Jacquie tried the woman to woman approach. 'I need a phone number, urgently. That of one of your employees, Richard Underdown. Do you have it here?'

'I certainly do,' she said. 'Waste of space, that lad. Bill, don't sit there on your high horse all night. Make these good folks a cup of tea. It's freezing on this doorstep.'

There was no reply from Richard Underdown's home phone. It was Saturday morning now, black and raw. Landline one, Jacquie Carpenter nil. All right, then. Richard Underdown was out on the town, at a party, stalking God knew who. She tried again and let the mobile ring.

It was a female voice who finally answered, just before the phone clicked over to voicemail. The voice was breathless, scared. 'It's Helen Marshall. Lewes. Red Astra.' There was a thud and the phone went dead.

CHAPTER TWENTY-ONE

This time, Jacquie did ring Henry Hall. She also rang Lewes nick and let the whole machinery of Sussex Law grind into action. It would be interesting, for those pundits who watched these things, to see how East and West Sussex would work this one. Those at the cutting edge didn't have time. Jacquie, Maxwell and half the CID on the south coast had a murderer to catch.

'Oh, Christ!' Maxwell flipped open Jacquie's phone for the umpteenth time in as many minutes. 'Jacquie Carpenter.'

'God, Jacquie, bollocks dropped at last?' a sexist DS Davies was chirpy at the other end, bearing in mind it was nearly one in the morning.

'Is there a point to this?' Maxwell growled, watching the road hurtle beneath his feet in the car headlights.

'Is that Maxwell?' Davies asked. 'Put DS Carpenter on.'

'You know better than I do, Sergeant Davies, that it is an indictable offence for a driver to use a mobile phone while his or her vehicle is still in motion. Were I to pass you across, that would constitute either a) abetting a felony or b) using the lure of entrapment. Either way, it wouldn't look very good on what I fancy must be your pretty tarnished reputation. Just tell me, Davies or I'll have to start reminding you who pays your bloody wages, mate.'

The last part of that sentence was uncanny in that it sounded like an echo of Davies himself. There was a silence and then, 'Could you tell DS Carpenter that the red Astra licensed to Richard Underdown has the registration Romeo 457 Whisky Sierra Foxtrot. We're closing in. Keep in touch.'

'Love you too,' said Maxwell, snapping the cover shut. 'DS Davies sends you his,' he said, 'and says what an honour it is to work with professionals.'

'Great.' Jacquie was concentrating on the road, her speed way over the limit. 'What did he really say?'

'They've got Lobber's number – but then, I think we all have. If my knowledge of arcane policiana serves, it's R457 WSF.'

'Where would he take her, Max?' Jacquie asked. 'And why Lewes?'

'Ambigram,' Maxwell said. 'It's poetic, really. Almost too poetic. Perhaps Lobber wants to make this one extra special. An ambigram victim in an ambigram place. Yet why...?'

'Do you know Lewes, Max?' she asked.

'I can't give you a grid reference,' he

401

admitted. 'I leave that to my sad colleagues in the Geography department. The name comes from the Saxon word Hlew meaning a hill – and it is, in fact, hilly. Called a spade a spade, did the Saxons...'

'Max,' she growled. 'I'm not sure we've got time for the History lesson.'

'Oh, I don't know,' he said, gesturing to the lights twinkling far ahead, 'that's Brighton over there; we've got a while yet. And there's always time for a History lesson. I was going to fill you in on the battle of Lewes in 1264 when Simon de Montfort kicked Henry III's arse on his way to setting up the first parliament. Tom Paine lived there for a while before he got up himself and started shouting about people's rights. The worst-ever recorded British avalanche occurred in the town in 1836, effectively burying Boulder Row – that's South Street today, by the way...'

'Max!' Jacquie wasn't growling now, she was screaming.

'Left,' he told her.

'I know, I know,' the indicator was already flashing. 'I was just wondering how in hell we're going to track down Underdown in a town the size of Lewes.'

'Point taken,' he said, 'but we're only looking for Lobber's car.'

'You reckon? He must have heard Helen Marshall give us the tip down the phone. He wouldn't be stupid enough to stay with it, surely.'

'Oh, yes, Jacquie,' Maxwell nodded. 'That's precisely what he'd do.'

Henry Hall was at Leighford nick as another grey February dawn broke. There was a time when, a colleague down, he'd have jumped into the nearest patrol car and hit the road. Now, he had people for that. Lewes Uniform and Lewes CID knew the town better than he did. Anyway, he had sent DS Davies and three squad cars as back-up and, since the call had come from her in the first place, he knew Jacquie was on her way. True, he had his reservations about Davies, but the man was good on the action stuff. There was an All Points out on Richard Underdown and a shaken and very disturbed set of parents were standing in their living room wondering where and how their upbringing had gone so tragically wrong. Across town, an equally disturbed Legs Diamond was helping police with their inquiries by letting them in to Leighford High School to comb the school files on the young man they were anxious to interview.

The light was creeping over the headland as Jacquie's car purred to a halt. Seconds before, Maxwell had grabbed her arm and pointed. It was a red Astra all right, its bodywork spotted with mud, parked at a crazy angle by the trees. Mist wreathed the hollows and Maxwell realised they were on the edge of a golf course, apparently in the middle of nowhere, the still-sleeping town a world away below them.

It was cold up here, on this lonely hillside. Maxwell opened his door.

'I suppose there's no chance of you staying here,' Jacquie said.

Her man just smiled and unbuckled his belt. He crouched by the half-open door. 'What do you see,' he asked her, 'in the car?' What with his age and the unaccustomed grey of the morning, he valued a second opinion.

'One figure,' she said softly, 'in the driving seat. Is it him?'

Maxwell strained his eyes. 'Could be,' he said. 'Could be Lord Lucan, for all I know.'

'Max,' she said, 'I'm calling for back-up.'

He nodded.

She spoke quietly into the mobile, linking with the uniformed branch she knew would already be combing the streets and prowling the suburbs.

'But I'm not sure we can wait,' he said. And was gone, scurrying out across the dew-heavy grass, rustling as he went, scarf flapping in the wind.

'Jesus!' she hissed and ended the call, running after him as the wet grass soaked her shoes and jeans-bottoms. Everything went through her head as she made that dash. Helen Marshall was lying in the back seat, her throat cut, her skull smashed. Or she was not there at all, but dangling at the end of a rope somewhere they hadn't looked yet. And what about Lobber? Had he blown his brains out in the front seat? Or was he sitting there with a knife to the woman's throat, nutty as a fruit-cake, ready for some climactic confrontation with the police?

Jacquie had the years on Maxwell and they reached the car together, he flinging open the driver's door, Jacquie going for the back. Helen Marshall was indeed lying there, bound and gagged with gaffer tape. But there was no blood around her throat or in her tangled hair and there was no sign of a rope. As for Lobber, he was sitting there, staring out of the windscreen at the lightening grey of the distant sea, a mobile phone in his hand. He felt the hands on his anorak, but failed to react except to turn his head to his assailant.

'Hello, Mr Maxwell,' he said. 'I'm glad it's you. I'm not sure what to do now.'

And Jacquie and Maxwell heard the wailing whine of the police sirens getting closer. Neither of them knew whether Lobber heard it or not.

It was nearly lunchtime at Leighford

General, as it was everywhere else in the town. This time, Peter Maxwell knew exactly where he was going and he timed it to perfection. He smiled at the Jamaican nurse and ostentatiously washed his hands in the goo. Then he positioned himself at the entrance to the ward and waited.

The bell sounded for the end of the visiting hour and the scattered remnants who hadn't already done a runner long before began to drift past.

'Hello, Nick.'

'Mr Maxwell.' The boy stopped in his tracks.

'He's looking better, I see,' and he waved to Greg Adair at the far end of the ward. The man was sitting up, smiling. He still looked grey and waxy, but the mask and tubes had gone and he was a human being again. A line from an old Great War poem crept into Maxwell's mind – 'And some Slight Wound sat smiling on his bed.'

'The fever broke last night,' Nick said, waving at the man too. 'They say he'll be fine in a day or two. He'll be coming out. Oops, no pun intended.'

'Good, good.'

'It's nice of you to check how he is.'

'Well,' Maxwell wandered with the boy along the corridor and down the stairs. 'That's not exactly why I'm here. I've just come from Lobber.'

The boy stopped in mid-flight. 'Lobber? Where is he?'

'About now, he's in Leighford nick, helping DCI Hall with his inquiries. Interview Room One would be my guess.'

'Thank God,' Nick sighed. 'And thank you, Mr Maxwell.'

Many people believed that was largely the same thing, but Maxwell let it go. 'Me?' he said. 'Why?' The pair were moving again, down to the ground floor and towards the main entrance.

'Well, you went to the police. Something I should've done, of course. They'll want to talk to me, I suppose?'

'Oh, yes, Nick,' Maxwell said. 'They'll want to ask you about ambigrams.'

'About what?'

Maxwell stopped and turned to the boy. 'Have you got a minute, Nick?' he asked.

'Sure.' The boy was smiling but his eyes told a different story.

'Tell me about Leopold and Loeb.'

Nick laughed, caught as he was in a corner of the hospital's vestibule. 'Mr Maxwell, we've had this conversation. You know more about it than I do.'

'Oh, now, Nick,' Maxwell smiled. 'No false modesty, please. You and Lobber researched it, remember. To me, it's only ever been one case, one tiny example of Man's inhumanity to Man along the Dead Man's Walk of crime. But to you guys ... well...'

'I don't know what you want me to tell you,' Nick shrugged.

'Well, for instance, who was who?'

'Sorry?'

'Leopold and Loeb. Which of you was which?'

'I don't...' Nick was frowning.

'Let me help you,' Maxwell said. 'They were both arrogant sons of bitches, as the Chicago press of the time all but called them. But the smartarse, the brains behind it, was Nathan Leopold. Linguist, ornithologist, homosexual and disciple of Nietzsche. He saw himself as a Superman, but *so* arrogant was he that he passed that accolade to Loeb, making him, Leopold, a super Superman, I suppose. Poor Richard Loeb, not so bright, not so arrogant. Just a teeny bit out of his depth. A bit like Lobber this morning. Manipulated all the way. Lobber's the puppet; you're pulling the strings.'

Nick looked nonplussed. 'No, Mr Maxwell; I told you...'

'Oh, I know what you told me, Nick,' the Head of Sixth Form said, both of them oblivious now to passers by. 'And most of it was a pack of lies. Yes, you and Lobber became obsessed with the Leopold and Loeb case. Yes, you both planned it to the letter. But then Lobber got cold feet, didn't he? Once in the kitchen, he couldn't actually stand the heat, after all. Not mixing too many metaphors for you, there, am I, Superman? Confusing my clichés? You see, I've got to take my hat off to you,' and he did, doffing it low. 'You're actually cleverer than Nathan Leopold, because he made his murder selection by random choice. The only criterion was that the target had to be a rich man's son, because part of the ploy was ransom. Neither of them needed the money, but it added to the torment of the Franks family and was good for a laugh. And what finer pranksters could there be but you and Lobber, the eternal jokers? So, you'd read Dan Brown – Lobber hadn't, I asked him – and you hit upon the idea of ambigrams for your victims; the letters of their first names forming a chain. As well as that, to make the chain more tightly linked, they had some connection with each other. Lara had met Darren in a club and they had exchanged numbers; Darren spoke to Dierdre Lessing in the street – an Old Highena saying hello to his old teacher. Helen Marshall was investigating Dierdre's death ...where would you have gone from there, I wonder?'

'This is rubbish,' Nick said. 'Look, I have to go now...'

But Maxwell slammed the boy back against the glass behind him. 'But Lobber let you down, didn't he? Lost his nerve at the last moment. He didn't ring you to tell you about each kill. You rang him. You'd met your darling Greg by this time, so what use was Lobber? Except, Lobber had betrayed you. And *nobody* betrays Superman. So you forced him to carry out one killing himself – an ambigram name killed in an ambigram place. Helen in Lewes. Too clever by half. You'd seen her on the telly, hadn't you? The press conference. Here was this bossy cow, a mere woman, coming across as if she'd got the whole thing sewn up. Well, you'd show her, wouldn't you? Or rather Lobber would. We don't know yet how he managed to grab her – that's not one she'll live down in a hurry. But we do know he didn't know what to do with her. I found him sitting in his car in Lewes. The right victim, the right place. But the wrong killer. Should've done that one yourself, Nicky boy, just like all the others.'

'You're fucking mad!' Nick broke way from the iron grip on his shoulder, striding for the door.

'Tell me one last thing,' Maxwell shouted to him, about the original case. 'What caught Leopold and Loeb in the end?'

Campbell stopped, hesitating. This mad old bastard had nothing on him. It would be his word against Lobber's. And that would be no contest. 'Glasses,' Nick said. 'Leopold dropped his glasses near Bobby Franks' body.'

Maxwell nodded. 'So much for Superman,' he muttered, closing to the boy. 'With you, it was timing.'

'What do you mean?' Nick blinked.

'When I talked to Lobber earlier this morning,' he said, 'he didn't have any answers. None at all. He couldn't remember where Lara Kent was killed or when. He was vague about Darren Blackwell, too and as for Dierdre Lessing, he only remembered her from school. But you, Nicholas, knew it all. You knew that Dierdre's body was dumped on a disused railway line at Arundel because that's where you left it.'

'Lobber's lying, Mr Maxwell,' Nick wheedled. 'Can't you see that?'

Maxwell's shoulders relaxed. It was the end of a long day. 'All right, Nick,' he said softly. 'One very last question. When did Leopold and Loeb kill little Bobby Franks?'

'Er ... 21 May 1924,' the boy said.

'Spot on,' Maxwell said. 'That's sixty-one years before a genuinely clever bloke discovered a little thing called DNA. The Chicago cops didn't have that advantage back in the twenties. Henry Hall has. Yours will be all over the teeth of Lara Kent's dog from that nip the poor bugger gave you trying to defend his mistress. That'd be enough to hang you in the good old days. We're not going to find Lobber's DNA anywhere near any of these victims, are we?'

411

Nick Campbell spun on his heel. 'You're as barking as her dog, Maxwell,' he called. 'You don't know what you're talking about.'

'I took my hat off to you earlier, Nick,' Maxwell called, 'That was a pre-arranged signal. If you'll look to your left.'

Across the grass ahead of him Jacquie Carpenter stood, wondering which way he would run.

'And to your right.'

The uniformed constables were approaching from the rise to the lily pond. Still others were trickling over from the car park. In the event, it was Maxwell who reached the boy first, because he'd stopped and stood stock still on the hospital forecourt. His old Head of Sixth Form looked into his eyes. 'Why, Nick, why?' he asked. 'There'll be no Clarence Darrow to save you now. Great advocates are a thing of the past. He saved those boys from the electric chair, but you know as well as I do that Nathan Leopold was fifty-three when he got out. What a waste.'

'Why, Mr Maxwell,' Nick repeated. 'You asked me why.' He stood up tall as they clicked the cuffs on his wrists. 'Because I could, that's why.'

Maxwell and Jacquie stood on the first landing of their sleeping house. The Troubridge sisters napping on the sofa were making small whiffling noises in their sleep, almost indistinguishable from those they made when awake. Nolan's post prandial mutterings, eerily amplified down the baby alarm, were as yet lacking in his usual urgency. With luck and a following wind, he would sleep for a few more minutes yet. Metternich, having availed himself to the maximum of the Troubridges' generosity in the pilchard and lap stakes, was stretched full length on the chair and was noisier than the other three put together, snoring down his battle-scarred nose in a rhythmic rattle and hum.

Maxwell turned Jacquie towards him and enfolded her in his arms. She leant in to his warmth and snaked her arms around him, inside his coat. She could have happily stayed there for ever. So what if there would be a mountain of paperwork? So what if the press would be all over the nick, Columbine and Leighford High for weeks? Here, for the moment, time could stand still.

After a while, Maxwell stirred and pulled away slightly, looking down into her tired, but still frank and open eyes. He cleared his throat, very quietly, so as not to waken the sleepers. 'Jacquie,' he said, seriously. 'I've been giving a problem a lot of thought lately and I've got to ask you...'

He saw her eyes widen as she looked over his shoulder through the landing window. A grin broke over her face and transformed her into the seven-year-old he had never known. She shook herself free and ran to lean on the sill, her nose pressed against the cold glass. She turned, eyes sparkling. 'It's snowing!' she said, and so it was. Those same big, lazy flakes of years before were spiralling down and already covering Leighford with a blanket of purest white. They stood there and watched for a moment.

'Nolan's first snow,' Maxwell said, quietly.

'And ours,' she said and turned to put her arms round him again. He kissed her on the head and laughed.

As if on cue, Nolan's muttering became a torrent, Metternich wandered by and clawed Maxwell's ankle in an absentminded sort of way. The Troubridge twins both broke into a cacophony of coughing but even so, beneath it all, Peter Maxwell heard his true love say, 'And yes, Peter Maxwell, I will marry you. But only on one condition.'

'Name it,' he said, 'And it's yours.'

'Bill Lunt has to be the photographer.'

He breathed a sigh of relief. 'That's a mercy. For a moment, I thought you were going to ask that the Troubridges could be bridesmaids.'

'How lovely,' came the chorus from the sitting room.

'A spring wedding,' added Mrs Troubridge. 'How romantic. And we'd *love* to be your bridesmaids, Mr Maxwell.'

The publishers hope that this book has given you enjoyable reading. Large Print Books are especially designed to be as easy to see and hold as possible. If you wish a complete list of our books please ask at your local library or write directly to:

Magna Large Print Books
Magna House, Long Preston,
Skipton, North Yorkshire.
BD23 4ND

This Large Print Book, for people
who cannot read normal print,
is published under the auspices of

THE ULVERSCROFT FOUNDATION

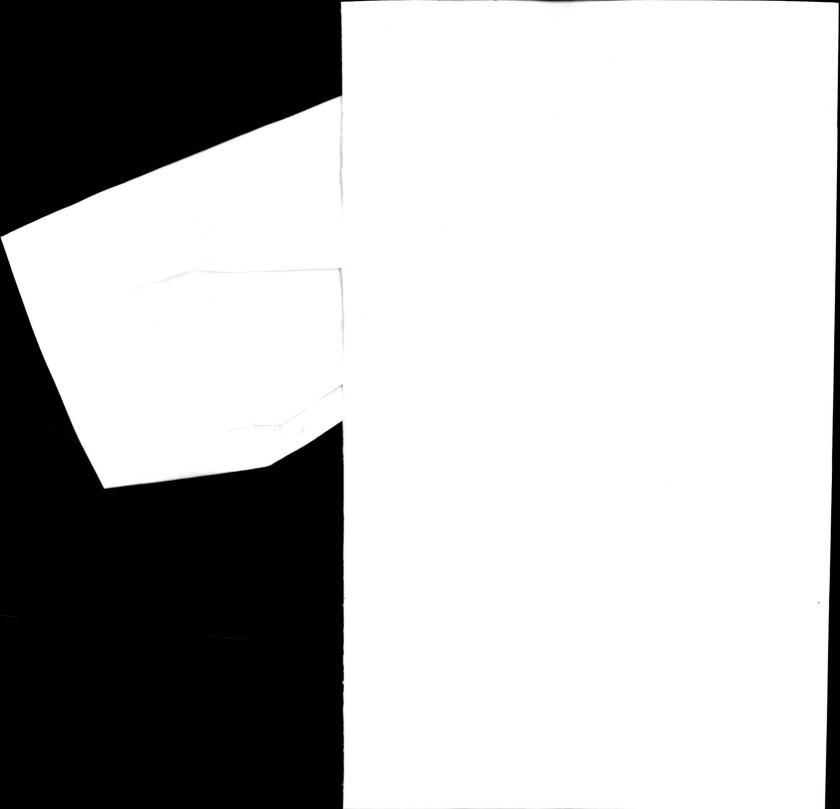

1001 1009 1016 1024 1083 1100
1001 1016 1031 1046 1061 1076 1091
1069 1084 1099 1100

1101 1110 1111 1126 1127 1142 1143 1158 1159 1173 1188
1116 1117 1125 1126 1141 1156 1157 1172 1173 1188
1131 1136 1139 1140 1155 1170 1171 1186 1187 1200
1146 1151 1154 1169 1184 1185 1199
1161 1166 1181 1196 1207
1176 1181 1195 1206 1222
1191 1196 1205 1220 1221 1222

1209 1211 1212 1213
1210 1224 1225 1226 1227 1228 1241 1242 1243 1257 1258 1272 1273 1287 1288
1207 1222 1237 1252 1267 1282 1283 1298
1206 1221 1236 1251 1266 1281 1296 1297
1205 1220 1235 1250 1265 1280 1295 1296 1300
1201 1216 1231 1236 1237 1252 1298
1246 1264 1279 1294
1261 1276 1279 1294 1295

1303 1304 1305 1306 1307 1308 1310 1311 1312 1313
1318 1319 1320 1321 1322 1323 1324 1325 1326 1327 1328
1333 1334 1335 1336 1337 1338 1339 1340 1341 1342 1343
1347 1348 1349 1350 1351 1352 1353 1354 1356 1357 1358
1362 1363 1364 1365 1366 1367 1368 1369 1370 1371 1372 1373
1377 1378 1379 1380 1381 1382 1383 1384 1385 1386 1387
1393 1394 1395 1396 1397 1398 1399 1400
1404 1405 1406 1407 1408 1409 1410 1411 1412
1419 1420 1421 1422 1423 1424 1425 1426 1427
1434 1435 1436 1437 1438 1439 1440 1441 1442
1450 1451 1452 1453 1454 1455 1456 1457
1466 1467 1468 1469 1470 1471 1472
1481 1482 1483 1484 1485 1486 1487
1495 1496 1497 1498 1499 1500